Chronicles of the Old Kingdom

Book One

The Siege of Castle Black

RS Johnson

Acknowledgements

This book is for the special people in my life who have listened to my tales – Catherine, Thomas, Robert, Jonathan, Daisy and in particular Jessica, who uniquely read the draft and whose encouragement mattered a great deal.

About the Author

RS Johnson was born in Liverpool. He has a multi-faceted background as social worker, family therapist, group worker and mental health worker, working with children and families of all ages; typically working in some of the poorest socio-economic environments of the UK.

He has also worked with colleagues and students as consultant, supervisor, trainer and teacher.

A storyteller for his own children and grandchildren. He is a big believer in encouraging creativity and imagination. This story began on walks with his granddaughters and grew as they did.

Prologue

The river of history for the Kingdom is long. Before it was ever called a Kingdom, it was wild and expansive with no boundaries and no names that apportioned ownership. There were large houses and castles, whose occupants fought over land, beliefs and family ascendancy. Gradually, some families laid successful claim to widespread tracts of territory where they developed prominence, gathered followers and made allegiances. Until, ultimately, hostilities subsided and most conflicts were resolved.

New oaths were sworn and loyalties forged, and a ruling dynasty emerged positioned in Venterra. An impregnable fortress was built, set against a mountain. Constructed from hard black stone and named Castle Black. It is where the rulers of Venterra have resided ever since. If viewing a map, it can be found close to Duskhold. A succession of kings nurtured the Kingdom and Venterra prospered. Then a different kind of king was crowned, King Perforll.

Unashamedly ambitious, under the guidance of Grandmaster Wizard Anzalum - who hailed from the great mage library – he set out to expand his kingdom. He ensured the Venterran army was efficient and well-drilled for his deployment. As a result, over time, the land ruled by King Perforll stretched far and wide. At its zenith, it included all or part of the lands we now know as Gritol, Yasrall, Tebira, Skovelenbar, Farkijal and Venterra.

In reality, its size was a constant challenge to oversee and rule. As humankind repeatedly fought about land and dominion, so claims about boundaries within the Old Kingdom ebbed and flowed. Yet, throughout such turbulent times, four areas remained outside of Venterran rule, despite being part of the same geography coveted by the king. These areas were Earthroot, Clinglewood Forest, the Dwarf kingdom – situated within the Ironspine Mountains - and Chimbleton.

However, in the recounting of these tales, the common erroneous assumption that all four areas were part of the Old Kingdom, will be acceptable. For each was integral to the geography of what we know as the Kingdom and played a part in the unfolding events within the domain.

The first and largest area not ruled by Venterra was the great forest of Earthroot, the home of the Faerie. It runs along the whole of the southernmost boundary of Venterra. Yet it continues beyond Venterra and is often referred to as the infinite woodland. No one can say where it goes or where it ends. That knowledge is beyond anyone within the Kingdom, perhaps even the Faerie themselves. Although there was never any expression of hostility from Venterra toward Earthroot, the Faerie queen, Tixlodel, was wary of King Perforll and his intentions. However, the heir to the Venterran throne, Cadmus, was always demonstrably more positive toward the Faerie, long before he was crowned king.

The second area not ruled by Venterra is the forest of Clinglewood, another deep, dark woodland that is home to many creatures not found elsewhere and a favourite retreat for wizards of the Great Library. Aside from wizards, few ever dared enter its ominous gloom. Those who did intrude, found that its few pathways ran into impassable dense woods, which led to being lost and confused. Such experiences discouraged further exploration. The great Clinglewood forest parallels along the eastern side of Yasrall, stretching the length of Seabreeze Lake.

Thirdly, there is the domain of the Mountain Dwarves, whose province runs underground throughout the Ironspine Mountains.

Rarely emerging from their dim abode, the dwarves confine themselves to their own dark world. Contact has always been on their terms. No king from Venterra has ever visited the dwarves under the mountains, although a select few wizards have done so.

However, at the start of this account, the vast halls and roads within the mountains lay silent. Without warning, the dwarves had upped and gone from their homes and dwellings. Traditionally, they would trade with, but did not trust, those living overground, including Venterra. Thus, they had shared with no one as to why they had emptied their underground abode or where they had gone.

Despite being robustly independent, self-sufficient and cautious when dealing with humankind, at times of major conflict, both the faerie and the dwarves had acted as allies of the Venterran kings. Nonetheless, there was an undercurrent of suspicion with regard to King Perforll.

This, and much more, changed significantly when Cadmus succeeded Perforll to the throne in Venterra. He had a wisdom that the old king seemed to lack. He recognised that trying to rule over lands as large and diverse as the Old Kingdom had entailed suppressing the indigenous inhabitants. He believed that this benefited no one and did not see a positive future in trying to maintain the remaining boundaries of the Kingdom. Thus, he took it upon himself to enable the various areas still within the Old Kingdom to regain their independence.

So, in a few short years, the Old Kingdom shrank. The rapidity of that change is evident even now; for there remain many who can still bear witness as to when it was at its largest. The pinnacle of its expansion being when the western lands of Farkijal were annexed.

At the time our tale begins, the Old Kingdom is already reduced. It now constitutes Venterra, Yasrall and in theory, Chimbleton. In fact, there are many who would argue that, in effect, it is just Venterra. King Perforll has passed and was succeeded by Cadmus. The Grandmaster Wizard, Anzalum, is also long gone and Grandmaster Olbus is the established leader of the wizards.

Yasrall is the closest neighbour to Venterra. Bordered on two sides by mountains, it is expansive and relatively flat, interrupted by a few gentle hills. Like a large green wall, Clinglewood Forest stretches along its eastern side. As much of Yasrall consists of hard, cold earth, difficult for farming, so the majority of its population lives in the south, where the ground and weather are more suited for agriculture. The northern part of Yasrall runs up to the Ironspine Mountains. It is a harsh place to forge a living and unsurprisingly sparsely populated. The area to the west neighbours with Gritol and is dusty and barren. It is aptly known as the Grim.

Yasrall had always allied itself to the king in Castle Black and had long considered Venterra as its protector. Despite this allegiance, King Cadmus himself is regarded as a stranger, for it was back in the early days of his reign when he made his one and only visit to Stonehelm, the largest town in Yasrall and the main area where the Rall thrive. Now, little contact is initiated from Venterra. Likewise, it might also be said that contact has not been encouraged by Yasrall, for the bulk of its trading is conducted through Bridgemouth, the connecting point and boundary with Venterra. In recent years, any Rall traversing the long roads beyond Bridgemouth to Duskhold would be regarded as a stranger there, if not a curiosity, so rare is their appearance. It is even more rare for a Venterran to travel in the opposite direction beyond Bridgemouth.

In the east of the Old Kingdom, lies Skovelenbar, where it would be equally unusual for any Skove to visit Venterra or vice versa. The Venterran preference for order and discipline has always clashed with the erratic nature of the Skove, where the whims and inconsistency of its tribal rulers dictate what is expected and acceptable. It is estimated that Skovelenbar narrowly surpasses Tebira as having the largest population within the Old Kingdom. It was only ever partially ruled by the Venterran king and not for very long. Predictably, the incursion into their land by the soldiers of Perforll was not welcomed and did not endure.

Skovelenbar was where the soldiers of Perforll did most of their battling in trying to expand the boundaries of the Old Kingdom. With a reputation for being merciless and quick to fight, the Skove ruling house led a consistent resistance against the invasion army of King Perforll. They fought not only to regain lost land, but buoyed by their success in this, to go further and conquer the Kingdom.

To begin with, the Venterran foray had progressed very effectively into Skovelenbar, but came to a halt when dragons were brought into the conflict. It was not common knowledge that a weyr of dragons existed in Skovelenbar. Decimated by the fiery beasts of the Skove, the Venterrans were driven back and eventually took to their ships on the Greenwater Straits to return home.

The Skove, heady with success, crossed Greenwater Straits in pursuit, landing on the southern coast opposite and west of Skovelenbar. Unfamiliar with the lay of the land, they mistakenly assumed that where they made shore was part of Venterra. It wasn't, it was Tebira. Mistakenly, they marched into that foreign land. The Teb responded and called upon their own weyr of dragons nested within Tebira at Dragon Mountain.

A battle followed between the Skove and the Teb, along with their respective dragons. This clash of the huge fire-spitting creatures is often referred to as the Dragon War. Many dragons perished, resulting in a much-reduced population. Fearing for the survival of all of her kind, the dragon matriarch, Vazzorg, intervened. Her message that dragons should not be killing dragons, resonated and the dragons from both sides withdrew from battling one another. Vazzorg led all the surviving beasts to nest peacefully on Dragon Mountain, removed from the human warring.

The Skove force attacking Tebira was smaller in number than the defenders, but had achieved some success from their advantage of having dragons. Once Vazzorg had persuaded all dragons away from the conflict, the Skove judged it prudent to retreat back across the Greenwater Straits. No peace treaty was signed. To this day, both Skove and Teb regard the conflict as unresolved. Although there has been no open combat between the two sides since.

Nonetheless, the Master Wizard Jevell once described Skovelenbar as being like a simmering pot of water constantly on the edge of boiling over. Importantly, at the time when our tale commences, there is a new Skove king, Durugen, who is eager to enhance his own reputation and expand Skovelenbar interests. Many expect that he may yet cause the boiling over that Master Jevell noted.

As already mentioned, Tebira is the largest area of all those lands referred to as being under the banner of the Old Kingdom. However, it was never part of the Old Kingdom. Despite this, as with Earthroot and the Ironspine Mountains of the dwarves, Tebira is commonly talked about as if it were.

More accurately, King Perforll had ventured into Tebira without understanding its size. Fortunately, before engaging the Teb in combat, he had recognised that he faced an army considerably larger than his own. He withdrew his forces.

However, the Teb were not seeking war, and cleverly interpreted the incursion by Venterran soldiers as a mistake; thereby affording an excuse for King Perforll to withdraw his army without loss of face. This mutual accommodation facilitated good relations, so that within three months, a trading agreement was signed between Venterra and Tebira. Some in Venterra viewed this as the king extending the boundary of the Old Kingdom, but that was politics and not fact.

Then there was the old foe, the Girngog. Like the Skove, the Girngog of Gritol had a reputation for fighting amongst themselves. Whilst renowned for their ferocious and fearsome battle skills, the divisions amongst the Girngog tribes meant that such energy was typically expended between one another.

Thus, the tribes were not sufficiently organised to withstand an invasion by the disciplined soldiers of Venterra. So, for a period, King Perforll was able to occupy and claim Gritol as part of the Old Kingdom.

Ironically, given their history of infighting, it was their collective experience of being governed by the king in Venterra that most effectively united the Girngog tribes. The Venterrans could derive little economic gain from occupying Gritol and that, along with the persistent rebellious challenges, eventually led to the decision in Castle Black that Gritol yielded insufficient benefit to justify its continued occupation. So, after a relatively short governance of a handful of years, the soldiers of the Old Kingdom were withdrawn and Gritol was abandoned to its own internal chaos.

Left alone, the warring and wild Girngog lacked leadership. The in-fighting amongst the tribes rumbled on once more. As futile as many considered the civil warring to be, it was this aggression that appealed to Merektar the Sorcerer. He estimated that he could harness such energy for his own purposes.

Merektar had been a mage in training at the Wizard Library located in the Pancake Lands. He was there striving to develop into a Master Wizard. However, corrupted by his desire for power, he had betrayed the trust placed in him. After stealing unique and valuable artefacts, he fled from the library. He killed those sent to return and bring him to account.

He was, in effect, a rogue sorcerer – naturally talented, malevolent and deeply ambitious. When eventually cornered, he relinquished the artefacts to facilitate his escape. He fled to Gritol. He had long decided that the Girngog would be the vessel by which he could quench his own ambitions. And it was not long before the Girngog were in his thrall.

Finally, there is Farkijal. Historians argue as to whether it can be accurately said that it was occupied. Certainly, the time spent there by Venterran forces was relatively brief.

The Venterrans had entered Farkijal from the west and found it a cold, hard and barren land. The population they encountered was sparse, just a handful of hill farmers. For many leagues, the Venterrans found western Farkijal an unfriendly and unattractive terrain. After progressing unopposed through unfamiliar territory, the invaders finally emerged from the rough rocky landscape into a luscious and green land, only to be greeted by a host of Fark soldiers.

A ritualistic and disciplined society, the Fark were reputed to be fearless warriors. Clad in shining armour and wearing fearsome face covers known as 'war masks', they battled with the invaders. Over several weeks, battles were fought without any clear conclusion. Ultimately, the Venterrans struggled to sustain their assault. A decisive factor occurred when the Venterran withdrawal from Skovelenbar impacted the supply lines to Farkijal. King Perforll recognised the danger. He did not wish to have a significant portion of his army split, cut off or isolated, so he decided to cease attempting to conquer Farkijal and recalled his forces.

The dream of Perforll to expand the Kingdom had enjoyed a short existence. For a brief time, it had subsumed all or part of six lands, which together are referred to as the Old Kingdom. But fate was not finished with the instigators. The cruellest blow came later, when within a year, both King Perforll and his mentor, the Grandmaster Wizard Anzalum, were dead. The king through illness and the wizard from an accident.

It was the new king of Venterra, Cadmus, under the guidance of Grandmaster Olbus, who recognised that the extended Kingdom was overstretched and built on warring, which he deemed to be unjust. He knew it to be a resented foundation which would undermine an extended kingdom in the long term. So, Cadmus set about extracting Venterra from foreign lands.

All conquered territory was returned to self-governance. It was a strategy that worked well, garnered him much goodwill and for some years Venterra no longer waged war. Its people did not march off to fight in strange lands; instead, they enjoyed peace and focused on their own prosperity.

Life settled in Venterra, routine prevailed and soldiers no longer fought. So it was that King Cadmus took half of his army and visited Tebira to reinforce friendship. He stayed much longer than expected, but resulted in extending the treaty of trade and mutual support, that existed between the two kingdoms.

Moving to the point where our tale commences, we find the soldiers of Gritol, the Girngog, are in the early stages of invading Yasrall. Led by the sorcerer Merektar, he is directing matters from the Blue Tower in Gritol. He is astute and has mulled over his plans for a long while. He has gauged who might oppose his manoeuvres.

He is aware of the strengths of his foes. Invading Yasrall was the first step in his plans.

Yet, despite his fierce intelligence and his thorough scheming, he did not envisage that any threat to his plans would come from one particular and unexpected source. That source being Chimbleton. The simple reason for this being, that he had never heard of Chimbleton or of Chimbles. Likewise, the people of Chimbleton were unaware that a Girngog invasion had begun.

Chimbleton is different from anywhere else and requires a little explanation. Situated to the south of Yasrall, within a long day or so walking, it is accessible to Stonehelm, Midmoor, Bridgemouth and Clinglewood Forest. But almost no one knows where Chimbleton is. There is no road or path to follow. The heavily wooded hills that lead up into the Ironspine Mountains do not suggest that there is anything beyond. However, partway up, through the trees and out of sight from below, the land becomes more amenable. Somewhat isolated and almost hidden away, positioned on the other side of the mountains is a long, lush valley.

It is there, a world apart, that Chimbleton can be found. It is a collection of small villages spread across both sides of the river Wispy, which runs the length of the valley. It is a place of tradition and culture where the optimum expression of conflict is displayed at its fairs and fetes. It is not riddled with struggles for power, has no soldiers and no army. The name Chimble does not exactly suggest a fearsome foe. In fact, Chimbles are content and peaceful, not infected by the endless wish to have more, more of this and more of that. Uniquely, no royalty or ruler from outside has ever travelled there. Secretly, it has always been under the exclusive protection of the mages at the Wizards' Library.

Whilst it could be said that the history of the Old Kingdom is one of intermittent conflict, Chimbleton has never participated in any of that. It has no ruler and no wish to expand. Yet, most curiously, two of the main protagonists in this tale are Chimbles.

The Chimbleton knowledge of the world beyond its valley, is at best, partial. In good part because much of the information that does reach the Chimbles is not official in any way. Mostly, it derives from individuals who bring the rumour and gossip of taverns. Of which the usual culprit will be Ned Fludge, who carries news and tittle-tattle. He is very partial to Rall beer and is well known at the inns of Stonehelm and Midmoor. However, barely anyone realises that he is a Chimble and he prefers it that way, which avoids him being asked any awkward questions.

Common understanding across the Kingdom is that Chimbleton is a myth; it does not exist! Yet, privately, Master Jevell will admit that it is his favourite place. Its mythical status has been accentuated by the contentment of the Chimbles, who prefer to stay within the confines of their hidden haven. It is a rare Chimble who copies Ned Fludge or ventures beyond Chimbleton into the wider world. Though occasionally some do, as our story will reveal.

1

Captured

She was running as fast as she could, heart pounding, knowing that if she were caught, then tonight she could be eaten. She knew little of the Girngog and had no idea how quickly they could run. They all knew that there was a risk of encountering them, but considered it was the kind of thing that happened to others. They were wrong.

They were running for their lives, Ceridwen, Tansy and Ruffle. Scared and desperate. They were making for the safety of the trees in Clinglewood Forest. At least they hoped it would be safe. They could hear their pursuers grunting and yelling. A gaggle of Girngog were enough to encourage anyone to run. They all sensed their pursuers were closing, so they split up. Ruffle and Tansy had veered left as Ceridwen went to the right. The Girngog gang split up in response, with most following Ceridwen.

It was soon clear that Ceridwen had selected an awkward route, littered by tree roots, divots and fallen branches. She ran and jumped, now breathing hard, her throat raw. She could hear the Girngog, and a shiver of panic ran through her veins.

'Ouch, that hurt!' she squawked as something hit her leg. She slowed to rub her thigh, but one glance behind and she sped up again. She knew that she could not stop running, unless, of course, she wanted to spend the evening sitting in a pot of boiling water accompanied by carrots and potatoes, which had no appeal to her at all.

Consider yourself: Would you want to be the main ingredient in a Girngog stew? I don't think you would, and neither did she.

The shouts of her pursuers seemed closer. More alarmingly, she could hear the sound of big feet thudding through the grass. She wanted to look behind again, but equally feared what she might see. Then 'whoosh' sang the wind by her right ear, as something thrown by the chasing mob whizzed past her head.

'What was that?' she thought to herself, but didn't pause and kept running.

Closer to the woods and shelter, she was now constantly having to skip over tree roots and duck under branches, dodging in between bushes; her breathing was loud, and she gasped for every morsel of air she could get. Yet the snorting and smell of the Girngog was vivid, as if it clung to her nostrils. The land had slowed her down, and dread got the better of her. She dared to look behind. Then immediately wished she hadn't.

Her anxiety exploded. She felt as if she were living in a nightmare. Without doubt, they were closing on her. She had never seen Girngog up so close and at that moment never wished to again. They were all shapes and sizes, fearsome and frightening. Ugly, mishappen, slobbering and in their fashion, running toward her. They waved their arms and shouted, a savage mob, thought Ceridwen. She had no understanding of what they said. Once again, the stories of them eating their prisoners came to her mind and fed into the panic she felt.

Some Girngog tripped over tree roots or ran into one another, falling down and arguing, but there were enough of them to keep up the chase. Their voices were wild and excited, as was the slap of their feet on the ground. They were enjoying the hunt. Ceridwen wasn't. She told herself not to look behind again as the grunting grew and their unwashed smell filled the air. Her legs were getting heavier, as if her energy was leaking away. She struggled for breath and moved her head left to see where Tansy and Ruffle had gotten to. It was a mistake.

The glance was barely a couple of seconds but now the ground was cluttered with the detritus of the forest. Having diverted her eyes from the ground, her foot clipped something and over she went. Despite demonstrating a half somersault before landing with a bump, she got to her feet quickly. Feeling bruised, breathless and sore all over, it seemed she had broken no bones, and off she ran again. 'I will have some lovely bruises,' she muttered to herself. But the fall had cost her valuable time.

Running was now painful, and before she had gone much further, something hit her legs. The impact caused her to topple over, falling onto her side, shouting out in pain. She looked down to see a rope tangled about her ankles. Sitting up, feeling dizzy, she quickly set about removing the rope, but almost immediately the air around her was filled with the noise of heavy breathing and a powerful odour, which she later described as a stinky pong! She lifted her head and her fears were realised; she was surrounded by Girngog.

They were grinning, panting, sweating, and worst of all, they were so smelly. Some were rubbing their stomachs, and it was clear to Ceridwen that they were suggesting that dinner had arrived and that she was it! The ugly, misshapen gang around her were stomping their feet on the earth, clearly pleased with themselves, and they now stood catching their breath as they watched her remove the rope from her ankles. She looked up horrified and helpless, still gulping down air as a big hairy hand grabbed her arm and yanked her to her feet. Ceridwen had been captured by the Girngog.

2

Picnic at Big Sprout

In the telling of this tale, a little context might be helpful before we progress. After all, you don't know who Ceridwen, Tansy or Ruffle are, or indeed anything about the Girngog. So let me explain how the Chimbles were drawn into this tale, and as a result, their lives changed along with many others.

For the Chimbles it began on a warm summer day in Chimble Thistle in Chimbleton. As you will have guessed by now, Ceridwen and Tansy are Chimbles. Secreted away from the wider world, Chimbleton can be found nestled in a long valley on the fringes of the Old Kingdom. That said, you should understand that it is not easily found. Its wide valley is walled by high mountains, and is rather out of the way, so to speak. There is no well-trodden road to lead you there. There are no signposts in the Old Kingdom and visitors are rare. So much so that it is considered a myth by many. This is accentuated as very few Chimbles ever travel out of their valley. They are as common as spotting a yellow dragon, which is why most assumed Chimbles only existed in stories told to children.

If you ever were to find your way to Chimbleton then you discover a collection of villages, such as Apple Hollow, Trug and Chimble Thistle, set along the lush foothills of the valley and close to the river Wispy which ran the length of the green haven. Chimble Thistle was where Ceridwen and Tansy lived.

Whichever village one hailed from, all living in this peaceful abode were known as Chimbles. They were a contented people and all they required could be found within their own surroundings.

They were proud of their large valley lands and grew everything they ate. Few wished to explore beyond their own borders. They were peaceful and settled. Strangely, most got along very well. Of course, there were some disagreements, but Chimbles never drew weapons on one another.

However, with those who did express a more prickly disposition, it tended to show itself in valley competitions. In particular, when it came to judging who made the best beer, or who grew the prize-winning vegetables, or cheating in the annual duck races. Disputes about such decisions would linger for half the year, but the worst that happened was illustrated by Mrs Limpson when she took a walking stick to the marrow of Mr Buddle, when his pride and joy was awarded first place ahead of her effort at the Apple Hollow fair. Tongues wagged for a long time in the village taverns over that, many speculating that somehow Mr Buddle had cheated, though no one suggested how.

This inward-looking dimension was typical of Chimbles, for truth be known, they were genuinely uninterested in what occurred outside of the valley.

Curiously, they aged more slowly than people beyond the valley and typically lived a lot longer. Thus, it was hard for an outsider to gauge the age of a Chimble. Although resembling human kind, it was always a tricky task gauging the age of a Chimble.

It was not unusual for there to be five generations of a family living. And so it was with Ceridwen, who had lots of cousins; though not all were very friendly, as a good number of them considered her too clever. Her best friend, Tansy, said that it was just pure and simple jealousy. However, throughout the valley, Ceridwen was a popular young woman, regarded as naturally helpful, intelligent and always ready to smile. She was known to most as Ceri, so for the rest of this tale we too shall call her Ceri.

Ceri was learning about plants and herbs that were used in medicine and healing. She had tended to many cuts and sores of the villagers when Nossy Leaves, the most skilled of healers in Chimbleton, was not available. Though she always suspected he used a touch of magic. But he laughed it off, if Ceri ever suggested it.

She also liked to write and teach. In fact, she was the reason so many children in Chimble Thistle were able to read the common language of the Kingdom. She was a talented cook and often created new recipes; for which Tansy volunteered to be her assistant, usually by eating the outcome, for which she awarded herself the title of 'official taster'. In fact, Tansy regarded Ceri as the most clever person in the valley.

Tansy was a contrast to Ceri. She was always on the move, building things and exercising. It seemed that the only time she was not moving, was when she was fishing. There were many streams running through the valley and one wide river, the Wispy. Tansy was arguably the best swimmer in Chimbleton, having won the annual river race three years in a row. She was also a good horse rider and had ridden the length and breadth of the valley more than most. Traversing the valley was her way of quenching her restlessness. As a result of these jaunts, many people in other villages recognised Tansy, having seen her riding. Her various skills combined with her striking appearance and she was noticed. She long golden yellow hair, which she rarely tied back, and piercing blue eyes which seemed to be always smiling. She was popular throughout the valley and considered to be a generous soul, often stopping to chat or help others.

They both lived peaceful and contented lives, seeing no need to go out on adventures or anything beyond the valley. Their friendship was a meeting of two contrasting personalities. On the day our tale takes shape they engage in one of their favourite activities, which was to share a picnic. Many of their best conversations had occurred on a picnic and they had always been a source of enjoyment. And on this particularly warm day, Ceri decided it was perfect for another one at their favourite spot, Big Sprout. The largest tree in Chimbleton. Unbeknown to either, it was to be an ominous day.

So, she went into the garden, whistled and within a few seconds a small silvery bird flew down and sat on her outstretched arm. No bigger than a peach it was a Starlight bird, indigenous to the valley. Gently stroking the bird Ceri said softly 'I want you to deliver a message to Tansy'. She spoke to the bird because the Starlight possessed the unusual ability to understand Chimbles. She sometimes wished that they could also speak. But they couldn't, so she resorted to scribbling a few words onto a tiny piece of paper. She then attached it to a small leg band. 'This is for Tansy' whispered Ceri. Once the band was attached to its leg, the bird flew off. Ceri was totally confident that Tansy would receive the message within a few minutes.

She now turned her attention to the enjoyable task of deciding what to pack for the picnic. She often made the mistake of packing too much, so she decided she would try to take just enough. But then, how much is 'just enough' she thought, and started by choosing to let her stomach decide. Assessing how hungry she felt at that moment, she packed accordingly.

Opening her knapsack, the first item she packed was a jar of honey, followed by a big cob of her own homemade crusty bread. Then a small jar of strawberry jam, made by her Aunt Dilly; a big chunk of yellow cheese made in Dale, lettuce leaves, tomatoes, a jar of pickled onions, two apples, and a handful of grapes, plus several pieces of liquorice. Finally, some oat biscuits, a small carrot cake and a flask of water. She tied the flask to her belt. Finally, the knapsack was full and then Ceri pondered - is this too much or just enough?

She quickly decided it was just enough and that she would forego taking her patchwork blanket. It had not rained for some days and the ground was dry to sit on. But she did fold and pack a small tablecloth on which to lay the feast. As she closed the bag, she remembered to include a couple of small knives to cut the cheese and the cake. She and Tansy enjoyed regular picnics, sometimes taking the blanket, other times not, but forgetting a knife usually meant they would end up with sticky fingers.

Feeling ready, she threw the knapsack on her back, put on her floppy hat, closed the front door and set off on the short walk to Big Sprout. In the warm sun, she felt happy, singing to herself and expecting another lovely picnic. She was curious to know where Tansy had been riding of late, as she had not seen her for two days, although she knew she was now at home.

Meanwhile, the Starlight bird had arrived at the kitchen window of a small house that looked out upon the river Wispy. The house had a long garden that ran down to the river shore, where Tansy lay looking up at the few white puffs of cloud drifting across the blue sky. Her fishing rod leant on a stool, its line dangling in the water. She had never caught a fish but that was not the point. She was there for the quiet, to absorb the world and allow her thoughts to drift like the clouds. It was one place where she gave herself permission to keep still and relax.

Almost dozing, she nonetheless heard the faintest noise which stood apart from the hazy buzzing flutter of summer insects who were enjoying her garden. Turning her head, she saw the little Starlight bird land on the window sill. Then in a slow unwinding fashion Tansy stood. She recognised the little bird, knowing it was a favourite way by which Ceri would convey messages. Ambling back toward the house, she noticed the tiny leg band on the bird and knew it would be a missive from Ceri.

She was correct, of course. Speaking quietly, she chatted away to the bird whilst gently removing the message. It consisted of three words, 'picnic Big Sprout' and she knew exactly what it meant; Ceri was heading to Big Sprout for a picnic and asking Tansy to join her there. Big Sprout was the nickname for the largest and oldest tree in Chimbleton, and their favourite place to picnic. It was less than a ten-minute walk away, positioned at the edge of Chimble Thistle where the road ended.

The two Chimbles loved their picnics together and most often met at the old tree. They would sit and lean back against the thick tree trunk, which offered delightful refuge from the sun on a hot summer day. Twenty steps away from the tree was the Wishing Well, once a popular meeting place for courting couples. Many Chimbles had tossed lucky charms into the well and made a wish, including both Ceri and Tansy. But that was a long time ago and now the well was quite overgrown. Several planks of wood lay across the top, covering the hole. The over growth around it now meant that it was possible to walk past the well without realising it was there.

There was no need for Tansy to reply to the invitation. Their arrangement was that unless, for some reason, she was not able to meet then she would simply make her way to the huge tree. If the little bird returned the message to Ceri, then she would know Tansy could not be there. On this day, all was fine, so she thanked the bird and began to ready herself. What made their picnics so easy for Tansy was that Ceri always prepared the food, so she simply had to ready herself.

She had intended to repair her rocking chair after she was done fishing, but instantly decided that that could wait. Grabbing her small knapsack, she added two dandelion lollipops, a whistle – which she considered always to be useful; a small folding knife, as Ceri sometimes forgot cutlery and Tansy preferred cutting cake rather than breaking off pieces. Finally, she added a towel, thinking that she might wash her hands if Ceri brought jam or something sticky, or she might need it if she decided to take a dip in the Wispy. The river ran past the tree, just fifty paces from the wishing well. Closing her bag, she grabbed her straw summer hat, stepped out and set off.

With perfect timing, the two friends met on the road and approached the tree together. The road that ran through Chimbleton petered out at the tree. Thereafter the ground was strewn with trees and fallen boulders, wild with flowers and uninhabited. There was no discernible path. It simply ended.

'What a delightful idea Ceri and on such a lovely day,' said Tansy.

'I thought you would like the idea' Ceri replied.

Reaching the huge tree, they sat on the lush grass at the edge of the shade provided by Big Sprout and Ceri began to unpack her knapsack. Tansy kept smiling as her friend placed the food on the little tablecloth. There was not a single item she did not enjoy and as each was revealed; her stomach began to rumble. In the warmth of the midday sun, they ate their picnic and talked. They chatted and laughed. When sated and content, they moved to sit propped against Big Sprout. On a clear day, the view from the ancient tree looked right down the valley. This day was clear and warm, even in the shade. Gradually, their conversation dwindled, and they both closed their eyes and dozed in a light sleep. Birds and insects provided the background music to their blissful slumber.

Relaxed and content, their reverie was suddenly punctured. It was a noise which did not belong and it woke both. Not a loud noise, but enough to cause their four eyes to open.

'Did you hear it?'

They sat up straight and looked at each other, all was quiet.

'Did we imagine it?' queried Tansy.

'Both of us!' said Ceri.

'Probably a squirrel,' proposed Tansy.

'Of course,' Ceri smiled, but not really convinced.

Then there was more noise, a scraping sound, a muffled shout and what seemed to be deep heavy breathing.

'Maybe it's a big squirrel!' Tansy suggested.

Ceri hauled herself up and looked around. Listening. She pointed to the old wishing well.

'Your big squirrel seems to be in the wishing well.'

Slowly, they both walked toward the well. Cautiously, they pulled back some of the overgrowth and old planks of wood covering the hole. They hesitantly peered down into the darkness. It was deep and they knew water remained at the bottom. But it had been a very long time since it had been used. Staring into the dark hole, they could see nothing. There was no noise.

'As I thought, we just imagined it,' said Ceri.

Then they heard something, like scratching. A clawing on the walls of the well and what sounded like laboured breathing. Mouths open but making no sound, they stepped backwards. They looked at one another eyes wide.

'What animal climbs down a well, I don't think squirrels do,' said Ceri.

'Perhaps it's lost or fell down by accident,' said Tansy.

Then they both jumped as a voice echoed from inside the well.

'Stay there, please, and help me get out,' it spoke.

Their first impulse was to run, but they remained, looking at one another.

'It's a ghost or maybe a spirit living in the well,' whispered Tansy.

'Or a talking squirrel!' said Ceri, 'Don't be silly it's, it's........ something, I don't know, let's try talking to it'.

They removed the remaining wood covering the well and very slowly leaned forward to look into the hole once again. This time they could see something moving in the gloom.

'I think I see a hat, or maybe it's a head,' whispered Ceri.

Tansy said nothing but then pointed into the hole. Hands emerged, gripping the side walls of the well. Someone was climbing up. It was deep—everyone knew that—and the walls were slimy and overgrown. But it had not rained for days, so they were much dryer at that moment.

'Who are you?' called Ceri.

'Please wait until I reach you' a voice replied, 'I am out of breath climbing, this is hard work for me, but I won't be long'.

'Of course,' responded Ceri, and then added in a whisper to Tansy, 'he is very polite for a ghost'.

Tansy looked at Ceri, hands on hips, 'shall we push him back down the well when he gets near the top, he might be dangerous, an evil spirit!'

Ceri gave out a small laugh.

'Goodness Tansy, how unfriendly you are. I think anyone who uses the word *please* has some good in them and he sounds friendly enough'.

'Sorry, but you can't be sure it's friendly,' said Tansy, feeling abashed that she had suggested it. 'It is just that we never get visitors to Chimbleton from outside; and when we do, they don't arrive via an old wishing well.'

'Yes indeed, but I am curious that the ghost seems to know this secret passage from Yasrall, which is one of the most difficult ways to get to Chimbleton. It must have put in quite an effort in order to find its way here through the rabbit warren. Whereas I thought ghosts just appeared in a puff of smoke!'

'I didn't know there was a secret passage in the well, or about the rabbit warren or that it was a way to reach Yasrall. Why didn't I know?' said Tansy folding her arms to show she was cross.

'Few people know of it and I don't think it has been used for many a year. I have never used it. But I should watch what I say. Old Nossy Leaves told me about it when he was showing me what plants I needed to gather for use in healing.'

'Well, it still might be a talking rabbit down there! As I doubt anyone from Yasrall knows of the passageways you clearly know about,' said Tansy.

Ceri looked at Tansy and smiled, 'well you may be right, as Nossy told me that nobody outside the valley knew of them. Let's wait and see, shall we!'

They did not have to wait long to find out. Emerging from the well, pulling himself over the side onto the grass was a slim bearded man; dressed in a red tunic, black trousers, knee-high boots and a thick shock of black hair. He was now all covered in dirt. He greeted them with a smiling face camouflaged with soil. He stood catching his breath and bowed toward the two surprised Chimbles.

'My name is Ruffle Cragstone and I am a Rall, from Stonehelm in Yasrall, and I am so pleased to meet you, very pleased in fact,' he said.

'My name is Ceridwen but everyone calls me Ceri, and this is my best friend Tansy' was the greeting he received. 'We did not expect anyone to come climbing out of the well today, so we have a lot of questions for you. But maybe we should sit down first as you seem to have expended much effort in climbing up our wishing well'.

'Thank you' said Ruffle, 'that sounds like a splendid idea. But I spy a lovely river behind you. Given that I feel very warm and sticky, would you mind if I took a quick bath in that river before we talk - I am exhausted and uncomfortable dressed in all this dirt.'

With that, Ruffle strolled down to the Wispy and, fully dressed, plunged into the water. The two Chimbles stood watching as the Rall lay on his back soaking up the sun and the water. He then took off his shirt and breeches and scrubbed them thoroughly. He thrashed about scrubbing his face and hands. Finally, he emerged dressed in his wet trousers carrying cleaner, though dripping, soaked clothes.

'That feels so much better. Thank you. If the sun is happy to dry my clothes, then I am quite happy to sit in my wet breeches,' he declared as he rejoined the Chimbles by the giant tree. 'Though I do apologise for my appearance.'

'There is no need to apologise,' said Tansy.

The Rall was wet but drying quickly in the warm sun. He walked about for a short while before he sat down with the Chimbles. They had moved the tablecloth out of the shade and into the sun and invited him to tuck in to their picnic.

'Where shall I begin with my story?' mused the Rall as he chewed some bread and cheese. 'I think I should start with a little bit of history. Sometimes it's hard to know where a tale begins and even where it finishes?'

3

Rabbit Holes

For a few moments Ruffle said nothing, he just savoured the Yellow Dale cheese and chewed. He was thinking.

'Ah yes, let us start with the 'Great Girngog War when the Girngog tried to enslave all lands in the Old Kingdom, only to be eventually defeated by the wizards and Cadmus, the King in the North. I assume you have heard of that?'

'Yes, I know of it but little of any substance,' replied Tansy.

'I also know of it, but only from the reminiscences of some old Chimbles who talk about it when they have had a honey dew beer or two' added Ceri. 'Oh, by the way I meant to tell you, if you did not deduce it already, that you are in Chimbleton and we are, of course, Chimbles.'

'I did wonder exactly where I was, so thank you for explaining. Some say Chimbleton is the stuff of myth but I always knew you were real,' said Ruffle, 'after all who hasn't heard of Salos the Swift.'

Ceri and Tansy looked at one another, but said nothing. Ruffle continued.

'Well, it is many years now and I was no bigger than a stick of rhubarb when the Great War ended. But I can still recall hiding with my mother and seeing huge Trolls swinging their big clubs as they marched alongside those ugly Girngog. I remember it was very scary and smelly. I always thought that it was the beastly animals, but now

I think it was the Girngog themselves. Anyway, it was not nice at all.'

'Ultimately and happily, the Girngog lost the Great War and the king got them to sign a peace treaty. The treaty said they could return to the lands where they came from, which is Gritol, on condition that they never took up arms to fight in the Old Kingdom again. At that time the lands of the Kingdom included Yasrall, my home. The jeopardy for the Girngog was that if they could not agree these terms, then soldiers from the victorious armies would take charge of their lands. But of course, the Girngog accepted the treaty. In hindsight the treaty was poorly thought through and did not provide for a way forward for either side. Moreover, nobody realised then, that the master manipulator was already at work, albeit out of sight or knowledge.

'For many years thereafter, the Girngog kept to themselves. The land between Stonehelm and Gritol which is part of Yasrall, is mostly desert; dry, flat and sandy. Little grows on such land. It is aptly known as the Grim, though I am sure you know that already.'

'Actually, we didn't, but do continue, said Ceri.

'Then, about seven years ago, the Girngog crossed the Grim and began to trade with some in Yasrall. Nowadays, and for a long time now, Rall have become farmers and craft people. We grow and make things. Although we are in fact descended from the Mountain Dwarves. However, we have not lived within the mountains for many generations. Our way of life is simple; we look after the land and the land looks after us. We get the rain that Gritol doesn't get, along with plenty of sunshine.'

'Away from the Grim, we can grow almost anything somewhere in Yasrall - oranges, strawberries, potatoes, grapes, carrots, onions, in fact anything, and we are proud of it. We trade with all people.

So, although the Girngog had not been seen in Yasrall for many years, it seemed a natural development that they would wish to trade with us. By that time the Great War was becoming a distant memory for most. Whilst nobody I know of has spent time there, the story is that Gritol is very large and has a coast. That it has fertile land, though but the Girngog are poor at farming. So, their desire to trade made sense.'

'As Rall we are skilled with our hands, our old traditions involved creating things with metal and wood – things that are useful and sometimes things that are just nice to look at. Nowadays, we continue to be craftsmen but we more often create things from the earth. Then again, we also make things that are pointless! Anyway, it was not a surprise that the Girngog liked our wares.'

Over the past few years, trade between the two peoples has steadily increased. Then, they started building small structures in the Grim, halfway between Stonehelm and Gritol. The Grim is a large area of land owned by us, but having temporary dwellings for travellers to rest during long journeys made sense.

In fact, the buildings were very similar to small forts in appearance, though nobody noticed at the time, as very few Rall journeyed toward Gritol. The bulk of trading was conducted in Stonehelm. And for a good while all was amicable, despite the hygiene shortcomings of the Girngog.'

Ruffle paused, had another bite of his cheese and bread, and then drank some of the refreshing water before carrying on with his tale.

'Well, gradually things changed, and then one day we heard things from a traveller passing through our village. He had moved out of Stonehelm to live in the farm lands, which is where I live, as he felt safer. He told of how the trade with the Girngog had grown so much that some of them were now living in Stonehelm itself. At first it had all been very friendly but he did not like the way things were going. He said suspicions of the Girngog were growing.'

'Anyway, more and more often discussion of the old peace treaty was occurring. Most specifically, the condition that stated the Girngog should keep to their own lands. But having traded with them for some time it was a little late to be pointing this out. It became noticeable that more of them seemed to be settling in or near Stonehelm and predictably, tensions increased. The biggest concern was what they were doing to the area where they had built their so called 'stopover buildings' along the road to Gritol, they had begun digging holes, deep holes and as this was discovered, everyone gradually realised that they were digging for coal and gold. They were creating mines. Arguments broke out and fairly soon relationships between us became fractious.'

'These were things that Rall had never sought. We have always cared for the earth. Digging or mining would mean creating huge holes and damaging the land. Rall simply did not do such things. Besides, nobody had ever thought that gold or coal lay under the ground near Stonehelm or anywhere else in Yasrall. The Girngog were asked to stop their digging and to return to their own lands. But, of course they didn't. By that time there were considerable numbers of Girngog living in Stonehelm. Unlike Rall, they carried swords and axes, weapons that the old peace treaty had forbidden. Alas, it was all too late.'

Again, Ruffle halted, drank some water and bit into his cheese.

'Sorry, but I am hungry and I do appreciate your sharing your picnic with me. But I will continue,' he spluttered in between chewing.

'Now Girngog are ugly, let me be honest. They are usually smelly and their clothes are dark and unchanged for months, if ever!

To begin with they had been tolerated in Yasrall because, as I said before, we are a friendly and generous people, plus the trade had been good. But their numbers had slowly increased until they almost outnumbered us. I am told that some Rall spoke up to protest but soon disappeared. We discovered later that many had been imprisoned or put in chains; whilst others were put to work in the mines away from Stonehelm, often to make swords, shields and armour. Eventually, but too late, it was realised that their intention all along had been to occupy our lands. The trading had lulled us into letting our guard drop.'

'They began to mine deeper and deeper holes in their search for coal and gold. They opened up great caverns and destroyed crops and trees. More Girngog came and they spread out from the town to the countryside, taking whatever they wanted, no longer bothering to trade. The situation was deteriorating and there was nothing we could do to persuade them to leave Yasrall. I am told that once upon a time, we had been fierce warriors, but alas, now we are a peaceful people. We could not force them to leave, they are much bigger than us to begin with. So, Stonehelm was effectively occupied by Girngog and some argue that we brought it upon ourselves.'

'It was a vain hope but my friend Beryn and I went to see the King's Voice, to find out if he had informed King Cadmus about the Girngog. He is supposedly the direct link to the king, authorising laws and such. Though many say it is years since any direct contact took place. Nonetheless, we were shocked by what we found. I had not been to Stonehelm for some time and it seemed the Girngog were everywhere, doing whatever they pleased, getting drunk and causing damage. The guards commanded by the King's Voice were unable to control them. So, it seemed sensible that during our visit we did nothing to attract any attention.'

'The building where townspeople took their grievances to the Kings Voice, normally busy, was now unusually empty. When I had lived in Stonehelm his office had always been thronged with people. But now it was the opposite, as if it were avoided. The truth being, that the role of the Voice had been ineffective for some time once the Girngog began occupying the town. However, we got inside and found him sitting at a table and writing.

'It's Ruffle Cragstone isn't it?' he greeted us and for some reason recognised me. 'You're the man I need. Here take this and hide it from sight.'

He handed me a small seal; it was the one he used to stamp and authorise official rulings on behalf of the king.

'I ask you to take this to the king, he will immediately understand that we are in jeopardy and we need his help,' said the Kings Voice.

'He looked a worried and frail man, as if he expected worse was yet to come. Before I could respond, two burly Girngog entered the room. The Kings Voice changed his tone straight away and said '*I am sorry I cannot rule on your dispute today but come back in a week by which time I will have had time to think on matters*', as if he had been in conversation with us.'

'We understood instantly what was happening and said farewell. The two Girngog looked at us as if about to challenge us, but the King's Voice spoke with them, which caused sufficient distraction, enabling us to take our leave and quickly slip out of the building and then the town, with me holding the seal in my pocket.'

'Beryn and I discussed what we should do. Presenting the king with the seal would give us credibility when informing him of the Girngog. We knew that it was part of the oath of the King's Voice never to be separated from the seal, except in an emergency, and this is an emergency. So, we agreed that we should do as he had asked and take the seal to the king.'

'Now the problem in delivering the seal was that the king lives at Castle Black in Duskhold, which of course is a long journey and further than either of us had ever travelled. In fact, there had been no soldiers in Yasrall for many years, so we didn't even know if King Cadmus was still alive. Yet we felt there was no choice, we had to get the seal to him or at least to whoever was now the king. That was quickly decided but our biggest dilemma was how to get there. To be blunt, we did not know the way.'

'We knew that we had to cross Seabreeze Lake then head east. Though we had no boats and knew nothing about sailing. But we did know that there was a bridge called the Necklace situated at Bridgemouth. That seemed our only option. Neither of us had ever been there but we did at least know the road to take. Although, after Bridgemouth we would be in the dark, because we had no idea which way to go from there.'

'Nonetheless, we knew it was urgent; we needed the king's help. So, we said goodbye to our families and set off the next day. That was a hard thing to do. Yasrall needed help from somewhere and the king was our only possibility. Whilst we knew it would not be a quick journey it was an essential one. We just hoped our people could survive until we could return with help.'

'The day that we set off, we had walked for less than an hour when we heard shouting behind us. We were still crossing fields, making our way toward the road that led to Bridgemouth. Turning to see where the shouting was coming from, we saw a group of Girngog, including a large figure, which Beryn said was an ogre, who were clearly following us. They were calling out as if asking that we halt. At first, we fell to the ground, hoping that we had not been seen, but we soon realised that was foolish. So, instead, we got up and ran. And the Girngog ran too. They were after us and we were running for our lives.'

'It did not take long to see that they were gaining ground, so Beryn suggested that we split up. He went north and I ran south, agreeing to meet up in Bridgemouth. The Girngog saw what we had done and in response, they also split up. All too soon, I could sense a group getting closer and I knew if I stayed in the open field I would be caught.'

'I decided my best choice was to make for the hills and Rabbit Woods as I knew it was riddled with rabbit tunnels and I thought I might hide in one. The lower reaches of the Rabbit Woods are not as thick as Clinglewood Forest, so I could still see my pursuers between the trees and bushes. I ran for the higher ground and came across many rabbit holes, but most too small for me to hide in. However, Rabbit Wood is known for having some very big rabbits, as I am sure you know. In Yasrall there are frightening stories about them, which is why most people keep away. Thankfully, I found a large hole, preferring to meet a big rabbit than the Girngog. But I could not get in wearing my pack, so I flung it away between some bushes, hoping that the Girngog would not realise which hole I had chosen. Then in I went.'

'It was a squeeze and I thought it would simply be a hiding place. But to my surprise, it was larger than I expected, so I just kept moving forward. To begin with I could hear the Girngog, they sounded as if they were at the entrance and my heart filled with dread, but they are much bigger than me and I hoped none could follow. I went deeper down the tunnel and into sheer darkness. It was then so quiet, very quiet. Slowly, I moved forward, increasingly confident that I was not being followed. But I had no sense of direction, I was lost in the darkness.'

'The darkness in those tunnels was truly dark. I could not see my nose in front of my face. I used my hands to guide me, sliding them along the walls. I came across more openings which I assumed were more tunnels. At these junctions, I had to make choices as to which way to go, and of course, I had no idea which way to go. I knew I could not find my way back to where I had started. I had no idea where the tunnels would lead and most felt too small for me to crawl along, even if I wished to. Though my eyes adjusted to the darkness, I could see no detail.'

'Even the largest tunnel was a tight squeeze. I could not turn around. If the space allowed, I could crawl on my knees, but I had to stop and stretch as my back ached. I also wondered how big the rabbits were who needed such large tunnels. That worried me. Would I end up as rabbit dinner! After a while, I began to imagine I would be trapped there forever.'

'I had to fight with myself and control my thoughts in order not to panic. The whole thing was bewildering and I lost track of time. I don't know how long I have been in those tunnels but I was becoming mighty hungry and thirsty. My hands and my clothes were filthy; I could feel it even though I could not see it. And to be plain, there were times when I felt like just giving up. I also fell asleep at several points, but I am unclear how long I slept.'

'Perhaps the most surprising thing was the quiet; I could hear nothing. I mean on the one hand I expected quiet but I also expected to hear rabbits. Though once or twice I thought I heard a voice telling me to wake up. My spirit waned but I kept going, though I realised I was moving slower and slower. I had completely lost track of time. Famished and thirsty, I expected I would rot in there. At what felt like my lowest point, when I thought I might as well just give up, I then heard a sound. My body tensed. Lifting my head, I saw a dim light ahead.'

'At first, I thought I had imagined it, so I closed my eyes and looked again. It was still there. It was dim and very small but it was a light. My heart raced and my hopes rekindled. I made for the light as quickly as I could, which was probably no faster than a snail. As I crawled and drew nearer the light, it grew larger. It seemed an eternity to reach it but when I did, I looked out and could see nothing at first, mainly because it hurt my eyes, it felt so bright. I gave it some time, allowing my eyes to adjust and then peeped through the hole again. I realised that it was a hole in the side of a wall. It was plain that I was partway in the hole; it dropped down, but it was too dark to see what lay below. So, I knocked some dirt into the hole and waited before hearing a splash. It took a few seconds but I decided that I was looking into a deep well.'

'I confess that I cried with joy and relief. But my challenge now was to try and climb out. As my eyes adjusted to the light, I looked up and could see the sides of the well. It was old and crumbling in places, and bricks had evidently fallen out. It looked daunting, too treacherous to climb but I had no choice. I had to get out; there was no other choice. I could not stay any longer in those tunnels.'

'Looking up I could see that the opening above had something lain across the top, but there were gaps in the covering through which the sun seeped through. That opening became my target. I tried to shout but my throat was sore. Deprived of water, I could not muster much more than a whisper.'

'So, I gathered my strength and began to climb; my heart pounding. I felt exhausted. Fearful of falling into the water below, I focused on one step at a time, not looking up or down. As I climbed,

I was breathing hard and I knew I was being rather noisy in my efforts. Several times I almost slipped but I was determined. One mistake and I would fall to the bottom. Yet it was taking all my strength to progress. Then I heard a voice, so I stopped and listened. I was sure that I heard someone talking about a squirrel or a ghost in the well. I confess that those words were like a song to my heart, they brought tears to my face, for I knew, to my relief, that I was not hearing the voices of the Girngog.'

4

The Request

So that is how I come to be sitting here with you. And in the circumstances, I am delighted to be here. Of course, I have heard of Chimbles but you are the first I have met. In truth, many in Yasrall think that you do not exist. Certainly, I know of no one who has any idea where you might live. And though I am here, I don't know where I am.'

'Well, we do tend to keep to ourselves that is true. Few people know how to reach our land, most pathways in or out of Chimbleton are secret or at least not used very often' replied Ceri. 'Though it is also true that Chimbles rarely venture outside of Chimbleton. We do not encourage contact.'

'Nonetheless, I am glad I found you,' continued Ruffle, 'I was completely lost in those rabbit tunnels and I could never find my way back. I thought I was doomed to wander forever or become rabbit fodder.'

Both Ceri and Tansy smiled as they both knew how confusing the tunnels were. They had once ventured into that labyrinth themselves, but that is a different story.

'Anyway, you may have gathered by now that I am on a quest to reach the King at Castle Black. Though, I don't know how to get there. He doesn't know about the Girngog overrunning Yasrall and breaking the terms of the peace treaty. I make an assumption in saying that, but to my knowledge, no message has been sent to him and contact with the Kingdom is so rare these days, how can he know? We foolishly trusted the Girngog too much from the beginning. We thought after all the years of peace that they simply wanted to trade. We were lulled into thinking the trading was genuine, when it was all part of their plan. It is my quest to tell him what has happened.'

'What do you think the King will do when he hears about this?' asked Tansy.

'I don't know, but surely, he will do something to help us' muttered Ruffle looking long faced and in truth unsure.

'The Girngog War was a long time ago; he must be very old by now' suggested Tansy. 'I wonder if his army is very old too because there have been no wars or fighting that I have heard of since. But then again, we do not bother with the affairs of the world, so I doubt that we would know if there had been.'

Ruffle sat up and in a more serious tone of voice said, 'For my part, I have no choice but to find my way to Castle Black and plead with the King. There is no one else I know of who might stand up to the Girngog. If nobody fights back then Yasrall is lost forever, we are already overcome. It will be the same for the whole Kingdom unless he does something.'

Ceri tried to be encouraging.

'I am sure the King will want to help, after all, he is the King and Yasrall has been protected by the Kingdom in the past. He will listen to you, Ruffle. In fact, you may be surprised and find that he may already know. He might even be gathering his army as we speak.'

'Thank you for your kind words, but I do not believe that to be so. Duskhold is so far away and we have seen no soldiers for many years. If he did know what is happening, then he would have responded by now, surely!' answered Ruffle. He looked at the two Chimbles and said quietly.

'I know I am already indebted to your hospitality, but there is something I would ask of you.'

'Hospitality does not carry a debt, you are very welcome, Ruffle. But do tell us what it is that you would ask,' said Ceri.

'I have decided to seek out help from Jevell, the wizard who lives in Clinglewood Forest, but I do not know how to get there or how to contact him. I realise that we have only just met, but can you help me to get there?'

Ceri and Tansy were surprised by this request; it was not what they had planned for that day and it seemed only five minutes ago that they had met this stranger.

'We have never really travelled out of our lands. We visit other Chimble villages yes, but they all lay within the valley. It is highly unusual for a Chimble to go beyond the valley. I am not sure that we could be much help' responded Tansy.

In truth, she had not ventured outside Chimbleton so had never visited Clinglewood, so she was quite unsure how to respond. However, Ceri surprised Tansy with her response and revealed a secret at the same time.

'Well, I do know how to get to Clinglewood, but if the Girngog are seeking you, then the final part of that journey may be dangerous. And forgive me for asking, but are you sure that Jevell the wizard lives there?'

'It is well known in Yasrall that the wizard Jevell lives there, although I confess, I know of nobody who has met him. But I believe it is true.'

Tansy interrupted, her eyes wide and staring at Ceri.

'How do you know a route to Clinglewood? When were you there? You never took me!' she spurted out, looking a little hurt that she did not know this of Ceri before this moment.

'It was a long time ago, when Grandpa Brock took me looking for blackberries,' replied Ceri, smiling. 'We did not go into Clinglewood Forest itself but collected the berries from bushes on its fringes.'

'It would save me precious time and be so helpful if you could show me the way,' said Ruffle. 'I do appreciate that it might be dangerous and that I am asking a lot of you, having only just met. But I hope you can see how urgent my journey is and how I have wasted too much time stuck in those tunnels. I ask a lot of you, I know, and I apologise if you think me rude for doing so.'

Tansy was still dwelling on the news that Ceri had been to Clinglewood Forest and she wanted to do the same. So, motivated by jealousy, she quickly responded to Ruffle.

'Of course you are not rude Mr Ruffle. I am sure we can take you there, don't you agree Ceri?'

Ceri smiled and looking at Tansy she guessed why she was so enthusiastic to help.

'Well, no immediate thought comes to mind as to why we cannot help you, so if that is the plan, and I am quite happy if it is, then we should make ready. I think we have enough time remaining of this day to get you there, though I am unsure if we can return home before night falls.'

'Right, it's agreed then,' said Tansy.

'Thank you, thank you. I promise I will find a way to repay you,' enthused Ruffle.

'Well, if we are not to spend the night in the forest then we should go straight away,' said Ceri.

As they packed away the remnants of their picnic the two Chimbles chatted and Ruffle took his clothes to dress fully. Although it was just the middle of the day Ceri explained that it would take most of the afternoon to reach Clinglewood Forest.

'How often have you been to the forest?' asked Tansy.

'Only twice, and it's been a long while,' answered Ceri.

'Have you met the wizard who lives there?' asked Tansy.

Ceri looked about to see where Ruffle was and nudged Tansy. The Rall was laying by the tree and seemingly fast asleep.

'He needs rest,' observed Tansy.

Ceri nodded toward the river and two Chimbles ambled to its shore.

'No, I have never met the wizard and if I am honest, I am not sure that there is any wizard living there. But Ruffle believes that there is, and after his ordeal, I think helping him reach the forest is the least we might do for him. He will need to decide how to proceed from there. Unfortunately, we can't allow him to sleep if we are to get there in daylight.''

'I presume when he spoke of the danger, he was referring to the Girngog. I have heard enough to convince me that I do not wish to meet any; they sound horrible, not the kind of people I would invite for tea or a picnic. Let's give him a few minutes to doze.''

A short while later Ruffle awoke and sat up. It had only been ten minutes but the Rall looked brighter, his clothes drier. Though they were still in need of a good soapy wash after his underground adventure.

Walking back from the shore, the Chimbles rejoined Ruffle.

'Sorry about that, I am more tired than I thought,' said the Rall.

Ceri decided to leave her knapsack at Big Sprout as there was nothing in it that would be helpful for their journey to Clinglewood. Tansy did the same, though she insisted on bringing what she called her 'Faerie sword'. It was a tiny blade that she insisted the faerie had once used. Although, she had never met a faerie. Nonetheless, a trip to Clinglewood was an adventure for a Chimble and just might be dangerous. So, she decided it was better to be armed.

They set off following a path which Ceri knew, but not one that a casual hiker would ever recognise as a path. It was a mixture of trees and bushes with some open spaces, but they could not easily be seen as they wended their way downhill. Some parts of their route were steep but presented no difficulty to the hikers. As they walked, they talked and the new friendship grew as they exchanged stories of their respective home lands. It took several hours before they reached ground level. Tansy was surprised, admitting that she had not appreciated that Chimbleton lay on such high ground.

The trees thinned as they had got closer to ground level. Ahead of them stretched fields of flowers and long grass. Ceri ushered the group behind a large tree at the foot of the hill they had descended.

'If the Girngog are still looking for you, Ruffle, then this is where they might be patrolling. It is not obvious from here with this long grass in front of us, but the road to Bridgemouth runs shelter nearby. As you can see there is little shelter between here and that dark outline of trees, which is Clinglewood Forest. So, let us just pause and look about before we venture out,' said Ceri.

'That forest looks so big and dark,' observed Tansy, for which there was silent agreement amongst her companions. Though some distance away, the trees of Clinglewood stood large and imposing.

The tree line stretched as far as they could see, projecting an impenetrable darkness beneath the branches.

'Have you ever visited the forest?' asked Ceri.

'No', said Ruffle, clearly very thoughtful and not sounding confident.

'Are you sure there is a wizard there? Do you know if he is friendly?' quizzed Tansy.

'As I said before, I am not certain, but I am confident that a wizard lives there. The stories say that he is a kind wizard, a Master Wizard, who goes by the name of Jevell. Although I confess, I do not personally know of anyone who has met him,' said Ruffle. 'But my friends, I have no choice. I know I will need help and this wizard may be the one who can help me. The last thing I would ask of you, if you don't mind, is will you accompany me across the fields until we reach the trees?'

'Well having come this far, I was assuming that we should at least see you to the trees' answered Ceri, grinning.

Tansy was not so sure but said nothing. She suspected Ceri wanted to see if there was a wizard in the forest. However, she had an uneasy sense about the situation and it was a good distance to the tree line. Nonetheless she wished to be a good friend and help Ruffle. Privately she thought her sense of dread may be because she had never been away from the valley of Chimbleton before.

The three companions looked about for a few minutes, scouring the land, but could see nothing moving, so cautiously, they set off across the open fields. They chatted as they walked, frequently scanning the horizon for signs of Girngog.

'It has crossed my mind that if the Girngog overran these lands, then one day they might find their way to Chimbleton,' said Ceri.

'Well, they better not, for we Chimbles can fight if we need to' replied Tansy as she touched her 'faerie sword' inside her belt.

'Yes, but we are not soldiers, Tansy, we are peaceful and I hope we never lose that quality.' answered a thoughtful Ceri.

'We did not wish to fight either. And not only because the Girngog are bigger than us, some twice my size and more. I have even seen ogres and trolls amongst their number. But we are people of the land not warriors. I suspect only the humans are a match for them, which is why I have to let the King know our predicament and get some help,' said Ruffle.

'Shush!' said Ceri lifting her right hand wide to signal a halt, 'lie on the ground and don't move, someone is on the road'.

They all dropped to the grassy floor. The large fields were all overgrown except for the road which ran from Stonehelm to Bridgemouth. It was a little more than a hundred paces in front of where they lay. It was the obvious route for any travellers.

At that moment, they were thankful for the long grass and Ceri's acute hearing. There was definitely noise that grew louder with every passing minute. It was the sound of voices. Peering between the blades of grass, they spied a group. 'They are Girngog,' whispered Ruffle. They were coming from the direction of Yasrall, chanting, or perhaps singing; it was difficult to decide. They tromped along, five abreast, taking up the whole width of the dusty road.

It was the first time the two Chimbles had seen the Girngog and they decided Ruffle had described them well. They appeared to be all shapes and sizes, armed to the teeth, accompanied by a strong whiff – not dissimilar to dried sweat, even at a distance. They were led by several on horses, big unfriendly looking horses. The leader at the front continually looked about from his high elevation as if expecting to see something significant. Several other Girngog, walking through the grass beside the road, seemed to have the same job - to spy the surrounding landscape. It was a tense moment as the companions lay flat, hoping that they had not been seen. The procession trundled past, taking several minutes to do so. It was tense, and Tansy's face suggested that she had forgotten to keep breathing. Nothing was said between the three companions until the marchers were long past.

As the Girngog walked off into the distance, Tansy whispered, 'I think I just created a new record for holding my breath, there must have been five hundred and I reckon they were looking for something or someone.'

'I hope it wasn't me they sought,' said Ruffle, smiling sheepishly.

'Your description was accurate, Ruffle; they are a smelly lot and ugly with it. I have no wish to meet them again' asserted Ceri. She knelt and hesitantly looked about to check if all was clear.

'Though surely such a large force was not marching just to search for you Ruffle. Anyway, I think it's ok now, we should go before any more of them venture along this road.'

With that they stood, brushed the grass from their clothes and set off toward the forest. They crossed the road and were now on the side of the field that ran up to the forest. They continuously looked about as they walked, not wishing to meet any more Girngog. Their mood was becoming more relaxed the closer they got to the big trees. Then the mood changed.

'Boom, boom, boom' rang through the air - it was the drums of the Girngog. There were shouts and more 'boom, boom, boom'. Appearing as if from nowhere, the edges of the field were suddenly full of running Girngog and seemingly heading toward the three companions.

'Where did they come from?' said a surprised Ruffle.

'I have no idea but I think we ought to run' responded Tansy.

'Definitely, to the trees', agreed Ceri and off they sped.

The Girngog seemed to be coming from the road and the three companions had just a short lead on them, so without further comment, their legs whirred into motion. Whilst the long grass had helped them hide, it now made running more difficult. It was soon clear that the bigger Girngog were reducing the distance between the hunters and the hunted.

'Spread out,' shouted Ceri as they ran, and they did. Tansy and Ruffle were close together on the left whilst Ceri headed more to the right. Their only hope was to reach the forest first. It was increasingly clear that it would be a very close contest.

So, you may have now realised that this is where our tale began. Tansy and Ruffle did reach the trees together, hearts pounding and mighty relieved to find that the Girngog did not follow them into the forest. Unfortunately, as you know, Ceri did not. She was captured.

5

Clinglewood Forest

Tansy and Ruffle reached the forest before the Girngog. Before them, the trees stretched endlessly, dark and foreboding. The only light splintered through the canopy above, offering no clues as to which way they could go.

'Stop, Ruffle, stop,' called a breathless Tansy.

Ruffle gladly came to a halt, puffing and panting.

'What is it?'

'I don't think the Girngog are following us and I can't see Ceri'.

Turning, they walked back toward the tree line.

'I think you're right; I hear nothing other than birds, which honestly is a little unnerving.'

'But where is Ceri?' wondered Tansy.

'She must have entered the forest somewhere. Let's retrace our steps and see if we can see her. But watch out for Girngog,' he cautioned.

Carefully and slowly, they wound their way through the trees. They had not penetrated far into the woodland and felt confident that they were accurately retracing their steps. The forest was dense, as if the trees cuddled together, making it difficult to run. At the edge of the tree line, they hid behind some wide trees.

Peering across the fields they saw the Girngog retreating back toward the road, seemingly uninterested in entering the forest.

'There are many more of them than I thought. And look, oh dear,' uttered Ruffle, pointing and eyebrows raised.

Tansy gasped, Ceri was in the middle of the Girngog gang, being pushed along and looking quite small among her subduers.

'I must help her,' said the Chimble as she drew her small sword and took a step forward as if she was about to charge after the Girngog.

'Wait,' said Ruffle as he placed his hand on her sword arm, 'if you try to help her, you will be killed or captured, there are too many of them. '

Tansy knew he was right and stopped. She felt helpless watching her dearest friend being pulled and jostled by her captors.

'What are we to do?' she spoke aloud.

It was the first time Tansy had ever encountered danger of this sort and she was feeling she had let Ceri down, that she should have done more to help her friend. But even in her despair, she knew that blaming herself was not helpful. Nonetheless she felt despondent. The Girngog were so large and one big lump of a creature stood out, taller than the rest. Was he an ogre or their leader? Whatever he was, he alone would be difficult to defeat in battle and there were dozens more with him. Ruffle's words reverberated in her mind. She knew it would be futile to try and rescue Ceri.

Ruffle interrupted her woe.

'Tansy, there is nothing that we can do now but perhaps the Master of the Forest might be able to help us. After all he is a wizard and it may be that he has some idea as to how we might save Ceri. Let us go and find him as quickly as we can.'

She could think of no alternative, so reluctantly she accepted the suggestion from the Rall. Though she said nothing, she was doubtful that any wizard lived in the forest. She tucked the little faerie sword back in her belt and turned to face her companion, saying, 'Which way do we go?'

'Well, to be honest, I don't know. I've never been here before. But it makes sense that if we head for the centre of the forest, then we stand a good chance of finding the wizard' suggested Ruffle, who in truth had no idea which way led to the centre or if it did make sense!

'Do you think that there really is a good wizard here?' asked Tansy.

'Of course, that is the whole reason I am here, to find him,' answered Ruffle. Privately, he had more hope than belief.

Tansy nodded in agreement. So, they turned and moved back toward the forest. She felt desperate about the situation and could not imagine how a forest wizard could help, but she needed to do something to lift her spirits and the only option she could think of was to go along with Ruffle's suggestion.

They trudged through the trees speaking little. It was dark and quiet. They walked slowly, hoping that they were heading toward the centre of the forest, but they may have walked in circles as there was nothing to indicate where they were. It all looked the same. After some while Tansy stopped.

'I would say that we are lost but we didn't know where we were to begin with. Certainly, I see no sign of any wizard,' bemoaned Tansy.

'Sadly, I think you're right,' replied Ruffle.

'I worry what is happening to Ceri!'

'I would not worry too much, I think the stories about them eating captives are exaggerated,' said Ruffle.

'What stories?'

'Have you not heard them?' replied Ruffle, regretting that he had said anything.

'No. I know little of the Girngog. What are you saying?' asked a worried Tansy.

'Well, some say that the Girngog cook and eat their captives. But I think it is more likely to be their ogres. Though I don't think they ate anyone in Yasrall, so I am sure Ceri will be fine,' said Ruffle, trying to reassure Tansy and regretting that he had said anything.

'Was that big creature with the Girngog who were chasing us, an ogre?'

'Perhaps, though it was difficult to tell.'

'So, not only is she captured but she could be eaten by an ogre or a Girngog! We have to do something and quickly,' said Tansy.

Ruffle could think of nothing to add. He wanted the ground to swallow him. This was the beginning of his quest and already he had lost both Beryn and now Ceri. His confidence was punctured. He was still committed to reaching the king but he questioned himself – was he being foolish!

'Are you sure that there is a wizard in this forest?' asked Tansy.

'It's true that I can't be certain, but others say they have seen him.'

'So really, we only have rumours of his existence. Let us hope there is some truth in those stories, for we have no one else to turn to,' said Tansy, who was now feeling a rising anger.

'Though even if we do find him, I do not see how he can help us retrieve Ceri. In fact, we don't even know if he is friendly. This could become more of a disaster than it already is,' she added.

Ruffle was well aware of the upset Tansy felt but he was bereft of words to help her. He was blaming himself and now felt sorry that he had asked the Chimbles for help. He was at a complete loss as to what to do. His hopes now rested on finding the wizard. His silence signalled his own despair.

They both began to notice that the forest grew darker. Tansy thought that the fading light reflected their mood. They walked without speaking. The gloomy darkness of the forest contrasted with the loud noise created by the sound of their footsteps scrunching leaves underfoot.

'Let's rest,' said Tansy.

They were in a small clearing where an old fallen tree served as a bench. They sat and each took a swig of water.

'We are truly lost,' said Ruffle. 'It's getting so dark we will struggle to walk anywhere.' His optimism now acutely diminished.

''We have been lost since we entered this forest. There is not a semblance of a path that we can follow. There is nothing to suggest anyone lives here. But I doubt that we could find our way out now, these trees are all so close together, I have no idea what direction we came from. As for the wizard, it's probably just a tale of someone who doesn't exist,' responded Tansy.

'I am sorry, Tansy; it is all my fault. I should never have asked you to come with me.'

'Oh, do not blame yourself, it was our choice. I am sorry things have turned out this way. Ignore my whining, I just feel I should have done more to help Ceri. We are in a maze made of trees, lost and unable to help her. I fear that by now she may be chopped up or sitting in a pot surrounded by carrots and potatoes. The thought of someone eating my best friend upsets me.'

'Don't talk of food, I am famished. Besides, they will question Ceri before doing anything else, so there may be time yet. And I know they don't eat everyone they capture,' said Ruffle. 'If only we had some way to contact the wizard, at least then we could ask him if he could help.'

'Perhaps he already knows you need help' said a deep voice, that did not belong to either of the two companions. It came from the darkness and caused them both to jump with fright, falling off their tree stump seat. Tansy tried to find her small faerie blade.

The voice had come from the trees and its owner was not visible.

'Who said that?' asked Tansy, looking into the depths of the night.

'Not me', said Ruffle in a rather squeaky voice.

'It was me and I apologise for giving you both such a fright' came the voice out of the darkness.

They looked into the dark and noticed movement; a shimmering shape was emerging. Then, rising from the trees moving toward them was the biggest dog they had ever seen. It was more the size of a horse. It was black which made it hard to see where it began or where it finished. It came to a halt in front of the two petrified friends. Its big green eyes stared at them and Tansy felt it was smiling. She tightened her grip on the hilt of her small sword.

'Are you real?' spluttered Tansy.

'I will let you decide that,' replied the dog.

'You talk!' said Ruffle.

'Indeed, I do, thank you for noticing. My name is Shadow and I am here because Jevell, the Master of Clinglewood, asked me to find you. He invites you to supper. Would that be acceptable?'

The friends looked at one another. For long moments neither spoke.

'Very much so, please,' spluttered Ruffle. 'I could eat.'

'Who is this Jevell, is he the wizard in the wood?' asked Tansy, feeling suspicious and on guard.

'He is. In fact, he is a Master Wizard,' said the dog.

'Then your invitation is most welcome and warmly accepted,' said Tansy. Suddenly her suspicions had evaporated and instinctively she felt relief. For the first time since entering the forest, she felt hopeful.

'Which way do we go?'

'Please, just follow me,' said Shadow.

Looking at one another, eyes wide, the two companions stood up and began to follow the huge dog.

Ruffle was surprised, excited and relieved. Relieved because it seemed that the stories of a wizard were actually true; it seemed the wizard did exist and maybe, just maybe, he might be able to help Ceri.

As Shadow walked, it seemed that the trees parted, allowing a clear pathway that had not been there before. They followed. They realised that the dog was creating its own path as it walked; a path that had not existed until he created it and disappeared once they had passed.

The two friends struggled to keep up with the dog, not least because they were tired. Plus, the dog has such long legs. Shadow had noticed their weariness and halted.

'Please do not be offended but may I suggest that you both climb on my back, it will make our journey a little quicker!'

'Climb on your back, won't we be too heavy?' asked Tansy.

The dog made a sound which they later learned was his laughing.

'No, I will be fine,' said Shadow.

'I am not offended by the suggestion,' said Ruffle, who was feeling excited at the idea of riding a giant dog.

'Me neither and speed is important to us.' Tansy nodded.

Shadow crouched down on all four legs as if to invite the companions on board. They both obliged, although even when crouching the dog was still large enough that each had to assist the other in clambering atop their unusual steed. Eventually, they were seated on the huge animal.

'Hold onto my hair if it makes you feel more secure. But don't worry I will not let you fall' said Shadow as he stood up and began to walk.

After allowing the two riders a few minutes to adjust to their transport the dog began to steadily increase its speed. Before very long they were galloping through the trees at such a pace that the surroundings were a blur. Neither companion had ever travelled so fast. Briefly, Tansy expected that they would bump into a tree as they sped so swiftly. Yet soon both riders felt quite safe astride the amazing dog. It became plain to Ruffle that some magic was at work, for the dense forest and the uneven ground was no hindrance to Shadow.

The two companions barely talked as they clung to the back of the dog. However, it was not long before the journey came to an end. Nonetheless, they sensed they were now deep within the forest. Shadow had slowed and then emerged into a large clearing. The friends were lost for words.

Emerging from the dark of the forest the last embers of daylight were sufficient to illuminate what lay before them.

Their eyes immediately focused on a small cosy cottage, with smoke billowing from its chimney and a faint light evident in its windows. A garden of flowers spread around the cottage and for some unknown reason a gentle smile broke on the faces of the two companions.

It was a place of peace and it enveloped them. No words had been exchanged but both felt safe.

Smoothly, Shadow lowered and allowed his passengers to dismount. 'The Master is expecting you, just take yourselves in,' said the dog.

Wordlessly, they followed the instruction given by Shadow and took the path that wended through the flowers to the large wooden door, painted maroon with a large brass knocker shaped like an owl. As they drew closer and before they could knock, the door opened and the two friends stopped dead still and wide-eyed. Out stepped a tall man with long black hair, a short beard and wearing a broad smile.

'Welcome, my friends, come along inside and let us share some refreshments, I am sure we have much to discuss', he said, gesturing that they enter.

'Don't worry little ones this is Jevell, Master of Clinglewood Forest' encouraged Shadow as he followed behind. 'He is the wizard you seek.'

'I have been expecting you. I knew Shadow would find you. This woodland can be quite confusing for a visitor. Though we get few visitors nowadays. Oh yes, I am Jevell and you must be Tansy and Ruffle!'

'Yes, but how do you know our names?' queried Tansy with surprise colouring her voice.

'The forest has many ears and word travels quickly here' replied Jevell.

Ruffle had been silent as he stepped into the cottage. Wide-eyed he stood looking about the room. He then stepped back out of the door before returning inside again.

'Fludgebuttle wallop' he uttered, 'it may be my eyes but this dwelling seems much larger inside than it appears from the outside'.

'Well observed, Ruffle, you are indeed correct', smiled Jevell. 'A simple indulgence of an old wizard.'

Then it was the turn of Tansy to notice the peculiarity of the cottage. The room they stood in, with its open fireplace, chairs and large table, seemed larger than the entire building that they had observed when they had arrived. Furthermore, there was a passageway with doors along its walls and another room that was clearly a kitchen. How did it all fit in, she wondered? So, she too stepped back outside and then in again.

Jevell smiled a smile of welcome and reassurance.

'Come and take a seat, I am curious to learn why you are here,' said the wizard.

Large cushioned chairs faced a glowing fire, encouraging relaxation. As they made themselves comfortable both companions felt the tiredness sweep through their bodies. Tansy was a stew of feelings, fascinated, amazed, relieved and fearful. This was all so new and she felt a little overwhelmed.

In his warm welcoming voice Jevell asked his guests, 'now before we talk, would you like some dandelion tea or perhaps strawberry wine?'

'Tea is fine for me' said Ruffle as he wallowed in the comfort of the cushions and the heat from the burning wood; temporarily forgetting why he was there, he stretched his legs as if ready to drift into sleep.

'It's fine for me too, thank you,' said Tansy.

The wizard took himself off to the kitchen but soon returned. He carried a tray with an apple-shaped teapot and a plate of biscuits. Before he could lay it upon the table Tansy spoke.

'Please master wizard you must help our friend, Ceri, for she has been captured by the Girngog and even now they may be eating her. What can we do, can you help her? We are at a loss as to how we can save her. Please can you help?'

The words were tumbling out as her worst fears for her best friend took hold of her thoughts once again, disrupting her calm.

'Slow down young Chimble, let us have some tea and then tell me your story from the beginning,' said the wizard. 'Meanwhile, rest easy, I know about your friend's predicament, and a good friend of mine is assisting her as we speak.'

Once again Tansy was taken aback. His words were welcome but a host of questions immediately sprang to her mind; who was this 'good friend' and how could one person help Ceri captured by a small horde of Girngog? She had so many questions but she told herself to be patient, allowing herself the feeling of a smidgeon of reassurance from the wizard. She sipped the tea which was absolutely delicious and tried a biscuit.

'That is a scrumptious biscuit' she commented, doing her best not to keep asking questions.

'Blueberry biscuits, made by my own fair hands and without the aid of magic. Though my first attempts at baking were not so successful,' laughed the wizard. 'And trust me, the friend I speak of is a very sensible and capable ally. In fact, he should rejoin us tonight, I estimate.'

Tansy nodded. Quite perplexed, then feeling reassured with what the wizard had just said, she relaxed and munched a biscuit, adding 'this is the best blueberry biscuit I can remember having.'

Ruffle nodded enthusiastically but could say nothing as his mouth was so full.

'Well, we shan't eat too much, I have prepared supper for later,' said their host.

I just hope Ceri is not the main ingredient for some Girngog supper, thought Tansy as she took another biscuit. She knew she could not hold back her questions much longer.

6

Ozwill

Ceri was exhausted and annoyed. How could I allow myself to be caught, she silently scolded herself. She was now in the middle of a group of Girngog as they marched. She was consistently being pushed and shoved in order to keep up with her much larger captors. It was hard as they shuffled along at quite a quick pace, seemingly impatient to reach wherever they were heading. However, the jostling was not the worst of it, it was the smell. She thought to herself that Ruffle had not exaggerated when he had said just how smelly Girngog were. She had asked if she could stop for a wash, as if to drop a hint, but was answered by a slap to the back of her head, which hurt. Girngog do not like to wash.

In addition, they were singing as they marched, though she thought it better described as a chant. She did not like their singing or the song they all seemed to relish, which seemed pertinent to her situation. A number grinned at her as they sang, as if to confirm her suspicion. The words she could make out went like this;

We are the Girngog

It's time for us to eat

We like to chew the bones

And finish off with feet

Munch munch munch

The Siege of Castle Black

It's time for us to eat

Munch munch munch

It's time for us to eat

On your own or in a bunch

You'll fit inside our pie

Our favourite part is hands and toes

And sometimes pickled eye

Munch munch munch

It's time for us to eat

Munch munch munch

It's time for us to eat

You'll be warm inside the pot

You'll make a lovely stew

We'll cook your skin so tasty

Your bones and meat will do

Munch munch munch

It's time for us to eat

Munch munch munch

It's time for us to eat

The Siege of Castle Black

You can sit beside the carrots

Or potatoes if you wish

You can bring your friends along

There's room upon my dish

Munch munch munch

It's time for us to eat

Munch munch munch

It's time for us to eat

On and on it went, so many verses but she did not like the topic, so she tried to stop listening. She wondered, was it her destiny to end up in a pie? This was her first real adventure outside of Chimbleton. It was not going well and she preferred that it did not end this way. Besides, she thought she should point out to her captors that Chimbles don't taste very nice and they would be ill if they ate her. She decided to tell them that Chimbles are poisonous if eaten. That thought was cheerful and she hoped it might put them off cooking her!

The light had faded and they marched by torchlight. Suddenly, they halted and began to make camp. Bags, pots and pans were unloaded from the unfortunate animals they used to carry their equipment. Unsure where they were, Ceri estimated they must be heading into Yasrall. It was obvious that they felt there was nothing to fear, as they stopped and camped right beside the road. There were just a few trees and bushes, no need for them to find cover or hide. They had no tents or bedding; they simply lay on the ground.

Ceri was sat leaning against a tree, near a group that seemed charged with watching her. She was not tied up and there was no need of a guard - there was nowhere to run. It was dark and she was surrounded by Girngog. Small fires were lit by different groups and most appeared to carry some dried food and pouches which contained liquid. The more of the liquid they drank, the rowdier they became. Nothing was offered to Ceri, for which she was grateful. Then her bag which had been taken from her was flung at her feet. She took out her own flask and had a much-needed long drink of water. There was no food remaining in her bag. She decided that her captors must have eaten what was there. She did not want to ask for food, unsure of what they were eating, and preferred to go hungry.

Intentionally, she did not make eye contact with anyone, though she noticed that some stared or pointed her way. Her heart was heavy, for she knew escape was beyond her. She wondered if her friends had escaped or been slain. As for herself, she had heard that the Girngog were known for eating captives and the words of their chant reinforced her thoughts that she might be heading for an oven or a spit.

This fear was compounded when several Girngog came and stood over her, pointing and laughing. They rubbed their stomachs and seemed to be arguing, though she could not understand what was said. Voices were being raised and it was clear that there was disagreement. One drew out a long knife and started waving it in the direction of Ceri.

'Oh dear,' the Chimble said to herself.

Then it seemed as if some agreement had been reached and they took a step toward her. Fearing the worst, she was relieved when a booming voice stopped them in their tracks. A very large Girngog strode over, said a few words and then slapped the one holding the knife, spoke some more and then the group turned and walked away mumbling amongst themselves.

The big hulking figure looked at Ceri, 'We have not eaten you yet til' Irig see you, then we cook. For me, I have your feet' and he laughed a deep horrible laugh. At last, someone who spoke the common tongue, she thought. However, she was not comforted by his words.

'Well, I can assure you that you will regret it. I am a Chimble and many have been sick and poisoned trying to eat us. We simply don't taste very nice,' she splurged out, unable to think of what else to say, and desperately trying to negotiate.

The big Girngog pulled a face, an ugly face, as if he were worried by her words, then he laughed again, 'no matter, we will cook you until the poison is gone. Roasted Rall will be a dish for Irig, I make him pleased,' then he strode off.

'So, that worked well,' she said to herself! He thinks I am a Rall, but that doesn't matter. She knew exactly what he was telling her; she would be questioned by someone called Irig and then cooked. No doubt others were laying claim to different parts of her. At that moment everything felt hopeless and she begrudged a smelly Girngog laying claim to her feet. I need them she thought, not least if I am to try and escape. She struggled to hold back tears, not wanting to show her captors how upset she really was.

After a while the Girngog quietened, settled down and most went to sleep. Some were clearly meant to be guards and they stood around the camp looking out into the darkness. All was still, except for the snoring. It seemed to Ceri that most Girngog snore and many fart in their sleep. It was all a little overpowering and soon the camp reeked of extra smelly Girngog despite being outdoors.

Ceri was weighed down by the feeling of disappointment. She felt that she had failed and let down her friends. She considered how worried Tansy must be, assuming that she escaped. She dreaded the thought she and Ruffle were also captured? But if they were, then surely she would have seen them by now. There was no one she could ask, as the Girngog would or could not talk with her. Besides it was not a good idea to remind them about her friends, especially if they had escaped. She reasoned that they must have escaped. If they had been slain, then presumably these barbarians would already be cooking them. No, she decided that they had escaped. This gave her some small relief.

She tried to concentrate on good things, and felt warm inside when she thought of her dear friend, Tansy, and of all the fun things they had done together. She missed her. Plus, she was just beginning to know Ruffle and she liked him. She hoped that they were both well away and safe.

Leaning back against the tree, she tried to find some calm within her, but her thoughts whirled around and she could not find sleep. She stared at the sky with its endless canopy of stars and hazy moon. Then she blinked and looked again. Was that something moving across the moon? She stared. Some guards seemed to have noticed it too. They pointed to the sky and others were grumbling as the chatter disturbed their sleep.

Whatever was in the sky seemed to be in flight, circling the camp from ahigh. It seemed to be flying lower. Ceri could make out large wings. There was shouting among the Girngog and she heard someone utter the word 'demon' as panic spread and pandemonium broke out. Girngog jumped up and some were now fleeing, forgetting to grab their meagre belongings. Nobody was paying any attention to Ceri.

'Is that what a demon looks like?' the Chimble muttered to herself, puzzled by what she saw. She realised she was alone, her captors running away. Then the demon descended more swiftly, dropped down from the sky and landed a mere ten paces in front of a startled Ceri.

In fact, the so-called demon was a huge brown owl, as tall as a tree and wearing spectacles.

'My apologies for the dramatic entrance but I thought it might have more impact on those creatures if I arrived this way. Forgive me, I assume that you are Ceridwen Meldrim?' asked the demon.

Ceri, mouth wide open, simply nodded her head. The giant owl was speaking.

'My name is Ozwill by the way and Master Jevell asked me to collect you. You do know who Jevell is, don't you? I can see from your expression that you are surprised that I am wearing spectacles. Well, my sight is as good as any, except when I am too close to something, then I do need a little assistance.'

'You did say you know of Jevell, didn't you? He is, of course, the Master of Clinglewood and he explained to me that those smelly creatures had taken you prisoner. It was he that asked me to fetch you. Now, whilst I do like a decent conversation, at this moment your captors seem to have regained some courage and I see that they are turning to come back toward us. So, if you don't mind that is enough chat for now. Lie down and I will pick you up and I think we best be off.'

Ceri, still flummoxed by this huge talking owl, and having not said a word, did as requested. She lay on the ground, clutching her empty knapsack and wondered what was to happen next. She felt the large claws of the owl gently close about her; her eyes squeezed shut, she was off the ground. The wind blew across her face and she heard what she assumed must be wings flapping. She was moving and slowly opening her eyes saw she was already high in the air. She could not see the face of Ozwill but she could hear him.

'You can relax, it is not a long journey and I won't drop you. Oh, and your friends await you at the cottage. Close your eyes if you feel unwell.'

Ceri remained lost for words. Glancing below she saw that the Girngog had returned and loosed off arrows vainly hoping to stop the giant bird as it rose into the night sky, but their efforts were futile. The owl was too swift. She could see the Girngog arguing and fighting amongst themselves. No doubt none wished to be held responsible when it came to explaining to Irig, what had occurred.

She regained some calm as they flew over the land and then the trees of the forest. This has to be better than being an ingredient in a pie she decided. Then the thought crossed her mind, what if this giant owl also wants to eat me! But she comforted herself recalling what the owl had said, referring to Jevell and her friends awaiting her. So many thoughts rushed through her mind, she was confused.

Before long she felt comfortable and despite the great height, safe. So, she dared to look about. She looked down and although it was dark she could make out the ground. Suddenly it felt that they were impossibly high, and she instinctively gripped harder to the claw of the great bird. She thought she might be sick and closed her eyes.

Gradually she reopened them and calmed herself. She was filled with wonder as she thought, this is how birds must see the world. She marvelled, allowing herself to be amazed and less fearful. She had many questions for Ozwill but decided that it was not the best time to ask them, so she kept quiet. Instead, she watched the world whizz by, in silence and in awe. Her stomach became more settled, as long as she did not look directly below.

Her eyes were adapting to the darkness and she now trusted the giant owl. So much so that she was a little disappointed when Ozwill announced 'Here we are.' It had not taken very long.

The owl flew lower and Ceri could make out a cleared area within the trees. Dropping closer to the ground, she spied a small cottage with a whisp of smoke escaping from its chimney. Light shone through the cottage windows and as the ground grew near, she could see a large garden of flowers. Quite suddenly, Ozwill dropped swiftly, coming to rest on the ground.

'Here, you are as safe as you will ever be Ceri, for this is where Jevell lives,' the owl informed her. 'I hope that was not too unpleasant a ride.'

At last, the Chimble found her voice.

'Thank you, Ozwill, you have saved my life. That was simply amazing.'

'It has been my pleasure. Now, I think you should go and knock on the cottage door, for I am sure that they await you.'

'Won't you join us?'

'Thank you but no. The night is young and I still have my supper to catch. But fear not, you will not be eaten tonight, at least not by me, besides there are too many bones in people for my liking,' and he made a gruff sound, which Ceri deduced was likely to be laughter.

'Good luck,' said Ozwill as he rose into the air and flew off.

Ceri waved and said quietly, 'good luck, it was nice to meet you.'

High in the sky and rapidly rising Ceri assumed Ozwill could not hear her, but the owl turned his head and said, 'it was jolly nice to meet you too.'

Ceri stood watching him go. After a few moments, she turned and walking through the flowers, made her way to the cottage door. She could hear voices inside and wondering whom she was about to meet, she lifted the silver doorknocker set in the middle of the door which happened to be in the figure of an owl and knocked.

7

Gaining Friends

Before the knock at the cottage door, Jevell had asked a simple question. 'Now we are comfortable, I would very much like to learn what brings you to Clinglewood?'

Despite having consumed an endless supply of strawberry tea and blueberry biscuits Ruffle was enthusiastically garrulous in telling of his experiences so far. He explained how the Girngog had, over time, ensconced themselves into the fabric of life in Yasrall. It had been in effect a quiet invasion that had imprisoned the Rall before anyone recognized what was happening. He told of his meeting with the Kings Voice and that he now carried the Kings Seal.

Then, of his escape from Yasrall, his friend Beryn, the rabbit tunnels and being lost in darkness. How lost in the underground tunnels, he had almost given up before discovering the light leading to the well in Chimbleton. Then upon climbing out of the well he had discovered that he was in Chimbleton, where he had come upon Ceri and Tansy.

At that point, Tansy had not said a word but now she took over. She described the picnic at Big Sprout, where a dirty Ruffle had come climbing out of the well and how their encounter had led to an agreement to accompany him to Clinglewood. She concluded with an account of how Ceri was captured and emphatically repeated how worried she was for her friend.

The telling of the tale had taken a good while and the wizard had noted how sad Tansy had become as it unfolded. He offered some words hoping to reassure her.

'Ozwill is wise and brave; he will surprise the Girngog. I have every confidence that he can help Ceri.'

'But master wizard you don't understand, there were lots of Girngog, how can one person hope to rescue Ceri. They may have eaten her by now! Unless this Ozwill is a great warrior I don't see how one person can succeed.'

'I doubt that Ceri has been cooked and eaten already, for they will want to question her first. Ozwill is swift and, how do I say this, not an ordinary person, so don't give up hope on his being able to help,' said Jevell. 'Now, I am sure your storytelling has restored your appetite, so let me go and find something more to sate the hunger Ruffle appears to have!'

With that Jevell took himself to the kitchen and returned with cheese, bread, pickled onions, lettuce leaves, butter and elderberry wine. Both his guests did not hesitate to tuck in. As they broke bread, the friends took the opportunity to ask questions of Jevell.

'I know this side of Clinglewood faces Yasrall but what lays on the other side of the forest?' asked Ruffle.

'Well, the forest is wide and runs north all the way to the Ironspine Mountains. However, on the eastern side it grows close to Seabreeze Lake, though, not completely to the shore. From the trees, there is a stretch of flat and shrubby land that runs into sandhills, which lead down onto a sandy beach. The beach is the shore for Seabreeze Lake. The lake itself is enormous. To the north, the lake is fed by many streams and rivers, and although called a lake, to the south it actually leads to the open sea. For the most part, the lake is expansive and can take several days to cross by boat. To the south it narrows significantly at Bridgemouth, which is where sits the only bridge across the lake. The bridge is often referred to as the Necklace. I suspect that if the Girngog are indeed making war then they will be heading there, as it is the main route from east to west. In normal circumstances, you would cross the bridge when travelling to Duskhold from Yasrall. At this time, in these circumstances, I think we must assume it is occupied by the Girngog and consider alternatives.'

Jevell could see he had a captivated audience; the two guests were eating as they listened and had forgotten their worries for the time being.

'Seabreeze Lake is a huge expanse of water and over time many stories about its inhabitants have grown. Some say that it is so deep that a sea monster lives in its depths. But to my knowledge, none have seen it in living memory. You also may not know it but Clinglewood is the largest forest in the Old Kingdom. Earthroot, which is not considered part of the Old Kingdom, is the only forest that I know of which is larger. In Earthroot, the trees are the tallest and it is also the home of the Faerie. The tales of that great forest say that it stretches all around the world. As for the Faerie, you will never see them unless they wish to be seen.'

The voice of the wizard was soothing and his visitors were visibly relaxing. The cottage was warm, orange flames danced off the wood crackling in the fireplace and the two companions were entranced by Jevell's words; so much so, that they slipped into sleep. Even Shadow lay in front of the fire snoring, rather loudly at times.

Suddenly Tansy jerked awake. She was warm and snug. Turning to Ruffle, she could see that he was likewise soundly asleep. Jevell was sat in a big cushioned chair reading. Why had she woken, she wondered? She closed her eyes to return to her slumbers. But the peace of the room was then shattered by two knocks on the door.

'Would you mind seeing who is at the door Tansy?' said Jevell, without lifting his head from his book.

'Of course,' she replied.

Yawning, Tansy made her way to the door, wondering who might be knocking. She lifted the latch and, on opening the door, staring straight back at her and grinning, stood a ragged and dirty Ceri. They both shrieked with joy and reached out to hug one another. The noise brought Ruffle out of his slumber.

Rubbing his eyes, he looked toward the commotion at the door and shouted 'Ceri' as he jumped up. He ran over and hugged both of his companions, now all back together.

There were beaming smiles and lots of questions issuing back and forth, their joy at being reunited plain for the wizard to see. Jevell closed his book and greeted his latest visitor, 'You must be Ceridwen?'

'It is late but if you don't mind there is still time for Ceridwen to tell us what has transpired. But firstly, let me get you a drink and a little supper before you begin,' suggested the wizard.

As Jevell rattled around in the kitchen Tansy took the hand of her friend and spoke.

'I am sorry Ceri I should not have left you, I let you down'.

'Don't be silly, if you had been with me then you too would have been captured or worse. The plan had been to separate to make it harder for the Girngog to follow us and it worked, though my getting captured was not the intention.'

'Please let's not be sad, we are back together and I hope you are none the worse for the experience', added Ruffle.

Jevell returned with a pot of tea and some buttered crumpets.

'After what I saw the Girngog eat, this is a feast fit for a queen,' laughed Ceri.

'Alright, so tell us what happened and how did you arrive here?' said Tansy.

Ceri recounted her story and her audience listened intently. It was only when she had concluded her tale that the first question was asked.

'Where is Ozwill now?' said Tansy.

'I don't know, hunting for his supper most likely' replied Ceri smiling.

'A giant owl, how incredible, I would like to meet him,' said Ruffle.

'A giant talking owl!' added Tansy.

'It was a pleasure to meet him and he told me it was his first rescue mission', smiled Ceri. 'He hoped Jevell would be pleased'.

The wizard laughed out loud, 'duly noted.'

'Having been a guest of the Girngog I confess I am surprised that your people tolerated them at all in Yasrall' stated Ceri, looking to Ruffle. 'They seem naturally aggressive and I would not trust any for one single minute. Plus, they do stink.'

'I know, I know, but I think they were friendly in the beginning and we wanted to think the best of them', responded Ruffle. 'We did not want conflict; Rall are peaceful people'.

Returning the conversation to the present, Tansy said, 'I imagine that they were flummoxed seeing a giant owl whisk you away. Do you think that they will follow you into Clinglewood?'

It was Jevell who answered.

'The Girngog would not enter Clinglewood. There are protection spells that would increase their fears to an intolerable level if they stepped too close to these woodlands. Plus, although they do not know who I am, they do know a wizard lives here. That and other things would discourage them.'

'Thank goodness for that,' said Ruffle.

'Were you very frightened?' Tansy asked Ceri.

'To be honest, I was. The idea of being cut into pieces and cooked certainly felt scary. The Girngog are rough toward one another so I did not doubt that at some point I would be tortured to reveal anything that I knew. But the strangest thing was something that I initially dismissed. Despite my position, I had a feeling that everything would be fine. I thought it was simply wishful thinking on my part. But when Ozwill arrived, whilst I was amazed to see a giant talking owl; in some way, I was not surprised. However, I do admit that I was lost for words when he spoke. Maybe it was some kind of intuitive thing, I don't know.'

'Or perhaps it was something else. There is a realm of senses some wizards know of and you may have slightly opened the door to these. You may surprise yourself Ceridwen, we will see in time,' said Jevell stroking his chin and smiling.

'Please call me Ceri, no one really uses my full name,' she requested of the wizard.

'Of course, consider it done,' said Jevell.

They talked for a while longer before deciding that sleep would be welcome. To their surprise Jevell was able to provide each of his guests with a bedroom.

'This cottage is definitely bigger inside than it looks from the outside. Did you know that?' enquired Tansy of the wizard.

'Actually, my dear Tanzy, I was aware of that. It just shows that one cannot always judge things from appearances, don't you think!'

None of the travellers woke early the next morning but each eventually made their way to the big table in the main living room. Waiting to greet them sat a hearty breakfast of porridge, crumpets and a rack of toast, tea, jam and strawberries that soon had everyone restored and eager to face the new day. Strangely, the breakfast remained hot, just right for eating, regardless of the time differences each guest got up.

'I have been thinking,' said Tansy, as they sat around the table.

'Everyone be prepared, this is a special occasion,' joked Ceri.

'I think we have just had our first real adventure, and very few Chimbles can say that they have ever had an adventure at all, it is not a Chimble thing to do,' observed Tansy.

'Yes, I think you are right my dear friend.'

'Foolishly, when we left Big Sprout, we did not appreciate that we were going on an adventure, even though Ruffle had warned us about the Girngog. We thought it was a simple matter of showing him how to get to Clinglewood,' added Tansy.

'I know I was not expecting to actually meet any Girngog, so I thought it unnecessary to do any planning or preparation. So, yes, a simple trip turned into an adventure,' said Ceri.

Tansy warmed to her subject.

'So, it set me thinking exactly what is an adventure. To begin with, it must be doing something one usually doesn't do. I think it means that we have to deal with the unexpected and the new. It seems that it tests our resolve and our willingness to stick with a plan when faced with a problem; or perhaps put another way, it poses the question whether to stick with the adventure or to give up,' said Tansy.

'Well, you are a surprise, Tansy. I think in this instance that we stuck with it and for me at least, it has been an adventure,' said Ceri.

'You know you are both very right. I did not consider that it might be dangerous when I asked you to accompany me to Clinglewood. Now, in my situation, I have to decide whether to continue to try and reach the King and persuade him to help Yasrall; or recognise that it is now too much for me, maybe too dangerous, perhaps an adventure too far!' said Ruffle.

Jevell had been listening to the discussion and remained silent, seemingly curious as to where the conversation would go.

'Are you thinking of giving up?' Tansy asked Ruffle.

'No, not really. For the sake of my people, I can't, I must reach the king. It is just that I am not sure that I, Ruffle Cragstone, can get there. It has been scary to even get this far and to go further feels quite daunting. I suppose I am doubting whether I can do it.'

'I believe in you, Ruffle', said Ceri, 'you are a resourceful and brave person. Surely everyone embarking on an adventure must have that element of doubt, otherwise it is not really an adventure. Of course, it would be better if you knew that you would succeed, but if we only did things that we were certain of, then would anything ever change?'

'Puddleflum, I thought you were a Chimble!' said Tansy, smiling. 'Those are not the words you would expect to hear from a Chimble. Have you swallowed an adventure potion or a swig of wisdom wine?'

'Thank you, Tansy, but no. I know we are not renowned for our adventures and neither are the Rall, but perhaps this is a time when we have to choose to be more than we have been, to take a chance, to make it an opportunity for change,' replied Ceri.

'I am grateful to you both for your help in reaching Clinglewood and for your encouragement. I would like to think that I have gained two friends. I am also mighty relieved that no lasting hurt has been done to either of you; but now I must plan for how I proceed from here. It means a step into the unknown and in doing so I would ask for your guidance Jevell,' said Ruffle.

Before Jevell could reply, Ceri spoke.

'I too have been giving thought to your adventure Ruffle and I have a proposal for you'.

'Really, what is your proposal?' asked the Rall.

'I have not spoken with anyone about this, but I propose that I might accompany you on your quest to reach Castle Black and the king. I know little of fighting and less of the lands such a journey would take us to, but I am sure it must be preferable to have some company rather than strike out alone. Hopefully, I can prove to be of some use. At least I hope my company is acceptable!' said Ceri.

'You do appreciate that I expect the journey to be fraught with risk. Most likely life-threatening at times. But if you are prepared to accompany me then I would be honoured and delighted to accept your proposal' responded Ruffle.

'Hold on just one minute' interjected Tansy. 'Do you think it would be fair that you both go off on another adventure and leave me behind? Then come back with all the tales to tell whilst I have nothing! As the more accomplished warrior and a good friend, surely it would be the correct thing that I too should accompany you!'

'Erm, I am not sure 'warrior' is an accurate description for you Tansy, when most of your fighting has been with a beech tree in your garden!' laughed Ceri. 'That said, this quest would be so much more agreeable if my best friend were to tag along. I don't know about Ruffle but it would be a great comfort for me to have you with us.'

'This must be my lucky day. It would be a privilege to have both of you with me. I can think of nothing better. And if this confirms that I have gained two new friends, then that is the most valuable treasure I could hope to gather on any adventure,' said Ruffle.

They all clasped hands in agreement and turned to the silent wizard wondering what he might say.

'It seems there is nothing I can or should add. If you are all resolved to undertake this journey then I suggest that you have a restful day and sleep on it overnight. First thing tomorrow we can discuss how you intend to reach Castle Black,' concluded Jevell.

And so, it was agreed.

8

Explanations and Choices

The three friends slept soundly. They woke renewed, refreshed and eager for what lay ahead. After a hearty breakfast, they congregated around the big oak table in the kitchen, ready to plan their next steps. Jevell began, 'As much as I would very much enjoy travelling with you, I cannot leave the forest. I have cast spells to protect these woods and they are stronger when I am here. Any news of my absence would encourage the Girngog to broach the forest which would be destructive. So, for the foreseeable future I must remain here. But there are some of things that I can give you that may help and a few friends I know who will gladly assist you along your way.'

'Like Ozwill did,' smiled Ceri.

'Yes, just like Ozwill,' replied the wizard.

'That is a kind thought and for my part I did not expect you to accompany us, but I would value your advice as to the quickest route to reach the king in Duskhold,' said Ruffle.

'Yes, I agree. I know we are in Clinglewood but I have no idea whether we head south, west, east or north!' chipped in Ceri, 'or even how quickly we can move through the trees here to be on our way.'

'I echo that, for if it wasn't for Shadow, I don't know how we would have found our way here. This is also the furthest I have travelled away from Chimbleton,' said Tansy.

'My plan with Beryn was always to head to Clinglewood and find you,' said Ruffle, looking at Jevell. 'I hoped that you could then direct us as to the best route to take.'

'Getting you out of the forest is the least of your decisions, Shadow will lead you out once we have decided which way you should proceed,' said Jevell reassuring his guests.

'However, I have been giving your situation some thought. There are towns and castles across Venterra that do retain their own soldiers, though nothing like as many as the army at Castle Black. However, if we are indeed seeing the beginning of a campaign from Gritol then it would only be the garrison at Castle Black that could resist them. Town garrisons could not withstand a Girngog onslaught if they arrive in large number.'

'However, if the Girngog are already occupying Yasrall, then that alone is sufficient reason for the king to respond. But let us consider what we know. Is it the Girngog intention to progress beyond Yasrall? I think having already seen them on the road leading to Bridgemouth, suggests that it is. If they capture Bridgemouth and gain control of the Necklace, then they will effectively control the land west of the great lake. Which will, no doubt, include a threat to Clinglewood at some point.'

The wizard leant back in his chair, lit his thin pipe and between puffs of rising smoke seemed to be thinking. The three companions had listened and watched in silence, waiting. It was Ruffle who broke the quiet.

'Do you think this means the Girngog have started a war? If so, they would surely be resisted at Midmoor and Bridgemouth!'

'The Girngog traditionally gather in great numbers when being aggressive and as I stated earlier, they would outnumber whatever resistance those towns could put up. A slim possibility is that

Midmoor, being a small town and strategically unimportant, may be ignored. But if not then it would be overrun. More likely their priority would be the capture of Bridgemouth. All land traffic has to go through there. Thus, it would be a priority for them to acquire it, if they are indeed going to war,' replied the wizard.

'Why would the Girngog want to start a war?' asked Tansy.

'We do not yet know if they do, as they may be content to their aggression at the borders of Yasrall, although your experience close to Clinglewood suggests that is unlikely. As to why, I think we can only speculate at this point. Our immediate task in hand is to decide which way you should travel in order to reach the king. However, a little bit of history might be helpful for you, so bear with me.'

'I am sure that you have heard of the Girngog Wars, when they poured out from Gritol intending to overrun the Old Kingdom and depose King Cadmus. They were led by a young sorcerer called Merektar, who had been an apprentice mage at the Wizard Library. That in itself is a tale for another time.'

'The Girngog were in the thrall of Merektar who had united the tribes in pursuing one end, to achieve dominion over the Old Kingdom. He fabricated a tale that long ago the Girngog had ruled the Old Kingdom, saying he had seen evidence of this when he studied at the Wizard Library. It was a wholly false assertion. An imaginary history that the Girngog were all too eager to believe.'

'In truth, the Girngog had been a peaceful people, on good terms with their closest neighbours, the mountain dwarves, and had mostly kept themselves within Gritol. They did ebb back and forth in conflict but it was amongst themselves; quite simply the six tribes of Gritol had vied with one another for domestic ascendancy throughout their history.'

'They had long traded with Yasrall and that increased after the dwarves abandoned the mountains. Then unbeknown to others they built their Wall. From the east there is only one way into Gritol. It is a road leading into a V-shaped valley. The mountains rise either side of the road and it is at the entrance to the valley that the Girngog built their huge wall stretching from one side to the other. A high and formidable wall it is, with a magnificent broad gate at road level. The effect was that the Girngog had total control of who went in and out of their lands. One notable consequence of this construction was that contact with Yasrall diminished greatly.'

'Mostly the gate remained shut. Then one day, without warning, they opened it and the Girngog flooded out in great numbers, intent on warring. What followed was a bloody and terrible war. Nobody had foreseen this aggression as no information of what was happening within Gritol had seeped out. There was simply no warning.'

'And so, the Girngog poured out into Yasrall. They were merciless, plundering and destroying everything they came across. They had the element of surprise and they swept rapidly across the Old Kingdom, reaching Venterra before many appreciated what was happening.'

'Their army halted at Castle Black and laid siege. The castle was all that remained to prevent their conquering the whole Kingdom. Many small towns and castles across Venterra remained free, as the Girngog strategy was to make directly for Castle Black and defeat the king. That was all that stood in their way of achieving victory. So, a siege commenced. The king was trapped within his castle and his forces were heavily outnumbered. The castles and manor houses left untouched by the Girngog did not have the numbers to assist the king. Only one outcome seemed inevitable.'

'But the tide turned when the House of Wizards was drawn into the conflict. The Grandmaster felt the wizards were obliged to become involved when he learned who had orchestrated the Girngog invasion.'

'The Girngog invasion was the work of Merektar. He had learned much from his time as a mage at the Wizard Library and developed into a skilled sorcerer. As a mage he had excelled, demonstrating the ability to progress swiftly. But he had his own ambitions and secretly chose to follow a different path. This culminated in treachery. He stole and fled from the library. The pursuit of him resulted in the deaths of many young wizards and the loss of invaluable artefacts.'

'The Grandmaster blamed himself for the betrayal and for not perceiving the twisted path Merektar was choosing. Again, I will tell you more of that later. Olbus recognised the Girngog were in the ascendance so, taking it upon himself he created the three Instruments of Light – a crown, a sword and a wand. Together with the help of three Master Wizards, the Instruments were deployed to turn the war against the Girngog.'

'Were you one of those wizards?' asked Ruffle.

'Yes Ruffle, I was indeed one. Eventually, with the help of the Faerie and the Instruments of Light, which the wizards wielded, the Girngog were defeated. As helpful as they had been, it became clear that the power of the Instruments was enormous, barely controllable. The Grandmaster was deeply disturbed by this, for when used together even he found them almost beyond his skills.'

'So, Grandmaster Olbus set about discovering how he might destroy his own creations. Whilst he did so, he took the precaution of separating them in order that they might never be used together again. He feared what Merektar or his like could do if they had control of the Instruments. Even now he continues working to find out how they might be rendered harmless.'

'But let me add just a few words about Merektar, so you know a little of the person who may be conducting the Girngog manoeuvres.'

'From his time spent at the Wizard Library Merektar was beguiled by the Book of Shade, a collection of dark and malevolent spells. It was his fascination with that book that enticed Merektar to choose the evil road he now travelled. He had furtively gained access to the book when learning the ways of a mage. Then one dark night, he stole it and fled. This despite being secured deep within the library archives and thought to be safe. The once trusted Merektar nonetheless turned into its thief. No one knows when and why it was created. It had been kept at the library so none could use it. Unfortunately, it had not been destroyed for it does not burn and resists tearing or cutting. It is unique and defies destruction.'

'Merektar made off with the book until eventually it was retrieved, though at great cost. It took a long time to regain and by that point the Wizard Library situated on the edge of the Pancake Lands was gone, the building empty, abandoned. The shell of the building remains but there is absolutely nothing within it, other than the wind blowing through its empty corridors. To my knowledge nobody knows what happened to the library, if it moved elsewhere, was totally destroyed or even if it still exists.'

'So, the Grandmaster decided that the Book of Shade along with the three Instruments, should be separated and hidden to prevent their falling into malicious hands. Despite the secrecy as to their whereabouts, you may hear a rumour that the Crown of Connection, as it is known, is now in Castle Black. They say it is in the deepest rooms of the castle, guarded by soldiers and protected by spells. So, believe what you will.'

'What happened to Merektar after the Girngog lost the war?' asked Ceri.

'Nobody knows. Some thought he may have been slain in the fighting, though of course his body was never found. Faced with wizards brandishing the Instruments of Light, the Girngog assault failed. Their leadership disintegrated and most fled back to Gritol. Yet with this latest incursion into Yasrall I am thinking, did Merektar simply retreat to Gritol? None of the victors entered Gritol, so we do not know if that was where he took refuge.'

'Eventually the war was formally ended by a peace treaty that was signed in the shadows before the Wall of Gritol.'

'Before Merektar the Girngog had rarely been aggressive toward those outside Gritol. But now once again it seems they bring their hostility into Yasrall and by so doing, break the peace treaty. Unfortunately, one has to suspect that it may well be the hand of Merektar behind these recent events.'

'If it is him, do you think he wants to conquer the Old Kingdom again? Or maybe he wants the Crown of Connection? Though from what you have said, could he yield it even if he acquired it?' asked Ceri.

'I do not know the answer to your questions as yet Ceri. He was skilled enough to develop into a sorcerer and he may have grown his abilities since. Though I do know that keeping the Instruments away from him remains the most sensible idea,' mused Jevell. 'But enough history for now, let us return to your plans. I have something that may assist our discussion.'

At which point he stood and strode from the room. He went into a room near the kitchen from which they heard things crashing to the floor and the wizard muttering to himself. Minutes later, he emerged carrying a long canvas roll under his arm.

'Here, lay this out and place something on the corners to prevent it curling up.'

The canvas was rolled out to reveal a map. 'Wait, don't touch it yet,' said Jevell.

Within seconds, the map moved of its own volition. Hills, trees, lakes and buildings rose up from the canvas, all providing a true replication of the land, albeit on a small scale. It was both exciting and scary, as it highlighted how little the friends knew of the Old Kingdom, which was mostly the area that the map covered.

'I drew this based on my own travels and for its time it was fairly accurate, but that was a good few years ago' Jevell explained, 'although I doubt that the broad layout of the land has altered much. But I admit the distances between places on the map may not be in correct proportion.'

'I have never seen such a map before, it is beyond something an artist might draw,' commented Ruffle. He then stood up and using his finger, moved it over the surface.

'How can it rise and take shape like this?' asked Tansy.

'You ask a wizard that?' said Ruffle, raising his eyebrows.

'Oh, yes, sorry,' Tansy replied.

Ruffle was clearly enjoying the unique map and made a proposal.

'Now my first impression looking at this, is that we should cross the great lake, then head to Springhaven, then through the Pancake Lands into Venterra and onto Duskhold, where the castle sits.'

Ruffle sounded decisive, which impressed all. In contrast, Tansy giggled and said, 'I like the sound of the Pancake Lands, can we eat them?'

'The map lacks detail but as you can see much of the Pancake Lands is flat and sandy, so not so tasty to eat. As you see there is a road from Springhaven to Venterra that runs along the edge of the land hugging the Haunted Hills on its southern perimeter. It is a faster route than travelling through the hills. North of that road, the gentle hills give way to the parched flat Pancake Lands. Much of it is barren, sandy and scrubby with just occasional clusters of bushes. It suffers from unrelenting sunshine and is hard on the creatures that call it home. The bones that are scattered across the land bear silent witness to that truth. Most travellers avoid the area, although crossing that way is a shorter distance. However, most who do choose to cross the Pancake Lands do so along the rough road that skirts the hills. They also prefer to travel in the cool of the night.'

'However, that way is also not without its dangers. There are some settlements across the Pancake Lands, although mostly temporary, as the people who choose to live there are nomadic. They wander the land and obey their own laws. It is not unknown for them to waylay travellers, which is why those using the road tend to travel together in large groups. Aside from that, you have the packs of wild dogs that scavenge through the night and disappear during daylight. They will attack animals and people.'

'Stop Jevell, please. I think an alternative to the Pancake Lands might make more sense,' pleaded Ruffle, at which point all chuckled.

'Well, looking at this map it seems to me that our first obstacle will be to cross the great lake,' said a more serious Ceri.

'Can't we just cross at that bridge, the Necklace, I think you called it?' asked Tansy.

'Given what we have seen, I am thinking that the Girngog may already be there,' said Ceri.

'I suspect that you are correct Ceri; if the Girngog are already on the march, it would be one place that they would wish to control,' said Jevell.

'So, can we swim across the lake?' said Ruffle.

'I doubt that I could swim such a distance, it looks huge,' frowned Ceri.

'Indeed, you may not wish to swim the lake. Aside from the fact it is so wide, other than where the bridge sits at Bridgemouth, it even takes a boat two or three days to cross. Plus, there are large fish that might regard you as a fine catch,' laughed Jevell. 'Some say that giant sea serpents still roam the deeper parts and they are not fussy what they eat!'

'Definitely no swimming for me then,' said Ceri firmly.

'Don't concern yourself with mythical serpents. As for crossing the lake, I can enlist some help for you to do that. The more difficult question is, where you make shore?' said the wizard.

'What are our choices?' quizzed Ruffle, who still felt a little crestfallen; he had hoped that crossing the Pancake Lands would be the simple and straightforward option.

'Once you reach the other shore, you have several choices as to which way to travel to Venterra. You could go north to Springhaven and that would be the way if you decide on the low-lying route through the Pancake Lands. However, you are not a large group and I have mentioned the dangers in going that way,' continued Jevell.

'Do remember that wherever you go ashore, the Haunted Hills loom over the lake. However, they are not as high as the Ironspine Mountains and for the most part, not so steep. You will have to go over, through or around them. For most travellers there is one main route, it is the one wide enough for wagons and it wends through the hills rather than over them. It is the longest way as it avoids steep inclines and is full of twists and turns. It begins at Bridgemouth, where a large archway sits. The point of that was to inform travellers that they were entering Bridgemouth. The plan was to charge a toll for all who entered that way. But it did not work. Traders refused to pay the toll and threatened to cease trading with Bridgemouth. So, the idea was dropped but the impressive gateway remains. You can't miss it, two massive figures holding swords crossed together to form the arch. Cold stone guardians without a purpose.'

'Then there is the small matter that the Girngog may already occupy Bridgemouth. And I think it wise that we assume that they do. So, that option won't work for us,' said Tansy.

'A good point Tansy. However, if you were ever to choose that road, then at its beginning, you would notice some large trees to your right as you go through the arch onto the mountain. Those trees represent the edge of Earthroot, the forest that some say never ends. The trees are large and high, dense and wide, and avoided by the Girngog. For Earthroot is the home of the Faerie, the most mysterious of races, who welcome few to their land. They are no friends of the Girngog.'

'Would they help us at all?' asked Ceri.

'I do not know. They have helped in the past but that was long ago. Part of Earthroot runs along the southernmost border of Venterra. In theory you could travel through the forest and reach Venterra that way, but I know of no one other than the Faerie who have travelled that route. However, I do know that the queen of the Faerie, Tixlodel, is a good friend to both King Cadmus and Grandmaster Olbus. But the Faerie have no wish to embroil themselves in the machinations of mankind.'

'The third alternative is to take the narrower track that lies midway between Bridgemouth and Springhaven. It climbs through and over the Haunted Hills. It is steep in parts and more open to the weather. It is also regarded as the most haunted part of the hills. The wind sweeps through the higher parts and creates a howl, which is what many take for haunted cries. However, it is also where the Whispies live. They are small monkey-like creatures who in fact are rarely seen. They inhabit that rocky world, living in large groups and keeping out of site, occupying caves and tunnels dug out over many lifetimes. They tend to avoid people but will slip into a camp and steal goods. They are very adept at keeping out of sight. They speak quietly, in tones that sound like whispers to you or me, which is how they obtained their name. Sometimes they can be heard screeching in the distance, a noise which adds to the belief that the hills are haunted. Few have seen the Whispies, which perpetuates the belief that there are ghosts in the mountains.'

'Which brings us to your final option, namely to walk and climb over the hills from wherever you wish, creating your own path. Of course, this has its own risks. The hills are rocky and steep. So, the higher that you ascend, the more your climbing skills would be tested. You would also be exposed to the cold wind and maybe rain when climbing away from the sheltered routes that the established pathways take. It is probably more dangerous and significantly slower, but it is an option.'

'I thought that escaping Yasrall would be the hardest part!' uttered Ruffle.

'What about north of Springhaven?' asked Ruffle.

'Well, there are a few small villages, and you could certainly go ashore there. However, landing further north and then going east will take you across and into the heart of the Pancake Lands. Aside from all other dangers, it is easy to get lost in those flat sandy lands,' said the wizard.

'I don't suppose that you could travel with us?' quizzed Ceri looking at Jevell.

'I am afraid not. As I mentioned before, I am the protector of this forest and all life within it. I know the Girngog would not hesitate to invade these woods if I were not here. My spells of protection could not protect all that lives here if I were away. I am sorry Ceri but you must undertake this quest without me.'

'I understand that and for my part I never expected you to be able to join us,' said Ruffle; then turning to look at the Chimbles, he added, 'I am grateful that you both are accompanying me, but if you choose to remain here, then I will not begrudge you. There is more risk here than I expected.'

'Don't be silly, Ruffle. We have come this far and we must see it through. I know Chimbleton may not be under threat today, but it may be soon. So, there is a larger purpose at stake here, possibly for all of the Old Kingdom,' said Tansy.

'I agree Tansy. Let us take one step at a time and with enough steps we will succeed,' said Ceri.

'Indeed. And furthermore, I propose that we take the narrow road through the mountains, Whispies or not. What say you?' said Tansy.

'That is a clear proposal and the one I would support, but let us spend a little time to consider all that Jevell has told us before we finally decide,' proposed Ceri.

Ruffle laughed and smiled.

'Little did I realise that I would find two brave souls who would become dear friends when I climbed out of that well.'

With that, they all stood and went in different directions, each occupied with their own thoughts. Ceri took herself into the garden and Tansy lay on her bed, eyes wide and deep in thought. Ruffle sat down again in one of the big, comfortable chairs and struggled to light his pipe. Jevell disappeared into the kitchen.

Some twenty minutes later the three friends found one another outside the cottage and sat together talking. Then Jevell suggested that they return to the table and their planning. It was Tansy who spoke first.

'Master Jevell, I think we seem to be agreed. The Whispies road it is.'

'We should hope that the Girngog are still this side of the lake and not advanced toward Springhaven. The route itself sounds as if it will challenge us without also having to overcome any Girngog,' said Ceri.

Jevell said nothing. Ruffle swiftly moved the discussion on.

'So, the first thing we must solve is, how do we cross the great lake?'

'Perhaps we can travel around it?' suggested Tansy.

'Unfortunately, that would be difficult. Whilst it is called Seabreeze Lake it is not fully enclosed; at its southern end, past Bridgemouth, it leads out into the sea. At its northernmost, past Springhaven, it continues to the Ironspine Mountains. There, many streams and waterfalls flow down from the mountain peaks. Those peaks reach high above the clouds. The upper regions are covered in snow throughout the year. The mountain range itself stretches like a massive wall the whole width of the Old Kingdom and then eastward beyond that. To the west, it runs into Gritol and it was the home of the mountain dwarves until they abandoned it. It would be no help to head that way.'

'The lake itself is wide and long. It narrows like the neck of a bottle at Bridgemouth, which is where its only bridge sits. A mighty and impressive bridge it is. High enough for ships to sail underneath and when lit up at night it glitters like jewels, which is how it obtained its common name, the Necklace. As I said earlier, south beyond the bridge the lake broadens again and leads out to the oceans,' explained the wizard.

'So, we have little choice. We cannot cross the bridge if the Girngog are there and yet we must cross the lake,' said Tansy crossing her arms.

'Did you not say earlier that you knew someone who could get us across?' asked Ceri.

'Indeed, I do and I have been a little presumptuous to have already sent word to him. His name is Captain Zim and he has a ship called The Dove. He is a good man. He will get you across the lake and put you ashore at the spot that you have selected.'

'From here, Shadow can escort you to the edge of Clinglewood. From there, it is a good half-day walk to reach the shores of the lake. You cross fields that lead to sand hills which run down to the beach. The captain will meet you there. I have told him to expect you around the middle of the day tomorrow. Does that sound satisfactory or is it too soon?' asked Jevell.

'It is excellent and it makes sense to begin tomorrow. I thank you,' said Ruffle.

'We all thank you,' agreed Ceri.

The rest of the day was spent in preparation and discussion. The Chimbles had originally set out for Clinglewood expecting that they would return home after escorting Ruffle to the forest. Now they had to rethink their plans. Talk of mountains, stony paths, cold winds and danger ignited the realisation that they were not prepared for what they had agreed to do. But they were quietly excited.

Their concerns were partially allayed by Jevell, who conjured up boots and coats, jumpers and a blanket for each. They were to carry small shoulder bags, in which blankets were folded and food was wrapped – a traveller's fare of crackers, cheese, dried meat, apples, celery and bread. By early evening, they were provisioned and ready, feeling as organised as they thought they could be, given their swift decision to undertake an adventure into the unknown.

That evening, packed and prepared, they sat around the warm fire in the cottage. All seemed lost in thought. Silence had descended, only broken by the crackling of burning wood in the fireplace and then by the snoring of Ruffle. Shadow lay with his head on one of his front legs while his eyes watched the group. Jevell was reading and puffing on a long-curved pipe. Ceri had her eyes closed and legs outstretched, though a long way from sleeping. Tansy sat in a big cushioned chair, hands cupped and resting on her belly as she stared at the orange flames dancing in the hearth.

Jevell closed his book, stood and stretched his arms.

'An early supper and to bed, I think.'

After a supper of crackers, cheese, and carrot cake, washed down with blueberry wine, all took to their beds. Ruffle and Tansy soon slept but Ceri turned and turned, with a hundred thoughts filling her mind. She drifted in and out of sleep but was far from refreshed when she rose early next morning. She was a mix of feelings – regret for having to leave the safety of Jevell and the forest, discomforted at not returning to Chimbleton - but also eager to take up the quest. She wondered if this mixture of feelings was usual when setting off on an adventure!

9

Race to the Lake

They woke early, excited and nervous to be venturing into the unknown. Nonetheless, a hearty breakfast was enjoyed. Bags packed, water flasks filled, with stomachs content, they were keen to make a start. Jevell brought out three swords with scabbards.

'There are some things I must gift you that may help with your journey.'

The wizard handed each of the companions a blade. The grip of each sword had a shiny stone in the pommel, each one a different colour.

'I like the look of my sword but I am not sure how much use it will be. I have no experience of using one,' said Ceri.

'Well, I have practiced and I do like my sword. I think I could put it to good use if I need to,' smiled Tansy as she swung her blade about and ran her fingers along its length. It was sharp.

'I know what to do with a sword but I confess I have few skills. I have rarely had need of one and never in earnest,' added Ruffle.

'Well, swords can be useful in many ways, not only in combat,' explained Jevell. 'You may have to fight for your life with some beast or at least give the impression that you would. If you never use them, then that would be wonderful, but I think it's best that you are at least prepared.'

'I think you're right' chimed Tansy, 'although I do already possess a sword'. She then took out her 'faerie sword' which was quite shorter and her face beamed, clearly pleased with herself. Then she compared the sword Jevell had given her and after a few moments said, 'I think I will use my faerie weapon as my knife.'

'The swords used by the Faerie are rather larger than yours Tansy. They are exquisitely crafted and highly effective. I think you're right, we best call yours a dagger, though if you meet any of the Faerie, I think you might refrain from calling it anything other than yours, you wouldn't wish to offend anyone,' laughed the wizard.

'Now, for you a coat, Ruffle,' said the wizard as he handed him a mustard-coloured coat having lots of pockets and two particular wide ones on the sides. 'This will keep you warm and waterproof.'

He then plucked a hair from Ruffle's head, rubbed it between his fingers and spoke some words very quietly. Nobody heard or understood what the wizard said. He then placed his hands on the shoulders of the Rall, tapped the two side pockets and closed his eyes. After ten seconds or so he withdrew his hands saying, 'That should do it.'

The companions were intrigued and wondering what the wizard was up to. He then took a pouch from his own tunic and gave it to Ruffle.

'Maybe the pockets are now full of gold' grinned Ruffle.

'Place this in a pocket, please,' he instructed.

Ruffle did so.

'Now take it out' and once again Ruffle followed the instruction and retrieved the pouch. He looked nonplussed, it was not what he had hoped.

The wizard then gave the pouch to Ceri saying,

'Now you place it in Ruffle's coat' and Ceri obliged. 'Now take it out' he asked of Ceri.

She reached into the pocket of Ruffle's coat but found there was nothing in there. She withdrew her hand.

'It's gone,' she said.

'Surely not,' chirped Tansy, who then put her hand into the pocket but also found it empty.

'Oh, it has gone!'

'You try Ruffle,' suggested Jevell.

Ruffle put his hand in his pocket and took out the pouch, looking surprised but pleased with himself and shared a big grin with everyone.

'It must be magic or rather a trick' said Tansy looking at Jevell, 'let's try again'.

So, they did, and the result was the same - once any item was placed in the pockets of his coat, then only Ruffle could take it out. They tried several more times whilst Ruffle grew delighted at the wonders of his magical coat.

'Am I becoming a wizard?' he joked with a beaming smile.

'It's not that easy, but it is a special coat. Once anything is placed in either of the two large pockets, then only you, Ruffle, can withdraw it again,' explained the wizard. 'You will also find it bottomless, although the weight of the coat will never change.'

'Well, it will be very useful if we are ever searched, as long as Ruffle stops grinning,' said Ceri.

'Exactly' replied Jevell, himself grinning.

The wizard then turned to Ceri and presented her with a narrow box similar to a case in which a wand could be carried. He then took her to one side and they spoke quietly. It was only his final words that Tansy and Ruffle could make out, *'let us hope that you have no cause to use it,'* they heard.

Jevell then rejoined the others and proffered an explanation.

'Forgive the secrecy but I have given Ceri something that has powerful magic but will hopefully never be needed. It is something that I believe she has the ability and judgement to know when to use it. It can only be used once.'

Then, from within the folds of his long robes, the wizard produced a shiny brass tube and held it out for Tansy. 'I suspect that this may become the most used of the items that I have given you' he commented.

He then pulled one end of the short tube which extended into a long spyglass and suggested that Tansy look through it, which she did. She placed it against one eye then, took it away and then looked through it again.

'Incredible' she uttered, 'how does it do that, everything looks so close.'

It was indeed a thing of beauty, crafted in brass and glinting in the light, with wizard symbols decorating the length of the tube. Tansy had been briefly disappointed to be given a small shiny tube, albeit one beautifully inscribed with flowers and shapes. But after using it, she was impressed and struck by its power.

'I will assume from your smile that the gift meets with your approval.'

'Approval given,' smiled Tansy.

'Good, I hope it comes in useful for you. It will fold up to hang on your belt. You will see it has inscriptions, some of which are there so that it will work even when it is dark. Anything you look at will be visible, almost as if it was a bright afternoon. It may well be the most powerful spyglass in the land. It will show you things in more detail than your eyes can.'

'Now I give you one final item and hopefully this will save you time as well as give you credibility.'

That said, the wizard put his hand into the swathes of his robe. He took out something in the shape of a small green leaf, which at first glance could have been a brooch. It was hard and shiny, intricately made, delicate to look at but in fact unbreakable, explained Jevell.

'Show this if your word is doubted and if you ever need to verify that you are friends of mine. For those whom I trust, it will verify that I trust you. For instance, King Cadmus will recognise it immediately. And for safety I suggest you carry it in the deep pockets of Ruffle's coat.'

'I am beginning to think that your robes are like my coat, full of treasures and bottomless,' suggested Ruffle.

'You may be more correct than you can imagine!' beamed the playful wizard.

After receiving their gifts, the companions were ready to start their journey. A range of emotions coloured their parting - excitement, worry, fear, determination and a shared hesitation about starting out.

'I wish you were coming with us,' said a wistful Ruffle to the wizard.

'I think he speaks for us all,' said Tansy.

'Alas, I cannot. There will come a time when I must leave the forest but it is not yet that time. I understand that you are stepping into the unknown, which can be frightening. However, as brief as they have been, these last few hours have given me belief in you. I think you may surprise yourselves on this venture you undertake,' replied the wizard.

Ceri addressed the wizard, 'It is not a Chimble habit to go travelling, we are a people who value home. We like the peace and tranquility of our valley. So, this truly is an adventure for a Chimble. I have no doubt we will see things and meet people who are new and strange to us. But the unknown is often frightening. I know it will test us. I just hope your belief in us is not misplaced. Not least because I would be delighted to come and stay here in Clinglewood again, if you will accept us Master Jevell?'

'Well, I endorse what Ceri has said. I now understand that we take this journey on behalf of many and I am expecting to come face to face with danger, but so be it. I intend to keep my companions as safe as I can. I also do not want Chimbleton drawn into this conflict, so I am ready to do what is needed,' added Tansy.

'Then it is my turn to add a few words,' said Ruffle. 'I also believe all our lands are threatened, and it is my deepest hope that we can persuade the king to come to our aid. What began as a lonely quest is now all the stronger due to my companions. Whilst what lies ahead is unknown, I do hope we can turn to you Jevell if needs must.'

'Should there be an occasion where I can help then of course you can call upon me. For now, you seem as prepared as I think you can be. No doubt you will encounter challenges we could not have foreseen, but I have faith in you all to persevere. You have one another which is no small thing and already I look forward to your return and to hearing the tales of what you overcame to succeed in this venture. But we have exchanged enough words; you really must get going.'

Hugs and handshakes were the final goodbyes and then, as promised, Shadow led them out of the clearing and in amongst the trees. There was no obvious path to follow. Even in the morning light it was gloomy, though shards of light seeped between the canopy of branches above them. Without being able to explain why, it was evident to the three friends that many trees had been there a long, long time.

They walked behind the huge dog in single file and Ceri in particular was amazed as it seemed the trees actually moved aside to create a path. Ruffle and Tansy looked at one another and smiled, as they had seen this before, Ceri had not. They walked steadily for an hour or so. It was warm, walking was slow and it was impossible to gauge how far the forest stretched.

Shadow suddenly stopped, turned and faced the three adventurers.

'We are making progress, but the forest is big and there is still some distance to travel. I think it might be useful for you if we were to travel more quickly, so I will lower myself and then please all climb on my back.'

Turning to Ceri, Tansy said quietly, 'believe me it will be quicker.'

However, they were a little unsure with all three sitting on the big dog.

'Are we not too heavy for you?' asked Ceri.

'No, not at all. Just get yourselves comfortable and leave the rest to me. Besides, you will need your energy for the walk to the lake.'

Pushing and pulling, eventually they were all mounted on Shadow. The giant dog began walking. It took a little while but the riders began to relax. It seemed as if the dog recognised this and increased speed. Soon they were hurtling between the trees. The open-mouthed and astonished riders held one another tight as they sped almost silently through the forest.

Whereas before it had seemed the trees almost hugged one another, now they leant back to allow a galloping Shadow through. Looking ahead the companions could see no welcoming path yet one constantly appeared as it was needed.

It had been gloomy, almost dark within the shade of the dense woodland, though not the deep darkness that the night brings. Shortly after adjusting to their ride, the canopy of branches thinned and Shadow came to a halt. They were still amongst the trees but just ahead lay the edge of the forest. They had a clear view of the open land sat before them. Shadow lowered himself and the travellers dismounted.

'For the moment, stay within the trees. We need to check the landscape before you begin the next step,' said the dog. Hiding behind tree trunks and bushes they all scanned the land thereabouts.

'And I was just beginning to enjoy that,' said Ruffle.

'The land seems clear,' suggested Tansy.

There was nobody to be seen and the only sounds that reached their ears were made by the birds singing and the insects busying their day away. Ahead were green and lush fields that rose gently up and down, but were essentially flat.

Shadow spoke.

'You should travel straight from here like an arrow toward the horizon. A hundred or so paces from this point will bring you to a road. It is not often used and in part is hidden by long grass. Few people travel the road nowadays, although it winds all the way to Bridgemouth. However, you should ignore it and cross straight over and make for the horizon. You should spot a footpath, which you should take. It will lead to the sandhills, the beach and the waiting ship.'

'As you walk other paths will cross the one you tread, but ignore them. Eventually the path will drop down onto the beach. It is the sand hills that prevent you seeing the shoreline until you are very close. Once on the beach, you will find Captain Zim and the Dove waiting for you. They will send a rowing boat to take you on board. Now, are you clear on which way to go?' asked Shadow.

'Yes, it seems straightforward,' said Ceri with the others nodding in agreement, 'thank you, Shadow, your instructions are helpful'.

'Remember. Once you are on the footpath stay on it, do not be distracted.'

They stroked and hugged the dog and said goodbye.

'Be quick now, time is imperative for you,' urged the dog. Then almost immediately he turned and disappeared into the trees. He was gone. Heeding his advice, they set off. Within minutes, they had found the road, but the path leading off it was less obvious. They searched.

'Here it is, rather overgrown but look, it goes straight through the field to the skyline, this must be it,' said Tansy.

'Yes, I think it is, let's go' urged Ruffle, 'I don't wish to wait for the Girngog to come along.'

'Are they likely to be here, really?' said Tansy.

'Yes, they don't give up. They are probably everywhere by now,' responded Ruffle waving his arms to indicate they were all around.

'Indeed, so let's all keep our eyes peeled, though I think from my brief experience we might smell them before we see them' smiled Ceri.

They set off, walking at a brisk pace as their destination appeared a long way off. The path was narrow and they walked in single file, Tansy leading. They talked as they walked, quickly deciding that they would not stop until they reached the sand hills.

'Makes sense,' said Ruffle, 'though it's further than I expected. I think a short stop might make sense. My legs might be rather achy by the end of the day.'

'Mine too,' agreed Ceri.

As Shadow had said, a number of other footpaths crossed their chosen path but they remained true to their instructions. The path followed the gentle rolling of the land. They were diligent in constantly looking about and increasingly confident that they had no pursuers.

'The grass is long enough for a herd of cows to have a feast,' commented Ruffle.

'Or for someone to hide in!' said Ceri.

'Don't suggest that, I could easily believe it so,' uttered Tansy.

However, it was uneventful as they progressed, and they relaxed. In the warmth of the sunny afternoon, they chatted and grew more confident.

'Have you ever crossed Seabreeze Lake before?' Tansy asked of Ruffle.

'No, this will be a first time for me and really my first time on a proper boat.'

'I have heard that some people get sick when travelling by boat, I think it must be because of the waves,' added Tansy. 'I hope I am not one of them.'

'Well let us hope that none of us do, for we have no other choice than the boat. Though truthfully, I am quite looking forward to it and we may be the first Chimbles to sail on the great lake, though I suspect others have done so in the past,' said Ceri.

'Yes, and when you put it like that, it makes me feel adventurous,' agreed Tansy.

'Well, I just hope it's not me who gets sick' said Ruffle feigning a curmudgeon manner.

They had been walking several hours and decided that they could afford a few minutes to have at least a bite to eat, reneging on their original plan. Stopping, they flopped to the ground, opened their bags and took out cheese, crackers and a small jar of pickled onions.

'A feast,' laughed Ruffle, 'and very welcome. After a little food I could just lay down here and fall asleep under this warm sun.'

'It is tempting', agreed Ceri.

'But perhaps not a good idea' said Tansy as she peered through her spyglass. After a few seconds, she handed it to Ceri, 'Look there, follow where I am pointing'.

'A dust cloud is what I see,' said Ceri as she passed the spyglass to Ruffle. 'It is some distance away but what would create a cloud of dust? I imagine it must be from someone on the road.'

'Well, you would get dust if they were moving across a very dry field, I suppose,' said Ruffle.

Tansy took the spyglass and peered again.

'Blast it. Unfortunately, it is a group of Girngog. Some are riding animals, followed by a larger group running behind. Let's hope they are just on the road and have not seen us.'

Ceri took the spyglass.

'You're right, come on I think it's time we got going. Our nightmare is too close.'

They swiftly packed away their food and set off at a faster pace, until they were almost running. They could see ahead of them that the land rose and agreed it must be the sand hills. Encouraged by this they jogged. Tansy stopped, looked back and noticed that the dust had settled down but that was because the Girngog were now running across the overgrown fields.

'They've seen us,' she exclaimed.

'Ignore them, keep going, we're not far now,' encouraged Ceri.

'We have a good lead and this time we stick together, no separating,' said Ruffle, who was blowing quite hard as their jog had turned to a run. 'I do not enjoy getting chased by those ugly beasts.'

Before long, they crested the sand hills and the beach stretched out ahead. It was much longer and wider than they had expected. Looking behind, Ceri could see that the Girngog who were riding animals had closed the gap considerably, but she said nothing.

The sand hills were not easy to run through, taking them up and down. Inevitably their pace slowed considerably, from having to tread the soft sand. But they were encouraged as they reached the flatter firmer beach. Sitting and bobbing in the shallow waters close to the shore, was a rowing boat. They assumed it waited for them. Further out, they saw a ship, hopefully it was there for their rendezvous. .

A man in the rowboat stood up, calling and waving. On the flat beach they ran toward the rowboat which was already being pushed into deeper water.

'Hold on,' shouted Ruffle. 'Don't leave us.'

'Quickly, quickly, they're coming,' yelled one of the sailors as the three companions drew nearer.

The three friends were now quite exhausted and blowing hard. The soft sand of the hills had been hard to run through. Now, on much firmer sand they ran faster. Without hesitation, they ran into the shallow water toward the boat, which now sat in a couple of feet of water, ready to be rowed. They threw themselves over the side as they scrambled aboard. Two sailors had jumped out and pushed the boat toward deeper water before climbing back in. Two others had begun rowing and it was just in time.

Galloping through the sand hills down onto the beach came the mounted Girngog, shouting, screaming, and angry. Some jumped from their rides and waded into the water, but the little boat was now too deep to be caught by a swimmer. Some Girngog had gotten waist high in water, trying to catch up but soon gave up. Arrows and spears flew toward the little vessel but splashed harmlessly in the water behind. The companions lay on the floor of the boat, gulping down air, exhausted and relieved to have escaped. Gradually, they gathered their breath and sat up. Looking back toward the beach, they saw a crowd of Girngog screaming as their prey escaped.

'That was too close,' said Ruffle as he gulped in more oxygen.

Minutes later, the rowing boat drew alongside the ship from which rope ladders hung.

'Be careful now friends, grab hold of the ladder before you step off,' said one of the rowers. It was Jabe, a slim man who was wiry in appearance but obviously strong, as he had shown when rowing.

'Thank you,' said Tansy turning to face Jabe, I am so relieved that you were there, otherwise we would be Girngog dinner.'

'A pleasure m'lady. The Girngog are not the best cooks I hear, but you're safe now,' he replied, injecting a little humour.

In turn, each climbed up the rope ladders, which was not as straightforward as it looked. The ropes swung about and moved with each step. It felt unsafe and more difficult than it appeared. But with a little help and encouragement, they scrambled aboard. The rowboat was then tied to the stern to be pulled behind the ship.

On deck it was a hive of activity. A big man with a dark reddish-brown beard barked orders and the anchor was hauled up, then the sails on the two masts were raised. The companions stood watching, not knowing what to do or where to go. The bearded man, long hair tied back, came over and, tipping his hat slightly, spoke to them.

'Welcome aboard The Dove, I am Captain Zim and I think the first thing we must do after your adventure is to get you comfortable and take some refreshment, follow me please.'

It was plain that he was the man in charge and despite his imposing size and commanding presence, his voice was warm and friendly. The companions immediately felt that they could trust him. He led them to the doors set directly beneath the helm, where, upon entering, they found a small hallway with more doors leading off it.

'You can make yourselves at home here,' said the captain as he opened one door and waved them in, 'that other door is my cabin. The bow or the front if you like, is where the crew sleep. Make yourselves at home, I must go and attend to things on deck,' and he left.

Muttering thanks to the retreating captain, the three companions looked about their cabin. There were four bunk beds, three chairs, a table and a bench, all nailed to the floor. There were small windows and one large one, almost the length of the cabin, affording a panoramic view of the sea. The light from the windows gave the cabin a bright sunny feel. And when the sun disappeared, there were several lanterns that could be lit. All three friends chose a bed and lay down whilst chatting. Soon they could feel the movement of the ship, something they had not previously noticed.

It was not long before Ruffle sat up.

'I am not sure I can sleep here; I feel a little queasy with all this swaying.'

Ceri dangled her legs over the edge of her bunk having already sat up.

'I find if I don't lay down then I feel better. Perhaps we will all adjust,' she said trying to encourage Ruffle.

'I hope I do and soon,' Ruffle replied.

'Maybe some food might help,' suggested Tansy.

'No thank you, I am not sure my stomach would welcome that,' Ruffle answered sharply. 'Please let's change the subject, the idea of eating is not helping.'

'I wonder what the captain knows of our quest and how much we can safely share with him?' pondered Tansy. 'But then again, he is, after all, a friend of Jevell and he is helping us, so I think we should trust him.'

'I assume you are not having this discussion just with yourself!' laughed Ceri. 'Though you do make a serious point Tansy. The degree to which we trust him will dictate how much we tell him. I think at this moment we should be cautious and find out how much he knows before we proffer too much,' suggested Ceri.

'I think I need some fresh air,' said Ruffle, standing up and wobbling toward the door.

Ruffle had no wish to look out of the windows; he stumbled toward the door, his single intention being to reach the deck. Once there, he leant his head over the side and emptied his stomach. He gulped air, welcoming the breeze blowing in his face. After a few minutes, his insides seemed to calm. He hoped his stomach was settling and the spasms abating?

He was joined by his friends who were a little concerned for him, as they were seemingly unaffected by the swaying ship. He took a long swig of water from a flask Ceri handed to him. The sails were high on the two masts; the wind was blowing and the ship sped quicker than the companions expected. Digesting their surroundings, the three travellers felt that they were now truly living their adventure. The captain strode across the deck to join them.

'I hope your cabin is satisfactory!' he asked.

'It's fine, thank you, captain,' replied Ceri.

'You feeling any better, Ruffle? I saw you feeding the fish. Hopefully, you will adjust soon. Being sick can leave you feeling drained of energy. You should drink water and try to sleep.'

'I think I feel a little better, though I am not certain as yet.'

'I will organise some food and drink for you all, as I am sure you must be hungry. Though perhaps Ruffle should eat just a little. But after that, I suggest that we sit down so you can tell me a little of your story. I am curious to learn why it is that the Girngog chase you.'

Several hours later the companions had returned to their cabin. Ruffle had spent most of the time out on deck where his stomach had calmed. Ceri and Tansy had taken a small meal and returned to their cabin. Soon after, Ruffle had left the open air of the deck and joined his companions, thirsty and tired. Cautiously he had eaten some dry bread and drank water. The ship was calm and quiet. This first evening aboard the sea was placid.

As suggested earlier in the day; the captain joined his guests in their cabin.

'Found your sea legs yet, Ruffle?'

'I don't know. Though I have not been sick for some time and so far I'm coping with being in the cabin,' was his reply.

'You will be fine,' the captain assured the Rall as he pulled out a chair and sat at the table. 'I was the same when I first went to sea, it should pass.'

The two Chimbles joined the captain sitting around the table. Ruffle remained stretched out on his bunk bed.

'Now I know your names, though which of you is Ceri and which is Tansy, you will need to remind me,' said the captain.

'I am Tansy.'

'So, I think it obvious which one I am,' said Ceri.

'Well, do tell me where you are bound and then we can agree on the best place to put you ashore,' continued the captain.

'Perhaps, I could begin, it may take my mind away from my stomach,' suggested Ruffle, sitting up on his bed.

'Good idea,' said Ceri.

So, Ruffle began to explain what was happening in Yasrall, why he had left and what he had set out to accomplish. Intentionally vague, he explained how he had met with Ceri and Tansy. More clearly, he described how Ceri had been captured, rescued and the consequences of their visit with Jevell. One of which was meeting up with the captain. The two Chimbles contributed some detail at certain points but left the bulk of the telling to Ruffle. Preoccupied with conveying the story, Ruffle was feeling a little better at its conclusion.

'So, captain, we surmise that the Girngog are likely in Bridgemouth already and heading for Castle Black. For the sake of the Old Kingdom and Yasrall in particular, the king should be warned so that he can prepare his army. We hope to get to Venterra before the Girngog and forewarn him. Most immediately, can you deliver us close to the road that leads through the middle of the Ghost Mountains? We will have to avoid Bridgemouth,' concluded Ruffle.

The captain leant back in his chair, took out a pipe and a small tobacco pouch.

'Yes, Jevell told me much of what you say. As for the road you choose, it's true we can make land fairly close to that route. However, you should know that being just three people, on that road it is most likely that you will encounter the Whispies?'

'Yes, we have been told about the Whispies, but on balance, we decided it is the least dangerous option,' responded Ceri.

The captain continued to stuff his pipe but said nothing. No one spoke and the waves slapping against the ship seemed louder in the silence. The companions all assumed he was mulling over what had been said. They waited. Then the captain sat up straight as if he had decided something, his hands placed one on each knee, still holding the unlit pipe.

'So be it, I will speak to my helmsman Dibit to head for that road. You do understand that it will take a couple of days to cross

Seabreeze Lake, so whilst on board do enjoy the freedom of my ship. Please make yourselves as comfortable as you can.'

With that, he stood as if to take leave of them. His pipe still unlit.

'Captain, do you think our plan foolhardy?' asked Ceri.

'No, for you are right, if the Girngog are afoot then there is little choice among the roads leading to Venterra. Each has its dangers. But my question might be, is it too late? If the Girngog are on the move and also heading toward Venterra, what is to be gained by your risking your lives to try and arrive there before them?'

'Well, I was hoping that King Cadmus might do something once he knows that the Girngog have broken the treaty and invaded Yasrall. If we can arrive at Castle Black before the Girngog, it would help him be prepared. He could lead his army out to repel them. And, I did give my word to the King's Voice in Yasrall that I would inform the king.'

'Sound reasoning Ruffle; and as I have little knowledge of what is transpiring on land, I cannot offer you informed counsel. I have no idea how matters unfold at Castle Black or thereabouts. Although, I do wonder if Venterra still possesses an army sufficient to repel the Girngog? Truth is, I don't know. In fact, there is so much that I do not know, thus I make no attempt to persuade you away from the plan you have chosen. You must do as you see fit. All I can do, is to offer you what assistance I can to speed you along your way.'

That said, the captain bade them goodnight and left the companions to consider his words. They did talk but not of their plans or the viability of their quest, instead it was about their first-time experience of being on such a big ship. They decided that tomorrow they would have a thorough look around the vessel. Gradually they each took to their beds, conversation dwindling to silence. Ruffle was not keen to discuss what Captain Zim had said or to reconsider their plans. It seemed his companions felt the same. So, they avoided discussion of their quest.

The Chimbles swiftly slumbered, Ruffle less so. He kept his eyes open, hands on his stomach, watching the shadows dance in the room to the rhythm of the ship swaying and the moonlight shining through the large window. Before long he could hear that his companions were asleep. He listened to the sea and told himself to relax. He was unsettled and pessimistic, his thoughts running amok. He lay awake a long while until sleep finally came upon him.

10

Demons and Monsters

Morning brought the sunshine and another fine day. Breakfast for Ruffle was porridge, bread and water, which he successfully managed to keep in his stomach, though he did feel incredibly thirsty. Happily, his body seemed more adjusted. He confessed that he had felt so dreadful the day before that he had considered jumping overboard; but knowing he could not swim very well, he thought better of it. His friends laughed.

The Dove was moving steadily through the water and the crew were in good spirits, with someone whistling merrily. Ceri was the more curious of the travellers and roamed the ship, concluding her exploration by joining Captain Zim at the wheel acting as helmsman. He greeted her warmly and to her delight suggested she could steer the ship. He offered a few simple instructions but little effort was required.

Meanwhile, Tansy was starboard side of the deck looking through the shiny spyglass gifted her.

'What is that?' she asked of nobody in particular.

'What can you see?' responded Ruffle, who was standing next to her.

'There, it's just a spot in the sky but it seems to be moving toward us.'

'Probably just a bird,' said Ruffle.

'Yes, I mean what else could it be?' mused Tansy.

They both continued to peer into the sky watching the black shape as it seemed to draw closer and grow larger.

'It's coming our way. Strange thing is that I think it's much bigger than a single bird,' observed Ruffle.

'It must be a flock of birds, a rather large flock and I think I am right,' said Tansy, still using her spyglass.

Dibit had taken the wheel once again, whilst Ceri and the captain joined Tansy and Ruffle.

'What a wonderful spyglass,' said the captain.

'Thank you, it was a gift from Jevell. But here captain, look out there, a big flock of birds flying our way' she said, handing the spyglass to the captain.

'What incredible magnification, this is a wonderful gift. Now, where are these birds? Right, now I see them. You are indeed correct, Tansy; they're crows, and such a group is referred to as a murder. But these are demon crows, so-called because they are much larger than ordinary crows, destructive and a favoured tool for many a sorcerer. That said, I have not seen nor heard of such a sizeable flock flying together for many a year, in fact not since the golden falcons of King Cadmus scattered them to the winds in the Great War.'

'However, their reputation persists and we should prepare as if we are their target. They can be deadly in such numbers. They are not shy in pecking people. Fortunately, your magnificent spyglass has enabled us to see them already, which affords us some time to organise ourselves. Jabe!' yelled the captain.

Turning to the companions his demeanour was now serious and business-like.

'Now you must go to the cabin and stay there whilst the crew makes the ship ready. These crows are large and have a vicious bite and for some reason I suspect it is us that they seek. They are unnaturally heading our way.'

'Us, why us?' queried Ruffle.

'I don't know but my experience tells me that a flock that size is likely the work of a sorcerer and it is not a good omen. Now quickly please.'

Almost immediately, the ship was busy, with the captain barking out orders to his crew. The sails were lowered, everything that could be was tied down, and loose items were removed from the deck. The captain was telling his men what to expect as they went about their tasks. Aside from the captain, only Jabe had ever seen demon crows before. Briefly, the captain considered trying to outrun the approaching flock but it was plain that the birds were moving more quickly than the boat. So, he abandoned those thoughts.

The three friends could do little to help, so they took refuge in their cabin and waited, wondering what the birds might do.

'Maybe they will simply fly past us,' said Tansy.

'Let's hope so, but I agree with the captain; I think they may be connected to the Girngog in some way and it is us that they seek,' replied Ceri.

'I hope not. Even in Yasrall they are renowned as nasty things. I have heard a few tales of them biting and wounding, even taking eyes out,' added Ruffle. 'But I thought they only existed in old stories.'

'If we do what the captain said and stay here, then surely, we will be alright. Though I wonder what damage they could do to the ship,' said Ceri.

'It's hard to imagine what damage birds could do,' added Ruffle.

'Well, I intend to be ready for them,' said Tansy, taking out her sword and swinging it around as if practising.

'Careful, you almost took my nose off with that swing,' laughed Ruffle.

'You see Ruffle, that's how dangerous I am, 'Tansy the Tormentor of crows,' will put them to flight.' She laughed at herself as she danced about the cabin fighting an imaginary foe.

Settling down, the three friends sat together on the bunk bed that afforded the best view through the long window. They sat huddled together listening to the banging and the running out on the deck. After some minutes, Tansy jumped up and pressing her face against the glass peered out of the window, trying to see if the birds were still heading toward them.

'I can't see them,' she said as she distorted her face on the glass.

'Come away,' said Ceri firmly, 'you will encourage them to look for us.'

'Oh, I take that back, they're already here. They seem to be circling above us' said Tansy, as she bent her neck to look directly above the ship. She withdrew and sat back on the bunk, now wearing a worried expression.

Up on deck the lowering of sails was almost completed. More and more of the birds were landing on the masts and rigging. Caws rang out growing louder like a painful chorus. Using their talons and beaks, the birds pecked and scratched at wood and cloth. The whole flock seemed to be descending upon the ship and the caws were deafening.

'Everyone below deck,' shouted Captain Zim, though his words were lost in the constant din.

He tied the wheel to keep the ship on course and drew his own cutlass. One of the crew who had been securing a sail had been caught on deck and was now being attacked by a group of birds. He screamed as they bit at him. He waved his arms like a mad windmill as he struggled to get away. He fell to the floor his arms covering his head, his hands scratched and bleeding.

Captain Zim ran over, swinging his cutlass and shouting. He caught several birds with his blade whilst others flew from the stricken sailor. It was Dern who lay there holding his head and groaning in pain. The captain pulled him up as the birds attacked again. He swung his cutlass with one arm whilst at the same time, dragged Dern across the deck with his other arm. They reached the bow cabin doors, pushed and fell inside bringing several birds with them. More attempted to fly through the open doors. But the crew already sheltered inside were ready and smote those that had deigned to follow. A frenzy of feathers filled the air. Confined by the cabin walls the birds retreated to the open doorway. Seizing the opportunity, the sailors closed the cabin doors, with the captain and Dern safe inside.

Meanwhile, more demon birds had lined up along the narrow sill of the long window in the cabin of the companions. Tap, tap, tap, tap was the refrain as the birds pecked at the window. It was a horrendous noise, so loud and threatening. The whole ship sounded as if it were being pecked to pieces. More and more birds swarmed outside the window, so much so that they blocked out the light. Combined with the torrent of cawing it seemed that the world had gone mad. The three friends clung to one another; this was beyond anything they had experienced before. Staring at the screeching birds and hoping the glass in the window would not give way, they were shocked.

After what seemed a long time, the cacophony of noise abated and the crows flew from the sill. Ruffle remembered to breathe again in his relief. When the window was clear Ceri slipped slowly over to peer out. The window was chipped in a hundred places but had held. She strained to peer upward and could make out the birds high in the air, circling. She sat back down and spoke.

'Oh my goodness. They were so much bigger than a normal crow. I thought the window would give way. They seem to have paused their attack and are flying above us. They may come back. So, I think it best that we wait for the captain to tell us when it is safe to leave the cabin.'

The silent nods from her shocked companions showed agreement, for they were in no hurry to meet the crows.

An eerie silence descended across the ship. The companions realised that they were talking in whispers, unsure why, except that it seemed appropriate. They sat waiting, listening and wondering. The ship was almost at a standstill. There was no sound outside. Then a trickle of voices - someone was talking, though it was not possible to discern what they were saying. Footsteps, then a knock on the cabin door and the captain entered.

'Are you all safe?' he asked.

Amidst reassuring him as to their own welfare, they noticed that the captain had a host of small cuts on his face and hands. He noticed that they had noticed.

'Nothing to worry about, I am in one piece. I collected these souvenirs when helping Dern. He was caught outside by those annoying birds. Thankfully, he is fine; worse than I mind, but now asleep and tended by Elam. If you will, do come on deck and help tidy the mess those creatures have created. It's safe now.'

Out on the deck it was chaos. The whole ship bore scratches. Holes had been gouged in the wood and most ropes looked badly chewed. Even though folded, the sails had been ripped and torn.

Tansy took out her spyglass and looked in the direction of the small black cloud of crows now moving away. Her special lenses confirmed that they were definitely flying away from the ship.

Everybody got involved in repairing the vessel, though the most telling damage had been done to the sails. That would take longer to remedy. The damage was such that the captain decided to drop anchor so repairs could be made. The three friends could do little but watch as the sailors demonstrated very impressive skills in sewing and patching the sails. It was not quick work and Ruffle began to wonder how much of a delay it would cost their journey. The captain answered his question before his thought had escaped his mouth. He took the companions to one side.

'This has slowed us but once repairs are complete, I estimate that we should reach land early tomorrow evening, perhaps a little after. If it is dark when we reach our destination, then I suggest you stay on board until the following morning. Although, in fact, it may well be safer arriving in darkness.'

The companions agreed that his suggestion made sense. They were also pleased to hear that repairs would be completed sooner than they had expected. Nonetheless, the repairs took several hours and deep into the evening. Finally, the captain felt the repair was adequate enough to raise the anchor and resume their journey.

That evening, the friends sat and ate with the crew. Inevitably, there was much conversation at the table and a sense of camaraderie pervaded the group, which stemmed from the shared experience of having been attacked by the demon crows. Even Dern felt well enough to join in and found himself the butt of a few teasing jokes to which he responded in kind. After plenty of food, laughter and relief, derived from having survived the day's events, all went to their beds and slept soundly. Throughout the night, the ship moved quietly across the sea with Captain Kim alone at the wheel.

The next day, the mending and the patching continued. One of the sails required more repair than the others, but the captain postponed any further refurbishing, preferring not to delay his passengers in reaching their destination. They set off again, patched up and making as much speed as they could muster. Several of the crew were busy with chisels, continuing to make good the damage to the wooden framework of the ship. The companions lent a hand, but there was little they could do to hurry things along. It was late afternoon when Kinter called down from his lookout position.

'Captain, there is something in the water, you should look.'

The captain crossed the deck to look where Kinter was pointing. Closing swiftly upon them, something was breaking the surface and it was enough for him to shout in a voice full of urgency and concern 'everyone grab hold of something, do it now or you will end up overboard.'

The three friends were in their cabin, unaware of what was happening on deck, when they were interrupted by a terrific noise that sounded like an explosion. A raw clatter of shouting followed and the ship lurched to one side. The two Chimbles fell out of their bunks onto the floor along with everything else that was loose in their cabin. A huge cracking sound pierced through the clamour that was coming from the deck.

'What in fiddlesticks is happening, it sounds like the ship is breaking in two,' said Ruffle as he stumbled toward the door.

The companions rushed through the cabin doors onto the deck to be greeted by utter chaos. Water was washing over the side and something massive was wrapped about the rear mast. More correctly, what was left of the mast, as two-thirds of it lay on the deck, starboard side and looking as if it were about to slide into the sea. Broken and splintered wood still connected to its base was all that prevented it from sliding overboard.

The culprit responsible for the chaos clung to the remaining base of the mast. Laying across half the deck it slumped like a huge reddish blob with two staring eyes set in a large bulbous head. Beneath the eyes was a mouth as big as a cave. The creature swayed and slithered as it spread its wriggling tentacles, causing the ship to rock and roll. The crew lay sprawled across the deck like fallen skittles. The slippery fiend was now slithering backwards off the deck and into the sea.

Somehow, the captain and Jabe had remained on their feet and were stabbing the creature with their blades. Though it seemed clear that their efforts were having little effect. The assailant continued slithering back to its watery home, its limbs flailing about. Suddenly, one flailing limb swept across the deck and caught Jabe, knocking him over the side into the sea.

'Oh no!' called out Tansy, 'Jabe, Jabe,' she shouted. But he was gone.

The ship slowed its swaying and the noise diminished almost to silence as the monster disappeared back into the water.

'Jabe has gone, did no one else see that?' pleaded Tansy.

'Yes, Tansy, but we can do little for him just yet. That thing is likely to return, be ready,' said the captain.

'What was it?' said Ruffle, 'something from the depths of hell?'

The warning was prescient as a great thud came from below deck and the ship rocked back and forth.

'What is that devil up to know?' mumbled Ruffle, more to himself than anyone else.

The ship steadied and everyone stood waiting, cutlasses drawn, bodies tensed and breathing hard. They were not to be disappointed. A tremendous splash of water rained across the deck as the creature lunged up and onto the ship once again. This time it hit the front mast. The ship tipped sideways as if it were about to capsize. The impact issued a loud bang, followed by a crunching cracking snap that fractured the remaining mast. The painful sound of wood splitting assaulted their ears, then the top half of the mast broke off and slid over the side into the sea. The ship wobbled dramatically but remained afloat.

In the commotion, most of the crew had found themselves on their backsides, and now on a deck awash with water many struggled to stay upright. Having slipped onto his back Captain Zim was nonetheless the first to regain his feet and once again he rushed at the creature stabbing it with his cutlass. There was no discernible reaction to his stabs. Angered at the futility of his attack the captain gave an almighty stab downward and his blade punctured the skin of a tentacle. The sword was embedded, so much so that he could not pull it out it.

Unarmed, the captain looked around for another weapon. Suddenly Ceri was by his side.

'I thought you might use this,' she said handing him an axe.

The captain grinned. He turned back to the monster only to find it was retreating to its watery habitat. Taking the axe he chopped and chopped at a tentacle whilst the fleshy monster slid away and he finally got a reaction. Suddenly the tentacles seemed to be waving all at once, up and across the whole deck. The whiplashing arms caught several of the crew and Kinter was swept overboard. Ceri was sent crashing against the walls of the bow cabin and lay flat on the floor unmoving.

The frantic thrashing abated as the creature finally returned to the water, the cutlass still protruding from one of its tentacles. Ceri lay unconscious. Tansy had been flung to the other side of the deck, sore but uninjured and still holding onto her sword. It was Ruffle who was closest and reached Ceri first. He turned and called out to Tansy, 'She's alive, she's alive.' Several crewmen were at the starboard side of the deck, peering into the sea, looking and calling out for Kinter and Jabe. There was no reply.

The captain carried the unconscious Ceri to her cabin, where Tansy tended to her, though unsure what she could do to help. On deck, the crew remained watchful for the return of the creature. With no sign of its return some had already begun throwing broken bits of wood overboard.

It was unspoken but all knew that another attack would likely sink the ship.

Whilst helping on deck Ruffle suddenly called out and began pointing to the sea. There were groans from the crew as most assumed he had spotted the creature again. The captain swiftly made for Ruffle and as he got closer, he realised that Ruffle was in fact calling out 'Jabe.' Swimming toward the stationary ship was Jabe. The captain patted Ruffle on the shoulder as if to say well done, though as Ruffle later said, he had simply spotted the swimmer.

The rope ladder was dropped over the side and soon Jabe was on deck, shivering and alive.

'How did you survive that?' asked Dibit as his fellow crew members gathered about him, clearly happy to have him back.

'I hit the water some way from the ship and I intended to swim back on board but that creature was still there, so I decided to make for the rowboat, which remains in tow. I climbed in and waited. I watched that thing crash into the ship and then escape back into the depths. I am quite sure it has gone, at least for the time being.'

'That is two lots of good news; having you back and the monster disappearing,' said the captain. 'I don't suppose that you saw Kinter?'

'No, sorry captain, I saw no one else.'

'Right. Jabe get some dry clothes and join us. As for everyone else, spread out across the ship and see if we can spy Kinter. We can clear the debris once we have him on board. Jump to it lads,' said the captain.

The ship was in a sorry condition. Both masts were demolished, like two stunted tree trunks, neither of any use. The top half of one had fallen into the sea along with its sails. The other was split in two, one half still dangling across the deck, attached only by splintered wood and a few ropes. It was just a matter of time before it would break completely. Sides of the deck were smashed, and water sloshed about, making it very slippery under foot. The biggest surprise for most was that the ship had not sunk.

However, the immediate task was to find Kinter. The sea was calm and all sides of the ship had crew looking out. Some time passed and silence cloaked the ship. There was nothing to be seen. No one said anything but most were thinking that Kinter had not survived.

'Right lads, Kinter is gone. We will pay our respects later. Let's repair what we can and be on our way,' instructed the captain. It seemed harsh but in truth there was nothing else they could do.

Unfortunately, there was yet more to discover as Dern drew attention to the behaviour of the wheel. It was not working. It was as the captain had feared. But he was in no mood to dwell on their misfortune and quickly decided that someone should dive below and check the extent of the damage.

Jabe had heard the exchange between Dern and the captain as he was about to go inside and change his clothes. Instead, he turned and spoke.

'Captain, I don't think I can get any wetter, so before I get dry, let me get wet again. I'll take a look' he volunteered.

The ship was bobbing in the water, straining on its anchor rope. Jabe tied a knife to his belt and dived into the deep blue waters. It was some minutes before he reappeared, his head and arms visible atop the surface, treading water.

The captain called out to him.

'What is the damage?'

Jabe did not answer but instead swam back and climbed aboard.

'I did not want to call out and run the risk of alarming the crew, captain. But the rudder is almost completely gone. And there are cracks on the port side midship. We should check if those are already leaking.'

The crew had gathered around and the captain had decided that they should hear what news Jabe had. There was nothing to be gained by doing otherwise. They all heard his news and few were surprised.

'Nevan, Berry, go check midship below to see if we are leaking,' ordered the captain. 'We're at the mercy of the sea, with no sails and no rudder. I need a few moments to think. Meanwhile, let's carry on and clear the deck.'

He then took himself over to the wheel and sat down, deep in thought.

Ruffle talked with Jabe, explaining to him what had happened to Ceri and that Tansy was now with her below.

'What was that monster?' he asked the sailor.

'I am not sure it has a name, though some call it a Kraken but that is because nobody knows what it is. Tales of long ago tell of a sea monster living in the lake but to my knowledge nobody has ever actually seen one. It is certainly the first time I have seen one, so I don't really know what you call it,' replied Jabe.

'So, it is unusual for it to attack a ship?'

'Definitely. But I sense that there is something odd going on. Firstly, we are attacked by Demon Crows, not a usual occurrence but not unique. Then a short time later a sea monster attacks us. I wager most everyone considered tales of a sea monster just a myth, but now one suddenly appears and almost sinks the ship. You may know more than I, but it is hard to believe that such things are a coincidence.'

Ruffle did not venture a response. Thoughtful, he left Jabe and sought out his Chimble friends. He entered the cabin and found Ceri sitting up and talking with Tansy.

'Are you feeling better?' he asked.

'Yes, thank you. I feel as if I have a nasty bump on my head but otherwise, I am fine.'

At which point Ruffle brought his friends up to date with what had been happening up on deck. Then there was a knock at the cabin door. It was Dibit.

'The captain is addressing everyone and he asks if you could be there too.'

'Perhaps you should remain here until you are fully recovered,' suggested Tansy to Ceri.

'No Tansy, I am alright, but I appreciate the thought,' answered Ceri.

The companions joined the crew who were gathered together. The captain began by saying a few words about Kinter, who had been lost in the encounter with the sea creature.

He continued, 'Our purpose was to transport our three guests across the lake and that remains our purpose. The plain problem is that we now have no mast, sails or rudder. There are cracks in the body of the ship to which Berry and Nevan have made some repairs; they believe that they will hold for the rest of this journey. After completing our mission, we must then get The Dove to a place where she can be properly repaired. For now, we are at the mercy of the wind and the sea, we can do little to control our direction or speed. Fortunately, we have one saving grace and that is our rowing boat, somehow, it remains intact and still tied to the Dove.'

'We can bring the rowboat to the bow and pull the Dove as best we can. It will be hard going. We have oars enough for eight so that will have to do. We will make for the shore and drop anchor as close as we dare. Then we can drop off our guests. From there we can row north and hopefully enlist the help of some fishermen in the villages. We will need some help to get to Springhaven where we can commence the serious repair of the ship.'

Everyone realised that it would be difficult to tow The Dove, so the captain ordered that anything broken beyond repair be thrown overboard in order to lighten the weight of the vessel. At the same time the crew set about recovering the rowboat and making it ready. The captain took his three guests to one side.

'Let me be blunt, for you must deal with the reality of what lies ahead. I believe that the sea monster and the Demon Crows were sent to delay or thwart your quest. I do not know why and I have no proof, but somebody does not wish you to reach Castle Black. The power to conjure up the creature that attacked the ship, along with the ability to mobilise the Girngog, is most likely the work of one person, and to my mind it must be the dark sorcerer Merektar. Tell me, do you know of him?'

It was Ceri who responded.

'None of us know him but we have all heard of him. After talking with Jevell we suspected that he was behind the Girngog aggression in Yasrall and our being chased when leaving Clinglewood Forest.'

'But I don't understand why he feels we are a threat to him!' exclaimed Ruffle.

'I confess, I don't know,' said the captain.

'Could it be that he thinks our reaching Castle Black before him will allow Venterra to be prepared? Which makes sense if it his intention for the Girngog to attack the castle,' suggested Tansy.

'But he cannot know that our purpose is to forewarn the king. We only decided that ourselves in the last few days!' exclaimed Ruffle.

'I have no answer for you Ruffle. But it does bring us to another serious consideration. It is my estimate that we cannot now deliver you to the point that you desired. Being towed by the rowboat will be slow and given how the currents flow I am afraid that we will reach the shore closer to Bridgemouth than anywhere else. I calculate you will be at least two days' walk from your preferred route through the Ghost Mountains. Of course, you are welcome to remain on board, even until we reach Springhaven but that would delay your travel by several days.'

'Do you have an alternative suggestion at all captain?' asked Ruffle.

'You are going to lose time, that is now unavoidable. And as we know, the quickest route is to cross the Ghost Mountains from Bridgemouth. However, we do not yet know if the town is occupied by the Girngog, or whether they guard the gate at the start of that road. But if they are at Bridgemouth then I would suggest that you reconsider your plans. To be plain, if they intend to march on to the castle at Duskhold, then it is hard to see how you can expect to reach it before them. It will be safer to relinquish your quest now. However, if giving up is not an option, then it may be that passing through the Bridgemouth gate and taking that road may be your only choice for getting ahead of them. Though, it may already be too late to do that. It is your business to decide but if speed is important to you then you should abandon your plan to take the Whispies road. I will leave you to decide how you wish to proceed.'

The companions took his advice and withdrew to their cabin to discuss what they should do.

'Well, for me I do not think there is much to discuss. We are on a quest and we knew that there would be dangers, so we carry on,' asserted Tansy.

'Thank you, Tansy,' replied Ruffle. 'But we did not know it would be this dangerous. We have only just survived two attacks and we have a long way to go. I am unsure that I can ask you to go any further. Plus, the whole effort may be pointless, as the captain implied. If we cannot reach Castle Black before the Girngog then our journey will have been in vain and we will be stranded amongst the enemy. Perhaps we have to consider returning to Cricklewood.'

Ceri stood up and began pacing slowly across the cabin.

'Firstly, we do not need to go over old ground. You are not responsible for our decisions Ruffle. We all accepted the journey would be difficult and we are all committed to continue. Secondly, you do make good points, but this is not the time to be giving up. We knew we would encounter challenges. However, now is the time for us to use our minds and take action.'

'Yes, absolutely, I like that,' said Tansy.

'We can only take one step at a time, so let us do so. We cannot foresee the conclusion of our quest, so we keep going. I am just as concerned and I suspect as scared as either of you, but that cannot be a reason to stop. We go forward despite those thoughts and feelings. Such thoughts will only bring worry. I say let us continue, let us concentrate on achieving what we set out to do. Giving up will always bring regret,' concluded Ceri.

Her voice and words were full of defiance and passion. Although within herself she felt daunted at the task ahead.

'You both put me to shame. I wonder where I would be if I had not met you. Let us go forward together, how can we not!' said Ruffle, who stood up smiling, whilst both Chimbles gave him a hug of encouragement.

'We agree on that but we are not yet decided as to which way to travel through the Ghost Mountains. Though, it seems we have little choice,' said Tansy.

'Given what the captain said, the only option is to make for the gate at Bridgemouth. Do either of you see an alternative?' Ceri asked of her friends.

Ruffle shook his head and said nothing.

'I am not sure how we might do it but I agree. It seems that the most dangerous way is the only way we might beat the Girngog to Duskhold,' agreed Tansy.

'I think we have a consensus. Let us tell the captain of our decision,' said Ceri.

The companions went on deck. Although it was slow, the ship was moving forward. The captain stood with hands on hips looking down at the rowing boat now pulling the wounded ship. He turned to face his three passengers and spoke.

'It was difficult, we had to shorten the rope and create sufficient tension to affect a tow. Nonetheless we are moving. Progress will be slow but we will reach the shore,' he reassured them. 'Of course, that depends on your continued wish to do so.'

'Indeed, it remains our wish, captain. We choose to persist with our quest, that is our resolve,' said Tansy.

'We will leave the ship anywhere that you can get us, though not Bridgemouth of course,' added Ceri.

The captain gave a small laugh.

'Somehow, I am not surprised. I doubted that the thought of being pursued by hordes of Girngog would stop you.'

They all laughed, a hesitant and restrained laugh.

'Well, it is difficult to predict exactly where we might make land, but hopefully it will be sufficiently north of Bridgemouth for us not to be seen. I will need to drop anchor a little way from the shore. If we go in too close, then we may not have enough power to pull out to deeper water again. So, once we are near the shore, the rowboat can take you on the beach and the next part of your adventure can commence,' explained the captain. He wore a slight smile, not because he was amused but because he was full of admiration for the bravery of the companions.

'That sounds just fine captain,' said Ceri.

'It will have to do my friends. Perhaps, one day I can make it up to you and show you that being assailed by sea monsters is not our usual experience at sea,' said the captain.

11

Foreign Land

Despite the calm sea, it took a mighty effort from the crew to tow the rudderless Dove toward land. The companions offered to take a turn in the rowboat, but the captain insisted that they save their strength for what awaited them on shore.

Progress was sluggish. The approaching darkness came as a welcome relief to the weary oarsmen, who had been labouring under the sweltering sun. As dusk settled in, the distant lights of Bridgemouth began to flicker into view. Tansy brought out her gift from Jevell, the spyglass, that even in darkness displayed a scene as if it was the middle of the day.

'This is a fine gift from Jevell,' said the captain, once again admiring the spyglass and peering toward Bridgemouth. 'I can see movement around the town, and I think, if I am not mistaken, I can see the flags of Gritol. Fortunately, they will not be able to see us in this darkness, even with our lanterns alight; we are too far away unless they possess a spyglass such as this.'

'It seems our assumption about the Girngog being in Bridgemouth was correct. How far are we from shore, Captain?' asked Ruffle.

'At the rate we are travelling, I would say about an hour. Although the shape of the shoreline means we will lose sight of Bridgemouth within minutes and happily they will not be able to see us. That said, we are still closer to the town than I would have preferred. Once we set you ashore, you will be just a few hours' walk from the town. But we will be a long way from the road you originally chose to take. I am sorry about that. It has proven difficult to prevent the currents tugging us south. Once you are ashore, I will take the ship north to find a safe haven to make repairs. The further we are from Bridgemouth, the better I will feel.'

'We will be ready to leave once you deem that we should. We have no wish to delay you,' said Ceri.

'I appreciate that. And one thing you should bear in mind is that you can walk the shoreline from here all the way into Bridgemouth. So, beware of anybody else on the beach, as they could be Girngog. For now, excuse me as I must attend to the crew. A short rest is in order.'

The companions returned to their cabin. They were ready to leave as soon as they could. In fact, they were eager to do so. Inevitably, their thoughts and conversation turned to what lay ahead.

'I think the first thing we should do once ashore, is take stock of where we are and then decide how we proceed,' said Ruffle.

'That sounds sensible,' said Tansy.

'Yes, we do not know what we will find. I also suggest that we assume the Girngog are looking for us,' added Ceri.

'I agree. Jabe told me that on leaving the rowboat, we will be on a beach. He said that it runs back into sand hills and if we climb atop those, we will be able to see the road that connects Bridgemouth to Springhaven,' said Ruffle.

'If that is the position where we land, then we will be vulnerable. The Girngog could come at us from the town either along the beach or from the road, or both,' said Tansy.

'Yes, but Jabe said the sand hills would afford us cover and a view of the road. Plus, the beach gives us access all the way to Bridgemouth, which could be helpful. Hopefully, they are not expecting anyone to approach the town. It would be foolish,' argued Ceri with a small laugh.

'In other words, we are going to be fools,' chuckled Tansy, folding her arms and leaning back against the cabin wall.

'Well, we can only decide when we are actually ashore. And then, like so much these days, we will have to react to what we find. But at least we have the element of surprise on our side!' said Ruffle.

'So many decisions. I wonder if all adventures require dealing with uncertainty? I think ours do,' said Tansy.

'Maybe it's the uncertainty that means it is an adventure?' mused Ceri.

'Without getting too philosophical, is all travel an adventure? Or is it just when being chased by Girngog?' posed Ruffle.

'Enough, this talk is not helping,' exclaimed Tansy, 'we don't have to get philosophical; we just have to get on with it.'

'Spoken like a true adventurer,' said Ruffle, grinning.

Tansy looked at Ruffle with a stern face as if about to argue, then she laughed. Then all three friends laughed together and without saying as much, they silently agreed to discontinue discussing the subject any further. Instead, they talked of how glad they would be to step on land again.

It was not so long before Dibit knocked on the cabin door to say the captain was about to drop anchor and that they should come on deck. Within minutes, the companions were standing next to the captain, packed and ready to leave.

'We are as close as we dare be,' said the captain. 'Any closer and the ship may be at the mercy of currents and tides that our rowboat cannot pull us through. So, in a few moments, climb into the boat. We will drop you on the beach, but then we must make a hasty retreat. We must be as far away from Bridgemouth as possible come the morning light.'

Soon, a shout from below signalled that the rowboat was beside the Dove. Brief farewells were exchanged, then the three friends clambered down the rope ladder and took their seats in the rowboat. To their surprise, Captain Zim joined them, along with five of the crew.

Ceri was about to ask the obvious question, but refrained, for it was plain that the captain intended to accompany them. Fortunately, there was little wind and the sea was placid, although the ship lay further from the shore than any of the friends had expected. Nonetheless, the rowboat progressed quicker than she expected. They were soon in shallow waters, shallow enough for the captain and crew to jump out and haul the boat close to the beach. The three friends clambered into the trickling waves and onto the sand.

'No offence, captain, but it feels good to place my feet on firm ground once more,' smiled Ruffle.

'No offence taken,' the captain laughed.

Both Ceri and Tansy gave the captain a hug as they said goodbye. Ruffle shook his hand, muttering that a Rall does not do much hugging. There was little time spent saying goodbye. The captain was eager to return to his ship.

The friends were keen to seek shelter where they could not be easily seen, and immediately began a reconnaissance of their position. They found refuge against the side of a sand hill; bowl-shaped like a naturally formed den. Looking back at the sea, they could make out very little in the darkness, so Tansy grabbed her spyglass. She could see that the rowboat was close to the ship, and the captain would soon be back on board.

'First, I suggest we climb on top of this sandhill and take a look at where we are, then we can better decide which direction to go,' said Ceri.

So, that was precisely what they did, all the time being careful not to stand upright fearing someone might see them. Noiselessly, they crawled atop the sand hill and found that they were in a good position to spy out the landscape. It took a minute for their eyes to adjust to the gloom, and again Tansy took out her spyglass.

Their cautious approach had been a good decision. Little more than two hundred paces away was the road. They realised that the sandy den they had occupied, dampened sound as well as offering protection from the wind. But within a few minutes, they could hear a low grumbling which soon became plain as to what its source was.

'Keep down, it's the Girngog' whispered Tansy.

Lying flat on the sandhill and straining their eyes, they could all see a mass of figures moving along the road.

'There must be three hundred or more,' observed Ruffle.

The companions lay still and silent, with only the thud of clomping Girngog ringing through the night. A murmur of mumbling accompanied the marching marauders. It was not until they had passed that anyone dare speak.

'I think it is a fair assumption that they are headed for Springhaven,' whispered Ceri.

'Why would they be marching at night?' queried Ruffle.

'Perhaps they are in a hurry. They probably think that the sooner they attack, the less time there is for any defences to be organised.'

'I agree,' said Tansy. 'So, I think that we should avoid the road. Because if you are right, then there will be more following them.'

'Tansy, use the spyglass and see what you can of the direction from whence they came,' said Ruffle.

Spyglass in hand, Tansy peered back in the direction of Bridgemouth.

'I cannot see as far as the town; the road turns and twists. But I can see many lights and tents, which I think must be close to the town. And I think I see the top of the Necklace, at least its lights. Here, see what you make of it,' she said and handed the spyglass to Ruffle.

Ruffle took a turn and then passed it to Ceri. She viewed their surroundings and then suggested that they return to the beach den below to decide what to do.

'We were guessing before, but now that we are actually here, I think it is clear that we cannot take the risk of travelling on the road, north or south. Which obviously affects our speed in trying to reach Bridgemouth. However, we are close to the town and the mountains. So, it should not take long to reach the gate even if we do not use the road. And whilst haste is important, we must be careful not to rush and make mistakes,' cautioned Ceri.

'You're right, Ceri. We cannot avoid getting close to the Girngog in order to get through the gate, but somehow, we must remain undiscovered. Though given how many of them there are, it may not be possible.'

'Well, there is clearly no good choice. Whatever way we go is risky. The problem might be that the Girngog may have set up camp near the gate.' said Tansy.

'Well, whilst we still have the cover of darkness, why don't we go closer and take a look at the camp. We need to know if the gateway through the mountains is approachable or if it is guarded.

There may be a way we can get past them. But we cannot know unless we take a look!' suggested Ruffle.

'Yes, that seems a good idea, albeit dangerous,' agreed Ceri.

'Yes, I agree, it has to be better than sitting here speculating. Let's go and take a look. I just don't want to be caught and then eaten!'' Tansy replied.

Off they set, stealthily and silently. All three were used to stealing through undergrowth, creating no more disturbance than a breeze might. Nonetheless, their progress was slow as they were vigilant. They kept off the road and made for the foothills of the Ghost Mountains that loomed high over the land. They were rocky and steep. The earlier option of climbing across the mountain which had been dismissed, was now seen to have been a wise decision. So, they crossed the fields and used what trees they could as they approached the town. Sneaking closer the situation became clearer.

The Girngog had set up a camp consisting of hundreds of tents, small and large. Some were still being erected, suggesting that more Girngog were continuing to arrive.

The Girngog they had seen marching, had been no more than a small mob compared to the numbers tromping about the encampment. The ragged, undisciplined crowd they had spied heading north did not, by themselves, point to an invasion, but the sprawling village of tents they now looked at certainly did.

Like silent slithering snakes, the companions moved into a wooded area and peeked into the camp from behind trees. Using just her hands, Ceri silently indicated to her companions that they should move back and confer. Stealing away from the camp, they sat on the soft grass behind a large boulder, pensive and quiet.

'If ever we needed proof, then I would suggest that this camp tells us that we are in the midst of a Girngog invasion. There are thousands of them,' whispered Ruffle.

'It will be difficult getting past them, never mind finding the gateway. But they are still arriving, and it all looks chaotic, which may be good news for us. I am thinking that we could take advantage of their chaos in getting past them,' suggested Ceri.

Ruffle's face indicated he was doubtful, but he said nothing.

Then Tansy spoke with her old enthusiasm.

'I agree that their chaos could help us. Ordinarily, I would doubt that we could sneak through hundreds of Girngog. But given that they are still sorting out their camp, it can give us an advantage. I noticed that they are not camped very close to the foothills. That may leave us enough space to approach between the mountain and the tents. We could use the darkness to go around the tents and not between them. It will be risky and only possible in the darkness. We need to blend in with their confusion. What is more, I think I spied the gateway, at least the two stone figures that overlook it.'

'But they must have guards all around the camp? It seems very dangerous to think that we can slip through their camp.' said Ruffle.

'Of course it's dangerous, Ruffle, we all know that. But a quick look through my spyglass showed that there were relatively few guards on the mountainside of the camp, which is no surprise, as they obviously don't expect anyone to come down the mountain to attack them. We can approach that way, close to the mountain. It might be our only chance as more of them keep arriving,' argued Tansy.

'Well, it seems we have little choice but to find out. It may be our only hope of reaching the gateway unseen,' said Ceri.

'Well, it looks like there are boulders and trees along the foothills which will afford us some cover,' added Tansy.

'Alternatively, Tansy could fight all the Girngog to provide us with free passage. But if she is not going to fight all the Girngog, then I think we ought to give this idea a try,' grinned Ruffle.

'If I am to fight all the Girngog, then I would only do it on condition that you have tea and crumpets waiting for me when I finish, agreed?'

'Definitely, as you would also be my heroine!' said Ruffle with a chuckle.

'More seriously, you two, we need to decide whether we go now or wait until tomorrow?' wondered Ceri.

'I think we should go now. There are still several hours of darkness remaining, and I see no gain from putting it off,' proposed Tansy. 'Let's go and take another look. Then we can make a plan.'

'Agreed,' said Ruffle.

12

The Gateway

Gathering themselves for what lay ahead, the three friends set out toward the mountains overlooking the camp. The night was cloudy and the moonlight was weak. It helped their concealment as they stole across open land. Moving quickly and silently, they slipped over the road and into the fields that stretched up to the mountains. A persistent hum of activity came from the large Girngog camp. In contrast, they were light-footed and noiseless, a trait common amongst Chimbles and often amongst the Rall.

Reaching the trees that hugged the base of the mountains, they paused with relief.

'So far, so good,' said Ceri.

After taking some moments to estimate where the gateway sat, they set off in a single file. Ceri leading. Tansy had been correct in suspecting that there was good space between the Girngog camp and the mountains. Taking advantage of the natural camouflage provided by rocks and bushes, they moved within the shadows. They progressed in parallel with the camp perimeter.

A constant drone of noise emanating from the camp accompanied them, as did a pungent aroma. Ruffle squeezed his nose to block the smell, which almost started a fit of giggles among the three. It stemmed from the danger and tension they were feeling.

But fortunately, Tansy had been right.

'You were right, there seem to be very few guards,' whispered Ceri. 'They must be assuming there would be no need, as no one would be coming down from the mountain to threaten them.'

'Or perhaps it is the Girngog perfume that they rely on, no sensible person would wish to go near that aroma,' grinned Tansy as all three squeezed their noses in response to the smell pervading the night air.

'It is definitely a deterrent for any attacker,' said Ruffle, scrunching up his face further as if he could taste the smell.

'I can state from experience that that scent is Girngog perfume,' commented Ceri, smiling.

Tansy suppressed a giggle again. Their demeanour contrasted with what they felt within.

'Maybe that's why so many are still awake. There seem to be hundreds still about; I wonder if they ever sleep?' Tansy added.

'Oh, they do, I can tell you that from the short time that I was captured. When they are all asleep, it is like a pig's chorus and I don't know how they manage to sleep through it,' said Ceri.

In a more serious tone, Ruffle spoke.

'I think the area we are approaching may be where new arrivals are putting up tents and settling. It definitely looks busier than the other side of the camp. But it can be our advantage,'

They set off again, this time not giggling. Continuing to use the undergrowth and small boulders as cover, Ceri suddenly stopped and pointed.

'It must be the gate,' said Tansy.

Two towering figures loomed high in the darkness. They were unlit except for firelight dancing about their legs. The figures stood feet astride, as if on guard. Their stances were the same and mirrored each other. One hand lay on the top of a long shield held on the ground in front of their legs, whilst the other arm held a long sword reaching across to touch the sword of the opposite figure, thereby forming an archway.

'Without doubt that must be the gate,' said Ruffle.

Now knowing where they must reach, they moved ahead. Before long, they had a better view of the monolithic guardians.

'Thunder, look what sits all around it, Girngog tents,' whispered a disappointed Tansy. 'In their chaos, they have made sure that the gateway is guarded. How annoying!'

'What do we do? There are too many for us to fight, and it's not as if we can just walk past them. If we don't try tonight, then once the sun rises, we will need to hide somewhere. But we will be faced with the same problem tomorrow! Do either of you have any ideas? I am afraid I don't,' stated Ruffle.

At that moment, they were flummoxed, bereft of ideas. They shuffled behind some trees and sat down to consider what to do next.

'I have an idea,' said Tansy, 'though I am sure you won't approve of it straight away. Be it day or night, the Girngog will remain here, as they are clearly camped and likely to stay for some time. So, waiting for them to leave is not a viable idea. Thus, I propose that I cause a distraction and draw them away from the gate. Then you both can slip through unnoticed. After all, the priority is to get a message to the king.'

'No Tansy, not a good idea; though I appreciate your bravery, lass. But it is I who should cause the distraction, for you are here because of me, and it is my responsibility to do this,' said Ruffle, and slowly nodded his head.

'You are both brave fools, but there may be another way,' said Ceri.

'Oh, please say that you are going to surprise us and produce a wizard from your pocket, that would be so useful,' teased Ruffle.

'Alas, I have no wizard, but we do have wizardry that we can use,' grinned Ceri.

'Where? Did I miss him, is he travelling with us?' scoffed Ruffle, turning his head to look around as if to spot such a wizard. His sense of helplessness had soured his mood.

'I said wizardry, not an actual wizard,' replied Ceri. 'Please find that slim box Jevell gave to me which sits in your coat pocket.'

Ruffle put his hands into his pockets and in a few moments exclaimed, 'aha, here it is.'

'What is it? A wand?' wondered Tansy aloud.

'Not a wand but a *Time Stick*,' smiled Ceri.

Even in the dim moonlight, it was evident that the box was decorated with symbols and from it, Ceri carefully removed a blue stick, which was also liberally inscribed with gold runes and symbols. It looked like a wand, but Ceri explained its true use.

'This, my dear friends, is a magical stick, for it carries a time spell. It can be used only once and then it will turn to dust, as will the box that holds it. Jevell said it must not ever be allowed to fall into the hands of the enemy, for it would be misused by those practitioners of dark magic.'

'What does it do?' asked Tansy with a puzzled expression.

'For the person holding the stick, it stops time. So, whilst everyone else is frozen in time, so to speak, the stick holder can move normally. The world stands still whilst the holder can move normally. There are no magic words; it simply has to be snapped for it to begin. Unfortunately, it only lasts for a few minutes,' explained Ceri.

'Oh, so that would be just for you? Well, I suppose it is better that at least one of us can use it,' stated Tansy, who felt disappointed.

'No, it is better than that,' Ceri continued. 'The stick has to be snapped in order for it to take effect, but anyone touching the stick holder at the moment it is broken is also able to move freely and not be frozen in time. So, if we are linked together, it can help us all. It will give us precious minutes to move without worrying about the Girngog.'

'Will it be enough? How far can we go in a few minutes?' queried Ruffle. 'It sounds like the advantage would be brief. Not very long?'

'Yes, I wish it were more, but it should give us time to run through the gate. It can give us a lead if the Girngog chase after us, better still, they may not even notice that we have gone through once the spell wears off.'

'Well. It does seem our best option so far, perhaps our only option,' said Tansy as she examined the blue stick, which seemed to be pulsing softly. 'I suppose all these symbols and signs are the wizard's spell?'

'I imagine so,' said Ceri.

'Honestly, I can imagine that it can help, but I wonder how far we can get along the road before the enemy pursues us, for I have no doubt that they will. A few minutes sounds such a short time,' grumbled Ruffle.

'Well, it does mean that neither of us needs to sacrifice ourselves as a distraction; we can all escape together, or not. Really, in these circumstances, I don't think we have much choice but to try it,' proposed Tansy.

'Yes, I suppose you're right. So, we'd better get as close to the gate as we can before we use it, so that my legs can carry me as far as possible before the spell wears off. I just hope it's enough time to get away!' said Ruffle.

'When you think on it, we can cover a good distance in minutes of running,' encouraged Tansy.

'Hush!' whispered Ceri, putting a finger to her lips to signal be quiet.

The others now heard what Ceri had, heavy footsteps crunching the grass. They could just about make out a large, big-bellied Girngog coming toward the trees where they hid. Immediately, the tension between the three friends was tangible. They lay down, barely breathing. The big, blubbery Girngog was sauntering directly toward them. Ceri decided they were, as yet, unseen. The manner of the Girngog was too casual to suggest he had noticed them.

However, the tension rose as the noisy soldier stopped just arm's length away from where they lay sprawled. The companions were rigid and tense. The Girngog burped and muttered something inaudible, then undid his belt as if about to relieve himself. Tansy's eyes went wide. If he toileted, it would be directly at them, barely two good steps away. Then a shout came from the camp and another large Girngog came tromping toward them. The second one called out, and the first pulled his trousers back up. The two exchanged words, but nothing was understood by the friends. It was clearly a disagreement. The two then walked quickly back toward the tents, grumbling at one another.

'Thank fiddlesticks for that, I did not fancy a drenching from that fat beasty,' said Ruffle.

'That was a close thing,' said Tansy.

'Absolutely. We must do what we must quickly. Getting back to what we were saying, I know you are both trying to make the best of it, but I don't see a better choice for us at this point than using the *Time Stick*. I think that we are all in agreement on that, if I am not mistaken. So, let us go and get as close to the gate as possible. We should use the darkness as cover as much as we can,' urged Ceri.

Her two companions nodded their agreement. With Tansy taking the lead, they took to sneaking and slinking behind the boulders and bushes. The cover was good as they drew closer and closer to the Gate. But the trees thinned, the ground changed, becoming flatter, with no large boulders and tents blocked their path.

'Keep your hoods up. Weaving between the tents is our best cover now. We must stay out in the open for as long as we can before I use the magic,' whispered Ceri.

Tansy seemed to be responding positively to the danger, her attention more focused than Ceri had seen for some time. They kept as close together as they could, stepping over guy ropes and creeping between the tents. But then it became unavoidable to take the road leading up to the Gate. Although the camp was quieter now, many Girngog milled about.

'Stay close to one another. Remember, we must all be touching when I break the Time Stick, that way the spell can work for us all,' said Ceri. 'Now just walk steadily, no rushing, we do not wish to draw any attention. Put your hoods up.'

Though Ceri felt determined about the plan, her stomach churned with tension. She thought, 'What are we doing, walking openly into the belly of the beast,' and she would have happily turned and run away, if it were possible. She told herself that being brave does not mean one does not act on fear; rather, it means carrying on despite it. She gritted her teeth and got more determined.

Keeping slightly apart, they emerged from between tents into the open space of the road. As they walked, it seemed that no one was interested or curious about the three hooded figures now strolling side by side. Despite the lateness of the hour, a constant drone of noise permeated the camp. Some Girngog were sitting around campfires eating, others sat about and talked, whilst even more seemed to be arriving. Bursts of laughter and brief shouts punctured the night. They friends were getting closer to the gate and daring to think that they might progress unchallenged.

Then someone called out, a shout that they knew was directed toward them. They tried to ignore it. Moments passed, then another shout, followed by another. Someone was clearly hailing them. They kept walking, not turning, pretending not to hear, hoping to be left alone. Then a large soldier seated on a big chair set outside a tent entrance stood up – he had been eating, but threw his food to the ground, wiped his hands on his tunic and started to move toward the companions. He had noticed the hooded figures and that they had ignored the hails - unlike the guards who were slumped and dozing at the gateway. Now, several Girngog were moving toward the companions, blades not yet drawn but obviously intent on accosting the intruders.

'Link my arms,' whispered Ceri with an urgency in her voice.

On either side of her, they each grabbed an arm, and Ceri could feel the tension ripple through their grips.

'Not so tight, Ruffle,' complained Ceri. 'I need my hands free.'

'Sorry, though we'd better use it soon or we will need to draw our swords,' he replied.

'You! Where you going? Who are you?' barked the big Girngog who had interrupted his feasting.

None of the companions responded. Ceri took the *time stick* from its box and tried to snap it. But it did not break. Her face had a horrified expression and Tansy looked at Ruffle, both wide-eyed and a little shocked. They had assumed that the stick would break easily. Ceri tried again, and this time a cracking sound punctured the air. It was a grating sound that felt almost painful, certainly uncomfortable to hear. The stick broke and was now in two pieces, one in each of Ceri's hands. Then instantly, each piece turned to dust, which slid between her fingers.

Suddenly, there was no sound at all, no birds, no wind, just complete silence. The Girngog stood, statue-like, as if made of stone, and the three friends could only hear their own heavy breathing.

'Run,' shouted Tansy, and they did. Despite knowing what to expect, the whole event had startled them and valuable seconds had been lost before they began to run.

Through the gateway formed by the enormous stone figures and past the frozen-in-time guards, they could see the road as it wended its way into the mountains. It was not steep, but it clearly had an incline and they knew the running would become harder the further they went. Nonetheless, they were away from the Gate, panting and already blowing hard as they sprinted. It was a long stretch of road and the mountain offered no shelter to avoid being seen from the Gate. To the right of the road was a wide stretch of grass that ran away to trees, but itself provided no possibility of cover.

'We have to get as far away as we can and hope the darkness affords us cover,' uttered a breathless Ceri as she ran.

'We don't do a lot of running in Yasrall, so next time I must practise,' puffed Ruffle.

Suddenly, the silence was shattered. Shouts and screams could be heard. Mere minutes had passed so swiftly. Ceri glanced behind.

'They're coming, they've seen us. Keep running.'

They ran, but already the incline in the road was slowing them. Tansy looked behind.

'Why are so many of them suddenly wide awake at this hour!'

'Stop. Stop. It's no use, they'll catch us,' said Ceri. They all stopped. Breathing hard and looking back, the Girngog were coming for them and closing the gap. Ruffle bent over, hands on his knees and gulping in air. There was nowhere to go but forward, nowhere to hide.

'Why are we stopping? They'll catch us, especially as I have a stomach stitch,' panted Ruffle.

'Indeed. So, change of plan. Let's get to the grass and make for the trees, it's our only hope, go' Ceri insisted, in-between gasping for air.

There was no argument, and the three friends sped off the road and onto the grass. All the advantages gained from using the *time stick* were fast disappearing. Now they were running for their lives, and the screaming gang behind was drawing closer. What was I thinking, thought Ceri as she ran - this must not be the end.

'They will catch us before we get there. We'll have to fight,' yelled Ruffle between breaths.

'Just keep going,' said Ceri.

Their hearts beat faster and their breathing was loud, as several spears and arrows whizzed past their heads. The shouting and screaming of the chasing horde was growing louder. The three friends were close to the trees, but the enemy was almost upon them.

'I'll fight them, you get to the trees,' shouted Ruffle as he stopped running. He stood gasping for air, drew his sword and turned to face the pursuers.

'No Ruffle,' called Ceri, also stopping.

Then the three friends all drew their swords and turned to face their pursuers, just in time. The first clash of blade upon blade rang out. The five Girngog arriving first were all large. It was unlikely that this little battle would last very long, thought Ceri. Ruffle's swordplay was immediately holding two at bay, but blood dripped from his head where a Girngog swipe had scratched him above his eye. Likewise, Tansy was fighting two and keeping them occupied until she slipped on a tree root, falling backwards. Ceri was losing her battle, being driven backwards by a large foe swinging an axe. Behind these, other Girngog were getting closer, running to join in.

Then a loud collective 'twang' rang through the air. Three of the Girngog in front of the companions slumped to the ground. Each felled by green feathered arrows. Almost instantly, a number of tall figures sped from behind and past the companions to engage the enemy in combat. Tall, slim and agile, it was immediately clear that they were swift and lethal warriors who displayed poise and calmness in their swordplay. Almost immediately, the companions were relieved of fighting the Girngog. These impressive strangers had engaged them on their behalf.

'It's the Faerie,' said Ruffle, breathing hard and leaning over with his hands on his knees.

Then all three companions jumped with fright at the sound of a voice close to their ears. It was one of the faeries who appeared as if from nowhere. He had long yellow braided hair, deep green clothing and wore no armour. He placed his sword in its scabbard as he spoke.

'Let us get you to safety, more Girngog will be upon us soon. Please follow me.'

He beckoned them toward the trees, and without hesitation, all happily and hastily retreated into the wood.

Startled by what had just happened, the friends followed in single file, still breathing hard and watching where they trod. It was dark and they were wary of tripping over a tree root or the like. Then another faery appeared with lanterns to lead the way. They walked for some minutes, and the leading faery seemed quite unhurried and relaxed, so Ceri asked, 'Won't the Girngog follow us, should we not run? And what about your fellows, shouldn't we help them?'

The yellow-haired faery turned, halted and smiled at Ceri.

'Have no fear, the Girngog know better than to follow us or venture into Earthroot. My 'fellows' are fine, they are already back with us, though you may not have noticed them.'

The three friends felt slightly reassured, although they did not fully understand what was happening. Tansy was perhaps the least reassured and kept her hand on the pommel of her sword as they threaded their way through the trees. She thought to herself, 'Are we safe?' The three companions began to take in their surroundings, absorbing the fact that if this was Earthroot, then they were in the largest known forest, and incredibly, for the very first time, they were in the presence of the Faerie.

It was soon apparent that Earthroot was quite different from anything that they had experienced before. Most obviously, the trees were impossibly large. Some were comfortably wide enough that a horse and cart could be hidden behind the trunks. Many were so tall that it was incredible to see how high they grew. The fascination of the three companions was increased when they noticed movement within the branches and realised that some of the faeries high above were running or leaping from branch to branch, even in the darkness! The clothes of the faerie blended so well with the forest colours that it was difficult to see how many were accompanying them. After walking some distance, the lead faery stopped and faced the three friends.

'Forgive my manners, but the situation by the High Path did not afford us time to make proper introductions. My name is Yollondos Wynperden, but I am known as Yollo. The settlement here at the western end of Earthroot is under my command. We are Faerie and our queen is Tixlodel; and on her behalf, I welcome you as our guests.'

'Well, firstly let me say on our behalf, thank you, for I think you may have saved our lives,' said Ceri.

'Yes indeed, I think we may have been the main ingredients in a Girngog stew if you had not helped us,' added Ruffle, with a little smile, shifting his feet about and feeling quite uncomfortable at the thought.

'How did you know we were there?' asked Tansy, still feeling unsure of their hosts.

'We did not, we are always on guard here, even more so since the Girngog appeared in Bridgemouth. However, we did observe that you were escaping the Girngog and that someone had used a *Time Stick*. So, helping you and discovering who it was that was capable of using such a powerful spell, piqued my curiosity. Then, when we saw you being chased by the Girngog, it behoved us to help,' replied Yollo.

Ceri had already grasped that meeting the faerie could be helpful in several ways.

'Once again, we are grateful that you did. And we can explain what brings us here, but for the moment, let me show you something that may reassure you about us,' she said.

She turned and spoke to Ruffle, who reached into his coat pocket and brought out the small green leaf given to them by Jevell. Ceri handed it to Yollo, 'Do you recognise this?' she asked.

'Yes indeed, I know this to belong to Jevell, and as you have it, then I assume that your journey has his endorsement,' replied Yollo. 'The three powerful wizards who were the closest allies of the Master Wizard each had one of these. They were actually given to them by our queen, Tixlodel. Ralissa had a blue leaf, Arc a brown leaf and the Grandmaster a white leaf. This green one belongs to Jevell. Finding that you carry his emblem increases my curiosity about your story, but that can wait until you are rested. Though it would be helpful to know your names at least,' said Yollo as he handed the green leaf back to Ceri.

'Well, my name is Ruffle Cragstone, and it is a pleasure to meet you, Yollo.'

'Please correct me if I am wrong, but Ruffle, I think you are Rall?' smiled Yollo.

'You are correct, my friend,' answered Ruffle, puffing his chest out a little more, happy to be recognised.

'I am Tansy Trundlebit and I hail from Chimbleton.'

'And I am Ceridwen Meldrim, also from Chimbleton. Though everyone calls me Ceri.'

'Well, I congratulate myself as I did think that you might be Chimbles, though I confess I have never actually met a Chimble. You are a mysterious people.'

'That is a very good guess on your part, but likewise, we have never met a faery before, and you too are mysterious to us,' smiled Ceri.

'I confess it was a guess; my first thought was that you could be from Springhaven, but I soon realised otherwise. Yet these are curious times when a Chimble is in Earthroot. I have never known of a Chimble venture outside of Chimbleton,' responded Yollo.

'But let us continue walking. A short walk ahead is our settlement, where I can offer you a bed. It is the middle of the night, and I am sure that you are tired. Let us go and get you settled, and in the morning we can talk. I am most interested as to what possessed two Chimbles and a Rall to burst through a Girngog camp in the middle of the night.'

They walked along the path threaded between the trees until they suddenly came upon a wide clearing. What greeted them left the three companions open-mouthed.

'It is an enchanted forest palace,' said Tansy.

The clearing was large and enclosed by huge trees that disappeared into the sky. Entwined within the trees were dwellings with doors and windows. They were connected across all heights by walkways, like bridges between the branches. The trees were strong and wide, effortlessly holding the hundreds of dwellings. The trees were alive with faerie. Lights shone from windows and doorways, creating a twinkling effect as if they were decorations. If Yollo had said that they were stars that had fallen from the sky and dropped into the forest, they would have believed him. It was impossible to see where the whole thing began or stopped. The companions were amazed, having never seen anything like it before.

'This is beautiful, beyond my imagination. Are those houses growing on the trees or were they added?' asked Ceri.

'I am not sure it matters, it is such a wonderous sight, magical even,' replied Ruffle.

'Beautiful and impossible,' added Tansy, forgetting her caution momentarily as she peered, transfixed. 'I am not sure if I am dreaming.'

'I am pleased you approve of our abode, but now let me find you somewhere to sleep,' said Yollo, smiling.

The companions would have been quite content to continue staring at the wondrous palace, but they were interrupted by the approach of another faery.

'This is Osonia, she will show you where you can sleep.'

Osonia was slightly taller than the Chimbles and moved with the grace that all the faerie seemed to possess. She introduced herself to the three visitors.

'Please, come with me,' said the faery.

A thought struck Ruffle as he gazed up at the tree palace. He turned to Osonia with a request.

'Would you mind if we did not go very high to sleep, perhaps there might be somewhere at ground level where we could rest?'

'Don't concern yourself, Ruffle, we have a room for you at ground level. In fact, for your own safety, we would not ask you to be up within the trees. It is natural for us, but we would want you to feel comfortable at such heights before we ask you to experience life in the tree tops.'

Reassured, Ruffle happily followed as the faery led them to a doorway set between two massive trees. It seemed as if their accommodation connected to the trees on either side. The door opened into a large room, in which chairs were set behind a table. Several doors led off the room and Osonia opened the first one, which was bright blue in colour.

'This room is where we can have breakfast. That orange door is where I will be, should you need anything. And do not concern yourselves about disturbing me, faerie sleep less than humankind. Now let me show you to your room.'

The faery then led them to a room with a bright green door.

'This is yours, please be comfortable and take some rest,' she said.

The room had six beds, overflowing with patterned blankets and pillows. It was lit by sparkling lights which they were later told were small faeries. Too bright for the companions to observe their tiny bodies or that the light came from their wings. The decoration in the room was beautiful and soothing, with painted flowers and skillfully carved furniture. The companions each chose a bed, and if they had intended to chat, they did not; for very quickly, all were asleep.

In the Girngog camp, the mood was rather different. In the hours after the three companions had escaped, fresh orders had been received. The guards patrolling the great gateway in Bridgemouth had been reinforced. The new directive made it clear that the ultimate price would be paid by the guards should anyone else enter or leave through the gate without official permission from Gritol. More significantly, the order was given that no Girngog should attempt to enter the great woodland of Earthroot, even if giving chase to a foe. No explanation was provided as to why. The soldiers knew that failure to follow the orders from Gritol could be fatal - they had experienced it before.

Having issued his commands, Merektar resided in the Blue Tower of Gritol, considering if he needed to adjust his scheming in the light of the new information. His suspicions about the three who had fled from Clinglewood occupied his thoughts. What was their significance, and do they matter?

He had intended to blockade Clinglewood and prevent anyone from leaving or arriving. So, he was slightly surprised that the three had successfully left the forest and boarded a ship. He sought to delay and capture them on Seabreeze Lake but that was only partially achieved. His curiosity deepened when he learned that the three had used some form of wizardry to avert capture as they fled through the gateway at Bridgemouth.

His estimation of the three unknown escapees had grown; they were plainly more resourceful than he had expected. But who were they? More importantly, what was their intention? Were they wizards? He doubted that. He had many questions for which he lacked answers.

In all his planning, the dark sorcerer had intended to give the Faerie no cause to become involved in the coming conflict. He knew that violating the forest of Earthroot would achieve the opposite. He did not wish for the enchanted folk to become involved. Their capabilities were beyond his knowledge and he feared them.

Consequently, his anger had raged when he learned of the encounter at the gateway and the skirmish with the Faerie. He made sure that within hours, all his commanders had received the strict order with regard to violating the Earthroot boundary; it was simply unacceptable.

He was quite sure that his old nemesis, Jevell, had not been one of the figures fleeing the wood. The reports he received suggested that there were two young women and a male. Nothing indicated that they were wizards. Yet the Faerie had come to their aid. Was it intentional or a coincidence due to violating Earthroot?

His soldiers reported that the three who were escaping on the High Path had only made for the forest when close to being caught. So, the Faerie involvement was more likely a coincidence.

Whoever the three were, Merektar was confident that they were not wizards. His thoughts reached a conclusion that reassured him. Namely, whoever the three were, they could not impact his plans significantly. Ahe concluded that there was no reason why his larger intentions and strategies should be altered.

Nonetheless, he was not completely comfortable with his conclusion. He lacked sufficient information to be wholly satisfied. He continued to ruminate on the significance of the three. They annoyed him. He consoled himself with the thought that in time, he would learn who the three irritants were and their purpose. For the time being, they did not matter.

13

Earthroot

'What a delightful sleep. My dreams were full of music and dancing, quite unusual for me,' said Ceri as she sat down for breakfast.

'I could say the same,' muttered Tansy in between mouthfuls of toast.

'It must be this place. I slept like a stone,' added Ruffle.

'You always sleep like a stone!' grinned Tansy.

By the end of breakfast, the settlement was already a hive of activity, alive with life and a vibrant spirit that was infectious. The companions felt a sense of joy and contentment, as if the jeopardy of their quest was behind them. Earthroot was different from Clinglewood, not only because the trees were larger, but it was like a different world. The faerie blended into the forest as if they were part of it.

'It's as if the faerie and the woods are as one entity, inseparable,' observed Tansy. 'And I had always expected the faerie to be small, judging by the sword I found, but clearly they aren't.'

Ceri looked at Tansy and laughed, 'You are funny about that sword.'

They were sitting outside, on long blocks of tree trunk, with splinters of sunshine breaking through the trees. They were joined by Yollo and Osonia, who had clearly heard what Tansy had said.

'Ah, but you are correct, Tansy, at least in part. There are faeries not much larger than my hand, to whom we are related but rarely talk. However, they live here amongst us. They are called sprites by many. Unlike ourselves, they can be found in many lands, but few will ever see them. They are thought by some to be invisible, but more than that, they are capable of becoming part of any background. They blend in so well as not to be seen. They can change colour and are very different from us; they fly. They are all around us now, but you will not see them. If you wish to see a sprite, then it will only be if they wish it. Then it would most likely be at night, for that is when they fly, like tiny shooting stars. They are curious beings, so perhaps they might surprise us, though I am doubtful. It is rare that they carry swords, and it would have to be very small,' said Yollo.

Tansy turned to Ceri with a big, smug smile, and then stuck her tongue out as if to say, 'there, told you so.' Both Chimbles laughed.

'But it is your turn to tell us a tale. I am eager to know of your journey and what brought you to risk your lives running through the gateway at Bridgemouth,' requested Osonia.

As requested, the three companions told their story from Yasrall to Chimbleton, to Clinglewood and across the great lake. They explained the importance of reaching Castle Black to warn the king of what was coming. They also revealed how the time-stick had helped them run through the gateway.

The tale clearly fascinated the faery, although Yollo rubbed his chin as if in deep thought at its conclusion.

'I am puzzled,' he admitted. 'I do not understand why the Girngog put so much effort into capturing you. I appreciate that they would prefer that Castle Black not be warned, especially if it is their intention to attack it. But why would it be such an important concern for them? After all, an invading army will soon get noticed. I am more inclined to think that your visit to Clinglewood is the significant thing for them.

'And that might be significant for one person in particular, Merektar. If he is conducting the Girngog invasion, then Cricklewood is probably part of his focus. He will know that Jevell resides there, and I believe that there is unfinished business between them. Whilst your escape from Cricklewood would explain his curiosity about you, it does not fully explain the invasion. There is surely more at play here than we know of.'

'Of that we cannot say. My own motivation is purely practical, Yasrall needs help. We merely carry a message of warning and a plea for assistance. Hopefully, a plea that can be answered,' said Ruffle.

'I appreciate your mission, but there have been changes at Castle Black, though I know few details. I do not know how your news will be received there. However, I will convey your story to Queen Tixlodel. I have little doubt that she will want to hear your story, and she knows much more of these matters than I do,' said Yollo.

'Is she near?' asked Ceri.

'She resides in Kebelos, which is not close if measured by distance, but our contact does not depend upon distance.'

'Kebelos is a place?' queried Ceri.

'It is a place of peace and beauty, the ancient heart of Earthroot. It is crafted from the best minds of the faerie, created long, long ago. Its trees, streams, dwellings and waterfalls express the magic of our land. Few outsiders have ever been there, though your Master Olbus is one.'

'Does Earthroot stretch near to Venterra at all?' asked Tansy.

'Indeed, it does. The forest forms the southernmost border of Venterra. Am I correct in thinking that it would be your preference to enter Venterra from Earthroot?' speculated Yollo.

'Yes, please, that would be wonderful,' said Ceri enthusiastically. 'It would be our safest route to reach the Old Kingdom.'

'That is assuming that you allow us to travel through Earthroot!' said Ruffle. 'Although I am not sure that we could find our way without your help, what with the forest being so large.'

'Well, if you travel through the forest, you could reach Venterra in about three days. Then you would have to travel north to Duskhold and the castle. Which with a horse would take another couple of days,' explained Yollo.

'But that assumes that we do not get lost, doesn't it?' said Tansy.

'Yes, it does, Tansy. But I think we can help you with that. I am prepared to have someone escort you through the forest whilst we wait for permission from the queen. If you wish to accept my offer, then I suggest that you start soon. I would do this because I am confident that the queen will be happy to help you.'

'That would be so good, not having to worry about Girngog chasing us. Though I don't know how we could repay you,' said Ruffle.

Yollo gave a small laugh.

'My dear Ruffle, no payment is needed. We all know of the Girngog and I am certain that the queen would expect nothing from you in return for any help we can offer.'

'So, if we travel with your assistance, then we may be five, or more likely six days, from Castle Black. But are the Girngog not likely to reach Duskhold before us?' wondered Ceri.

'Possibly, but unlikely. The high path over the Ghost Mountains is typically a week's journey for most travellers. It is a long and winding road, steep in parts and difficult to travel speedily. It would be a close thing, but with a little assistance, you could reach the castle at least a day ahead of them,' explained Yollo.

'I was hoping for a bigger lead, but in our circumstances, any lead will be welcome,' sighed Ceri.

'Then I think we should start right away,' said Tansy, rising as if to get going there and then.

'Before you rush off, there is something else that you should be aware of,' began Yollo. 'King Cadmus is not at Castle Black; he has been gone three years.'

'Is he dead?' quizzed Tansy.

'Not as far as we know. But he took his family and half of his army and travelled east out of Venterra. It appears his intention was to establish stronger trading links and allegiances with dominions in the east, especially Tebira. He left his brother, Prince Hewl, to manage in his absence. However, all has not gone as I think the king would have wanted.'

The mood changed with this news. Ruffle's grin disappeared. Tansy sat down. The three friends waited to hear what else Yollo had to say.

'There was an expectation that the king might be away for a year or so, but it has become much longer. Inevitably, the rumours have spread that the king is dead. Albeit there is no evidence to support such gossip. Despite this, it is planned that the king's brother, Hewl, will be crowned as his successor next month.'

'But how will this affect Earthroot?' queried Ruffle.

'Well, we do not believe the king has perished. For many years, Earthroot and Venterra have enjoyed good relations. King Cadmus and our queen, Tixlodel, are dear friends. But under the rule of Prince Hewl, things have deteriorated. Both Castle Black and Duskhold have changed since the king left.'

'Hewl has dismissed some of his best military people, along with key advisors appointed by his brother. Instead, a man previously unheard of, has emerged as his key advisor. He is known as Rillet. He seems intent on antagonising the queen. In one instance, woodcutters were sent from the castle to cut down trees at the perimeter of Earthroot. There exists a long-established understanding that such a thing should never happen. Of course, we prevented it. Which displeased Prince Hewl.'

'Apparently, the reason they sought the wood was for building in Duskhold. It has grown into a large, chaotic town, and the wood was intended to create more dwellings. The town is not the safe haven it once was. This is compounded by the castle soldiers having lost much of their discipline. Inevitably, this is reflected in the streets. Petty crime is increasing, and it appears that the prince has little idea what is happening around him. This is because, as is well known, Rillet controls what comes to the ears of the prince.'

'But surely the prince will wish to protect the kingdom and repel the Girngog,' suggested Ruffle. 'For our part, we simply have no other option. If King Cadmus is gone, then we must approach the prince.'

'Of course, you must do so, Ruffle. But you should understand that things are different from when King Cadmus was in Duskhold. He may not want to hear what you have to say,' commented Yollo.

'Well, I hope he has enough sense to heed a warning; otherwise, he might lose his castle,' said Tansy.

'It is my understanding that the prince has no liking for the Girngog. But he has little idea of what is happening within Duskhold or indeed within his own castle. He was a likeable and intelligent youth, but now he seems wholly under the influence of Rillet. So, I do not know how he will react to your news.'

Yollo abruptly stopped speaking and stood.

'At this moment, I think we have talked enough. Given the urgency of your purpose, you had best be on your way. Osonia will be your guide through Earthroot and show you a suitable place to enter Venterra. Please make yourselves ready and you can commence your journey straight away.'

The companions were still absorbing the information Yollo had shared as they gathered their belongings. They needed little time to make ready, but welcomed the opportunity to talk together.

'I think this is our best alternative, don't you?' asked Ceri of her friends. 'Not least, we should be safe from the Girngog travelling through the forest.'

'I see no other choice. The faerie saved our lives and now they are giving us safe passage to Venterra. What more could we ask!' said Tansy.

'I agree, of course. But I am worried about this Prince Hewl, what if he ignores us? Does he even know Yasrall exists?' Is he likely to be inclined to help us?' wondered Ruffle.

'Listen, we cannot worry about that before we even meet him,' said Ceri. 'I am more concerned that the Girngog do not get to Duskhold before we do. Castle Black could fall before we have a chance to warn them! Then there would be no prince to speak with!'

'Absolutely, you're right. We need to get going. Come, let us be off,' urged Ruffle, already heading out of the door.

Tansy looked at Ceri, half smiled, said nothing, shrugged her shoulders and followed Ruffle out of the door.

14

The Blue Fortress

A wide road ran along the bottom of a V-shaped valley, which sliced through the steep Ironspine Mountains. At the beginning of this road, an impressive wall had been constructed, with a rampart that stretched the width of the valley entrance. In the middle of the wall stood two large gates, where guards controlled who came and went. This was the only known entrance from the east into the lands of the Girngog, Gritol.

The sides of the valley were stony, unfriendly and bleak. The road stretched for several leagues between the harsh slopes before the terrain gradually softened, giving way to gentler, flatter ground. This was Gritol. It had never fallen to an invasion, and this lone point of entry was widely regarded as the chief reason why.

Travelling into Gritol and emerging from the valley, the first town was Kirinvig. A typical Girngog settlement. A large, rambling mess of ugly construction. The original houses were solid, typically made of brick. In more recent times, as the town had grown haphazardly and the population increased, so did the variety of dwellings. Made of stone, wood, mud or combinations of these materials, the resultant habitats looked a mess. They were of varied quality and shape. It was not unusual for some to fall down, and many looked as if they were about to.

Nonetheless, Kirinvig was the location of the Girngog military command. However, they would not be found within the ramshackle abodes that most of the population lived in, but in its singular, most magnificent masterpiece of architecture reaching into the sky, the Blue Fortress.

In contrast to the rest of Kirinvig, it was a palace, the embodiment of order and design. A great wall encircled its five towers. The wall separated the Blue Fortress from the hubbub of the town. It was like a huge compound, though, looking at the fortress from the outside, the true dimension of the building was not visible. For not only did it surge skyward and wide, it burrowed deep below ground where a maze of tunnels and caves hid a hive of perpetual activity; activities purposed to create weapons and beasts of destruction.

Inside the fortress the central and largest tower was built from blue stone, hence the name. Its diamond shaped stained-glass windows contrasted strongly with the grey morass of the town. The towers reached toward the clouds and it was said the whole of Gritol could be seen from its windows.

The Blue Fortress was not only military headquarters, but it was also the home of Merektar. Many years previously, the sorcerer had, by fair means and mostly foul, ensconced himself as leader of the Girngog. It was where his own circle of mages toiled alongside the Girngog to bring to life the imaginings of their master.

It was Merektar who had united the Girngog tribes and propelled them on an invasion into the Old Kingdom. The first Girngog War, as the offensive was known, had progressed swiftly, then stalled when laying siege to Castle Black. Merektar had anticipated and prepared for a siege, but it had endured longer than he had estimated. It effectively halted the advance of his armies and cost many Girngog lives.

Regardless of the holdup, he believed that the siege was succeeding. At least he did so until his fortunes diminished. His armies were repelled and then forced to retreat when the Grandmaster Wizard, Olbus, who had overseen Merektar's own learning at the Wizard Library, intervened. Assisted by the three Master Wizards – Arc, Jevell and Ralissa – along with the forces of the Faerie, led by Queen Tixlodel, the Girngog were routed. Key to this reversal were the Instruments of Light and Power. Unique creations crafted by Grandmaster Olbus.

Although he had grown in his powers, Merektar found that he was no match for Olbus. His own circle of wizards was routed, vanquished and fled from the battlefield. The Girngog were driven back to Gritol. Merektar, who had been leading the siege at Castle Black, was wounded, and many thought he had succumbed to his wounds. The wizards under Olbus triumphed. There was no victory for Merektar; his plans were in tatters.

Although defeated and frustrated, his ambitions remained unquenched and his determination reinforced. During his long recovery, he again set his mind to plotting. He vowed to himself that he would get revenge.

He set about rebuilding his army on a larger scale. He created a network of spies, determined to be better prepared and informed in regard to the strengths of his foes in the future. He began anew to recruit and train his own circle of mages.

He made it a priority to learn about the Instruments of Light that had been so effectively used against him. After some time, he learned that there were three Instruments – the Crown of Connection, Sword of Light and the Red Wand. Also, that Master Olbus had initially wielded all three. He learned that they were created by Olbus. That the Master Wizards had used one each and they were the same Instruments Olbus had used.

He deduced that if he were to fulfil his plans, he should possess these so-called Instruments of Light and Power. It became a priority to acquire them, or at least one.

However, he could not unearth where they were being kept or who possessed them. His intuition suggested that they were held by the wizards, but he had nothing to confirm this. And were the rumours that Olbus had died true? If he were, then Merektar was confident he could defeat the other wizards.

Added to this, his most passionate and deepest desire was to regain the Book of Shades; the same tome that he had stolen from the Wizard Library and then lost again. But the library was gone from the Pancake Lands. All that remained was a dusty shell of a building. Was there another Wizard Library somewhere else?

He had no inkling of where the library or the book now was. Both had been under the protection of Olbus, but if he had perished, then what had happened to the library and the Book of Shades? Obtaining this information was the primary objective of his network of spies.

Instinctively, he doubted Olbus was gone. He was very old, but was he dead? He thought not, though he hoped otherwise.

To compound his puzzlement, he could find little trace of the three Master Wizards who had successfully led the resistance to his aggression. He spent many long hours pondering these questions.

His spies had identified that Jevell resided in Clinglewood Forest, though no one had seen him. He had no clues as to where he could find the others.

Spikily frustrated by the holes in his knowledge, these continuing uncertainties undermined his scheming. He smoldered with anger. He wanted facts and good information. He had extended his web of spies right across the kingdom and beyond. His thirst to find these answers was linked to his thirst for power.

Meanwhile, for the outside world, it appeared that Gritol had accepted its loss in the war and complied with the terms of its surrender. That the Girngog were now content to live in peace. Their growing trade with Yasrall had affirmed such a perception.

But his foes had made a significant error. They had not entered Gritol to seek him. They had assumed that he had died in the war. A few suspected that he had returned to Gritol, but no action had been taken to check if this was so. Thus, he had been able to return to his Blue Fortress and recover.

Inevitably, he had resumed his hold upon the Girngog. He had waited, quietly planning and preparing, planning and preparing.

Gradually, the Girngog emerged from their land and interacted peacefully with their nearest neighbours in Yasrall. As trade slowly increased, fears about the Girngog lessened. Yasrall enjoyed the benefits of this trade and a minimal level of trust was re-established.

Unbeknownst to him, this was Merektar's scheme unfolding just as he had planned.

Complacency about the Girngog lulled even the concerns of King Cadmus. Merektar had delighted in the news that the King had travelled east with his family and half of his army, leaving behind his brother, Prince Hewl, to oversee Venterra and the command at Castle Black. He considered the situation to be a bonus, an opportunity that he could take advantage of.

He identified Prince Hewl as a point of leverage. It was common knowledge that the prince was frustrated living in the shadow of his accomplished older brother. This discontent was fed and encouraged by his closest advisor, Rillet, a handsome nobleman who had emerged from nowhere to feature prominently in the court of the prince. This began shortly after King Cadmus had gone east.

Through flattery and compliance, Rillet connived a position of being the indispensable friend and confidant to Prince Hewl. It was at the instigation of Rillet that the prince was persuaded to discard the advisors whom King Cadmus had entrusted as guides for his younger brother. Before long, Rillet became Hewl's sole confidant.

As if in a game of chess where the opponent does not realise the underlying strategy of his opponent, Merektar was moving his pieces into position for checkmate.

Further advantage was gained when one evening, as wine loosened the tongue of the prince, he told Rillet in confidence, that deep in the dungeons of Castle Black a crown was locked away. The prince confided that it was guarded, but did not explain what the crown was. Rillet drew his own conclusion.

At that time, the prince had no suspicion that Rillet was not whom he appeared to be. He was, in fact, an agent of Merektar, a shapeshifter by the name of Opik, a minor sorcerer and a member of Merektar's circle of mages. His singular ability was as a shapeshifter. Eager for approval, Opik reported the information about the guarded crown to his true master. Upon hearing this, Merektar instructed Opik to steal it.

It was some while later when Opik executed his theft. He did so at the same point in time when the Girngog invaded Yasrall. In the dead of night, Opik assumed the guise of Prince Hewl, visited the dungeons and stole the crown. The guards never knew what it was that they guarded, as the crown sat behind closed doors in a room without windows.

Overnight, back in the guise of Rillet, Opik disappeared from the castle along with the crown. When questioned later, the guards insisted that it was the prince who had visited the locked room. For a time, confusion reigned in Castle Black when it was discovered that Rillet had also disappeared. Prince Hewl was confused as to where his advisor might be. As it later transpired, the shapeshifter had escaped from the castle just in time.

Initially delighted with Opik and his theft, Merektar's mood changed when he found that the stolen crown possessed no magical qualities and was of no value whatsoever. In truth, this came as no great surprise to Merektar, who suspected that acquiring one of the Instruments would never be so easily accomplished. This magnanimous attitude saved the shapeshifter from the wrath of his master.

Nonetheless, Merektar remained confident that if he could wield even one of the Instruments, then his fortunes would be mightily improved. So, he intensified his approach and in particular, with regard to Clinglewood Forest, where he was almost certain Jevell lived.

He had the woodland watched day and night, eager to see who came and went. It was a result of this constant watch that three strangers had been seen entering the forest. Considering this unusual, he ordered that they be captured and brought before him. He was eager to learn what business was involved. He convinced himself that their business concerned the Instruments of Power.

Shortly after the capture of the worthless crown, Merektar's patience diminished. For a long time, he had schemed, waited, plotted and planned, all the while growing his Girngog armies. He had been patient, but that virtue was exhausted. He decided that his plans were moving too slowly. It was time to be bold. He needed to know if the Instruments were still in use.

Without warning, his forces poured through the gates of Gritol and swiftly overran Yasrall. From there, they marched on Bridgemouth. He intended to take control of the Necklace bridge.

In the early stages of this assault, it was also reported to Merektar that the three strangers who had entered Clinglewood had now left the forest and taken to a ship on Seabreeze Lake. The news was not received well by the sorcerer. His anger exploded further when he learned that his soldiers had failed to capture them.

His displeasure increased his impatience. More than ever, he was curious to speak with the three mysterious figures and instructed his minions that he wanted them taken alive as soon as possible. He intended to interrogate them. He suspected that they had information about where he could find the Instruments and perhaps even the whereabouts of the wizards. So, he decided to halt their progress whilst on the Great Lake. He sought to immobilise their vessel but not to kill those aboard. Once done, his own ships could then take them captive.

So, he sent his Demon Crows and then summoned the lake serpent. He was informed that the ship was scuppered but his fury burst forth when it could not be found.

His anger peaked again upon learning that the three people he sought had subsequently gotten through the gate at Bridgemouth and onto the High Path. When he learned that the faerie had helped them escape into Earthroot, he could contain his outrage no longer and destroyed, on the spot, the unfortunate messenger who had carried the news.

Merektar knew that, as powerful as he now was, he could not successfully venture into Earthroot. He did not wish to involve the Faerie. He doubted that there was little appetite among the Faerie for becoming involved in the affairs of man once again! This latest development was likely to inform him how accurate that assumption might be.

He hoped that he would soon discover the identity of the three figures scurrying across the kingdom? What role did they play in the affairs of kings, queens and wizards? He had yet to understand. He did not like that so many questions lingered which could threaten his intentions. Still, he reasoned that, in the days to come, he would learn all he needed to know.

15

The Faerie

The companions were eager to continue their journey, so farewells and thanks were swiftly exchanged. They were to follow Osonia, who was accompanied by several faeries, whilst others followed high above, skipping through the trees.

'First, we walk and then shortly after midday we will leave the woods and take to a road. I have arranged for horses to meet us there. Then we can ride, and once riding, we can make better time. For most of tomorrow we ride, but the day after our journey will take us back into the woods, which are too dense for horses to travel,' explained Osonia.

The faery conveyed a 'no nonsense' attitude as she led the group, which set the tone for the trek. There was little conversation. Despite the seriousness and brisk pace set by Osonia, it was a peaceful walk amidst the background of forest music performed by the birds and insects, humming, buzzing, flitting and singing amongst the flowers and trees.

Each of the travelling party seemed preoccupied with their own thoughts. The silent trek brought a calmness that soothed the adventurers; so much so, that they would have happily walked all day. Eventually, their reverie was broken by Osonia.

'In a short while, we will reach the road, where we will take to horseback. We can take a short break before commencing our ride,' said Osonia.

The three friends listened and nodded.

Just as the faery had said, they emerged from the dense cover of the forest and found themselves beside a road. It was a sight the companions had not expected, for the road wended its way over rolling grassy knolls into the distance. Wide open spaces lay ahead. Yet they were deep inside the forest.

Osonia noted the reaction of her guests.

'Earthroot does go on endlessly, so much so that I have never travelled to its end. But my friends, the forest is part of an even larger area that extends south and eastward; and within it, there are roads, hills and open spaces that are not dressed in trees.'

'I had assumed Earthroot was just forest; I mean, I know it is huge, but I did not realise that there would be so much open space,' admitted Ceri.

'Yes, there is a great deal of open land in some parts of the forest, and what you might call towns or villages. Though they are not like those built by humankind. They lie deep within the woodlands and cannot be seen from outside. Alas, we do not have the time to visit such places now. But do be aware that Earthroot borders many lands. most of which I doubt you have seen or heard of.

'So, do Skovelenbar and Earthroot meet? Asked Tansy.

'They do,' smiled Osonia. 'Skovelenbar is a large country, a long way from the lands you call the Old Kingdom. Although some say it was once part of the Old Kingdom. I do not know the truth of that. Their people are very different to us and we have a delicate relationship with them. You see, the Skove like to hunt and a long time ago began to do so in faerie woodlands. We do not hunt; in fact, we protect all living things as best we can. But the Skove enjoy the chase and the kill. So, we stopped them using our woods and the Skove were unhappy that we did so. It took long discussions and negotiations to resolve matters. The result was a treaty between us.

They are forbidden to hunt in Earthroot, though I presume they now hunt elsewhere. Their reputation is that they have plundered the sea and emptied it of fish, something we have no wish to see repeated on land.'

'I know almost nothing of the Skove and I think I have no wish to meet them,' commented Ruffle.

'Your words make me feel both wary and curious. But more than that, it shows how little I know of the world beyond the Old Kingdom,' added Ceri.

'You are not alone in that, Ceri. I have never encountered the Skove and I know that there are lands that lay even beyond their borders, of which I know nothing. But we faerie keep to ourselves, so it is unlikely that we will go exploring such places.'

Although their minds were brimming with thoughts, their tongues were still. Ahead, they saw a group of faeries with several horses, clearly waiting for them to arrive. The faeries greeted one another warmly before introducing the companions. The sun sat high in the sky. Sweltering, they took cover under some shade, where they ate before meeting their mounts. The break was brief. It was agreed that a meal could be taken in the evening, and they should ride before the day drew down.

The horses were calm as the friends drew near. Ceri and Ruffle were a little apprehensive, but Tansy, being the most experienced rider, relished the prospect. It transpired that there was no need to worry as the horses were amenable and made it easy for the companions to mount.

Osonia led the party, which included several mounted faeries. To allow the companions time to adjust, they set off walking the horses. Gradually, they picked up the pace and, though refraining from a full gallop, they were moving significantly swifter than hiking would have achieved. The road was wide and clear, and as confidence grew, they galloped. Unused to being in a saddle for a long ride, as the afternoon wore on, the friends began to feel saddle sore.

Other than a very short stop for a drink, they rode continuously until it the night began drawing down. Osonia halted the group close to trees and set about organising a camp. It was obvious the faeries were used to such things as they quickly assembled a shelter, lit a small fire and began cooking. A hot soup, filled with vegetables, together with chunks of bread, was soon ready and the group settled around the fire to eat.

'I confess that I'm stiffening up, being unused to spending so much time on a horse,' said Ceri.

'Hopefully, a good sleep will see your limbs recover,' suggested Osonia. 'We might also do some stretching before we set off in the morning.'

A broad conversation ensued with Osonia keen to learn more about Yasrall and Chimbleton. The companions were happy to describe where they were from, although it left them rather wistful for their homes. They repeated why they had undertaken their quest, making no secret of their purpose. At its conclusion, Osonia complimented Ruffle.

'You are a brave man, Ruffle. I hope your people come to appreciate what you have done on their behalf.'

'I am not especially brave, I am doing what any Rall would have done, it just happens to be me. Besides, nothing is achieved as yet,' he replied.

'You do yourself an injustice, Ruffle.'

'Well, I confess I have doubted the wisdom of our journey. There have been a number of instances when I have feared for my life and that of my friends,' said the Rall.

'But that is what bravery is. You were afraid, but you kept going, you persevered when others would have given up,' answered Osonia.

'I second that,' said Tansy. 'For I have felt afraid more often on this quest than I have ever done living in Chimbleton. Indeed, your determination was one of the things that drew me to be part of this quest.'

'Thank you, Tansy, but I think you have both been as brave as I have, probably more so given that this was not your mission in the first place, but here you are alongside me. And you are here out of choice, whereas I am here from obligation,' said Ruffle.

'I disagree, Ruffle. You being here is a choice, a brave choice. I know that Chimble folk would not believe what we have already been through. In fact, I hardly believe it. And I suspect that the same can be said of the Rall. Of course, I realise that there is more that we have yet to encounter, but I believe that we have gotten this far by facing these challenges together, don't you?' said Tansy.

'Well, I certainly do,' added Ceri. 'And I endorse what Osonia says, that you are one of the bravest people I have ever met, Ruffle.'

'In hearing your tale, I also wonder if all Chimbles are as fearless as you both? Your friendship and generosity toward Ruffle is something that I have seen little of amongst humankind,' observed Osonia.

'That is kind of you, but we are just ordinary Chimbles. It is just our way to help a neighbour. How could we ever have foreseen that meeting up for a picnic at Big Sprout would deliver us here, sitting and sharing a meal with a faery in the middle of Earthroot. Who knows what the future holds!' said Ceri, grinning.

Standing up, Osonia signalled a halt to the conversation. 'I could ask you a hundred more questions, but I think they'd best wait. We have a day and a half riding ahead, then another half day when we must take to foot again. So, you should rest and hopefully sleep away some of that stiffness. I have asked enough of you for one day.'

In fact, the three friends were grateful for the suggestion as they all recognised that they were tired. The faeries accompanying them had taken care of the horses, so the whole camp was ready for sleep.

'Do we need to post a guard?' Tansy asked.

'There is no need, Tansy, we are perfectly safe here. No Girngog or, in fact, anyone but faeries venture into Earthroot. These woods are ancient and living entities. They are wise and if ever there was danger, they would alert us. So, rest easy, you are in a place of peace,' smiled Osonia.

Tansy had half expected this reply but now felt wholly reassured, though she did wonder how the trees would alert the faeries to any threats! She wondered about this and how her own feelings had changed from the caution she had first felt when meeting Yollo. She realised that she now trusted the faeries. And that was her last thought before she fell to sleep.

The next morning, the friends slept later than they had intended, but the morning was still young by the time they had finished breakfast and were ready to ride. To alleviate stiffness, Osonia had them do some stretching exercises before they began. It helped. Having ridden so much the day before, they felt they were more comfortable in their saddles, at least to begin with. The disposition of the horses helped, as they seemed to make allowances for their inexperienced riders.

They made good time, riding past the middle of the day before stopping for food and water. They continued for the rest of the day and set up camp just before the sun disappeared. They made much progress, but found that they were just as stiff and sore as the previous day. They were busy stretching when Osonia approached with a small wooden bowl that contained a brownish coloured cream.

'Use this, but only a little at a time. It will help and hopefully you will feel better come the morning.'

As the companions tended to their aching limbs, the faerie set up camp. Supper was a simpler fare than the night before, consisting of dry foods. There was no hot food tonight. Soon after eating, they lay down, feeling weary. Before closing their eyes, Osonia gave them some welcome information.

'You have done well, my friends, for today was the longest part of our ride. Tomorrow we will need to take to foot at some point. We will then say farewell to the horses. So, rest and replenish your energies.'

Without prompting, they took to their blankets and dropped into sleep almost immediately. The next day, the ground was uneven and not suitable for galloping. This final ride was more a bumpy walk, until mid-afternoon when Osonia called a halt and declared that they could go no further on horseback. It was time to walk. Time to trek through the trees. After dismounting, they took the opportunity to eat and drink. They said goodbye to the horses and to their accompanying faeries. Now it was only Osonia and two other faeries who were to be their guides.

'We have a good walk ahead of us, so any remaining stiffness will hopefully disappear with the exercise,' smiled Osonia as she led them off the road and into the shadows of the forest.

Before long, they were deep within the great woodland. The three friends followed in a single file, constantly looking down to avoid roots and fallen branches. There was no obvious path; they simply followed Osonia and trod where she did.

'It would be so easy to get lost here, there are no clues as to which way to go and the path that Osonia treads is not one I could discern if I were leading,' observed Ruffle.

'It is as baffling as Clinglewood and I thought I was adept at finding my way through woods,' Ceri concurred.

Osonia heard the conversation and replied.

'You must remember that I have lived amongst these trees my whole life. I find that if I ever have cause to leave the woods, it is not long before I yearn to be back here. I know these trees. I feel their breathing and it is as if they lead me. It is difficult to explain, but I have a connection here, so I know instinctively which way to proceed. It may sound odd to you, but it is as if I am part of this great wood. Which may be true for all faeries who live here.'

'It is not odd to me. Having spent just a short time here, I believe I can feel the power and the life within these ancient woods. There is a tranquility that I can sense. I would enjoy spending more time here just relaxing and exploring,' Ceri responded.

'You could include me in that. I, too, am familiar with woodland, but I endorse what Ceri says; there is something unique about this forest. It feels ancient, as if the trees have existed here just as long as the mountains have,' added Tansy.

A gentle smile was the faery's response. And on they walked, round some huge trunks and over small trickling streams. Woodland flowers decorated the forest floor and small creatures for whom the woods were home, scurried away as they approached. Birds called and sang and Tansy spotted an owl sitting atop a branch, watching intently as the strangers intruded through his territory.

'He looks quite put out that we are here,' said Ruffle, looking at the owl.

The afternoon wore on, and the sun was sliding from the sky. The evening was waiting to make an entrance.

'We can stop soon and rest for the night,' said Osonia.

As before, they set up a simple camp. The two faeries accompanying them went into the woods and foraged ingredients to add to water in making a soup. The hot food was welcome. They sat around the small fire after eating.

'This travelling is a tiring business,' said Ruffle.

'I endorse that,' mumbled Tansy between bites of an apple.

'You have done well, my friends. If it is any comfort, we are now on the final part of our trek. By the middle of the day tomorrow, we should reach the border with Venterra. Knowing the Ghost Mountains, I doubt the Girngog will have gotten near Venterra as yet. The mountain route twists and turns and climbs; it is not a quick route. In comparison, our path through the great wood has been more direct,' stated Osonia.

'Look!' said a startled Ceri, interrupting, 'what is that?'

All turned to where Ceri was pointing. In the dark of the forest, glittering above them, were hundreds of small bright lights.

'It's like a swarm of stars, what can it be?' wondered Tansy aloud.

'It is the sprites. They have come to look at us and are gracing us with a dance of light. We are indeed favoured,' Osonia explained.

'It is beautiful,' said Ceri.

The sprites moved as if coordinated and formed into various shapes. All in the camp watched, transfixed. Then suddenly, the lights dimmed and vanished.

'They're gone. What a shame, I was enjoying that,' said Ruffle in a sad voice.

'We have been privileged. Only twice before have I seen the sprite dance. It is a good sign. We are all fortunate,' observed Osonia.

Everyone was impressed and the light display was the only matter they discussed before laying down to sleep.

The next day, they followed Osonia through the maze of trees, knowing that without her, they would be completely lost. It was close to midday when they emerged into open land. Waiting for them were several faeries who stood beside a wagon and two horses.

Greetings were exchanged and the companions were delighted to see that hot food had been prepared. Introductions were made and all chatted as they ate. Osonia talked with those who had brought the wagon and were not partaking in the meal. They conversed in the faerie tongue, so the companions could not understand what was being said. Once she had finished her conversation, Osonia came to sit beside the three companions.

'So far, there is no sign of the Girngog. Now we will take the wagon and I will travel with you as far as I can. As has been said before, the faeries are not so welcome in Duskhold nowadays, but I will be able to take you close to the town. It will take the best part of two days to reach that point, then Rabeek and I will leave you.'

'Rabeek?' asked Tansy.

'Rabeek is the chestnut horse I have cared for since she was a foal. The black horse, Peret, will stay with you. She is strong and fast and when you have no need of her, she will find her own way back to Earthroot.'

'Duskhold is where Castle Black sits, does it not?' asked Ceri.

'Yes, though you will see the castle before you see the town. The castle is set against the mountains of Ironspine and its walls rise high above any buildings within the town. However, it is the inner towers that rise highest and they will be the first thing that our eyes will see of the castle.'

'We are grateful to you, Osonia, for the help you have afforded us. One day, I would hope we can repay your generosity.' Said Ruffle.

'There is nothing to repay, and besides, your quest may benefit us all and so we wish to see you succeed. In fact, I have the message that our queen, Tixlodel, not only approved our escorting you, but also sent her good wishes for your fortunes. But now, if you have had your fill, we must be on our way.'

Minutes later, the camp was packed away so effectively that no one would have known it had been there. Peret was the horse pulling the wagon whilst Osonia rode her horse alongside.

The wagon was covered like a caravan, similar to the kind that might be the home of wandering musicians or a circus performer, suggested Ruffle. It was enclosed with a door at the back and a folded step for entry. Inside were cushions and a box holding a number of items, including the elements for a makeshift tent. The bench seat at the front was wide enough for the three friends to sit beside one another. Ruffle had driven such transport before, so it was he who took the reins as they set off.

'Venterra is large and has a good many castles and towns. However, we will avoid such places. I think it's better that we attract as little attention as possible, especially with one of the enchanted folk, as you say, accompanying you,' smiled the faery.

'That makes sense, we are in your hands, Osonia,' said Ceri.

For several hours, there was no road, so the caravan rumbled across the grassland, which made for a bumpy ride. It was late afternoon when they came upon a road.

'Do we take this road?' asked Ruffle.

'No, we should not take to the road just yet,' said Osonia. She pointed toward a hillock. We head for that clump of trees after which the land dips and we cannot be seen from the road. We should stop for the night once there.'

The faery had said that she hoped that they would not encounter other travellers, but she had taken the precaution to don a hooded cloak. She did not wish to draw attention to the fact that she was a faery. She led the way, riding just ahead of the caravan and shortly after cresting the hillock, she called a halt to their travelling for that day.

The caravan proved to be a natural shelter and they found that the faerie had stocked it with food. They ate and talked. The companions asked Osonia many questions about Earthroot and would have continued deep into the night; but it was Ceri who said she was in need of sleep. The faery suggested that they all sleep. There was no dissension. However, Osonia insisted that she would keep watch and settled herself next to her horse.

The next morning, they set off early, continuing to avoid the roads. The land rolled out gently before them like a rumpled carpet. It was sufficiently uneven to make for a jerky ride. From time to time, they used Tansy's telescope and could just about make out buildings across the land, but they made sure to keep well away. Chatting as they rode, the three friends revealed to one another that they were a mix of emotions.

There was relief that they were nearing the end of their journey, mingled with pleasure to have escaped the Girngog and to have met the Faerie. Yet, they were anxious as to how they would be received at the castle. Quite simply, they did not know what to expect.

'Have you visited Duskhold very often?' Ruffle asked Osonia, who rode alongside the wagon.

'In the last few years, no, but before that, faeries were welcomed by King Cadmus. Plus, the Wizards Library was always welcoming, but that has now gone.'

'Was the Wizards Library in Duskhold?' queried Tansy.

'No, it was a few miles away, close to the edge of the Pancake Lands on the western side of Venterra.'

'Where has the Wizards Library moved to?' continued Tansy.

'Nobody knows. Although the building remains empty, it is often used by travellers seeking shelter. It once had a lush garden full of flowers, which contrasted starkly with its sandy surroundings. But now it is just the wind and sand blowing through its corridors. The garden is long gone. Master Olbus, the Grandmaster Wizard, oversaw the running of the library and he was a frequent visitor to Earthroot. He often stayed at the palace of our queen. In fact, I believe he is now somewhere within Earthroot. So, I am unsure that even he knows what happened to the library.'

'But what of the people at the library?' questioned Ceri.

'They too disappeared. Perhaps Master Olbus knows where they went, but he is certainly not telling anyone.'

'What about Duskhold, is it a large place?' asked Tansy.

'It is now. It has been growing for a few years. Increasing trade from the east has seen it double in size. Though it has been a rather jumbled growth, with different kinds of buildings popping up and its markets continually expanding. It is a rather noisy and dirty place, and now I doubt I could find my way across the town. In fact, if King Cadmus ever returned, I think he might not recognise the town he left.'

'Has all this growth occurred since the king went travelling? Isn't it a good thing for the town?' asked Ruffle.

'I don't know Ruffle,' Osonia responded with a tone of caution in her voice. 'I certainly would not wish to live there, but then I am a faery and the trees are my home. To me, it seems that the more people who move to Duskhold, the more chaotic it becomes. How can I put it, let's say, it does not smell fresh.'

'I thought Prince Hewl oversaw and managed the town for his brother?' wondered Tansy.

'From what I know, he has effectively left Duskhold to develop as it will. The town is close to the castle but is not part of it. The prince does have dominion over it, but he just concentrates on the castle. The town has its own mayor and it is he, together with the tradespeople, who undertake the running of the place day to day. For instance, I believe it now has several daily markets, one of which is held within the walls of Castle Black - an arrangement that I doubt King Cadmus would ever permit. However, it is said that one consequence of this expansion is that the royal coffers have swelled. So Hewl is happy to leave the town to the mayor and have his coffers grow.'

'Do you think the town is aware of the threat from the Girngog?' queried Ceri.

'Unfortunately, I do not,' replied Osonia. 'Just as I think your message will be news to the prince, so it will be news to the townspeople. I suspect that many of the newcomers have never heard of the Girngog. Those who do know of the Girngog will not be expecting to encounter them. For many, the Girngog was vanquished and there has been no reason to think of them since, which is why your message is so important. It can give them some time to prepare for what might happen.'

These insights from Osonia gave the three friends much to think about. Thus, there was little said thereafter and with the evening drawing in, they set up a camp. They had stayed off the roads and ensured that they could not be seen from any passing travellers.

In the evening, after they had eaten and were soon to seek rest, Osonia reminded them of where they were.

'We have made good time and I estimate that by mid-afternoon tomorrow, I will be taking my leave of you. Then you will be a short distance from Duskhold. We will be on the road that you follow straight into the town. At some point in the morning, we should be able to see the highest towers of the castle, but it will still be a long way off. You simply stay on the road which will take you into Duskhold. Once you enter the town, be watchful, for nowadays Duskhold has a wild edge to it. Use your wits and keep your own counsel. Try not to attract unwanted attention; it can be dangerous. In short, don't trust anyone.'

16

Duskhold

Finding sleep was like trying to grasp smoke. Thoughts came and then escaped. Each of the companions had recognised the words of Osonia as a warning. Yet, despite such an elusive slumber they rose early, ate breakfast and made ready to resume their journey.

This morning the faery led them back to the conventional route to the town.

'You should be able to see the towers of Castle Black very soon,' the faery suggested as they regained the road.

'I think I can do so already, though I'm not sure; but if I am right, they must be really high. It's difficult to make them out against the black mountains,' observed Ceri, holding her hand across her forehead to block the glare of the sun.

Tansy took out her spyglass.

'Osonia is right. I can see the towers and the walls, I think. And I agree, Ceri, they are hard to make out against the mountains. They seem almost part of the mountain. But to be able to see them from here, they must be tall.'

Borrowing the spyglass, Ceri confirmed for herself what she saw.

'Now if my eyes don't deceive me, Osonia is right, there can be no other building of comparable size in the kingdom.'

'Yes, that is correct, Ceri. The castle is huge and it has two outer walls, one higher than the other. Plus, there is a moat wrapped around the wall like a scarf. It is no surprise that the castle has never been breached by any foe.'

Ruffle took a turn with the spyglass.

'I see it. Jiggedy woo, it is indeed massive, I know that you warned us, but it is still much bigger than I expected. How did they ever build it?'

'I have no idea, Ruffle. It was built long before I was born. For the rest of this journey, it will always be in your sights. You will have no problem knowing which direction to take,' said Osonia.

'We couldn't miss it,' laughed Tansy.

'Likely by the middle of the day, we will reach a small tavern known as the Travellers Rest. As the name suggests, its main customers are weary travellers, it being the last inn before Duskhold. It stands alone and is less than an hour from the town. However, I do not think it is wise for you to stop there. It does not have the best reputation. But it is the place where I will leave you, for there is a crossroads close by and things will be much busier there. Too busy for a faery to linger. However, it is a straight road into the town from that point,' Osonia repeated.

She continued, 'Your caravan will not draw any attention, as you will see a number similar to it. None of you should attract undue attention, for there are a good many travellers who are not from these parts. The increased trade with the East is the main reason for this. However, your appearance is sufficiently human to pass unnoticed. But one thing I am sure of, is that you will not see any faeries.'

'I cannot advise you as to which way to take through the town, as the place is now a maze that I am no longer familiar with. But the castle is obvious, so just keep heading toward it. When you arrive, you will find that there is only one entrance, the mighty gate. And finally, I would advise you not to share the purpose of your visit with anyone except Prince Hewl. I am led to believe the court at the castle is now a place of scheming and politics, so your information might get misused if it fell into the wrong hands.'

'Well, that seems excellent advice, Osonia, thank you. Though my trepidation is not lessened. Before I even see it, I can imagine that the town will be much larger than any we have in Chimbleton, so that alone may take some getting used to, but it is good to be forewarned,' said Ceri, shifting about in her seat.

'There will be no tongue wagging from me, as there is just one person with whom I must speak and that is Prince Hewl. I will not be chatting to any fair-weather friend that I encounter,' declared a determined sounding Ruffle. The others nodded their agreement.

Their journey continued without event. Predictably, the closer they got to Duskhold, the more people they saw. Even at a good distance from the town, the castle loomed large.

'That castle looks as if it is part of the mountain,' observed Ruffle.

'It almost is,' replied Osonia. 'The castle wall is half-moon shaped and built against the mountain, so there is no rear wall and thus no possibility to attack from behind.

'That is clever,' said Tansy.

'Well, it is the largest building that I have ever seen and easy to understand why it has the name it has, for the castle walls are black, perhaps more so than the mountains behind it.'

'For some reason, it makes me nervous. It is huge and foreboding. I can only imagine how many people must live within it. I don't think I was made to live in such places,' said Tansy, who was feeling as wary as she was excited.

About an hour later, Osonia brought their procession to a halt. The tavern was close by. She leapt down from the wagon where she had been sitting, talking with the companions.

'There lies the Travellers Rest, my friends and now it is time for me to take my leave of you. Remember, do not stop at the tavern, just follow the road and you will be within the outskirts of the town in a short while.'

It was a wrench for the companions to be saying goodbye to Osonia; they had become fond of her and her serious businesslike presence had helped them feel safe. They had relied on her for the last few days, but now their protective guide would be gone.

'Hopefully we will meet again under more pleasant circumstances,' the faery said.

'I think you speak for us all,' agreed Ceri.

The companions watched as Osonia rode back in the direction of Earthroot. Suddenly feeling vulnerable, they shared a mutual hesitation about starting the final part of their trek to the castle.

'This whole journey seems to have been a collection of hellos and goodbyes, but I suppose that is the nature of our venture,' pondered Tansy as she watched Osonia disappear into the distance.

'Indeed. And I confess I am not looking forward to this next part, but I think we should push ahead now. I do not wish to enter that big town in the darkness,' urged Ceri as she took the reins.

They gave the tavern as wide a berth as the road permitted. It was noisy. Men spilt outside, laughing, shouting and carelessly sloshing beer about. Happily, for the three friends, they showed no interest in their small caravan. Not tempted to stop and recalling what Osonia had said, the companions continued on to Duskhold.

As the faery had foretold, the road became a busy thoroughfare as carts, caravans, riders and walkers travelled the same route in and out of Duskhold. It was not long before they were in the streets and maneuvering between the flotsam and jetsam of the town.

It was the sound that Tansy first noticed, like a constant cackle of noise. A mixture of shouting, traders broadcasting their wares, the hum of continuous conversations, laughter and angry voices. She decided that it was all the consequence of so many humans thrust into one place. She could never imagine there would be anywhere in this town to find silence. The assault on her ears was combined with an assault on her nose. It was a confusion of odours. It was difficult to be sure what was which – people, horses, pigs, donkeys, cooking, rotted food, sewage, perfumes and more - created a cacophony of fumes. Some she liked and some prompted her to hold her nose.

Though it was expected, the most striking thing for the companions was the sheer number of people. There were so many people and they all seemed so busy, as if they had somewhere to go and someone to see. Ruffle speculated that 'this is what it would be like for a bee living in a hive,' but then rejected that idea as he thought that there would be less chaos in a hive.

How do people exist in such a place, wondered Ceri? She felt suffocated. Essentially, she was finding it a difficult experience; she wanted to turn and get out as quickly as possible. She looked at Tansy and her face informed her that something similar was crossing the mind of her friend.

Ruffle had observed the changed demeanour of his two companions. He spoke, hoping his words would help.

'I had the same feeling when I first visited a major town; it was a shock. You might feel unsure, even frightened, but it will pass. Just allow yourselves to soak in these new surroundings. It is what happens when many people are living so close to one another. Most will ignore us, just let me do any talking that must be done. I promise you things will get easier.'

Without comment, the two Chimbles listened to Ruffle and sat quietly, watching and absorbing this new world. They heard languages that were completely new to them. They saw animals they had never seen before, some growling from inside cages that were barely large enough for them to stand. They saw things being sold on the streets and had no idea what use they had. Most curiously, many people were dressed in strange clothes, the styles and colours of which were wholly foreign to anything they had ever seen before. But strangest of all were the people, the like of which puzzled them - from which lands did these strange people come?

After the initial sense of being overwhelmed, it turned out that Ruffle was right. The time it took to wend their way through the streets toward the castle allowed them time to get used to the strangeness of it all. In fact, the town's unusual character worked in their favour, as the three companions attracted no attention at all. Compared to many of the inhabitants, they were not unusual in the slightest.

It also became quite clear which parts of Duskhold had been built more recently. The haphazard structures on the outer fringes of the town contrasted with the more orderly and larger dwellings closer to the castle. The fringe dwellings emanated a sense of disorder, having been constructed in an unplanned and speedy fashion; a reflection of the new wealth pouring into Duskhold and the its subsequent rapid growth. Street markets had sprung up in several areas, but not in the older sections of the town. The older structures closer to the castle evidenced more wealth, they were quieter and much easier to navigate, especially for inexperienced travellers.

After navigating their way through the myriad of dwellings, they eventually arrived close to the towering gates of the castle. The walls were so high that they could no longer see the towers within or even the top of the walls. The black outer wall was smooth and featureless, offering no assistance to anyone who might attempt to climb it. The castle gate itself was vast and imposing.

'It is obvious why the castle has never succumbed to a siege. Though less obvious how the thing was ever built,' said Ruffle, as he marvelled at the giant structure.

'I know what you mean. And that dirty moat makes it difficult to get close to the walls,' said Tansy.

'It is incredible, by far the biggest building I have ever seen. And there seems to be a lot of activity within, so let me go and speak to the guards to check that we are able to go inside,' suggested Ruffle as he jumped down from his wagon seat.

He spoke to one of the slovenly guards, who looked over to the wagon and the two female Chimbles. Shortly after, he returned to the cart.

'That guard says no caravans or carts are allowed through the gate. There is a market inside and it is now full. He said that if we wanted to set up a stall, then we should arrive early in the morning. I told him we did not wish to set up a stall and he said we could enter as visitors, but only on foot. No horses are allowed in.'

There were several unkempt soldiers slumped near the gate, seemingly to enforce the rules and to watch who came and went through; although they gave the appearance of looking uninterested in checking who entered. Music and laughter wafted from within the castle grounds. Many exiting the castle were carrying an assortment of trinkets and foodstuffs, and the unmistakable aroma of warm food hung in the air. The untidy and bedraggled guards were doing more eating than guarding. Ceri suggested that it should be easy to slip into the castle grounds.

'It may be straightforward after all to meet the prince!' she observed.

'Happily, the gates are open and I assume that the prince lives within. So, shall we try to see him today or wait until tomorrow?' Tansy asked of her companions.

'Surely, we should try to see the prince today. We need to inform him about the Girngog as soon as we can,' responded Ceri.

'Absolutely, it has to be now. Time matters; the Girngog may be close. Given that we cannot take our caravan into the castle, might I suggest that two of us go in to speak with him. The other one can find a place to stable the horse and somewhere for us to sleep tonight. What do you think?' Ruffle asked.

'A splendid idea, Ruffle,' agreed Tansy. 'I propose that you and Ceri to go in and I will find a stable somewhere to stay the night.'

'I don't like us splitting up, but it does make sense,' conceded Ceri. 'Then after we have spoken with the prince, we can meet up and assess what to do next.'

'Right, that seems like a plan. I will meet you back here at nightfall,' said Tansy.

Ceri laughed.

'That was the quickest hatching of a plan we have ever done.'

'It sounds good to me,' grinned Tansy.

'Indeed, what could go wrong!' said Ruffle.

With the plan settled, Ceri and Ruffle stepped away from the caravan. They had been stationary for a few minutes and had caught the eye of a particular soldier at the gate. However, once the two friends bid farewell to Tansy and made their way into the castle, the soldier resumed eating the pie he was holding.

Once inside the castle grounds, the two friends could see why there was such noise and merriment. The large courtyard was filled with market stalls at which much haggling seemed to be taking place. Dogs barked, children ran in and out of the crowd and music from small drums, pipes, mandolins and tambourines filled the air. Was this a celebration, Ceri wondered to herself?

Standing next to a stall selling cakes, scones and pies, Ceri decided to inquire and spoke to the stallholder, 'Is it a special celebration today?'

'Yer must be a stranger to these parts. We have this market most days. But then there are many strangers afoot nowadays. I shouldn't be surprised at yer question. So, what yer after? If yer got coin, then you'll find what yer want here. You hungry?' the woman said, waving her hand over the pastries on her stall.

'Maybe later,' said Ceri, as Ruffle tugged her elbow to encourage her to come away.

'Coin, I have never used coin,' confessed the Chimble.

'Have you forgotten? Jevell gave us each some coin as we left him,' Ruffle reminded her.

'Oh yes, you're right. It must be in one of your pockets. I completely forgot.'

'Let's leave it for now. Our priority is getting into the castle. Though I do like the look of those pies,' said Ruffle.

Having been distracted by the vibrancy of the bustling market, the companions took pause to take in the wider surroundings of the castle. Mouths agape, they stared in silence at the sheer size of the black citadel. The courtyard that contained the market would comfortably hold hundreds of soldiers. The walls were rock solid and high, with soldiers standing on the ramparts, gazing down at the crowds below. The main building was equally imposing and so wide they could not see where either side ended. Then Ruffle nudged Ceri gently. 'There,' he said, nodding toward broad steps that led up to two big wooden doors.

They jostled their way through the crush, almost losing one another. Ceri was feeling increasingly uncomfortable. She had never experienced so many people in one place. She did not enjoy the pushing and shoving. She had to make an effort to control herself, to suppress the urge to get out and away from the herd of people.

Finally, they stood at the bottom of the stairs leading to two enormous doors. There were no crowds on the stairs, but instead a dozen soldiers with a lackadaisical demeanour slouched across the steps.

'Let's ask these guards where we should go,' suggested Ruffle.

Ruffle could not discern who was the senior soldier, so he asked the one with the largest belly.

'Excuse me, is this the way in to see Prince Hewl?'

He must have said something funny, he thought, as all the soldiers guffawed and giggled. The big man with the matching belly stood up, still chewing something.

'What do yer want with the prince?'

'We have an important message for him,' replied Ruffle, wondering what he had said that these soldiers found amusing.

'An important message is it!' and the group of soldiers all laughed again. 'Well, you just whisper it to me and I'll whisper it to the prince.'

Again, the soldiers guffawed and giggled.

'I am serious,' said Ruffle.

'Listen, my friend, he won't see the likes of you. Now take yourself back to the market or leave the grounds,' the soldier said, turning as if to walk away.

'We have travelled a long way and it is a message he will want to hear. He will probably reward you,' Ruffle said before the soldier could turn away.

The fat soldier hesitated and rubbing his chin, looked at the Rall.

'A reward, yer say. Well, just give me yer message and I will make sure he gets it, alright?' he said with a sly smile. 'Or come back tomorrow and I will see if he is free' - at which point the group of soldiers burst out laughing again.

'Fine,' said Ruffle, 'just give me your name so I can let him know who it was that cost him his kingdom.'

Now it was the turn of Ruffle to move, as if he were about to walk away.

The feign worked. The soldier stopped grinning and became attentive.

'Listen, my little man, I can't just walk up to the prince, soon to be king, and say some fellow you don't know wants a word! He would have my head for dinner. So, give me your name and what it is about and I will speak with my commander. Maybe he will speak to the prince.'

Ruffle considered this and realising it may be the best he could get at this moment, he said, 'My name is Ruffle and I am from

Yasrall. The message I carry is about the Girngog and I must be the one to deliver it.'

Ceri had watched this exchange with the soldier without saying a word. She was feeling very proud of her friend and thinking that Ruffle had managed the situation very well.

'What's a grin dog?' asked Big Belly.

'Not grin dog, the Girngog. Your prince will know what I mean. They are a danger to the kingdom,' responded Ruffle, who now felt as if he was getting control of the conversation.

'Stay there,' ordered the soldier, as he scratched his head and walked up the steps, pushed open the doors and went inside.

Almost whispering, Ruffle turned to Ceri.

'I think that may do the trick, but if not, we will have to find another way. I forgot that kings have all these people around them. It makes it so hard to actually talk with them, or in this instance, it's a prince, though it sounds like he is soon to be king.'

The two friends stood at the foot of the steps, shuffling about and anxious as to how they might be received or not. Then the big soldier reappeared at the doors. Looking directly at Ruffle, he said, 'Come with me,' and gestured for him to follow.

Ruffle smiled and said to Ceri 'It seems to have worked'. But Ceri said nothing; she felt uneasy about the invitation from the big-bellied soldier. Hesitantly, she accompanied Ruffle.

Stepping through the doors, they entered a cavernous room where several soldiers stood. They were led to a soldier who had a large twirling moustache and whose armour was more polished than others. The fat soldier stood them in front of the man wearing polished armour. After a few seconds, he turned and looked at the weather-worn companions.

'Who are you, what do you want and where are you from?' he barked in a 'no nonsense' voice.

'I am from Yasrall and my name is Ruffle Cragstone. I have business with the prince, important information to deliver.'

'I will decide how important your message is,' the mustachioed soldier snapped back. 'Am I correct in believing that your message concerns the Girngog?'

'Yes, it does. They are on the march once again,' replied Ruffle.

Ceri decided that there was no need to point out that she was not from Yasrall. It did not seem important given how it was already proving to be difficult to have a conversation with these soldiers.

'There has been no mention of Girngog for many years. They are a spent force. However, I am Lord Quintorn, the Commander of Castle Black. Give me your news and I will ensure that the prince receives it.'

'I am sorry, but I must speak directly to the prince. I have proof that my information is genuine,' Ruffle responded. He was thinking that the green leaf from Jevell would afford him the credibility he needed.

'I appreciate how concerning such rumours must be, but I can guarantee that the prince will only hear them from me. I have his ear,' said the Commander.

Ruffle was becoming annoyed as he felt he was not being taken seriously.

'I assure you that I do not deal in rumours. I have seen and experienced the things that I must report. There is danger and Yasrall needs help from the kingdom.'

'No doubt you exaggerate. I think you are playing games with me, young man, though I do not know what you hope to gain.

Perhaps a night or two in our dungeon for you and your wench may clarify your thoughts and then you can tell me what it is that you really seek. I will then decide what is to be done with you.'

Before the companions could react, two burly soldiers stepped forward and held each of them by their arms.

'A night in the dungeon might restore the truth. I cannot have your scaremongering. Take them away and show them how uninvited guests are treated,' ordered the Commander.

'I speak the truth, it is vital that I speak to the prince,' spurted Ruffle as he was led away. 'Stop this, you are making a mistake,' he shouted.

Ceri said nothing. This was what she had feared upon entering the castle; she knew pleading would be useless.

The Commander waved his arm as if to dismiss the Rall. 'Enjoy our hospitality, it will straighten your tongue for when we next meet.'

The soldier with whom the Commander had been speaking before the interruption, now spoke, 'Sir, who are the Girngog? Do you think they might be genuine?'

'My dear Costine, the Girngog are long gone. They were a foe of the kingdom, vanquished many years past and rumours of their revival would not be good for Duskhold. However, do not worry, I will find out tomorrow what these scoundrels really seek with their malicious stories,' the commander reassured his officer, who saluted and walked away.

From out of the shadows slinked a cloaked and skinny figure, shuffling up beside the commander.

'Well done, Quintorn. Troublemakers spreading falsehoods can only be harmful to the prince,' said Rillet, patting the commander on the back.

17

Troublemakers

The two friends were taken deep into the bowels of the castle, down cold stone steps into a dungeon lit by torches that hung from the walls. It was chilly and eerie, illuminated by wavering shadows cast by fluttering flames from the torches. Moans and groans rumbled from dark cells, conjuring a frightful atmosphere. Chains hung from the walls, instruments of torture lay on a table, and a pervading smell of damp intermingled with stale sweat accosted the senses. This was not hospitality as Ceri understood it. She was shocked that such a place existed. Her only consolation was that Ruffle was thrust into the same cell as she, so at least they had one another.

The only furniture consisted of two wooden stools. The floor was cold stone, condensation ran down the walls, cobwebs filled the corners, the cell stank and something with a long tail scurried across the floor into the shadows. Iron hoops were screwed into the wall, which Ruffle said must be for chaining prisoners. In the dim, flickering light, they could not make out which cells were occupied.

'What just happened?' exclaimed Ruffle, plonking himself on a stool. 'He gave us no opportunity to explain our mission. Clearly, he did not want to know what we had to say. He was not fair. Maybe you should have spoken and not I. Perhaps I should have insisted on speaking to the prince!'

'No, I don't think it was that. If he thought what we had to say was just gossip, then he would've simply had us thrown out. Instead, he has imprisoned us and I think it is because he is afraid. I believe the mention of the Girngog may have been it,' said Ceri.

Little did Ceri realise how accurate her suspicions were. High above them in a small meeting room, the Commander was in conversation with Prince Hewl.

'You did the right thing, Commander,' said the prince. 'If rumours spread that the Girngog were afoot and coming this way, then our trade would be ruined and my throne undermined. Duskhold would empty quicker than rats from a sinking ship. The prosperity we are enjoying would end. I might even have to take charge of the army. But there is no word of such a thing, that the Girngog are on the march, is there, Commander?'

'None at all, Majesty. Such rumours are baseless. The Girngog have lived in peace for many years now. They were decimated by the last war. If anything had changed, then my spies would have informed me,' the commander replied.

'That is what Rillet advises. He said there is nothing to fear from the Girngog; they slumber in their own lands. But where is Rillet? Have you seen him?'

'No, majesty. I saw him last when the troublemakers were here spewing their lies,' answered the commander.

'Well, at least they are now locked away. The last thing we need is panic. I will soon have the bounty a king should have when I assume the throne. Growing Duskhold and its trade are vital for my plans. The last thing I want is to frighten the traders away. Do make sure that nobody speaks with the prisoners. I will talk to them and decide what is to be done. But it is crucial they do not have the opportunity to spread their rumours. Do you understand?' quizzed the prince of the commander.

'Yes, of course, majesty, though I could do the questioning on your behalf, which would save your grace from such unpleasant matters,' the commander said with a slight bow.

The prince had been pacing the floor as he talked, rubbing his chin and thinking. Suddenly, he stopped, wheeled about to face the commander and spoke with concern in his voice.

'Yes, Quintern, you can question them. But do we know if they are alone? Are there other conspirators with them? Were they accompanied by others who might spread such foul rumours?'

'I do not know majesty, but I can check easily enough. I can do that immediately,' said the commander.

Responding to the nod from the prince, he left the room and made his way to find the guard who had brought the troublemakers to his attention. He questioned the guards at the castle doors, who said that they had only seen the two companions, no one else; but the commander was astute enough to also speak with the soldiers at the castle gate. His thoroughness was rewarded as one of those guards said he had seen the two arrive on a caravan with a third person. He reported that the third person was female and had driven back into the town. The commander returned and informed the prince of his discovery.

Prince Hewl wrung his hands together, his face showing his concern.

'I have no doubt that this woman is part of their scheme. She must be caught before she starts to spread the same rumours. Find her commander. Organise search parties. I want her found as fast as possible. She can join her fellow plotters in the cells. I want to question them all and find out who put them up to this. But be discreet, I don't want it known that we seek saboteurs. Make sure your men appreciate that.'

'Yes, your majesty. I will personally organise the search and start immediately.'

It had taken Tansy a while to find a stable where she could leave the caravan as well as get the horse fed and groomed. She had something to eat and then decided to make her way back to the castle gate. It would soon be time to make the rendezvous.

However, returning to the castle proved to be less straightforward than she hoped. Finding a stable had taken her some time and now she had to find a way walking through streets that she could not distinguish one from another. Once again using the walls of the great castle as a reference point, she eventually found herself near the monstrous gates. She waited.

The town buildings were fifty paces from the castle moat. She stood in a doorway, trying not to be noticeable. She had a good view of the gate and was content to watch the ebb and flow of people around the castle. It had been an uncomfortable experience making her way through the busy streets. She did not enjoy being in crowds.

Darkness descended. It occurred to Tansy that finding her way back to the stable would be harder in the dark. Or perhaps she might be welcomed to stay in the castle. She waited. No sign of her friends. She kept out of the guards' sight, not wishing to arouse their curiosity. She continued waiting as the crowds thinned and noise lessened. She thought to herself that there could be a hundred reasons why her companions had not yet appeared. Nonetheless, after several hours, she decided that she had waited long enough. It was time to go back to the stable, sleep and return refreshed tomorrow. Her mind was filled with wondering why her companions had not appeared.

It was late, but in the streets close to the castle, people milled about. Taverns were lively and soldiers patrolled in leisurely strolls to deter the pickpockets and rogues waiting to prey on the inebriated patrons falling their way home. Though she noticed that once past the older part of town, things changed; there were significantly fewer soldiers policing the mayhem. Which made sense to her as there were fewer taverns the further she got from the castle.

Despite losing her way at several points, she eventually found the stable where she had left the horse and caravan. It had taken her a good while to get back. Exhausted, she climbed into the caravan and before long drifted off to sleep.

It was the general noise of the town that woke her. She lay listening to the slowly increasing hubbub as more and more people took to the streets. Using the coins given by Jevell, she had paid for two nights' stabling. Warm and relaxed, she reluctantly climbed out of bed, consumed her dry breakfast and decided to make her way back to the castle.

Walking slowly in order to be able to recall her route, she felt rather pleased with herself. She was adjusting quickly to the crowds of people, the noise, the size of the town and even using coin. Pleased with herself, she bought a pie. It had all been so new and intimidating. But she was adjusting. Although given the chance, she would prefer to be in Chimbleton. She consoled herself with the thought that once the quest was complete, she could make her way home.

Her positive mood was enhanced by finding the way back to the castle gates quite quickly. She found a position where she could observe the comings and goings at the great gate, again in a doorway out of view of the guards. She folded her arms, watched and waited. The morning passed slowly and still there was no sign of her friends. By the middle of the day, she was hungry, impatient and worrying.

A boy was walking past with a tray hung around his neck from which he was selling food.

'I have bread and dry pork, but I can get yer a potato or rabbit pie. And if you want something else, my da' has a place in the castle where we have all kinds of meat and pies,' the lad informed Tansy.

'Thank you, but bread and a bit of meat to chew will be fine,' said Tansy as she handed over some of her coins. She had no idea how much she had paid. She trusted the boy to take what was required.

By late afternoon, her patience had all but vanished. She felt sure something was wrong. After observing their behaviour, she was convinced that enquiring of the guards about her friends was not a good idea. She decided to return to the caravan and consider what to do next.

Deep in thought and not paying attention to where she roamed, she became lost. Feeling she should sit down and collect her thoughts, she entered a narrow alleyway next to a tavern. Keeping to the shadows, she sat upon some cold stone steps set before a door. She needed to think and had noticed that silence was unusual in such a busy town. However, the alleyway was a little quieter, so much so that she could hear snippets of conversations from a yard. From the smell of ale, she guessed she was at the back of a tavern. One voice in particular she heard clearly and it piqued her interest.

'This is a waste of time. She's probably long gone, ridden out of town, me thinks,' said a male voice.

A second voice replied.

'Well, that's as maybe, but orders are orders. The commander was angry about those two that big belly took in. He stuck 'em in the dungeon, poor blighters. And the one we're chasing was with them. He said there could be a promotion or coin for whoever found the third rascal.'

'But we won't get it if he finds us sitting here drinking,' said the first voice, guffawing.

'Alright, alright. Let's go look in the stable areas, 'cause they said she had a caravan and horse.'

'You're right, mate, we definitely don't want to be the ones that miss her. This place has got so big that it would be easy to do that. Let's drink up and get going. Don't forget he wants her alive but dead if we have to,' at which both laughed.

Tansy pressed herself into the shadowy doorway, which was only a few steps from the street. She realised the soldiers had left the yard. She stood back, unsure whether to move or not. Seconds later, she saw two burly guards walk past the alley entrance and fortunately they did not look her way. As they passed, she realised she had been holding her breath and exhaled with relief. She allowed a few minutes to pass, then crept along the wall to peep into the street. They had gone. She knew that she needed to stay calm, but felt anxious about finding her way back to the stable. She walked hurriedly, keeping a keen watch to avoid any soldiers. She followed landmarks she had noted to help find her way back.

The conversation of the soldiers had given her some sense of what had become of her friends. She decided that being imprisoned in a dungeon was an acceptable reason for their failure to make the rendezvous. Now the soldiers were after her. It seemed alive or dead would do. She wondered how many soldiers were searching for her, she could not imagine. She also realised that if she stayed at the stable, they would eventually find her, it was just a matter of time. So, she decided that the first thing to do would be to flee the town.

Despite her thoughts racing as she walked through the winding streets; she recognised that she was on the correct route to reach the stable. Relieved, she arrived back to find her caravan and horse not yet discovered. There seemed to be no soldiers in the neighbourhood. Fortunately, the caravan was inside a stable and could not be seen from the street. She asked herself, should she leave now or wait until the next morning?

Her preference was to stay and to gather her thoughts on all that she had learned. But if the soldiers found her in the stable then escape was improbable. They were not yet in her district, but the longer she waited, the greater the risk of being captured. She needed time to think. Then, quite suddenly, she made up her mind that she had to go.

She took a saddle from several that hung on the wall in the large stable. She left all her remaining coins as payment, though she was unsure of their worth. Saddling Peret, she led the horse into the streets and headed for what she thought would be the outskirts of the town. Keeping calm, she walked, leading Peret by the reins and attempting to appear casual. In the outermost area, the number of people dwindled. There was a smattering of soldiers, but none paid her any attention.

Not knowing the town at all, she was wholly uncertain where she was heading. Her only plan was to walk as far away from the castle as she could. After what felt like an interminable walk, she recognised that she was on the edge of Duskhold, with few dwellings and fewer people. A wide and obvious road stretched away from the town, so she mounted her horse. Not wishing to attract attention, she simply walked the horse to begin with. She started to relax. It seemed as if she had at least escaped the clutches of the guards in the town.

But her relief was punctuated by the sound of shouting. She turned her head and looking behind, saw three soldiers riding on the same road. There was nobody else between them, so clearly it was she that they were hailing. Wasting no time, she encouraged her mount to speed up and soon she was galloping. The riding that she had done recently now benefited her, as her horse sped away as fast as she had ever ridden. The soldiers remained in pursuit.

The road ahead was clear and her pursuers did not seem to be gaining on her. Yet she wondered where she was headed! She did not recognise the road. At the same time, she thought that it did not matter, for she had no choice but to continue. Unbeknownst to Tansy, she was speeding along the east road away from Duskhold. The road then ran alongside the mountains for a distance and turned out of sight of the town. 'I am riding into the unknown,' she thought. Glancing behind, she could see that the soldiers were still giving chase.

'Please don't let this day get any worse,' she spoke aloud to herself.

18

A Surprise Return

Tansy had never ridden a horse so fast and despite all her practice, she struggled to stay in the saddle. She could not let them catch her. Ahead, the road curved and briefly, the pursuers were out of sight. She had no notion of where she was headed and it was a shock when her horse slowed and pulled up. But there was no choice. The road was blocked. Taking up the entire width of the road in front of her was an army.

Dozens of flags held aloft fluttered in the breeze, mostly yellow with a black castle emblem in the centre. Lances were held pointing to the sky and the sun glistened on the bronze armour of hundreds of soldiers. At the front, leading this procession, sitting astride a white horse, was a considerable figure in gold armour. The host of soldiers on horse and foot, intermingled with wagons, came to a halt.

Tansy's horse came to a stop in front of the mass of soldiers. The big man in the gold armour smiled and looking directly at Tansy. He spoke.

'Not so fast, young lady. You might hurt yourself or someone else. You ride as if your life depended upon it.'

'It does,' squeaked Tansy, gasping for breath and awed at the sight of the procession.

Then suddenly, the three soldiers chasing Tansy came hurtling around the bend only to pull up abruptly, just a short length behind her. They stared at what lay in front of them and then, without being asked, they dismounted. Kneeling on one leg, they bowed and almost in unison said, 'Your Majesty.'

Quickly realising what was happening, Tansy turned and without thinking said, 'Are you King Cadmus?'

Laughing, the King spoke.

'Indeed, I am. Now, who do I have the pleasure of meeting and do tell me why my soldiers are pursuing you.'

'I am Tansy Trundlebit and they are chasing me to lock me up, your majesty. It's because the Girngog are coming and my friends are locked in a dungeon, and they want to do the same to me, or kill me,' blurted Tansy.

'Slow down, Tansy; catch your breath. Nobody is going to hurt you. Do not worry about these soldiers, just take your time and explain to me what has happened,' the king reassured her.

So there, at the front of the king's army, Tansy told an abbreviated version of her story. She was aware of all the soldiers standing and waiting. The king and his commanders listened without interruption, though their expressions grew more serious as the tale unfolded. There were details missing from her account, but she thought that they could be filled in later if the king wished to know. The soldiers who were close enough and thereby privy to the tale Tansy told, listened enthralled. A warm smile spread across the face of the king when she mentioned the help they had received from the Faerie.

At the conclusion of the story, the king sat in silence. After a few minutes musing on her words, he simply said, 'Tansy, you shall ride here next to me.'

He then asked the soldiers who had been pursuing Tansy, what their orders had been and from whom. He listened without comment.

The pursuers were then placed in line amongst the following procession and told to be quiet.

Sitting upright, the king spoke to those around him.

'Let us continue our journey. I am eager to see my brother again.'

Like a gigantic snake, the army began to move. Tansy was a mix of feelings and thoughts. Her overriding feeling was one of relief and now hope. Here was the true king and he was alive. He also had a considerable army with him and perhaps that would be enough to repel the Girngog. Though more immediately, she felt positive and excited. How could the Girngog match this colourful force behind the king! Most immediately, she hoped that she was in time and her friends were safe within the castle.

Very soon, the procession reached the newer and poorer dwellings on the outskirts of Duskhold. The inhabitants were agog. Most had never seen King Cadmus before, nor such a vast host of soldiers as that which followed. It didn't take the watching crowds long to realise who he was.

'My, Duskhold has grown in my absence,' said the king, looking about.

From the ramparts of the castle, some soldiers, not distracted by the market within the walls, had spotted the encroaching army. They recognised the flags and the king. The captain of the guard had been alerted. He told the soldiers to stay in position and to make themselves presentable. He also decided not to inform any other officers and thus Prince Hewl. He was an older soldier and had missed the order and leadership that had dissipated in the absence of the king. He thought it a good thing on this occasion that the prince be surprised.

A number of horsemen were at the front of the cavalcade, clearing a path for the approaching king. Tansy could hear people uttering surprise and many saying, 'I thought he was dead.' She did not enjoy feeling hemmed in by the crowds packing together to catch a glimpse of the returning monarch, but she also felt quite safe at the side of the king. By the time they arrived at the castle gate, word had spread of their approach. The guards were no longer slouching around. They stood erect and to attention.

One of the leading horsemen rode up to speak with the king.

'We cannot enter the castle grounds easily, Your Majesty. There is a busy market being held there.'

The king did not look best pleased. His smile flew from his face. Then he issued instructions.

'Captain, take your men and clear the market completely from the castle. Then bring our soldiers in, organise food, barracks and care of the horses. Major, please take personal care of my family and escort them into their home. Meanwhile, I will take my guard and greet my brother. Tansy, please accompany me.'

The king crossed into the castle accompanied by Tansy and twenty soldiers in blue cloaks. The immaculately polished armour and blue cloaks signified that they were the king's personal guard. Dismounting, the king and his guards vaulted up the steps and through the big doors that Ceri and Ruffle had passed through. Tansy was with them and well aware that the good mood of the king had been replaced by a more business-like attitude. The castle guards stood stock still at the sight of the returned king as his long strides indicated this was not a time to interrupt him.

The king strode through the doors into a large entrance hall and straight to the far end through another pair of ornately decorated doors into the throne room. At the far end of the room, sitting on one of two large thrones, sat a man who chose not to rise as the king approached.

The sitting man spoke.

'This is a pleasant surprise, brother. I thought you were dead.'

'Wishful thinking Hewl,' replied the king, not breaking his stride and walking toward his brother.

Several guards stood close to Prince Hewl and one in particular looked to be their commander. It was Quintern. He touched the hilt of his sword.

King Cadmus looked straight at him with a coldness that was clearly a warning. Likewise, the Royal Guards echoed the king's warning by their own demeanour. They were battle-hardened soldiers who emanated a fearless aura. Quintern did not need a second warning. He moved his hand away from his sword pommel and took a step backwards.

The king stood before the prince, who had remained seated on the throne. He looked at him and waited. In a small act of defiance, the prince did not move but half-smiled at his brother. Then he stood up and with a sweep of his arm gestured for the king to take his seat.

'I am sure that there is much you have to tell me, Hewl, but first things first.'

'I simply managed things on your behalf and I did rather well, I might add,' retorted Prince Hewl. 'As you have no doubt observed, the town is thriving.'

'So, why were there no guards posted on the road to alert you to my approach? Why have you allowed the castle grounds to become a marketplace? And what have you done about the Girngog?'

The prince opened his arms as if to suggest these matters were of no importance. Then, before he could reply, the king spoke again.

'Why did you order that this young woman be captured or killed? I presume you have her companions in the dungeon and have done nothing worse than that!'

'It was for their own safety. Spreading such rumours would be dangerous and might cause panic if widely distributed,' explained the prince.

'You are a fool, Hewl. Did you not listen to what they had to say? Did you not understand why they had risked their lives to deliver such information?'

'I do not believe them. Scaremongers and troublemakers, that is what they are. Trying to make a coin out of our fears. A few nights in the dungeon would straighten their tongues,' suggested Hewl.

'We are not scaremongers and you should have listened,' insisted Tansy, who was angry and worried.

'Be quiet, you speak out of place,' scowled the prince back at Tansy.

Before Tansy could respond, the king spoke in a firm, threatening voice.

'Enough, do not insult my guests, Hewl. One more offensive word from you and the dungeon will have a new occupant.'

Prince Hewl scowled silently and crossed his arms, glaring at Tansy, who also crossed her arms. This little exchange was broken by the doors swinging open to admit two dirty-looking friends. Tansy ran to her companions and hugged them both.

'You've looked better!' said Tansy, smiling at Ceri. 'This is King Cadmus; he knows of our purpose here.'

'Tansy has told me why you are here and I apologise for the welcome you have been afforded so far. I can see our dungeon is not the cleanest place within the castle. But let me make amends. My captain will find you some quarters where you can freshen up and then join me for some refreshment. I have questions that I hope you can answer.'

'What a waste of time,' snorted Prince Hewl.

'Yes, I can see such information is wasted upon you, Hewl. I have no time for your foolishness. Leave me now. We will talk, but not now.'

Hewl opened his mouth as if to reply. He looked toward Quintern, but the King spoke again before his brother could reply.

'Fibert, escort my brother to his rooms and keep him there. He is to have no visitors until I have talked with him again.'

Fibert was a captain in the king's Royal Guard and he, along with two others, insistently led the prince from the throne room.

The king turned to Quintern.

'Return to barracks. Touch your sword again in front of me and I will have your head. Go!'

Quintern glanced at his own soldiers and then thought better of it.

'Yes, Majesty,' he said and left the room.

'Sergeant, escort my guests to suitable rooms.'

Turning to the three companions, 'Please freshen yourselves and let us meet back here within the hour.'

'Before we go, please let me show you this,' said Ruffle.

He reached into his pocket and brought out the green broach.

'So, you have the blessing of Jevell. That is good. Be quick if you will, as there is much I need to know,' added the king.

So, feeling much happier, the three companions followed Valaya, a commander in the Royal Guards, as she led them to the most comfortable rooms any of the companions had ever known. In their chambers, they found a tub filled with water, allowing them to bathe, and they were provided with clean clothes. A guard stood outside their rooms and, once they were ready, escorted them back to meet the king.

As they entered the throne room, Ruffle commented to his friends. 'I now feel much more optimistic that the king will help.'

'Definitely,' added Ceri, 'yesterday it seemed that all our efforts had been in vain. Well done, Tansy, bringing the king to our rescue.'

'Well, I was actually riding away from Duskhold when I bumped into his army. So, I am not sure how much credit I can accept. But it does seem that we have had one lucky break at least,' she smiled.

Upon reaching the throne room, they were shown to a smaller room, though one still large enough for a herd of cows to feel comfortable in. Already seated was the king and several soldiers.

'Come in and take some food. I am sure you must be hungry,' invited the king.

The table was laden with cheeses, pies, meats, bread, grapes, apples, wine and water, more than enough for all. The soldiers had begun to partake of the little feast, for they were clearly hungry.

The King spoke.

'I will have you know that I retain the utmost admiration and respect for Chimbles. I have only ever met one before, though I was little more than a babe in arms. I suppose it was the influence of my father, for Salos the Swift was a very dear friend of his. I realise it was before you were born, but I assume you know of Salos?'

'Of course,' said Ceri. 'He is renowned in Chimbleton as an explorer, though some say he is a myth, just a character from stories for children.'

The king laughed.

'Well, I guarantee you he did exist. My father described him as the most skillful swordsman he had ever seen. But he could never stay in one place for long. Such an intelligent man, too. It is said that he designed the Necklace, the bridge over Seabreeze Lake. Forever restless, he took a ship on an expedition and was away for several years. Eventually, he returned with all kinds of knowledge and things nobody had seen before. Which also included foodstuffs, seeds and tools. He had even learned a new language. He told tales of his adventures that captivated everyone. Then he left again and I believe he returned to Chimbleton. He was gone a year or more, returned again and then within six months, he was off on a new venture. It was another expedition. Another sea journey, but one from which he never returned, at least to here anyways. An extraordinary person and a Chimble.'

'Goodness, we know so little of him. I don't believe anyone in Chimbleton realises that he led such a life,' said Ceri.

'So, Tansy, perhaps you can take me through your tale again and please anything that you know of the Girngog intentions would be appreciated,' said King Cadmus.

Flabbergasted to hear of Salos and eager to learn more, the Chimbles deferred their curiosity to focus on the matter in hand. This time Ceri and Ruffle were there to help embellish what Tansy was able to tell the attentive soldiers. Compared to the outline Tansy had given to the king upon meeting him on the road, in this setting, the telling of the tale took much longer, not least due to the number of questions that interrupted its unfolding.

At the conclusion of the account, the king was swift to take action. He instructed Fibert to send riders out in various directions to ascertain if there were any signs of Girngog approaching. There was still uncertainty as to when or whether they intended to cross the Ghost Mountains and progress to threaten Venterra! 'Better to be prepared' said the king.

Within the castle, there were barracks unused for several years. The army stationed in the castle was now much smaller than it once was. The king ordered that the old barracks now be opened and cleaned, thinking it could form shelter for the inhabitants of Duskhold if the worst of their foreboding came to pass. Furthermore, there was much space within the castle that was now rarely used and could be storage space for foodstuffs.

Unknown to most, there were also cavernous rooms running below ground and these were built as shelters in anticipation of sieges. Although, they were rarely used as the castle had never come close to succumbing to any siege.

Ruffle was impressed by the swift organisation and busyness ignited by the king, who had clearly understood the need for urgency.

Whilst the castle became a hive of activity, the companions remained ensconced in the room where they had met with the king and his commanders. The afternoon seeped into the evening and the conversation ranged over a variety of subjects.

Of especial interest to the castle soldiers was to learn about Chimbleton and the Faerie. None of them had ever met a Chimble or travelled through Earthroot. The mood in the great castle was relaxed. Logs were placed on the fire as the heat of the day drained away, lamps were lit, wine cups refilled and food served. The wife of King Cadmus, Queen Liffilia, along with their three children, joined the king and his guests. There was laughter and storytelling throughout the evening.

The merriment was nourishing for the companions and their concerns eased. They were reassured by the decisive leadership displayed by King Cadmus.

For Ceri, it was no mystery as to why the king was held in such high esteem by his subjects. He inspired confidence and assurance. Nonetheless, she had other, more private thoughts of which she said nothing. She hoped that she was wrong, but wondered if this might be the most peaceful time that they would know for the foreseeable future.

19

A Decision to Make

After many nights sleeping in the woods and on the ground, the friends found sleeping in large bedrooms quite strange. Soft pillows and warm blankets felt luxurious. Most odd was sleeping in a big bed two feet off the ground. It was so comfortable that it took a while for each to find sleep.

Nonetheless, it took the noise of a castle abuzz with activity to rouse the visitors. The three friends gathered together in the room of Ceri. Peering down from a large window, they saw that the courtyard was full of soldiers and townspeople rushing hither and thither. The castle activity was clearly in preparation for hostilities.

The friends made their way to a separate room to eat breakfast. They were alone sitting at a long wooden table, surrounded by large, framed pictures of people that hung from the walls.

'Where is everyone?' Ruffle asked the man bringing their breakfast.

'Everyone ate breakfast earlier,' he replied.

'Do you think we should see if we can be of any help?' said Ruffle between mouthfuls of porridge.

'Well, we should at least ask, better than rattling around this stone castle doing nothing,' replied Tansy, rising and crossing the room to a window.

'Although everyone looks so busy, I wonder if we might get in the way. Hello, something may be happening. Some riders have just sped through the gates and sprinted into the castle. I think their urgency might suggest that there is news to be had.'

Putting down a large goblet of water, Ruffle wiped his mouth on his sleeve, stood up and said, 'Why don't we go and see if that is true?'

They made their way down the stairs and found the great hall where scores of people were talking loudly. They enquired after the king and were told he was in a smaller chamber adjoining the hall. The guard at the door initially denied them access, saying he must check before allowing them entry. He slipped inside and then minutes later opened the door and beckoned them in. Within, the king stood bent over a large table strewn with maps and small figurines positioned like pieces in a strategic game. He looked absorbed but turned as the door opened.

Looking at the king, Ceri spoke, 'Is it alright if we join you?'

'Yes, yes, of come in. We are considering our next course of action. The Girngog have been spotted. They are coming out of the Ghost Mountains and more have been spotted in the Pancake Lands. They are far sill enough away that we have some hours to prepare.'

'Is there anything that we can do to help?' asked Ruffle.

'Your arrival gave us early warning and we have been working through the night, so we have had some time to plan. For that, we are very grateful. At this moment, we are bringing the townspeople into the castle for their protection. Unfortunately, some are unwilling to believe the danger is imminent. Others have taken to the east road, fleeing the town as swiftly as they can. No one can blame them for that. So far, there has been little panic, but that may change. At this moment, my soldiers are organising our defences. Once we are agreed I have no doubt there will be plenty of opportunities for you to help.'

Feeling that they were surplus to the discussion, the friends took to Ceri's room, watching and listening from the window as the incoming townspeople swelled into the castle seeking refuge.

'Well, it would seem that if there was news, the king is not sharing it with us,' said Ruffle.

'I think everyone is preoccupied with preparing for a siege.' Observed Tansy.

'If that is true, then isn't it time that we consider what we ought to do,' suggested Ruffle as he sat down in a chair.

A flagon of wine, some fruit and bread were already on the table in Ceri's room, along with a small fire in the hearth. The friends sat around the warm fireplace, though it was not a cold day.

'Having enjoyed the advantage of travelling through Earthroot, I honestly thought that we would have a longer lead on the Girngog. And I had not considered that they would move so swiftly through the Pancake Lands,' said Ruffle.

'Given that all our routes home will be swarming with Girngog, I do not see that we have much to decide. It seems we have no choice but to remain here and fight,' Tansy pointed out.

'Yet, it seems to me that the king still has two choices. He can muster his army and march out to do battle. Or he can collect everyone within the castle, close the gates and choose a siege. Whichever path he takes has implications for us,' said Ceri.

'Looking at how deep the castle walls are, I doubt the Girngog possess any weapon that could break a siege here. One of the soldiers told me that they would have enough provisions to hold out for five years, which is surely enough,' added Ruffle.

'Yes. I think the way people are flooding into the castle suggests that the king won't be marching anywhere. It appears that he has already chosen a siege and it is likely to be a long encampment. But I am not sure I wish to be here for such a length of time. With their invasion of Venterra I confess I am concerned for Chimbleton,' said Ceri.

'Surely Chimbleton is too small and too hidden to be of concern for the Girngog. There would be nothing to gain by turning their attention to our valley,' Tansy pointed out, though in truth she felt quite unsure.

In a quiet, solemn tone, drenched with worry, Ceri replied.

'I hope that is true, but we really don't know.'

'Unfortunately, my friends, I see no alternative but to remain here and assist the king. Does Venterra have enough soldiers to take the fight to the Girngog? I don't think so. In fact. whichever choice the king makes, none make it easy for us to escape. And where would we escape to? Earthroot? I doubt that it's possible to travel that far. now that the Girngog are here!' said Ruffle.

'You may be right, Ruffle, but I cannot just wait here when Chimbleton may be in danger. I have decided for myself, I must find a way to get home,' Ceri declared.

Ruffle took his thin pipe and began the process of lighting up.

'Well, in my darkest hour of need, you helped and trusted me. You did not know me and yet you placed yourselves in danger on my behalf. Neither of you has uttered a single word of regret or reprimand. And I do believe that we have become good friends. I will not question your wish Ceri, as I know too well the pain of losing one's home. So, whatever you decide to do, even if it seems daft, you can count me in. I won't let you travel alone. Call me a fool, but I will be by your side,' said Ruffle.

'Well, you cannot exclude me Ceridwen Meldrim. If you think I would let you go home all by yourself, then your birds have left the nest. We have come this far together, so let's go home together,' said Tansy, feigning annoyance, then grinning.

'Well, at least it appears that we are agreed, albeit it may be a foolhardy decision. I have no idea how we might escape the castle, or Venterra. But we should go and explain to the king what we intend to do,' said Ceri.

'Which just leaves us with the small matter of deciding how we get home when the world is overrun by Girngog?' laughed Tansy.

They all laughed out loud, for they knew returning would be dangerous and perhaps impossible. In truth they were laughing at themselves as they recognised how foolish their choice was.

'Perhaps we start by asking the king for his advice,' said Ruffle.

'Good thinking, Ruffle, he may help us,' suggested Tansy.

'Right, I suspect that he will think us fools, but we should tell him immediately; time may be against us,' added Ceri.

They returned to the planning room, but the king was not there. They asked, but nobody knew where he was at that moment. Meandering through the corridors, they trudged up to the high ramparts of the inner keep. Looking down, they saw that the hustle and bustle had not ceased. People were continuing to enter the castle and as tempers frayed, voices rose. Many pushed and shoved, eager for sanctuary before the invaders arrived. In a different direction, a long line of carts and caravans continued to roll along the east road, keen to leave Duskhold behind.

'There, look, the king is striding toward the main hall,' said Ceri, pointing.

They watched him reach the main hall, where he entered the room being used for planning and coordinating.

'Come, we can catch up with him there.'

The friends ran down through the castle, crossed the courtyard, and hurried into the chamber. As they burst through the door, the king glanced up from studying a map of the castle.

'Hello, young friends, what hurries you here?' he asked.

'Your majesty, may we seek your advice?'

'Of course. I won't be sitting down very much today, so best do so here and now.'

It was Ruffle who took the lead in explaining what they had decided. The king listened without comment.

'So, in conclusion, we ask your opinion as to what route would offer us the best chance to evade the Girngog?' said the Rall.

'Well, I understand why you wish to go home, but allow me to advise you that your safest choice would be to remain here. All routes away from the castle are now very dangerous. However, try as they may, the Girngog will not breach the castle, so I reiterate that my best advice would be to stay here until this is resolved,' said the king.

'We do appreciate that your majesty, but we feel we could be of most use if we could go home and defend Chimbleton. If there were to be a battle here that can be won, then we would wait and fight beside you. But if a siege is more likely, then of course that could linger on for a long time. Our worry for Chimbleton would run deeper and deeper. We do understand the risk in leaving the safety of the castle, but we accept that risk if there is a slither of a chance to get home,' said Ceri.

The king leant back in his chair, scanning the faces of his three guests before he spoke.

'There will be no battle. My scouts suggest that the Girngog outnumber us greatly and more are arriving. So, it would be foolhardy to ride out into battle at this point. Thus, we are preparing for a siege.'

'Is there any route we could yet take to avoid the enemy?' asked Tansy.

'Well, it seems that you have given the matter some consideration and I understand your feelings. Having risked your lives to come here and forewarn us, then it would be churlish of me to persist in trying to dissuade you from your new intentions. Let me outline what I perceive as your choices.'

'The Girngog continue to arrive from the mountains and across the Pancake Lands. Consequently, neither direction would be a sensible choice. The east road remains open, but that takes you in the wrong direction. You could travel south-east across Venterra to Earthroot and appeal to the Faerie to escort you back to Bridgemouth. But I now hear that the towns and villages across Venterra are under attack, which includes the road to Earthroot. Even reaching Earthroot and making it to Bridgemouth, you would have to cross the Necklace or sail the lake. A difficult challenge given the Girngog now control the town and the bridge.'

'There remains just one slim possibility. I hesitate to mention it, as few ever attempt or succeed when traversing it. I refer to the northern path, which travels up and through the Ironspine Mountains. It is the old way used by the mountain dwarfs when they traded with Venterra. It is long unused. Aside from the stories of ghouls and monsters living in the snowy peaks, it is treacherous underfoot, with ice, hidden precipices and a difficult rocky terrain to cross. It is a cold and challenging route.'

'In fact, I know of no one in recent times who has succeeded in making that crossing. It climbs high into the mountains and is the coldest place within the Kingdom. The route runs near the mountain tops, which are always covered with snow and ice. It is said to be the domain of the Snow Trolls, who hunt along the path. If they do not catch you and eat you, then it is likely that you will freeze to death. The mountain dwarves always travelled in big groups for safety. Then I have no idea if it ever descends and if so, where that might be. Of course, there are roads and pathways within the mountains, but they are the domain of the dwarves, now abandoned and secured. The doorways to those passages are closed, sealed by the dwarves before they left. So, travelling over the mountains is the only possibility. Returning to my earlier suggestion, I urge you to remain here; we might successfully resolve this sooner than you imagine.'

'Your majesty, I think we need to consider things again, in the light of what you say. We should leave you whilst we discuss this further,' suggested Ruffle, looking to his two Chimble friends, who were nodding to show their agreement.

The king stood up.

'Do take as much time as you need. You can tell me what you decide when you are ready. I will be somewhere about the castle.'

He then returned to the group organising the siege preparations, whilst the friends took themselves to a corner of the room and sat leaning against a wall.

'What do we do?' posed Tansy to her companions.

'It seems to me that we have one more option than we had before. I did not know of the Ironspine road and perhaps neither do the Girngog. Obviously, the sensible thing to do is to stay here and help with the siege. But a new possibility now presents itself. As dangerous as it sounds, it is one I am willing to consider. I choose the mountain pathway,' said Ceri.

There was a brief silence as Ceri's statement was digested. Then Tansy declared herself.

'The safe choice, at least the relatively safe choice, is to take the advice of the king and stay in the castle. But then we would be worrying about Chimbleton, our families and friends. I am not sure how long I could tolerate the feeling of not doing anything for Chimbleton when it could be in danger. And the longer the siege lasts, the more I would worry. It might go on for years! I don't like the idea of the mountain road, especially the thought of being eaten by snow trolls, or maybe dying from the cold. But I see no other real option. Unfortunately, it has to be the mountain path.'

The Chimbles looked to Ruffle, who, with arms crossed and one hand on his chin, was plainly thinking.

'History tells us the path was once used by the mountain dwarves; therefore, it must go somewhere. Although that is likely to lead into the mountains. But it seems it has not been used since the dwarves abandoned it. From what the king said, it is also fraught with danger. However, it could be a long siege and if we remain here, then we only get to leave when the Girngog lose and give up.'

'Or if the Girngog siege is successful,' Tansy piped up and got a friendly thump on the arm from Ceri.

Ruffle continued.

'Well, without repeating what you have already stated and rambling on some more, it seems to me we have just one choice, as our fate shows that we are meant to have adventures together. So, let's give it a try. I am in for the mountain path.'

'Right,' Ceri said as she stood up. 'That is unanimous. Come, let us tell the king of our final decision.'

She sounded sure and confident, but she wasn't. There was little enthusiasm from the three adventurers. They all felt that their choice was not a choice, it was their only option other than remaining.

The king sat in a large chair and said nothing as the three friends gathered about him. They told him what they had decided. He said nothing. He looked to the floor, his hands cupped together. Finally, he spoke.

'Truthfully, I am not surprised. Though I fear for your safety, I cannot blame you for caring about your homes. I will refrain from trying to dissuade you any further.'

He stood up.

'Right, if you are to leave, then we need you prepared as soon as possible. We are readying for a siege and the main gate is soon to be closed. There is just one remaining exit from the castle, which will be sealed very soon after the main gate. It is a small side entrance which cannot be seen from the front of the castle. It is just about sufficient for a horse to walk through. You can exit there and that way draw no attention. You will be able to ride along the mountain path for a while before it becomes too steep and too cold for the horses. I will send an escort to show you the way and he can return with the animals when you have to abandon them. Hopefully, in good time before we seal the small entrance.'

'You will appreciate that I cannot accompany you, for I must oversee the closing of the castle gates. I will have warm clothes and food prepared for you immediately. Though I caution you to take extra care, as the mountain is very unforgiving of mistakes and it will be a long hike. I cannot add more as you go somewhere that few are familiar with. I sincerely hope to meet you all again one day and in more convivial circumstances. Now, go, get ready and cross the Ironspine. If anyone is to prove that it can be done, then I suspect it will be you,' said King Cadmus.

20

The Road of No Return

Less than an hour later, the companions were gathered and ready in Ceri's room. A knock on the door and a young soldier appeared.

'His Majesty said you should go to the kitchen, where food and clothing have been prepared for your journey. Then I am to lead you to the side gate where horses await. I will show you how to get onto the road leading into the mountains and travel with you for a while. Then I must return to the castle. My name is Wyll Storm, by the way.'

The soldier then led the three companions through the winding corridors to the castle kitchens. A place they would never have discovered on their own. Long before they reached the doors, the rich aromas wafted through the passageways, and the heat warmed the air. Unsurprisingly, the kitchen was very large and full of people rushing about. The hot ovens caused the walls to run with condensation, or sweat, as Ruffle joked. Tray after tray of food sat on racks. Bread, pies, soup, stews and much more were spread throughout, some cooking, some cooling, whilst more food was placed in the ovens and more removed.

'By the door, Wyll Storm,' yelled a big woman wearing a long white apron and pounding a block of dough as she spoke.

On a table by the door, wrapped in canvas, sat three small packs.

'They must be for you,' suggested Wyll Storm to the companions as he waved his hand in the direction of the parcels. 'Mistress Maud must have already prepared them.'

'Who is Mistress Maud?' asked Ruffle.

'The woman who shouted to us. She is the head cook in charge of the kitchens. They say the castle was built around her,' said the soldier with a small laugh.

Along with the parcels of food were three leather bottles. Walking toward them and rubbing her hands on her flour-spattered apron came the large woman.

'It's Mistress Maud,' whispered Wyll Storm.

'There is mushroom soup in them bottles; you got about a short afternoon before they cool and once you open them, you'd better eat them, it won't stay hot. You got bread and some white cheese, along with berry biscuits. All more filling than it sounds. You got more things in there, but you can find 'em yourselves. You could do with a good meal, Wyll Storm, you're as skinny as a hay fork. Anyway, I got a town to feed so best I be back to work, good luck to you all.'

And off she went back to the dough, calling out instructions to the multitudes toiling in the hot kitchen.

'I think we ought to go; they might seal the gate,' said the young soldier, turning away from the den of cooks. The companions followed, wondering how the gate would be sealed.

He led them through the stone maze that comprised the corridors and halls of the great castle. Some were empty and dim. Ghostly in their silence. Whilst others were boisterous and busy, reflecting the commotion caused by preparations for a siege. They climbed one set of stairs and then went down another. Winding through endless corridors, the sheer size of the castle further amazed the three companions.

'How long did it take you to learn your way through these long passageways?' Tansy asked Wyll.

'Well, I grew up within the castle so I can't rightly say, but for anyone new like yourselves, I think it would take a goodly long time,' he replied.

Eventually, they reached some half-lit corridors and went through a door that opened onto a row of stables holding many horses. The bright light of sunshine seeping into the stables was a sudden contrast to the gloomy walkways of the castle. The immediate reaction from the companions was to shield their eyes. In addition, the aroma from so many horses was overpowering. Ruffle instinctively squeezed his nose to suppress the smell.

'Good for the garden this stuff, so they say,' squeaked Ruffle, pointing to what the horses had deposited on the floor, but still holding his nose.

Many stable hands scuttered about feeding and cleaning the animals. Several called out greetings to Wyll, who was clearly well known. Walking out of the stables took them into a large yard where horses were being exercised and riders practised manoeuvres. Making for a door at the far end, they were greeted by another soldier who had five horses waiting for them.

'Take the reins of a horse and lead it through this door; it is too low to ride through,' instructed Wyll.

The companions each led a horse and followed their guide. They passed through a short tunnel, which was in fact the castle wall. Wyll explained that the inner wall was so thick that a carriage could be driven along the battlement above. Then there was a moat between the inner wall and the outer wall. The outer wall was also as thick as the inner wall but ten feet shorter in height. It enabled bowmen to be able to stand on the outer wall and others on the inner wall at the same time. There were also towers spread along the walls and they were now walking underneath such a tower. A soldier stood before them as if awaiting their arrival.

'This is our exit. Be careful leading the horses as the first few steps are on a temporary and narrow bridge across the moat,' explained Wyll.

He opened the door which led out of the castle. Several planks of wood had been laid to form the narrow bridge he had mentioned. Once all had crossed and stood by their horses he spoke.

'I will lead you along the road that climbs into the Ironspine Mountains. When it becomes too cold for the horses, I will leave you and return with the animals. Once I return, this doorway will be filled with stone and brick; it will cease to be a door. However, if I take too long, then they will seal this door before I get back. In which instance, I will have to travel to the front of the castle to the main gate, but that is due to be closed before this little gateway is sealed. As you will appreciate, if I return too late, I could become trapped outside whilst the enemy are arrived at the walls of the castle. So, please mount up and let us be on our way, I have no wish to be locked outside the castle,' said Wyll.

It was clear that Wyll's preference was to return through the same entrance by which they were leaving. Understanding the risk to Wyll, the companions complied without question. They were quickly on their way.

'Why do we have five horses?' asked Ruffle of Wyll.

'You can see four are saddled, the fifth carries extra clothing which you should put on once we stop and you have to proceed on foot. The fur clothing is to keep you warm, but they are rather bulky to ride in, so we carry them on a spare horse. Genuine snow troll fur, so don't let them see you wearing it!' Wyll grinned.

'You must be teasing us!' said Ruffle, aghast.

'Don't worry, I am teasing you. There are no snow trolls,' Wyll grinned at the Rall. 'At least none that come trading in Duskhold.'

Ruffle grinned.

They had exited the castle on the western outskirts of the town, where few dwelled. The place was dark and uninviting, hardly the most appealing part of Duskhold. Nestled so close to the castle walls and the looming mountain, it lay in perpetual shadow. Even without the threat of the Girngog hardly anyone lingered there.

The beginning of the road leading into the Ironspine Mountains was barely recognisable as a road; it was so rarely used that it appeared no more than a rough track. In fact, the friends did not realise that they were already on the road until Wyll pointed it out.

'No reason for anyone to be hereabouts, nothing grows here in the shadows of the Ironspine. Everyone knows this way leads into the mountains and it is a rare thing that anyone ever wishes to travel this way, at least if they have any sense. So, as you can see, it is quite deserted, which suits us. Whoops, I apologise. I was not referring to yourselves, of course, just ordinary folk, if they were trying to escape the Girngog, it would not be a good idea to go this way,' fumbled Wyll. 'Whereas my understanding is that you have chosen this route for good reason, at least I assume so.'

'No need to worry, Wyll, we're not offended. We've been told how foolhardy it is to take this road,' said Ceri.

'But we're taking it anyway,' Tansy said, half laughing.

None of the companions wished to explain any further as to what they were about. Silence descended. It was Wyll who broke the quiet.

'The horses will take us quite high. But they will go so far and then it becomes too cold, or they may feel spooked and refuse to go further, which has happened for me. At that point, I will leave you and return to the castle. What spooks them, you might ask me, but I don't know. There are stories, but perhaps it is just gossip, so I won't say more. Except that many do believe that the high peaks are the domain of snow trolls. I have never seen one myself and I would guess that you won't either.

'Well, that sounds frightening enough for me!' chimed Ruffle with widening eyes.

'What you are really saying is that nobody knows what is up there, if anything?' suggested Ceri.

'Well, I suppose so,' answered Wyll.

'How long does it take to cross these mountains?' asked Tansy.

'I have no answer for that question. To my knowledge there is no one who has crossed in my lifetime. Though I do recall seeing dwarves, so they must have crossed somehow. The only clue may be in the old song with the chorus line *a week to cross the Spine* which suggests it takes a week.'

'I don't know that song,' exclaimed Tansy.

'Oh, it's just an old tavern song. But if it's accurate, then you have a week in the mountains,' answered Wyll.

'Wonderful,' said Ruffle. He was feeling the temperature drop as they moved up the road and not enjoying it at all. He pulled his coat tighter about him and wrapped his scarf securely about his neck. He had felt overdressed in the castle, but now felt the opposite. 'I think I will be glad of those furs you carry,' he intimated to Wyll.

Steadily, they made their way up the lower slopes of the mountain. The peaks were hidden in the cloud, but below that, the rocky terrain was covered in snow. Soon they were high enough to look back at the town. They had a partial view of the castle, making out the inner buildings and battlements. Further away toward the horizon, Ruffle was sure he could make out the Girngog camp, but the others suggested he had been drinking wine before breakfast. The good humour was welcome, for they could all feel the cold beginning to test out their clothing.

They continued to trudge higher, but conversation was sparce now as the cold bit. The road was still discernible, but narrow, more like a broad footpath. The horses had become skittish and Wyll called a halt.

'This is as far as I can go,' said Wyll. 'The horses will become unmanageable soon and I think you should take the furs before you get colder. And I must return to the castle. I don't suppose any of you will join me!'

'Sorry, Wyll, we appreciate your offer, but we are committed to our purpose and to one another. You never know, perhaps we will be the first to return from the Ironspine. Now that would be a tale to tell,' smiled Ceri.

'Indeed,' said the soldier, looking very dubious.

They all dismounted and the friends donned the fur-lined coats. They also had over trousers, which were welcome. When fully dressed, only their eyes were exposed to the weather. The timing was apt as a dusting of snow drifted lightly from the sky.

'Thank you, Wyll, now you should leave us. I would not wish you to be caught outside of the castle. That's enough goodbyes, take yourself off and be safe,' urged Tansy.

The soldier gathered the horses and mounted his own.

'Good luck up there. I hope that one day you will be able to tell me the tale of crossing the Ironspine. But forgive me, I must make haste if I am not to be locked outside the castle,' said the young soldier.

He gathered the horses and sped off. The horses seemed quite happy to be getting off the mountain.

'Good luck,' he turned and shouted as he disappeared down the patchy road.

'Well, we are back on our own again and I think we should keep moving. I am warmer wearing this fur, but it is cumbersome to walk in. Perhaps our first effort now should be to find somewhere sheltered where we can make camp for the evening,' said Ceri.

'Good idea. I think it's better that we walk whilst it is light, but for tonight the sooner we find shelter the better, hopefully before this snow becomes heavier,' said Ruffle.

'I regret saying it, but I think the snow will be with us for the whole journey,' observed Tansy.

With heads bowed so the light snow did not blow in their faces, they placed one foot after the other and walked on into the mountains.

21

The King

In Castle Black, King Cadmus stood alone on the inner ramparts looking out over Duskhold. Half the population of the town had taken flight; the other half were scurrying into the castle. From his vantage point, the wagons and caravans heading east looked like a long snake. Considering the panic ignited by the news of the approaching Girngog, the procession was surprisingly orderly.

Those choosing to seek safety behind the mighty stone walls jostled one another in their eagerness to get inside. Yet there were some who had remained in town, refusing to leave their property and possessions stubbornly not willing to believe that the Girngog would carry their fight to ordinary people.

From his lofty perch, the king looked on with a heavy heart.

He knew he could not show his dismay at what was happening, at the anticipation of the sorrow that was inevitably coming with war. So many lives were in jeopardy and he was especially troubled by the fate of three. He had hoped to persuade his three visitors to remain within the safety of the castle, but despite his beseeching, they had chosen to leave. He feared the worst for them. He expected that one day in the future, he would have to explain to Jevell why he had helped them leave by such a perilous route.

Raised voices signaled an argument playing out at the great gates and reminded him that this was no time to brood over his concerns; too much remained to be done. He left the ramparts and returned indoors. He gave orders for his commanders and captains to gather for a meeting.

The planning room filled up and buzzed with the incessant chatter of his officers. The king rose up from his chair and raised his hand; the chatter ceased, 'Reports please' he commanded as he sat down.

There followed a variety of reports: about readying the army, organising the townspeople sheltering in the castle, arranging the supplies in preparation for a siege and ending with a question put to him about closing the great gates.

'Is there a set time that we must close the gate by?' asked the gate commander.

'No, but as soon as possible would be preferable, and definitely today,' said the king. 'We have had little time to prepare for this situation or assess the threat that we face. To my knowledge, we had no indication that the Girngog were about to invade. Trying to provide refuge for all those seeking it with such a short warning inevitably takes a little time.'

'In hindsight if we had more contact with Yasrall, then perhaps we might have anticipated something. I have played my part in that neglect. With some foreknowledge of their intent, then we might have marched out to engage the Girngog before they landed on our doorstep. But, we didn't. Thus, we are now faced with the consequences.'

'They have come over the Ghost Mountains and across the Pancake Lands to now swarm across Venterra. The latest report indicates that they occupy much of the land between here and Earthroot. Quite simply, we are surrounded. Our saving grace is that we have this castle. No one has ever successfully laid siege to Castle Black and I have no intention that the Girngog shall be the first.'

'For that to remain the position, it is imperative that we are organised and all soldiers understand the part they must play. We have to ensure that the townspeople are also organised amongst themselves. It is important that as few soldiers as possible are embroiled in managing the townspeople. Not least because battle is a new experience for most of our army and I want them to concentrate on their duties.'

'In fact, a large proportion of our force have never experienced the blood spill of conflict. I think that might also be true for some of you sitting here. Thankfully, I would say, but now things will change. You should prepare yourselves as best you can.'

'The Girngog can be a frightening enemy and they will bring war beasts few here have seen. They can be terrifying to behold. So, informing our soldiers as to what they can expect, will be a vital part of our preparation. At the same time, we should be confident. Our swords will cut Girngog just as well as they do for any foe. You should remind them that this castle has never been breached. Do make sure you impress that upon them. It will give them confidence.'

'At this point, we do not know what the Girngog seek. As yet, there has been no communication received from them. I suspect that they are in no hurry to contact us. Ultimately, it does not matter. They are the enemy, the invaders and we must defend ourselves. At some point, they will make their demands clear and I will inform you when they do. For now, please return to your posts and continue with preparations. We will meet again tomorrow morning. In fact, we will meet each morning whilst the siege lasts. Are there any questions?'

'There was silence.

'Right. Thank you. Let us be about our business,' said the king as he stood and the meeting began to disperse. He then spoke quietly to one of his captains.

'Adelia, I have no doubt that the demands of the siege will shred what time I can spend with my family. So, I would like you to be a conduit between us and also their protector. I need to know that they are safe or in need of anything. Would you accept that role?'

'Of course, Your Majesty, I would be honoured,' she replied.

'Thank you. I will inform the queen tonight. We can agree on how this can operate this evening. If it is not practicable at any point, then do not hesitate to inform me. Once again, thank you,' said the king.

In the war room, the king leant back in his chair; he was alone again with his thoughts. He had not expected to return home from his expedition in the east and be immediately thrust into a war. In his absence, Duskhold had grown chaotically. The army discipline had become sloppy. His brother had replaced good advisors and succumbed to the influence of Rillet, a mysterious figure who had strangely disappeared.

Hewl had focused his attentions on growing Duskhold and filling the royal coffers. The old communication lines across Venterra that enabled the king to oversee his lands had withered. Unused and then abandoned, they had been of no interest to Hewl. He had focused solely upon Duskhold, which had grown but had simultaneously become isolated within its own lands, only preoccupied with itself. In times gone by, messengers across Venterra would have alerted the castle to the advance of the Girngog. Now it had taken three brave strangers to warn the king of what was coming to his doorstep.

However, he considered that even if forewarned, it was doubtful that Hewl would have known how to prepare for the Girngog. So, in one sense, he had returned just in time. In another sense, having to go into battle again was not a welcome prospect. He had hoped his people would never go through another war. Personally, he felt that he had fought quite enough battles for one lifetime. But here he was, once again, having to mobilise in order to defend against an old enemy and he did not understand why this had come about!

Had Merektar returned to the Girngog? Was this all to do with his scheming? Whilst he was confident about the castle being able to resist any siege, as things stood, there were no allies ready to fight alongside Venterra. The Kingdom stood alone. It seemed inevitable that a long siege lay ahead. Then a knock at the door interrupted his thoughts and a soldier entered the room.

'Your majesty, you are needed at the great gate.'

'Right,' said Cadmus, straightening his tunic and marching out of the room, ready to do what he must.

22

The Ironspine Mountains

The snow was light, swirling in the wind but not settling on the ground. Tansy turned to see if she could still see the castle, but with the bends in the road and the blizzard-like conditions, she could not see any great distance. Ruffle saw her turn and he copied her. His words expressed her thoughts.

'Hopefully, Wyll got back before they closed the small gate.'

'I think he will be fine. We have not travelled very far or taken too long to do so. Plus, it is unlikely that the Girngog have attacked the castle as yet or that the side door is already walled up,' said Ceri. 'Which should allow sufficient time for him to enter the castle again. At least I hope so.'

'Yes, I am of the same mind. Our finding somewhere to shelter might prove to be a bigger challenge than Wyll getting back in time,' added Tansy.

On they went, feeling rather small and insignificant surrounded by the towering mountain peaks. The wind was rising, and the sky grew darker. Sheer rock faces loomed on either side of the path as they pressed deeper into a world of cold stone and sparse bracken.

'I have trodden some lovely mountains, full of wild life and splendid vistas. But these mountains are different; they do not welcome visitors. These are mean and lonely. I do not have a good feeling about this road,' stated Ruffle ominously.

Suddenly, Tansy stopped. Her companions stopped, looking at her, unsure why she halted.

'I confess I am wondering if this is rather foolhardy of us to pursue this path. The road ahead continues to rise and the temperature continues to drop. Is this a fool's journey?' said Tansy. 'I think we should consider returning.'

'What in this icy heaven has prompted that thought? I thought we had all agreed, we knew that this would be a mighty challenge, we were warned how risky it could be. This is not like you, Tansy,' asserted Ruffle.

'I know. I know. It's just that now we are here, I am finding it so intimidating and cold. And it's likely to become even more so. I just thought that we ought to be sure, we might be making the biggest mistake we could make. After all, there is no failure in altering our plans, especially if our lives are at risk,' said Tansy.

'That is a fair comment and to be honest, it has also crossed my mind. We are in a most unfriendly place here; dark, cold, forbidding and goodness knows what awaits us further along. So, it is sensible that we should consider our plans. It may be our last opportunity to return to the safety of the castle. That is assuming that we have not travelled too far already. What say each of us? We must decide quickly. We cannot linger here; it is too cold,' said Ceri.

'Well, it's straightforward for me. I expected this, I know mountains and I admit I do not like these. However, I have travelled and survived cold, snowy mountains before, although on those occasions I knew where I was going. Nonetheless, I am willing to proceed as planned. I know how much you both desire to return to Chimbleton. Equally, if it is your preference to return to the castle, I will not argue against that. It is your land that we seek to reach, so I bow to your wishes' said Ruffle.

'I also realise I made the choice to go this way, but this is all more hostile and menacing than I expected. Yet I know it would be churlish of me to renege on my decision. I am sorry to have raised it again. It's just at this moment I am torn. However, if we choose to go on, then you will hear no more whining from me,' added Tansy.

'Well, it seems you are leaving the decision to me. Now I also share the misgivings that you both speak of. I ask myself, would I prefer to be safe within the castle and definitely, part of me would. Albeit we cannot know what may have been asked of us if we had remained. In truth, here and now, looking at our way forward, it fills me with trepidation. But I am reminded that our purpose is surely larger than our personal comforts. I am confident that swathed in these furs, we can overcome the cold; and if we can find shelter along the way, then all the better. The hard fact is that we cannot know what lies ahead, so I have no words of reassurance on that. But my dear friends, it is my experience that when we work together, we can overcome any challenge. That said, I recognise your fears. Yet my intuition says we should persevere. Either way we should move before I get any colder,' said Ceri.

'If the only cost is bearing this cold, then it is a simple choice, but the cost could be our lives,' warned Tansy.

'True. But we knew this beforehand? I believe that we will survive. It may seem flimsy, but I trust my intuition in this, I believe in us, I believe we can do it' replied Ceri. 'And there is one more thing. I do not think that we have a choice. The gates into the castle will be closed before we could arrive back. With the Girngog surrounding the walls, I doubt we could get back into the castle even if we wished to.'

'Right. I think your words are true Ceri. I feel a fool. You're right, the reality is that we have no choice, we have come too far. One thing I do believe in is you, Ceri. I trust you, your judgement. So, I will go with the words of Ceridwen the wise! We have to go forward,' said Tansy. 'You know, it would not surprise me if one day you became a wise wizard.'

'Right, well, that is all clear to me, I'm in. Now let us move before I freeze and can't move anywhere,' said a shivering Ruffle.

They started to shuffle along once again.

'By the way, I am not wise, Tansy. You are the one who raised the matter and we did need to speak about it. This place tests our resolve. And now that we have spoken of it, I think we are stronger for doing so. Maybe it should be Tansy the Wise,' smiled Ceri.

'Fine, I like that, Tansy the Wise. I think it might suit me,' she laughed.

'I'll be Ruffle the frozen one, because if we do not find shelter, then I will definitely be turning to ice.'

'So, are we agreed? We carry on?' said Ceri, already moving forward. Her companions nodded agreement as they trudged through the falling snow.

'Good. Please keep moving, no more stopping. We need to stay warm and more urgently, find somewhere that can provide shelter for the evening,' said Ruffle.

'Absolutely, we do not wish to see you turn into a snowman,' said Tansy.

On they trudged, ever watchful for somewhere that could serve as a shelter. The light was starting to fade quickly and the wind howled through the rocky landscape. A few more heavy flurries of snow forewarned them of what they might expect to face as they climbed higher. Though completely swaddled by fur, the cold wind found gaps within their clothing that it was not entitled to

They walked as steadily as the wind would allow, for it consistently blew directly at them. 'It's doing it on purpose,' muttered Ruffle as he tightened his scarf. The road twisted and turned, but there was nowhere offering shelter. Too cold to talk for long, it did not need to be said that their survival depended upon finding somewhere out of the snow. Having seen nothing remotely useful for shelter, it was a welcome surprise when, rounding another corner, a yawning cave mouth lay right before them. Large enough to simply walk in, the three friends approached it but hesitated at the entrance.

'What if someone else calls this place home?' queried Ruffle, expressing why they had hesitated.

'Then we should check,' said Tansy as she struggled to draw her sword from beneath her layers of clothing. It was almost frozen and came out of its scabbard reluctantly.

Ruffle and Ceri did likewise. All three trod carefully and quietly, their bodies tensed and poised, ready should a cave owner appear. To their relief, they met neither person nor animal.

It was a large cave that went deep into the mountain. The three friends explored inwards as far as they safely could, before the absence of light made it too dangerous to go further. They returned closer to the entrance and finding small dry broken pieces of wood inside the cave, they tried to create a fire. Ruffle ventured outside, close to the cave, to find more bracken and natural debris, which he hoped to use in prolonging the life of the fire. He returned quite soon with disappointing news. .

'Even though the snow is not yet settling, it has dampened everything. There is little outside that we can use tonight, so we will have to make do with what is in here already.'

'Our kindling is little but I see no sign that we are trespassing in someone's home, so I definitely think this is where we should spend tonight. There might be enough here for a small fire to last most of the night, assuming I can get it started and it stays alight,' stated Ceri.

'I agree. We can't go out now, the wind and the snow are getting stronger. It is already warmer in here and who knows where the next shelter might be. Let's get the fire going. I for one, am pleased we found this place,' said Tansy, eager to see some dancing orange flames.

Before long, the fire was lit. It was small, but it made a welcome difference. It offered some warmth, a little light and an uplift for their spirits. Some replenishment was taken and greatly appreciated. Sitting around the little fire, they were just ten steps back from the entrance through which they watched and listened to the weather. The snow was falling heavily, and the wind whistled and moaned. They felt thankful that they were not outside. The night drew down and soon the only light came from the fire, casting flickering shadows on the cave walls.

'Those shadows could be dancing demons, they would play havoc with my imagination if I let them,' said Ruffle, staring at the walls.

'No need my friend, they are just shadows. I have no idea of the time, but it might make sense for us to go to sleep. We can put as much as we dare of the kindling on the fire, but the temperature will drop and I would rather be asleep at that point. I know the light through the entrance will wake me early. Then tomorrow is likely to be a long day, but the more hours we can devote to travelling, the better,' said Ceri.

'And let us not forget, we must allow time to find another shelter for tomorrow night,' said Tansy.

'Definitely,' agreed Ruffle, 'I would not wish to spend a night outside.'

They huddled together for warmth, sitting with their backs against the rocky wall. Walking had been cumbersome, having to wear several layers of clothing, but they were glad of the furs, the hoods and scarves. They judged that they were just about warm enough to sleep and wake up.

'Should we take turns at being on watch?' asked Ruffle.

'Looking at the weather, I doubt anyone would be outside tonight. And who would be foolish enough to be out on a mountain? No, I suggest we all just sleep. I sleep lightly, so any noise and I am confident that I will wake,' said Ceri.

'Accepted,' smiled Tansy. 'I am off to sleep.'

The ground was hard and getting comfortable took some fidgeting, but eventually all three welcomed the escape into sleep.

Ceri woke first, but she did not move. She was pressed warm against Tansy. Her eyes were open and she could see her breath in the cold air. Looking toward the cave entrance, the sun had risen and it was not snowing.

'We could stay snuggled up and sleep, which strikes me as a good plan,' said Tansy.

'I know what you mean, but it would get colder as the day unfolds,' said Ruffle in a rough, sleepy voice.

'I thought you were both still asleep. I could stay here too, but I think our bones would stiffen up. Come on, we should get going. The fire is out, so a little dry breakfast and then let's be on our way,' said Ceri.

They quickly ate and then set off walking. Their footsteps crunched the fresh snow, the sun not being warm enough to have brought any melt.

'At least the snow is soft and shallow enough to walk on; it would be treacherous if it were icy. It is not so deep, which I suspect tells us that it stopped snowing early on during the night,' observed Tansy.

'Don't be fooled, there may still be ice beneath the snow, so we have to watch where we tread,' said Ruffle.

Despite the white blanket covering everything, the way ahead was obvious; there was only one road. It soon became clear that they were steadily climbing. The incline was subtle enough so that they were not breathing hard. Nonetheless, they could feel the effort in their legs. The pleasant walk in the morning sun became a slow trudge.

'I wish this path would simply go flat for a while. It gradually keeps creeping up and up, always demanding we go higher, with no let-up for my poor legs,' said Ruffle.

'It is quite deceptive how it climbs. It makes sense that we should have a little break soon,' suggested Ceri.

'I was thinking about the castle and whether the fighting has begun,' said Tansy.

'I have no idea. I have no knowledge of how a siege proceeds and no way to give you any news. You may not have noticed but I have been travelling with you!' replied Ceri.

'If the king had decided to march out to the battlefield, then I would imagine he would have done so by now. But if they opted to remain in the castle, I have no idea when the enemy would be ready to commence attacking. I've heard it said that the Girngog bring monstrous beasts when they battle, and they may have siege machines. So, in short, I also have no insights to help your wondering. I doubt the king will start hostilities. If there is to be any fighting, then it is likely to be initiated by the Girngog,' commented Ruffle.

'I only said I was wondering,' exclaimed Tansy.

This little explanation from Ruffle was him thinking out aloud and brought chuckles from all three companions, though none could say why. The conversation abated as they each fell into their own thoughts. Onward they scuffled through the snow. It was an hour or more later when they paused for a break. Sitting on small boulders alongside the path, they indulged in some food - hard cheese, bread and an apple. The sun was shining, but too weakly to provide any warmth.

'We must be careful to make our food last, especially if Wyll was correct and we are here for a week,' said Tansy.

Ceri mused in between biting her apple, 'My bread won't last much longer before it becomes stale. Did anyone see any animal tracks?'

No one had.

'Why would any animal choose to live up here! The food pickings are so sparse,' stated Ruffle. 'Were you thinking of catching something? What wouldn't I give for a hot stew and some dumplings right now!'

'That is true what you say about animals, which may be a good thing for us. I would not wish to meet any animal tough enough to be living here,' said Tansy.

'Let's hope you're right. And no, I was not thinking of catching anything. Come, we should get going again. We cannot leave it too late to find somewhere to shelter, though I have not seen anywhere suitable since we left last night's cave,' added Ceri.

They set off and, before long, were presented with a dilemma. The route ahead split in two, offering a choice of veering right or left.

'I didn't expect this. Which way do we go?' said Ruffle as they stood at the point where the path divided.

'I feel that if we veer right, then we go deeper into the mountains. To me, keeping left seems the better choice,' advocated Tansy.

'Why would there be two pathways?' pondered Ceri. 'It must mean someone or something uses these paths, as otherwise they would not exist. A path doesn't just appear; it is created by use.'

'I would prefer that you don't continue with that way of thinking, Ceri. We have seen no other animal or people, plus there is no sign that either path has been used recently. The snow is untouched,' observed Ruffle.

'Then I think it must be an old path that the mountain dwarves made. For they say that they often used these mountains before they upped and left,' added Tansy.

'Yes, that is certainly a possibility, in fact, more likely than any other explanation,' said Ceri.

'It will do for me,' said Ruffle.

'For my part, although I have no reason to be confident, I too prefer that we take the left path. I agree with Tansy, for it seems the one to the right takes us deeper into the mountains,' advocated Ceri.

'Fine, I can live with that. But I think we should get going, I am cold standing still,' said Ruffle.

They chose the left path and continued on. The sun had barely smiled most of the day and the wind was now a caress that barely stroked their faces. By late afternoon, when the sun was getting ready for bed and slinking slowly down, the friends were feeling slightly worried. It was getting colder and they had seen nothing all day that was suitable to use as a shelter. Now quiet and concentrated, they looked every which way for a haven. Albeit feeling more intense would make no difference as to whether they fund a shelter or not. Then, from far off, they heard a sound.

'Stop. Did you hear that? Listen!' said Ceri.

They listened, but all was silent except for the swirling gusts of wind.

'It was a howl. Did you hear it?'

'I heard it,' said Ruffle.

'Was it a wolf?' wondered Tansy.

'I don't know, but it is more reason for us to find a shelter and soon,' said Ruffle.

'Let's move,' said Ceri. 'There is something living up here besides us and I have no wish to meet it.'

Their footsteps quickened as did their sense of urgency to find refuge. The path was enclosed on both sides by mountains, which meant that they could not see very far ahead. Then the snow began to flutter down from the sky; sprinkling at first, it soon became thicker. It was not having to walk with lowered heads that felt uncomfortable, nor the obvious drop in the temperature, but the most eerie aspect was that the more it snowed, the quieter it became. There was no discernible wind just the silence of falling snowflakes. Before long, it was snowing so heavily that it limited visibility.

'Stay close, or we lose one another,' shouted Ceri as a blanket of white engulfed everything.

'What?' shouted Ruffle in response. The snow deadened the sounds.

'Stay close, look for shelter,' Ceri shouted back.

Ruffle nodded.

Suddenly, Tansy grabbed Ceri by the arm and pointed. Through the white curtain of snow, she could see what appeared to be a large black hole set into the mountainside. Ceri grabbed the arm of Ruffle. She pointed, then shouted, 'Shelter, there, a shelter.'

Ruffle could not hear her words but saw where she pointed. They fought through the curtain of snow, but as they drew closer, they realised that it was no cave, but a boulder set back where snow had not yet settled.

Once again shouting at her companions, Ceri cried out, 'Keep hold of one another, the snow will separate us.'

She had to repeat herself to be heard. With heads bowed, they pushed forward. The snow was fast becoming a thick blizzard. All around the shape of things was blurred into white. They could easily walk past a cave without realising it.

 They walked and walked, increasingly exhausted and cold. Each step was becoming harder. Shivering and weakening, their hopes of finding a shelter were diminishing. Then Ruffle shouted, but his words were lost in the damp silence. He grabbed both friends, pointed and then pulled them toward the mountainside. Moving closer to the stony walls, they all saw it. The mouth of a cave, not as large as the one they had slept in yesterday, but certainly one they could enter by stooping a little.

Without hesitation they went inside. Once past the threshold, they found that it was high enough to be able to stand up. They were shaking and shivering with the cold. They listened, but no sounds came from within the cave. They knew they should light a fire, but fingers and toes felt frozen.

'We need to warm up, let's huddle together and try to create some warmth,' suggested Ceri.

They tried but with little success. They continued shivering and shaking, teeth chattering and the frozen snow that now decorated their eyebrows was not melting; it was too cold. The wind had picked up as if from nowhere and now a blizzard danced outside the cave. Despite the incessant wind blowing hard and loud, suddenly a long piercing howl could be heard.

Ceri glanced at her friends, but it seemed that she had been the only one to hear it. She said nothing. Tansy and Ruffle were now sitting on the floor next to one another, with their backs to the wall and arms folded. Ceri thought it would not be helpful to tell her companions that wolves were close, for that is what she thought it was. She stood near the cave mouth, peering through the veil of snow, but saw nothing. When she turned back, her companions were slumped together, leaning on one another, their eyes heavy with sleep.

She was alarmed. She could not recall whom or when, but somewhere in her memory, she had been told that going to sleep when excessively cold was not a good idea; they would likely not wake up. She knew her friends were worn out, as she was, and sleeping seemed so attractive at that moment. But she thought that they should warm up before going to sleep.

She tried to wake them, but it was futile; they were already deep in slumber. Her own eyes were heavy. She was bitterly cold. She also wanted to sleep. It was a struggle and she huddled next to Tansy, hoping to find some warmth, but her eyes felt heavy and closing. She opened them again, but she was losing the fight, as her eyes closed all too easily. She thought, 'Is this how it will end?' Then she heard sounds which she decided must be her imagination.

Am I becoming delirious, she wondered? Then, through rapidly blinking eyes, she saw something huge and white coming toward her. It seemed to be grumbling, or was that her stomach? 'Am I imagining this?' she wondered again. She told herself to get up; she was afraid, but that was the last thing she remembered.

23

The Ultimatum

As the companions had slipped away out of the castle and into the Ironspine Mountains, they had left behind chaos. The chaos was within the castle as preparations for a siege occupied everyone. Duskhold was now a shell of a town. Most of its inhabitants had scurried into the castle seeking refuge. The remainder had fled away on the East Road. A tiny number had chosen to remain within the town.

The patience of the soldiers tasked with trying to create some order out of the chaos was stretched to the limit. Finding space for the townspeople to sleep and eat had meant opening closed areas of the castle that had been unused for years. Within the mighty fortress, voices were raised all day; arguing, shouting, crying and panic. Self-preservation was foremost in the minds of the refugees. It was a mighty effort to accommodate all, but by the time they lay down to sleep, each had been fed and provided with a bed.

Throughout the day, the soldiers on the battlements had watched the mayhem unfold. However, their primary attention was given to watching what the Girngog were up to. Hundreds of black tents and blood red flags had sprung up as the camp of the enemy took root. Their camp sat too far away to discern what was happening. In addition, news arrived of smaller encampments to the west, where more Girngog had arrived via the Pancake Lands. Brave scouts on horseback had returned, telling of the enemy establishing another camp in the southeast of Venterra. They had deliberately positioned themselves between the castle and Earthroot. In effect, Venterra was occupied and the castle surrounded.

In the early evening, the great gates of the castle were finally closed. The side door through which Wyll Storm had led the companions was bricked up and sealed, as if it had never been there. Wyll Storm had arrived back to find the small gate gone. But fortunately, upon his return, the main gate had not yet closed and he entered safely into the castle – much to the puzzlement of the guards who did not recollect seeing him leave. And where did he get five horses from? It was a puzzle that took their minds away from the looming conflict.

The gates were shut and the castle walls were patrolled. The soldiers were all but ready for the siege to begin. It was an unsettling sight for the guards as they gazed out over Duskhold. Usually so full of noise and lights, on this night it was dark, silent and deserted. No signs of life, just the wind blowing through empty streets. There were odd exceptions, the occasional dwelling where a light indicated the occupants had remained, hoping that they could befriend the Girngog.

Although the town had grown erratically, it had observed the ruling that no building could be constructed closer than a hundred paces from the castle. That left a strip of land between the town and castle where any foe would likely station their attack. This was now regarded as a strategic mistake by the command within the castle. But it was clearly too late to do anything about it. It was anticipated that the Girngog would occupy the town and launch attacks from there. Unfortunately, it was belatedly realised that the town could offer the enemy cover from castle bowmen.

The first evening, nothing happened; the enemy were content to remain within their own camp.

Overnight, there was nothing to report. So the king woke and breakfasted with his family. He then chaired a meeting with his commanders and administrators to discuss the day ahead. As the meeting began, there was a loud knock and a soldier entered. Apologising for the interruption, he informed the king that a message had been received.

The Girngog were asking for a parley at midday at the southern outskirts of the town. No reply was sought as it seemed they simply expected the king would wish to attend.

'Not even waiting for a reply. So be it. The enemy is correct this time. I will go, hopefully I should learn what it is that they want and perhaps forestall the unnecessary shedding of blood,' said the king to his meeting. 'Nonetheless, we must be prepared for any treachery. Have the archers be ready on the battlements. I will lead a small troop out to meet them.'

Shortly before midday, a hundred or so Girngog marched from their camp, stopping at the perimeter of the empty town. Among the small horde were a dozen riders, one holding a white flag. Unusually for Girngog, they were quiet in their waiting.

The great gates of Castle Black swung back and the king rode out, accompanied by thirty cavalry, all adorned with blue cloaks. They were the Royal Guard. They rode through the ghostly town and the echoes of the horses' hooves rang out as if to emphasise its emptiness. Reaching the southern side of the town, the king, accompanied by six of his horsemen, broke off and approached the waiting Girngog.

Most of the cavalry with the king had never seen the Girngog before and though they displayed no indication, the king knew that a number would be unnerved by the sight. As a foe, the Girngog were formidable in appearance. Mostly large, their bodies tattooed, they had wide, ugly misshapen faces and grinning yellow teeth, fearsome in their dishevelment. It was as if they had stepped out of someone's nightmare.

Sitting on a large horse in front of the enemy group was a big, heavy-muscled Girngog, his body inked with symbols and no hair. He smiled through crooked teeth and sat upright on his black mount.

The king rode within a few feet of him and stopped.

'What is it that you want and why are you here on my lands?' he said

'Straight to the point, I see. I am Trumvek and I am here to offer you this opportunity to surrender old king. If you accept, I guarantee all your people safe passage out of the castle and away from this land.'

The king paused, assessing Trumvek, before replying.

'I think you may have taken a wrong turn or mistaken me for someone else. You trespass on our land with ill intent and that can be costly even when done through ignorance. But I can be a forgiving man, so I offer you the opportunity to retreat and save us both from unnecessary conflict.'

'You are an old man and perhaps you cannot see so well. Do you think that we would be here if we were not certain of our purpose and victory? We will reduce your old house to rubble and feast on your feeble bodies if you resist. Your time has gone, Cadmus; your resistance will bring your people death. I will give you until midday tomorrow for you to accept my generous offer,' warned Trumvek.

'This is a foolish enterprise, Trumvek. I care nothing for your purpose, but you will suffer great consequences if you persist in this folly. For now, there is nothing more to be said, just leave whilst you can, you will not lose face,' said the king, who then turned his horse to re-join his troop.

Trumvek sat watching and grinning.

'So be it,' was all the Girngog uttered.

Leading his cavalry back into the castle, the king spoke to Commanders Pashorn and Fibert riding beside him.

'Prepare yourselves, for the battle will undoubtedly commence at midday tomorrow.'

As the last cavalry rider escorting the king entered the castle, the great gate was once again closed.

The king strode up to his chambers, deep in thought. He knew he was growing older, and truth be told, he had little appetite for another war. Yet he also knew that should anyone threaten his family or his people, the old warrior's fire within him would blaze once more. Castle Black had never fallen and he saw no reason it should succumb now.

As his page helped him out of his armour, he considered how this had all come about. Why this sudden aggression from the Girngog after years of peace? Had the apparent peace been a mere deception?

Perhaps there had been a clue in that parley with Trumvek, as he had noticed a cloaked rider sitting amongst the Girngog escort, a man dressed in the black attire of a sorcerer. It was not Merektar; he knew him by sight. But who was it? Was there now another sorcerer manipulating the Girngog?

The Girngog were a simple people, in some ways primitive, consisting of tribes that competed and fought amongst themselves. However, they were easily led, as Merektar had demonstrated in the past. Usually, they would not band together and had only done so when under the spell of a leader. Was it possible that Merektar had returned and united them, or was it someone else? Whoever it was, he felt sure that the cloaked figure sitting on a horse behind Trumvek was in the thick of this.

Or maybe he, the king, was to blame! Was it foolish of him to have travelled east and away from Venterra for so long? If he had been at home, then he might have spotted things brewing with the Girngog. He knew that contact between Venterra and Yasrall had decreased, and with it the opportunities of an early warning about the rise of the Girngog. Had he been too complacent about that? And had he compounded his complacency by leaving his brother in charge at Castle Black?

All of these questions ran through his mind as they had on multiple occasions in recent days. He decided that he could not know and would not discover any answers by sitting and thinking in his throne room. He drew on his own experience and reminded himself that now was not the time to dwell on such things. He had to deal with the situation that lay before him.

With his mind still full of questions, he was about to rise and go to speak with the Queen, when he heard a noise, one that he disliked.

'*Boom, boom, boom,*' it went.

He recognised the sound - the incessant throb of Girngog war drums. He knew that their war drums would continue throughout the night. It was the Girngog way of preparing for battle, intended to unsettle their enemies with endless drumming. '*Boom, boom, boom.*' It continued. It sounded a long way off, not near enough to prevent sleep but enough to disturb thoughts. And he knew it would achieve its aim with many in the castle. He sighed, stood up and made to go see his family. His mind now dominated by the one thought, that tomorrow, it begins.

24

Xynnar

Although her eyes were still closed, Ceri realised that she was awake. It was quiet, but she was warm and in a bed. How had it happened, she wondered? She recalled the cave, the cold and the snow. She could vaguely recall a large white figure, or was she imagining that? Beyond that, she could remember nothing.

She listened and could hear birds chattering away. And the sound of someone panting. Is this a dream, she thought? She opened her eyes and looked about, not sure what she expected to see. It was a room with sunshine streaming through the windows. She sat up and looked about. There was furniture, a table next to the bed. On the table, a jug and two cups. Two chairs, one of which was occupied. And that was all. It was the occupant of one chair who was doing the panting. Looking straight at her and wagging its tail sat a small, brown, floppy-eared dog.

'Hello, who might you be?' she asked.

With that, the dog jumped down and ran from the room.

'I must look awful to have scared that little dog away,' she thought to herself.

She leant over the table to see what was in the jug, but stopped in surprise as a black and white duck padded into the room. Where am I, she thought? Turning to greet the duck, she smiled and said 'Hello', expecting the duck to quack in response or run away. Instead, the feathered visitor responded by uttering the sound 'dub

dub, dub dub.' It was not what she expected. With a puzzled expression, she spoke again.

'Where am I, Mister Duck? Can you speak, as I think I might be in a dream!'

At that moment, a very striking woman entered the room wearing a wide smile.

'I see our 'dub dub' bird has already introduced himself. He is not shy; I'll give him that. He looks like a duck, but I assure you he is not. It's very good to see you awake; we were worried about you yesterday. It's been three days since you were brought down from the mountains and your friends have been rather anxious about whether you would ever wake.'

'Are they alright?' asked Ceri.

'Yes, they are fine and eager to see you.'

'The last thing I recall was that we were freezing in a cave and I think a big white figure was coming toward us, but I couldn't keep awake,' she explained.

'You are right, there was a large white figure; it was a snow troll. In fact, it was the snow trolls that rescued you and brought you to us,' said the dark-haired woman. 'The snow trolls patrol the mountain road and most people are afraid of them. The road itself is treacherous and many have perished trying to traverse it. The snow trolls do not harm travellers; it is they who save them when they can. They suffer from the poor reputation gained by the mountain trolls in Gritol. But they are quite different.'

'Oh, we were told to be afraid of them and avoid them, if at all possible,' replied Ceri.

'It is of no matter. We prefer that people fear them as it deters travellers from trying to cross the Ironspine. The constant climbing road, the cold and the thinner air, will usually overcome those who dare to use the old road. And once you start on it, then it is difficult to descend, as it runs at a great height for many leagues and then completely peters out. Originally an old mountain dwarf road, but long fallen into disuse, now it is little more than a path. It is only the snow trolls who still use it.'

'That is disappointing, does that mean we could not reach Yasrall by that route?' asked Ceri.

'Yes, your friends told me that was your purpose. But we can talk about that later. For now, you are safe here. I should have mentioned it sooner, you are in the village of Xynnar, which is within Tebira. And I am Adella. The people of Tebira are known as the Teb, which you may know. We are a peaceful people and you are most welcome.'

'Your fellow travellers are outside and will be happy to learn you are awake. They have asked many questions, but if you have any, please ask away. There is water in the jug and water for washing behind the partition. Your clothes have been cleaned, but you are welcome to wear the robes that are behind the partition.'

Ceri then noticed the partition, which she had thought was a complete wall.

'In your own time, come and join us outside. Call if there is anything you need.'

Ceri rose slowly, happy to find she felt well. She drank some cold water and freshened up. Her clothes were neatly folded on a chair behind the partition, washed and dried, so she dressed. Adella had worn a beautiful silk gown, yellow and decorated with flowers. Ceri had thought she looked like a princess. But the Chimble was quite content to put on her own jacket, trousers, and boots—though she left her furs aside.

Outside, she found her companions sitting by a small river that flowed close by. Upon seeing her, they both jumped up, ran toward her and exchanged long hugs.

'Thank the trees you are well. I cannot recall what happened, just the feeling of being so cold. Tell us, what do you remember?' said Tansy.

'I'm the same Ceri, I can't recall what happened,' added Ruffle.

'I remember very little. I saw you both sleeping and tried to wake you, but obviously, I couldn't. Then the cold got into my bones and all I wanted to do was sleep. I fought it, but my eyes felt so heavy. Then, it must have been just before I succumbed, I saw a big white figure approach, but even that was not enough to keep me from dropping off. I vaguely remember thinking it might be a snow troll, but I couldn't stay awake. Then the next thing I know is that I wake up in a lovely, warm and comfortable bed. Based on all the things said when we were in the castle, I thought the troll would eat us. I am rather surprised to learn that instead they were our rescuers.'

'We all owe them a debt of thanks,' said Ruffle.

'I have not yet seen any trolls hereabouts; do they live in Xynnar?' asked Tansy of Adella.

'No, they live within the high mountains. It gets too warm for them if they descend for any length of time. But be assured, I gave them fulsome thanks when they brought you down. One thing you should appreciate is that although they are related to the trolls that inhabit Gritol, they are very different. The snow trolls do not roast people and are much more intelligent than their cousins who mingle with the Girngog.'

'That is definitely good to know,' said Ruffle.

'How much sooner than me did you both wake up?' Ceri asked her friends.

'I think about three hours, though I did wake briefly yesterday. You do realise that we have slept for two days?' said Tansy.

At that point, two of the Teb emerged from the building with platters of food, which were placed on the ground where they sat.

'Let us eat and I will explain where you are,' suggested Adella.

Whilst they ate, Adella explained that Xynnar was a village, devoted to the teaching of creative and practical skills. It sat in the shadow of the Ironspine mountains. The river they now sat beside was the Xynnar River, which was fed by a high waterfall from water running off the mountains. The village derived its name from this, as it was known as Xynnar Falls. People from all over Tebira came to Xynnar to learn about painting, drawing, handwriting, sculpting, pottery and more.

Adella ran a special school for the most gifted children, who sometimes would stay for one or more years, living within the school. Some came with family members who would help with the school whilst their daughter or son studied. Others came alone.

'Once you are rested, I would be happy to show you around and introduce our pupils. I know they would be delighted to show you their creations,' suggested Adella. 'But first, I would appreciate understanding more of why you chose to venture across the mountains.'

Feeling grateful for being rescued and now warmed up, the friends were quite willing to talk. It was Ceri who responded first.

'Of course. I think it might make sense if Ruffle begins by describing what is happening in Yasrall, assuming he does not mind. As our story really begins with him.'

Ruffle was happy to begin and having told the tale before, he was becoming an accomplished storyteller. As he unfolded their tale, each of the friends contributed to explaining some details. Their account was comprehensive and took a little while. The Teb sat quietly, listening intently without interruption, waiting until the companions had finished.

'Well, I am sure that I have never met a Chimble before. It is a land I know nothing of. You may also be the first Chimbles to visit Tebira, so I welcome you. I also perceive from your tale that you have become close friends, not least after having shared such challenges in order to fulfill your quest. I truly admire and respect you all for your bravery,' said Adella.

She continued.

'You should also understand that we are aware of the Girngog transgressions in Yasrall. We do not become involved, but we watch. Tebira is a peaceful country and the world is much larger than the boundaries of the Old Kingdom.'

'Coincidentally, King Cadmus was recently in Tebira. He and his family stayed at the palace of our Queen, Polleema, for over a year. The queen is young and I think she will have valued the wisdom of Cadmus. I believe relations between our lands were strengthened as a result.'

'I also know that in the past we have been allies with Venterra to help repel the Girngog. I think it is referred to as the Dragon Wars. We had dragons who fought o our side. But that was long ago. Our old king has since died and Polleema is now queen.'

'Tebira is a vast area and our boundaries are extensive. In days long gone, we fought our own invaders who came from the east, mostly the Skove. My appearance here may be deceptive, but it is not so long ago that I was once a warrior myself,' said Adella.

Before she could say more, Tansy interrupted her.

'Adella, do you think Tebira might consider helping us now?'

Adella had not expected the question and paused.

'Honestly, Tansy, I do not know.'

'Yes, forgive me. It was not a fair question and I realise that you cannot speak for the whole of Tebira,' apologised Ceri.

'We are not a country that relishes war. We prefer to trade and learn. However, it is also true that we do have a considerable army. We have had to defend ourselves from invaders. In fact, we have three main armies and it is the Sudoorn who protect this area.

As to your question about Tebira helping you, I personally could promise nothing, but on your behalf, I could ask those who decide such things,' said Adella.

'If you could, that would be so helpful,' said Ceri.

'Please do not raise your hopes, it is likely to be in vain, though the fact that King Cadmus has established closer contact with Tebira may help your cause,' asserted Adella, not wishing to encourage false hopes.

'But you are all forgetting something,' chimed Ruffle. 'How can we possibly go from here to the other side of the mountains to help Yasrall. From what you have said, nobody could march across the Ironspine; too many would perish in so doing. Sadly, I also think it might be too late to help anyway, as it would take so long to reach my land. I fear it would be too late and Yasrall will be destroyed.'

'You are right, Ruffle,' agreed Ceri gloomily. 'We are on the wrong side of the mountains. An army would perish in trying to go over the Ironspine.'

'There may be a solution to both of your concerns, but I will talk of that later,' said Adella.

'However, you should understand that any decision about going to war would have to be made in Elenembos, our largest town, where the palace is situated and from where our land is ruled. When our old king died and his son succeeded him, he was killed fighting the Skove just one year later. He had three children who would succeed to the throne and the eldest is Polleema. She only recently came of age and was crowned queen.'

'Elenembos is in the middle of our land, past Dragon Mountain. Tebira is so big that it will take several days to reach the palace by horse. Then the Queen would call a Royal Council and they would discuss and decide about your request. Though crowned as queen, she must yet refer to the Council until she reaches the age to rule in her own right. How long it would take the Royal Council to reach a decision, I simply don't know. Under the old king, I would have little hope, but now, I don't know. It may be that any decision would not be obtained very swiftly, my friends. Perhaps too late for Yasrall.'

'What is Dragon Mountain?' said Ruffle. 'I mean, why is it called that?'

Adella gave a small laugh because she was expecting someone to ask the question.

'It is called that because that is where the dragons live.'

'Dragons! I thought they were just part of our history, now just something to frighten the children, surely, they no longer exist!' exclaimed Tansy.

'Oh no. Many generations of Teb have befriended the dragons. It is said that they have lived within the mountain since it was formed. Of course, there are less dragons alive now, but Vazzorg continues. She is the mother of all living dragons in Tebira and has been here for generations. She is the only black dragon and the one who speaks the common tongue. If we had time, I would take you there, for in the summer months, Vazzorg allows people to visit the mountain and they show off flying and roaring fire. It is truly a wondrous sight watching them take to the skies. They are so big and if within fifty steps, you can feel the heat emanating from their long bodies. As a testimony to the trust that has grown between Tebira and the dragons, we have a dragon rider. He is the only person the dragons will allow to ride them. Now his story is fascinating, but that is for another day.'

'What would I give to see a dragon! That would be something to tell my children,' Ruffle exclaimed, clearly imagining the event.

'Is Tebira the only place dragons exist?' asked Ceri.

'I don't truly know, for it is believed that there are living dragons in Skovelenbar. But that may not be true.'

'So, you have children, Ruffle? That is something you never mentioned before,' Tansy teased him.

'No, I do not have children. I do not have a wife. Although there is someone that I had begun stepping out with; that is before all this Girngog trouble began,' answered Ruffle.

'You have kept that quiet for some time,' said Tansy, lightly punching his arm. 'Who is she?'

'Not now. I will tell you once matters are more settled,' he said. Then he fell quiet and a look of sadness spread over him as his thoughts drifted. Trying to brighten matters, Tansy spoke.

'Well, one day I think we should all see the dragons.'

'I hope you do,' said Adella. 'For now, let me compose a letter on your behalf to seek the help of the queen. In fact, let us do it now,' suggested the Teb.

So, the companions, Adella and a scribe called Jobi, all sat down and spent the next few hours composing the message to send to Elenembos as a request for help. Adella proposed they also send a shorter copy with a bird, as that would reach Elenembos more swiftly. The full, detailed letter was to be delivered in person by Jobi, who, as Adella's assistant, had remained with the group throughout the day, listening as the friends shared their story.

Once the message was completed, Jobi wasted no time in saddling a horse and setting off.

'She is an excellent rider and I know she will make good time, but it will still be three days before she reaches Elenembos,' said Adella as she watched Jobi gallop out of Xynnar.

Ceri had become fidgety as the day wore on. Her thoughts dwelt on time. She worried that they were taking too long to reach Chimbleton. After being rescued, she had slept for more than two days, and then another day planning. Now they were having to wait for their request to reach Elenembos. That would be discussed before an answer was given. Then there were no guarantees that any assistance would be given. After all that, if the decision was favourable, how long would it take for the Teb army to organise and set off? If the decision was negative, then they would be in the same position as they are today, but having lost almost a week. It was quite unusual for Ceri, but her impatience was plain for all to see.

'You look like you have ants in your clothes. I have never seen you so twitchy, unable to sit still, do you want to talk?' said Tansy quietly, hoping to help her friend.

'I am fine,' was the reply.

'If you insist,' said Tansy. 'But if it helps, you know we can talk.'

Ceri touched Tansy on the arm, stood up and walked outside. They had been conferring in a large room as to what detail to put in the letter to the queen. Most had already left the room. She looked out at the river, plainly troubled by her thoughts.

'What do you think it is that disturbs Ceri so?' Ruffle asked of Tansy as they observed their friend.

'I think it is having to wait around. Plus, I suspect that all we have been through is taking its toll on her. She is the most sensible person I know and the captain of her emotions. She is usually so patient. But she is unable to affect anything at this moment and it does not sit well with her.'

'I have felt something similar for a good while now, ever since the Girngog asserted themselves across Yasrall. It is not a comfortable feeling. But my deciding to strike out to enlist help from King Cadmus restored me. It helped me to feel I was regaining some influence over my own destiny. She is doing something similar and perhaps she should be reminded of this,' advocated Ruffle.

'I suspect it is Chimbleton that she worries for rather than herself,' concluded Tansy. 'But I think your insight is well-founded, Ruffle.'

The next day the two friends spent most of the time looking around Xynnar. They left Ceri to her own thoughts. As the afternoon cooled, all returned to the dwelling they shared. An inviting smell informed them that the evening meal was being prepared. Gathered around a table, in between eating, Ceri spoke to her companions.

'I will ask Adella what it was that she referred to when she made the comment earlier that crossing the Ironspine may not be as difficult as it seems. I have made a decision for myself. I cannot sit and wait for something that may or may not be forthcoming. I must try and get back to Chimbleton as soon as I can. It is my decision, I ask nothing of anyone else. I will go alone.'

Ruffle responded.

'Forgive me, but as your friend, I need to be blunt. From what you have said, I believe now you may have a deeper appreciation of what I felt about Yasrall being invaded, how helpless I felt. But you will also understand I learned that, on my own, I could make little difference to the plight of my people. Sadly, I think the same must be true for you, Ceri. I know that is not what you wish to hear. Nonetheless, it is true. One person cannot stop the Girngog.'

'I know you speak sense, Ruffle and that you are right. I just feel so useless. We need the help of the Teb or King Cadmus. But neither looks forthcoming. What would be best is that Chimbleton is yet undiscovered. If that were true then I would be worrying unnecessarily. But obviously I cannot know this until I return home. My worry is like a splinter that I cannot remove. Chimbleton could not defend itself. So, I feel that I must return as soon as I can; it has become so important to me.'

'Ceri, you know that I share your worries, but you are not making sense. Of course, I also long to be home and to defend Chimbleton from the Girngog. But we alone cannot protect the valley. We must have help. That is why we must wait. We recognised that it was true for Ruffle, which was why we helped him get to Castle Black. And besides, I have to confess that even my battle skills might not be enough to protect you,' laughed Tansy as she tried to lighten the mood.

Ceri smiled for the first time in some while.

'You are right, Tansy the Wise, I know that. I think today, all that we have been through has caught up with me. In particular, I keep thinking of our succumbing to the cold of the Ironspine mountains with you both asleep and helpless. I felt responsible. I felt that I had let you both down. Will I let Chimbleton down, too? The only way I can clear my mind will be to take action. If Adella can show me a way to cross the Ironspine, I must take it. I must do something and soon.'

'Well, you are not alone in being desperate to help Chimbleton, but once again I put to you, is our time not better used in bringing along allies?' said Tansy.

'Yes, of course, Tansy, but where are those allies. We have none. At this point, it is up to us,' said Ceri.

'Forgive me in stating the obvious and practical, but we are the wrong side of the Ironspine mountains to be considering how we can help,' said Ruffle.

'Which is why I need Adella to clarify what she inferred this morning,' said Ceri.

'Well, I don't wish to see you upset, but it will be a mighty challenge for anyone to cross the highest mountains in the kingdom. Don't get your hopes up,' advised Ruffle.

And for some while, that comment ended the discussion.

Adella joined them soon after to say a meal was being served in a large dining area. She noticed the gloom in the mood of Ceri. Several of the children and their families ate with them and brought along examples of what they had accomplished at Xynnar. There were wonderful paintings and drawings. Ceri particularly liked those that had been done in black and white. Then there were cups, plates and teapots, all exquisitely hand-painted and glazed by the pupils. One small girl even offered to paint Tansy a portrait. By the time the students left, the three travellers found themselves bestowed with gifts and feeling more relaxed.

The evening spent in the company of the children had proven to be a much-needed counter balance to the serious and sombre mood that had prevailed during the day. Everyone had relaxed, their thoughts momentarily lifted from the weight of their task. However, once only Adella remained with the companions Ceri told her that she intended to set out for Chimbleton the following day. The solemn mood quickly returned.

Once again, there was a conversation in which Adella attempted to dissuade Ceri from leaving too soon, urging her to wait for a response from Elenembos. She was supported by Tansy and Ruffle, who put forward arguments as to the folly of attempting such a journey on their own, given none of them knew which way to go. But Ceri was unusually stubborn; it was not just her determination to make her way to Chimbleton but her refusal to listen to any other points of view. It was unlike Ceri and though she remained calm, it made the discussion difficult.

Like a dog with a bone, she persistently asked Adella what she had meant by her comments about crossing the Ironspine.

'Adella, you mentioned that there is a way to get to Yasrall, which I believe is the nearest land on the other side of the mountains. Which means it would bring me closer to Chimbleton. Can you explain this to me, please?' Ceri pleaded.

Adella paused, as if considering whether she should share such information or not. Her audience of three sat in silence, waiting and all curious as to her reply.

'In days long gone, Tebira traded closely with the dwarves who lived within the Ironspine mountains. They dwarves built extensively within the rock. Great rooms, tunnels, passageways, mines and roads were created and extended for leagues through the mountain range. It was an inner world of rock and stone, unknown to the outer world.'

'Then, without explanation, the mountain dwarves simply upped and moved away. Nobody knew why. But they were gone. Now the world within the mountain was closed to us and remains quiet. There is still a belief amongst some that the dwarves will return one day, but they sealed the entrances leading to the outside world with spells and enchantments. This included the roads that ran between Tebira and Yasrall.'

'Few realise that one of the entrances is here in Xynnar. It is a road that links to others within the mountains, but its main route is to Yasrall. If ever Tebira were to aid Yasrall, then it is most likely that it would do so using that road. That is what I was referring to.'

Nowadays, few people know of these entrances and you should not tell anyone about them. Most folk within Tebira do not know how close the world of the mountain dwarves is to Xynnar. Although, as I said, the ways in and out of the mountains are now closed, held fast by incantations that few know about.'

Despite the caution lacing all that Adella said, the faces of the three companions had brightened. All kinds of possibilities ran through their minds.

'Are you able to open any of these entrances, Adella?' enquired Ceri.

It was a question Adella appeared reluctant to answer. Her face was stern and thoughtful. Eventually, she replied.

'Yes, I can. I was honoured to be trusted by the dwarves. But it is forbidden to do so without the consent of the Council in Elenembos.'

'Surely you might open it for a few seconds to allow one person through?' quizzed Ceri.

'Two people you mean,' Tansy quickly asserted.

'Three, if you don't mind. We are committed together. Besides, three would make no real difference from one,' added Ruffle.

The three friends laughed and Ceri felt gratitude and relief that her closest friends had effectively told her that they would go with her.

Adella felt it necessary to remind her visitors of their position.

'After all that you said earlier about the futility of one person reaching Chimbleton, it is surely just as true for three! Please do not reach for false hope, the entrance is long sealed and as I have just said, permission would be needed before any entrance could be opened again.'

But Ceri was like a hound seeking a scent and she had just sniffed one. She posed a clever question to Adella.

'What if the Council say they will not become involved? Would you then still deny us access through these tunnels to reach Yasrall?'

Recognising how quick-witted Ceri was being, Adella smiled. Despite the stubbornness of the Chimble, she admired her.

'That is an unfair question, Ceri. You are asking me to break our laws. I should repeat that I cannot grant you access without Council approval. Besides, it can be very confusing inside those mountains and it is likely that you would soon become lost, probably forever. Besides, I am unsure if I can recall the incantation to unlock the entrance. Meanwhile, let us wait and hope the Council look favourably upon your request.'

But the conversation swung back and forth. Now, all three friends were urging Adella to open the entrance into the mountain.

Ceri was surprised to hear her two companions express their wish to join her, as she had been prepared to undertake the journey alone. They had changed their minds, and though she didn't know why, she was glad they had.

Adella held up her hands as if to stop any further talk.

'Let me say one final thing for today. The roads within the mountain are long and varied. It is now a dark and empty place. The entrance here is an ancient passageway that, if opened, would not go unnoticed. As I have said, I cannot violate the oaths I have taken without the permission of the Council of Government. You now ask too much of me. I must implore that you have some patience. I am sure the gravity of your situation will be appreciated at Elenembos, but there are wider implications involved. Not least if the gate is opened and the Sudoorn travel through to Yasrall, then it is effectively a decision to go to war. Such matters cannot be considered lightly. I would ask that we speak no more of this tonight.'

Her words brought home to the three friends the gravity of their request. They ceased pestering Adella. Frustrated and disappointed, but glad that they had discussed matters, the rest of the evening passed quietly without any more reference to the mountain entrance. They seemed to have accepted that there was no choice other than waiting for the decision from the Council in Elenembos, much to the relief of Adella.

25

Siege

The whole garrison at Castle Black was primed, ready for the first onslaught from the Girngog. Cadmus had no concern that the enemy would be able to breach the fortress, but he knew that for many in his army, this would be their first taste of warfare. War was never anything other than horrific and there would be a variety of reactions to the brutality that they would witness. So, he spent time briefing his officers to maintain discipline and make some allowance for the inexperienced soldiers adjusting to the bloody reality.

Understanding the significance of his own demeanour for his soldiers, the king toured the castle offering encouraging words and humour where he could. The mighty fort was too large for him to visit every section, but his presence boosted morale and word quickly spread that the king was in good spirits.

It was while striding through the castle and perusing the levels where much of the dry food was stored, that he saw two sentries on guard by the dungeon. There were no prisoners in the dungeon. But there was a locked door. Instantly, he recalled that behind the heavy door was the Crown of Connection. The Crown had been one of the three Instruments of Light wielded by Master Olbus in the Girngog war. The three Instruments had been separated and secured secretly. The crown was locked away here and supposedly, only Cadmus knew of its presence in the castle. In fact, his brother Hewl also knew.

There was just one key for the locked door, which Cadmus had left with Hewl. Hewl had handed the key back to Cadmus upon his return from the east. The king had the keys on him and decided to take a look at the crown. Accompanied by Commander Fibert and four of the Royal Guard, he bade them wait outside as he entered the room. Closing the door behind him, he allowed his eyes to adjust to the dim light cast by the flames of the torch he carried. A glass case had been made for the crown and it sat upon a stone plinth. He stared and then walked closer to look. His eyes had not deceived him. Quite clearly, the crown was no longer there.

Cadmus felt a quiet sense of alarm. He was not afraid for the crown, knowing it was merely a replica. It held no power whatsoever. That was a secret possessed only by the king, he had not told his brother. Still, as far as he was aware, only he and Hewl knew that this crown was within the castle. He had instructed Hewl to tell no one. But now it was gone; how had it vanished? He doubted very much that Hewl had taken it.

He said nothing as he exited the room and locked the door behind him. He questioned the guards as to who had been in the room. They kept a written record, although there was little reason to do so, as the only person who entered the room in the entire time King Cadmus had been away, was Prince Hewl on two occasions. He decided that he would speak with Hewl once his tour of the castle ended.

At that time, midday was fast approaching and the king was aware that if the Girngog carried out their threat, then the siege would soon commence. It was time to make his way up to the battlements. He emerged into the daylight to find the inner and outer walls lined with soldiers, many with bows, watching and waiting.

A sense of expectation permeated the castle defenders. What would the Girngog do first? For a while, nothing appeared to be happening. The incessant drumbeat in the Girngog camp that had begun shortly after dawn continued. Suddenly, a loud murmur rippled throughout the battlements. The Girngog were on the move, making their way toward Duskhold.

'A mistake, Fibert. Although barely half a league away, that damn town is in the wrong place,' said the king. 'It should have been built to the east or the west, away from the castle. Sitting in front of us, it will afford the Girngog some cover. If we end up fighting within the town, then that will be costly.'

'Indeed, Majesty. Though I suspect the town took root a long time ago, perhaps even before your lifetime, Majesty,' responded Commander Fibert.

'Yes, you are right. Besides, there is nothing we can do about it now,' said the king.

It was a fact. The Girngog moved closer, like a shadow darkening the land minute by minute. Upon reaching the town, they poured into every street and building. The occasional scream and shout signalled that the few who had remained in the town had been found by the invaders. In less than an hour, the enemy had spread all over the town and stood in a long line not fifty paces away from the castle wall. They stretched the entire width of the great fortress.

Without warning, it began. A barrage of arrows flew upward and rained against the outer castle wall. Soldiers scurried for cover and the castle archers replied. In return, the Girngog sent shafts soaked in oil and burning. They sizzled through the air. But the burning darts had little effect and simply bounced off the stone walls. The Girngog had recognised that there was little point in trying to approach the outer wall, deterred by the deep moat. It was wide and they quickly understood that in trying to wade across it, they would become easy targets for the castle archers.

As the king had expected, the marauders wheeled out machines, mostly catapults that sling stones, or big jars of oil that spread fire upon impact. But it was all with little effect. The walls of the castle were simply too thick. This first onslaught from the Girngog endured for several hours, but the main consequence was to increase the confidence of those within the stone fortress.

Early in the evening, the siege paused and the Girngog retreated. Most returned to the black tents of their camp. Though some were observed sheltering within the vacant buildings of Duskhold.

'Is that the best that they can throw at us?' queried one smiling soldier to another. They were standing between the ramparts, staring at the retreating enemy. Commander Fibert was walking past when he heard the comment.

'Do not be fooled, soldier. That was merely the enemy prodding. They were assessing us and estimating what it would take to properly assail the castle. Rest while you can, for things will get harder.'

That evening, the king met with Prince Hewl. He had not spoken with him at any length since his return. He questioned him about his actions in his absence, without disclosing that he knew the crown to be gone. He learned that not too long after the king had set off to the east, a man had risen to favour at the court. Hewl insisted that this man had proven himself to be astute and before very long, became his trusted advisor. His name was Rillet. Strangely, it now seemed that he was nowhere to be found; he had disappeared.

The king's questions were wide-ranging and though unhappy with some of the actions taken and conclusions made by Hewl, he displayed no anger and accepted what his brother was telling him. The king knew that Hewl was naïve, but he was essentially honest. Eventually, he asked how often he had been to view the crown secured deep within the castle. Hewl replied that not once had he done so.

That afternoon, the king had directed his own physicians and alchemists to inspect the room where the crown had been kept, for he had his own suspicions. Their findings confirmed what the king believed he had recognised. He told Hewl bluntly.

'I take no pleasure in informing you, Hewl, but in your guise someone visited the crown twice. In truth, I suspect it was your man Rillet and furthermore i believe he was a shapeshifter. He has now made away with the crown. You have been fooled, brother.'

Hewl questioned the king, for he could not accept that this was true. But after hearing from the king's counsellors and practitioners, who knew the tell-tale signs of a shapeshifter, he accepted the conclusion, that he had been duped. He had trusted Rillet and now he realized that he had been dancing to his tune all along. He was distraught and angry with himself, and at a loss as to how he could make amends.

'Are you telling me that an Instrument of Power has been lost on my watch? Why didn't you warn me what was at stake? I thought it was just a very valuable crown. Now all that befalls us will be of my doing.'

The king showed little sympathy, but within himself, he was pained to see his younger brother so troubled.

'My dear brother, as foolish as you were to disregard the advisors that I designated to guide you, all is not lost. The crown that was taken was not the real Crown of Connection. It was placed there to focus the attention of those who might wish to gain it. Very few knew that it was a false artefact. It was bait. It was meant to draw out those who seek its power. However, it has no power within it. It is simply coloured stones and metal. It has no intrinsic magical value.'

'Although this Rillet character has evaded us, we now know what we suspected - that there is an active force seeking to gain the power that the Instruments wield. Given what is now happening outside our own gates, I think it may be a fair assumption that we also know where such scheming originates.'

Prince Hewl was relieved, but disappointed that he had not been told that the crown was merely a copy. But then he understood why he had not been told, given that it had been stolen whilst he was in command.

'I will find a way to make some amends for my woolly-headed idiocy,' said Hewl.

'I believe that you will, brother,' said the king. 'I believe you will.'

Over the next week, the siege of Black Castle slipped into a routine. The Girngog would launch an attack led by their archers. The soldiers on the castle battlements took cover and in turn, responded with their own arrows. This repeated each day. The Girngog made no progress in encroaching upon the castle walls. They were not equipped to threaten its defences. Many of those inside the castle relaxed, confident that the castle was impenetrable.

But in the second week, matters changed. Within their camp, the Girngog had been busy. The evidence of this appeared over several days as wooden towers sprouted high above the black tents. Then, large catapults were observed being slowly transported from their camp toward Duskhold. During several nights, there were all kinds of sounds coming from the occupied town. Banging, shouting, and odd machine-like noises, carried on day and night.

Then, towards the end of the second week of the siege, it became clear what had been going on. During the night the groaning of wood and the grinding of wheels had generated such noise that it spooked many a young soldier. It was when the darkness lifted that it became clear what the enemy had been up to. Arranged along the grassy knoll in front of the castle sat the machinery of war.

Positioned between the towers were massive catapults and ballistae, some reaching as high as the castle walls. These posed a different kind of threat, and the complacency of many of the castle's soldiers would soon be tested. The danger of the Girngog was about to become all too real.

26

The Unused Road

At Xynnar, the three companions had no other option than to wait for the Council at Elenembos to make its decision. Adella would not open the mountain entrance. So, they busied themselves as best they could. Ceri decided to learn more about Tebira, its customs and history. Tansy and Ruffle opted for more practical pastimes. Having learned that Adella was an accomplished swordswoman and a master of unarmed combat, they persuaded her to teach them some new skills.

In fact, few Teb knew of her background as a warrior. They involved qualities that she did not need to apply in her role as leader of the Xynnar Falls school. Nonetheless, she agreed to teach the two friends. Unsurprisingly, she proved to be a very effective teacher and both companions made noticeable progress in a short span of time.

It was a struggle for Ceri to control her impatience, but understanding Adella could do nothing to quicken the decision-making of the Council, the three friends did not harass her on the matter. They had been at Xynnar ten days when Adella received word from the Council.

'You will be pleased to learn that the Council of the Queen have agreed to help. In their letter of decision, they stress that the friendship and partnership now established with King Cadmus was a key factor. They write that they are dismayed to learn Venterra is under attack. The Sudoorn are already in preparation. It is decided that they will advance on Yasrall entering via the dwarf roads. The old doorway here at Xynnar Falls is to be opened,' relayed Adella.

The three friends hugged one another and thanked the Teb warrior. Ceri felt a weight lift from her shoulders. But Adella punctured their joy with a point of caution.

'It is good news and I am happy with the decision. However, I do not know how long it will take the Sudoorn to get here. They have to organise and arrange provision for such a campaign. I would ask that your patience be extended, my friends, for it may take a good few days.'

'You have mentioned them before, but who are the Sudoorn?' asked Ruffle.

'The Sudoorn is the name of the army based on the southern and western side of Tebira. You see, Tebira is a very large land and the distance between the east and west is too great for one army to defend. So, in effect, Tebira has three armies. The Nordoorn, the Widoorn and the Sudoorn. However, the Sudoorn are not so near as to be able to arrive as swiftly as you would wish.'

'Are the Sudoorn enough to fight the Girngog?' wondered Ruffle.

'Oh yes, Ruffle. Tebira is a huge country and we have a big population. The armies were created following the invasion by the Skove in years gone by. One army based in the centre of Tebira was unable to react quickly enough across the whole of the land. Consequently, three armies were created situated at different points across the land.'

'Oh, I see,' said the Rall.

For the remainder of that day, the three friends were buoyant and talked of little else other than the journey they hoped to embark upon very soon. But overnight, Ceri felt her impatience wreak havoc with her emotions. Knowing they had been granted passage through the mountains, she was eager to make a start. She expressed her keenness to her companions and advocated that they could begin the trek knowing that the Teb army would be following. She convinced her companions that they approach Adella to propose the idea.

Adella listened to their proposal in silence and then replied.

'I realise how hard it has been for you having to wait, but having got a positive decision from the Council, I urge you to have a little more patience. I am sure the Sudoorn will arrive before too long.'

As sensible as the advice from the Teb was, it did not deter Ceri, who persisted in pleading with Adella.

'Adella, you have been a wonderful host and friend, and you have our deepest appreciation. We are also very happy with the decision your Council has made. But having to wait another ten days feels too long. All that we now ask is that you allow us to make a start. We could spy ahead so that the Sudoorn can be informed of what awaits them.'

'Ceri, please listen. It may not be ten days; in fact, I am sure it will be sooner. The message says the Sudoorn are already in motion. You should know that the dwarf tunnels running through the mountain are long and confusing. They are dark and unused for many years. If I let you in, then you would likely be lost forever. And that would happen if you simply took a wrong turn. And that would benefit no one. Plus, I would be disobeying my oath if I opened the doorway before the Sudoorn arrive.'

Being especially stubborn, Ceri continued to press Adella, almost as if she had not heard the words of the Teb teacher. After much back and forth, Adella felt worn down and a little annoyed with Ceri.

'Enough, Ceri, I will make a concession to you. I appreciate your strong desire to return to your people, but the journey involves much more than passing through the mountain. Have you considered what you might find once you arrive in Yasrall? The Girngog might be there waiting and that would endanger more than yourselves.'

'But there is something useful we can do which will speed matters along. We can begin to light the way for the Sudoorn. Although the dwarves did not need them, there are hundreds of torches alongside the road within the mountain that will have to be lit. As you will appreciate, in the depths of the mountain, there is, of course, no sunlight. An army moving through a dark tunnel, having to light the way as it proceeds, would be slow. However, I am most familiar with the mountain road, so I will lead the way for all of us, Sudoorn included, by lighting the torches. It will facilitate their progress. That is my compromise to your demands; it will have to appease you.'

'That sounds a splendid idea, thank you,' grinned Ceri as she rubbed her hands together. 'I am sorry, Adella, for being so annoying.'

'But and I mean this, we go no further than reaching the entrance that opens into Yasrall. We do not enter Yasrall without the Sudoorn. The benefit of this is that the army will not be slowed if the road is already lit. So, are you agreed?' asked Adella.

'Definitely. And again, thank you,' said Ceri.

'I would say that we are all agreed,' said Tansy.

'My foolishness will no doubt bring much trouble to my door, but that is what we shall do,' muttered Adella. 'Tomorrow, we will need horses and several of my people, for the road is long and there are many torches to light. But now let us have no more talk and instead concentrate our energies on preparation. Be ready to travel in the morning.'

With that, Adella took leave of the companions.

That evening, they saw little of Adella. Their own preparations did not take long and they sat by the river enjoying the warmth of the evening.

'I am glad that we are finally making a move. I admit I am intrigued to tread the paths that the dwarves created, although I am also a little nervous. I still wonder why they simply upped and went away. Was it something inside the mountain that we might come across? Then, once we get through the mountains, what will we find in Yasrall? Forgive me being blunt, but you do realise, Ruffle, we may well find your lands overrun with Girngog?' said Tansy.

'Well, if we emerge from the mountains in the area where I think we might, then it will be the northernmost part of Yasrall; probably the area I know least. Truthfully, I cannot imagine why the Girngog would be there. It is rough, colder than most of Yasrall and hard, unforgiving land. There are few people living there. It would be of no profit for them to occupy that area. So, I am doubtful we will encounter many Girngog, at least to begin with,' suggests Ruffle.

'Are there not farms or villages?' asked Ceri.

'Very few, it's not good farm land. But it's possible the Girngog have guards stationed thereabouts anyway,' mused Ruffle.

'I am not sure why they would,' disagreed Tansy. 'Surely they do not expect anyone to approach them from the mountains!'

'Yes, with the dwarves gone, the mountain roads closed, you may be right,' conceded Ruffle.

'How far is Clinglewood Forest from where you think we will emerge?' asked Ceri.

'Again, I can't say very accurately. I think Clinglewood stretches right up to the Ironspine, which would mean it cannot be too far. But then again, I have not been there and I am not sure where the entrance we will use is, so I don't really know,' replied the Rall.

Ceri crossed her arms and leant back, clearly sorting her thoughts before speaking.

'I know that it has been my urging and impatience that have badgered Adella into making this move. And now that we are to finally go, I find I am realising the risk it entails. I suspect that I'm being foolhardy and unfair to Adella. I know the wise choice is to wait for the Sudoorn.'

'No, I think the bigger risk would be for us to try and cross Yasrall alone. Lighting the road through the mountain in advance seems an excellent idea to me. We help everyone by doing this,' argued Tansy. 'What would be foolish is to think that we can avoid any Girngog in returning home.'

'And I will add my endorsement. At some point, I know we will come face-to-face with the Girngog, which I am not looking forward to. But nonetheless, I am ready to go. I have enjoyed being here and learning from Adella. But the opportunity to make a move is welcome. I admit that I dread what I might find in Yasrall. I suspect my heart will be broken by what they have done to my land. Yet if there is a possibility that we can warn Chimbleton or indeed help them avoid the same fate, then let us get there as soon as we can,' said Ruffle.

Ceri laughed half-heartedly.

'I am a fool. I realise it is ironic that it is I who is now getting cold feet. I hope my impatience has not prompted us to make an unwise decision.'

'My dear Ceri, I do not know whether to applaud you or kick you,' laughed Adella gently. She had quietly joined the friends without being noticed and heard most of what had just been said. She continued.

'You seek certainty and assurance, but no one can give you that. It is not a comfortable feeling. But the most helpful thing to do is to make a decision and deal with the consequences of that choice. It is no surprise that you are unsure, but you alone are not solely responsible for the decision. The Council of Elenembos and I have been party to these decisions. We are agreed, we all move ahead together. So, don't apportion all the responsibility on yourself; we all carry our share. Interrogating yourself will not help now that the decision is made,' said Adella.

'I agree, we are all in this together, we win and we lose together,' said Tansy.

'Right, well, I'm off to find sleep now. I came to tell you that I have received word that the Sudoorn are already on the march, so we may see them sooner than I thought. For now, I bid you a good night's rest. We will set off first thing tomorrow,' said Adella.

The next morning was spent on breakfast, packing, and preparing to meet their horses. Adella arrived with eight mounted Teb, and everyone was ready to depart. Much of Xynnar still lay in slumber.

'Now I will reveal to you the knowledge that few possess. The entrance we seek is unremarkable; there are no indications of it being a doorway. It is found on the flat rockface to the side of the waterfall feeding the river. The road we take runs up to the waterfall and then past it. The door is protected by spells which I must lower, assuming I can recall the words. It will take a little time, but once done, we can leave it open for the Sudoorn to follow us,' explained Adella.

'Is it an entrance the dwarves built?' asked Ceri.

'Yes, a very long time ago. It was a useful conduit to Yasrall. Few Teb ever spent time within the mountain. It is not a natural habitat for us. However, before the dwarves disappeared, several of us came to know certain roads very well. The road we take is one of those. Although the dwarves were always welcoming, many Teb have always found it unnerving to traverse the dark paths that wind inside the mountains. It was truly the world of the dwarves. Sadly, they are now gone and their subterranean world is quiet.'

'The hasty exit of the dwarves heightened the fears of those Teb anxious about entering the mountain. Rumours spread and many are fearful of what may still live there. But the dwarves sealed the entrances so those who are curious could not enter. There remains just a handful of us who know how to unlock the spell used to seal the entrances.'

'Well, I confess I am also wary of travelling underneath a mountain. Though I am also excited at the prospect of experiencing it,' Ceri responded.

'I admit I am curious. After all, my ancestors once lived within the mountains,' said Ruffle.

'After listening to you, Adella, my caution about entering the mountain is deepened. I have no enthusiasm for this route. Hello, what is that noise?' interjected Tansy, interrupting herself.

A roaring rumble could be heard.

'It's not my stomach,' grinned Ruffle, 'perhaps it's yours!'.

'That is the waterfall,' said the Teb.

'I thought it would be more of a trickle' queried Ruffle.

'It is small in comparison with others we have in Tebira. But I suppose it is rather loud. In fact, we are likely to find that once we are close, the noise will make conversation difficult. I will need to get close to the rock. Our voices will be drowned out. I will have to use simple hand signals to communicate.'

Adella halted the group of riders twenty paces from the glistening black rock. They could feel the spray from the falling water on their faces. Dismounting, Adella then approached the left side of the rockface. She began speaking as well as using her hands. As expected, the others could not hear what she said, although they did understand her hands gestures, instructing them to remain on their horses and wait.

Ruffle tried to say something to Tansy, but even when shouting he could not be heard. So, he gave up trying. Meanwhile, Adella moved her arms as if she were drawing shapes on the rock. Nothing appeared to be happening, though she continued as if drawing invisible lines on the rock.

After some time, everyone dismounted. They stood about, then most just sat on the ground. The horses chewed grass. And despite the constant roar of the falling water, Ruffle lay back, pushed his hat over his eyes and tried to sleep.

'It's been too long, the door must be stuck,' shouted Tansy toward Ceri, who lifted her hands to her ears as if to say she could not hear what she had said.

Tansy nodded to show that she understood she could not be heard. So, she tried once more and then decided not to try again. Pulling her legs up, she rested her chin on her knees and closed her eyes. She did not wish to sleep, but buried herself within her thoughts. Then, suddenly, she felt a tug on her arm. It was Ceri. She brought her mouth close to Tansy's ear and shouted, just enough for her friend to hear.

'I think she has lost the entrance. The rock face looks unchanged. She may have forgotten exactly where it is; this may not work.'

Tansy turned, looked toward Adella and replied to Ceri.

'It has to be there. She will find it,' she shouted.

Ruffle sat up, looked at his friends and nodded. He then moved his arms and shrugged his shoulders in a 'what's happening' gesture. Ceri shook her head to indicate nothing was happening. He then lay back again and Tansy copied him, eyes closed and arms crossed.

Some minutes later, Ceri tapped both her companions on the shoulder and pointed. They looked over toward Adella and could see a large part of the rock slowly moving, like a big yawn; heavy-looking doors were sliding open. Adella was walking back toward the group, rubbing her hands together as if she were washing them. She took her horse by its reins and waved to all to follow.

The company of twelve led their horses through the large entrance into the darkness of the mountain. Some of the horses whinnied, unsure about entering the blackness within mountain. It smelled dank. It was so dark and soundless. A few steps inside the mountain, the roar from the waterfall fell away. It was quiet enough to hold a conversation once again.

'Was it more difficult than it should have been?' asked Ceri of Adella, referring to the opening of the gates.

'It was probably rusty,' joked Ruffle.

'No, the doors do not get rusty. It was me. I forgot some of the unbinding spell. It has been some time since I last used it. I was the one who was rusty,' smiled Adella.

'But we are inside now. So, will the gate close behind us?' asked Tansy.

'No. It will remain open. It is not yet fully opened but it will be soon and then the Sudoorn can simply march in and follow us.'

Looking back, the doors continued to move silently and slowly open. Light flooded through the entrance but did not carry any great distance inside the mountain. A blanket of blackness lay ahead, and the first torches lit prompted short shadows that unnerved the companions a little.

'As more torches are lit, your eyes will adjust. We simply follow where the torches illuminate the road. Also, be prepared, the sounds that we make will echo once we are inside. It can be strange at first, but do not be alarmed,' explained Adella.

Despite understanding that they were within a mountain, the huge cavernous space surprised the companions. The road was surprisingly wide and the feeling of emptiness was exaggerated by not being able to see very far. This was accentuated the ghostly echoes rebounding back when any sound was made.

'This is rather eerie, even for me,' said Ruffle.

'You are not alone in thinking that and I don't have dwarven ancestors!' said Tansy.

Four of the accompanying Teb rode ahead and began lighting torches along the walls. The travellers could see the burning torches illuminating their route, but they cast limited light. The deep darkness continued to dominate the surroundings.

'Our eyes will adjust and the road will become more visible as we proceed,' said Adella, trying to reassure the three friends.

'Was it always so quiet in here?' asked Ruffle.

'On the contrary, Ruffle, the dwarves were a noisy bunch. When they were here, the mountain was filled with banging and shouting, with many songs, laughter and just as many quarrels. The contrast now is stark. The silence is sorrowful. I don't know why the dwarves left or where they went; it always felt like they belonged here. It now feels like a lonely place and has since the sad day they departed.'

'I feel the silence is ominous. It is not just plain silence. I cannot explain myself any better, but I am uneasy, I feel a sense of dread,' said Ceri.

'Wonderful, just what I needed to hear,' said Tansy, touching the hilt of her sword for reassurance.

'I have travelled here often and it is a long time since the dwarves went; in all that time, there has been no indication of anything amiss. So, I would not worry. Although if there were, then perhaps it might go some way to explain why they left so suddenly,' said Adella.

Little else was said for some minutes, as if all were occupied by their own thoughts. The Teb, lighting the torches ahead, were being very efficient. There was no moonlight to aid them, just the orange glow from the torches. As they moved, so their shadows danced upon the walls, huge and long and orange. The passageway they followed was wide and every so often, other roads would cross their path. If there were a ceiling, it could not be seen. The light from the torches did not penetrate to any great height. Which only added to the cavernous impression.

One of the Teb lighting torches rode back to seek advice about the crossroads up ahead, where five roads met and the correct path was uncertain.

'I will have to ride ahead and show them the right road to take. You continue straight ahead until you reach the crossroads. I will meet you there,' Adella instructed before galloping off.

'I would have preferred if she had remained with us,' observed Ruffle.

'We will be alright, we just stay on the road following the torches, then we can't go wrong,' said Ceri to reassure him.

'You should be fine in here, Ruffle, seeing as the Rall are descended from dwarves, you should be relishing this!' said Tansy, teasingly.

'That was a long time ago and not in my lifetime. This place is dark, quiet and creepy. I would not wish to be alone here,' replied Ruffle. 'And I was not raised in mines, so this is all new to me too.'

'It is a rather incredible place, you have to admit. It is its own world. I wonder how far and deep this rocky labyrinth extends. Though I have no wish to find out. It is too dark to go venturing off exploring. But I imagine there must be many rooms within, given that there were thousands of dwarves. Though one would not know it now, for this is feels deserted, just silently collecting dust.'

'You're right, Tansy and I feel I should be excited, but instead I feel quite uncomfortable. It may be deserted, but it has an odd atmosphere,' said Ruffle. No one replied. They were all gazing into the gloom, as if they expected to see something lurch out of the darkness.

Before very long, they could make out a huddle of figures ahead. It was the Teb. Adella hailed the companions and waved her arms to encourage them forward.

'This is one of several crossroads we will come across,' explained Adella, 'so we need to make it obvious at each one which is the correct road to follow.'

The Teb had already begun lighting torches along one particular road and thus it became obvious which was the one to take.

'This rocky world exists on different levels and it has the peculiar feature of winds that blow through the tunnels. When I first journeyed through here I did not expect any wind to be blowing through an underground kingdom, but believe me, there is. They say the wind never leaves, it just circulates perpetually around the tunnels and roads under the mountain. When it arrives, it does not last long and quickly slips away. However, it can be quite strong and when it is, then it's likely the wall torches would be extinguished.'

'That is a strange phenomenon, but interesting too,' said Tansy.

'If we encounter the wind, we would hear it before we felt it, for it is like a whistling howl. Then there is a predictable feature of the tunnels; namely, some roads drop to lower levels and some climb higher. Few roads run straight. Often, the incline or descent is gradual, so one can move off the road without realising it. Fortunately, the road we take is one of the straighter routes, which should make it easier for the Sudoorn to follow. We must hope no wind claims our torches.'

'But didn't you just say that we would hear it, so if any wind does arise, wouldn't we be able to prepare?' Ruffle quizzed her.

'Yes, but our road is long with twists and turns, so we may not hear it if it is behind us and we are far ahead. Plus, we may not know if any torches are extinguished as we cannot see backwards along the length of our travels,' Adella clarified.

'And I thought it was eerie enough without having some wind blowing out the lights!' muttered Ruffle, who assumed a glum look.

'Come on, Ruffle, let's not imagine the worst. We should just deal with whatever comes our way,' said Ceri.

'Yes, you're right,' and he mimicked a big cheesy grin.

The small procession continued on its way. In the perpetual dark, it was quite easy to lose any sense of time. There were no clues to indicate how long they had been travelling, although Ruffle suggested his rumbling stomach was a good guide. Taking the hint, Adella suggested that they eat as they rode, which was not as easy as they expected, despite their continuing to ride at a walking pace.

'Will the Sudoorn move any quicker than we do?' Ceri queried.

'Most likely as the road will be lit to show them the way. With the numbers they will bring, they will have to contend with the dust which will be churned up. Although that should not slow them unduly. So, they should progress much faster than we have,' responded Adella.

'A silly question from me, as I have lost any sense of time; but how much longer do you think it will be before we reach Yasrall?' Tansy asked Adella.

'I don't think I can give you a useful answer, Tansy. But if my memory is correct, then we are well past the halfway point. I understand that you would like to halt, but it would be of little comfort sitting about in the dark. We will rest once we reach the entrance to Yasrall.'

On they went. Conversation was light and infrequent, mostly speculating as to why the dwarves left the mountain. For which none had answers. Or wondering what awaited them in Yasrall. Once again, they could only speculate. Then they saw that the Teb, who were ahead lighting the torches, were stopped and dismounted. Briefly, they were unsure as to why they had stopped, but soon realised the obvious explanation.

'We have arrived. The door into Yasrall sits before us,' said Adella.

The end of their road was as black as the darkness within the mountain. There was nothing the friends could see to indicate a door. The road ran straight up to the mountain and came to a halt. Straight ahead was a solid wall of rock, like an impenetrable black curtain. If there was a doorway, then only Adella could see it. But they all knew they could not trust their eyes.

Adella dismounted and approached the wall. As before, she placed both hands on the cold, hard surface. She turned and spoke to her audience.

'We must be ready for anything. We have no way of knowing what will be revealed once the door opens. It might simply be the land that runs up to the mountain, or it could be a host of Girngog. Prepare yourselves,' she cautioned.

Stood before the dull black rock, she spoke quietly, as if confiding something secret to the wall. No one could discern what she was saying. Spreading both hands and outstretched arms, she drew invisible shapes as she whispered to the rock face. Based on the time it took to open the doorway in Xynnar, Ruffle decided that he had time to sit down and eat.

'Where are you going?' asked Tansy.

'I think we have plenty of time before the door reveals itself and I am hungry,' he replied.

'Perhaps not my good friend,' added Ceri.

Something was happening. The rock face was shimmering and brightening in the shape of a very large rectangle. It was not a doorway opening so much as the rock fading away. Increasingly, they could see through to the other side, as if it were a window. They saw shrubby fields stretching out and the sun low in the sky.

The light streamed through. Dull at first but brightening as the rock melted away. Instinctively, everyone raised their hands to shield their eyes. The contrast with the tunnel's darkness was stark and jarring. Although it took some minutes before the gateway was fully open, all remained where they were to allow sufficient time for their eyes to adjust. Even Adella, who had revealed the doorway whilst keeping her eyes closed, stepped back into the tunnel to allow herself a moment to focus properly.

Ruffle led his horse out through the opening. He stopped and turned, grinning, and spoke to all.

'Welcome to Yasrall, my friends, this is my home.'

27

Impatience

Ceri and Tansy smiled to see how pleased Ruffle was to be back in Yasrall. But nobody spoke; they were watching and listening. Other than birds and some fleeing rabbits, startled by the entrance appearing, there was nothing in motion across the land. The door was at the foot of the mountains and there was no sign of Girngog or anyone else.

'This is exactly what I hoped for,' said Adella, staring out at the empty fields.

'Well, as is obvious, this part of Yasrall is not favoured by many. The ground here is known to be hard, the weather is cold and it's difficult to grow much. Very few people live here and I doubt that even the Girngog can see any profit in occupying this barren area,' suggested Ruffle.

'That will suit us fine, as the Sudoorn can enter without encountering opposition,' Adella observed as she continued scanning the surroundings.

'I think it must be early evening here. Adella, I propose we make camp. Given the large boulders and the clusters of trees hereabouts, it seems to me to be as good as anywhere to offer us cover,' said Ceri.

'Indeed, that makes good sense. I think we could build a small fire without too much to worry about,' the Teb replied.

So, that is what they did. There was plenty of dry bracken for a fire and as the sun went down, so did the temperature. It was not so cold that a blanket did not suffice and together with some hot food, they settled.

'What do you think of us doing some scouting tomorrow?' Ceri asked as they sat around the little fire.

'I am not sure that is a good idea. It might be dangerous. It would be much safer if we simply wait for the Sudoorn to join us,' Adella answered.

'But we don't know how long they will be and surely it would be helpful for everyone to know what lies ahead,' persisted Ceri.

'Ceri, I realise that you continue to be impatient, but waiting for the Sudoorn is the sensible thing to do and is what we agreed.'

'I know. I realise it is impractical to think that we can forge ahead to Chimbleton on our own, but surely scouting to see what is ahead of us will be useful for the Sudoorn!' said Ceri. 'Besides, Ruffle knows the land as well as anyone.'

'Oh, so you include me in this scouting mission, thank you. Well, I do know the land a little, but I have not frequented this area very often and certainly not this far north,' he responded.

'Do you always put such awkward proposals to your hosts and friends?' asked Adella of Ceri.

'Yes, she does. It is a Meldrim family trait,' said Tansy with a big smile. 'She can be very impatient, as I think you may have noticed. She is like this with me.'

'Thank you so much, Tansy,' said Ceri, glaring at her friend.

'Well, your impatience is like a thorn in my side and as much as my instinct warns against it, I admit it could be useful if we did know what lies ahead. I think once arrived, the Sudoorn would send out their own scouts to gather such information,' mused Adella. 'If I were to consent to your plan, you must promise that if you spy or encounter any Girngog, then you return here immediately and do not attempt to engage them.'

'I can certainly agree to that,' said Ceri.

'Before you simply assume it, I will accompany you, but as Adella said, any sign of Girngog and we retreat,' muttered Ruffle, lifting his head from trying to light his thin pipe.

'As their bodyguard, it behooves me to travel with them, so that would seem settled,' asserted Tansy, much to the amusement of the Teb who were sitting about listening to the exchanges.

'Our bodyguard?' said Ceri, raising her eyebrows.

'Of course, Tansy, I would expect nothing less,' said Adella.

Early next morning, the three companions were soon ready to set off.

'Be cautious, where you can use the natural cover offered by the land to disguise your presence. Return by tomorrow evening and report,' instructed Adella.

Off they went, choosing to walk through the ferns and undergrowth, leading their horses by the reins. All the while, they remained watchful, eyes scanning for any sign of movement.

'Not sure why we brought the horses if we are going to walk,' mumbled Ruffle. 'You'll have me carrying the horse next!'

'You know why,' said Ceri. 'High on a horse, we are easier to spot. Once we are sure all is clear and the trees give us some cover, then we can mount.'

They walked until the middle of the day and saw nobody. There were clusters of trees and bushes which afforded them cover, but the open land was flat. They could be seen from a long way off should they choose that way.

'I think we can ride, though at a walking pace. The area seems deserted. But we should be careful anyway and keep close to the trees where we can,' said Ceri.

'Are we anywhere near Clinglewood?' Tansy asked of Ruffle.

'I think Clinglewood Forest is several leagues to the west. I know it runs right up to the Ironspine, but we are not moving that way,' he replied.

'And how far are we from Stonehelm?' continued Tansy.

'I am not sure, but again, quite a few leagues. The land will change eventually, becoming greener and we might see some farms. And if I recall, there will be gentle rolling hills. Though I wonder if we will also find the Girngog there!'

As they rode into the afternoon, the landscape became less strewn with shrubs or trees. As Ruffle had said, they came across grassland that rolled out toward hills. They found several deserted buildings, which were old farmhouses. Still, they saw no one.

As the sun began its slide from the sky and the evening was soon to make its entrance, they came upon a large cluster of trees. Venturing amongst the trees, they decided that it would be a good place to make camp.

'My suggestion is that we grab some sleep and then, before dawn, we travel a little way further. In the cover of darkness before morning arrives, we are less likely to be spotted. Though the further south we travel, the more likely it will be that we come across Girngog, so we must be extra careful today. But regardless of what we do or do not find, we should keep our promise to Adella. I suggest that at the end of the morning we start our return. What do you think?' Ceri asked her friends.

'A good idea, it makes sense, we should not take unnecessary risks,' said Tansy.

'Yes, though we have nothing to report, do we!' Ruffle stated.

'On the contrary, my good Rall. It has to be good news that we have found no Girngog and that is worth reporting. The Sudoorn can advance without opposition,' said Ceri.

They made camp among the trees, confident that they could not be seen from without. It was time to feed the horses and themselves, then they lay down under blankets, staring up at the star-laden sky.

'It is dark out here, but the faint smile of the moon and the sprinkling of stars make such a difference. Thankfully, it is not like the complete gloom that we found within the mountain. One positive thing came out of it; I now appreciate sleeping beneath the stars and the moon more than I ever did,' mused Ruffle.

'I share your thoughts, Ruffle,' said Ceri. 'But I am wondering if we should take turns being on guard.'

'We have not come across a soul, so I think we can legitimately sneak a short nap without having someone on guard,' he replied.

'I am not so sure. But equally, I see no reason for one of us to go without some sleep. It is likely that these trees should be enough to keep us hidden,' said Tansy.

'Well, it seems none of us are eager to be on guard. So, let us all grab some sleep and then do our final bit of scouting in the morning before we return to Adella,' said Ceri.

Without further discussion, each wriggled beneath a blanket, trying to find a comfortable position and close their eyes. The horses were tied to nearby trees and all three companions soon drifted off to sleep.

It was Tansy who woke first. She lay still, listening. There were no sounds. She turned, about to wake up the others, when Ruffle mumbled, 'Is it time to get up already?'

'I suppose so,' replied Tansy, who had no idea how long they had slept.

It was still dark. They had not slept long. Suddenly, Ceri sat up.

'What is it?' asked Ruffle.

'Nothing,' she answered. 'I mean, there are no sounds, not even the ones that usually fill the night. There is nothing.'

'Yes, I noticed that,' said Tansy. 'I think that is why I woke.'

None spoke. They listened but only heard silence.

'What do you think it means?' quizzed Ruffle.

'I don't know. Perhaps this place is so deserted that it is just normal. Or it could be a warning. Whatever it is, I am not comfortable. I suggest we get up and get going,' said Ceri.

Very quickly, their camp was rolled up and packed away. They were ready to leave. Little had been said, but there was tension in the air. They could all feel something was not right.

'Listen, I think if there were Girngog around, we would have heard them. They are big and clumsy, incapable of quiet or sneaking up on anyone,' said Tansy, trying to reassure her friends and herself.

There was no time for a reply as the night sprang into life. As if in response to Tansy, a sudden outbreak of shouting, stomping and noise rang through the night. Moonlit shadows danced across their camp area. Raucous roars and the thud of drums, '*boom, boom, boom*' shattered all illusions of being safely hidden. As if they had simply popped out of the earth, Girngog were everywhere and running toward them.

'The horses, ride, run, now!' screamed Ceri.

Pandemonium, chaos and panic. Ruffle pulled himself onto his horse, which was startled and already wanting to run. After struggling to climb into the saddle and before he could move, he was pulled off and onto the floor. Meanwhile, Ceri was mounted and encouraging her mount to move. It needed little encouragement. The horse sped off, but had barely travelled any distance when three large figures jumped out of the darkness right in front of her steed, bawling and waving their swords. The horse stopped abruptly, reared its front legs in the air and Ceri slipped back out of her saddle.

Tansy fared better, at least to begin with. She was up and riding swiftly. The Girngog were everywhere, she was surrounded and there was no obvious exit. So, she charged at the ambushers, hoping they would jump out of the way upon seeing a thundering horse bearing down on them. And they did. She was through the line of attackers, but then violently yanked from her saddle. She hit the ground with a hard thud. The horse did not stop. It was free and sped away into the night.

Immediately they had hit the ground, the Girngog were upon the three riders. A rope tied between trees had caught Tansy and yanked her from her mount. She lay on the ground winded, gasping for air. Before she could recover, her hands were tied and a big smelly Girngog stood with his foot placed on her chest. The same fate had befallen her friends. Within minutes, each had had their hands tied in front, were standing up and being led like dogs on a lead. The laughter and back slapping between the captors showed that they were pleased with their night's work. Then a voice shouted above the clatter and the Girngog cheered.

The companions were captured and this time, no one knew they were; for the three friends, there was little hope of rescue.

The Girngog marched to the rumbling sound they typically made, which may have been a song but was more of a chant. The prisoners were dragged side by side, positioned in the middle of the enemy gang.

'Now we know why things were so quiet,' Tansy whispered to her companions.

'What do you think…' Ruffle had begun to reply, but was interrupted by a roar from a large Girngog who made it clear that they should not speak. He separated them so that they were in a single file and pulling one another by a rope lead.

They were being pulled at a rapid pace, needing to trot to keep up. If they slowed, they would be swatted on the shoulder or the back by a wooden cane the big soldier carried. The captors spoke to one another, but no one spoke to the captives. None were heard to use the common tongue and the companions did not understand the Girngog language. Being captured was bad news, but being kept ignorant of where they were going or what was to happen, made it feel worse. As brave as they were, the three friends could not help but feel scared.

'I hope they don't eat us!' whispered Tansy.

It was difficult to assess how far they had walked, but it was long enough for the bumps and bruises, obtained when being upended from their horses, to begin aching. The sight of a campfire signalled that their walk might soon be ending. That thought was both welcome and dreaded. The Girngog had moved briskly and the friends were in dire need of a rest. But did stopping signal that they would meet their fate!

The darkness lingered, yet to give way to the morning light. The campfire was getting bigger as they drew nearer. Several tents were evident and the smell of something cooking.

The prisoners were led to the middle of the encampment, where more Girngog gathered. They were prodded and poked, as if being inspected. Their presence was clearly the main topic of conversation, providing much amusement for their captors.

Then, from one of the tents emerged a Girngog who was by far the largest of the enemy. He cut a fearsome figure. Hairless and tattooed, his body carried many old scars, a record of wounds received. Evidently, he was in charge and he barked out words that resulted in the three hostages being tied together around a tree. They were then left alone and Ruffle whispered to his friends that he thought he could escape from his bonds. The tree was on the edge of the camp, but close enough for them to observe all that occurred. Both Tansy and Ceri looked at Ruffle.

'And where do you think we could escape to? With no horses, they would soon catch us and it could make matters worse!' said Ceri.

'How can it get worse?' said a miserable Tansy.

But before they could say any more, a short, bulky Girngog approached with two animals. He spoke gruffly to the animals, which promptly sat down and stared at the prisoners. They were bigger than a wolf, similar to a dog, white and grey in colour, with four long protruding teeth at the front of a slobbering mouth. Plainly, they were there to guard the companions.

The three friends sat, leaning against the tree, quiet and dismayed. Meanwhile, the Girngog made merry. Drinking, eating and arguing, it seemed the whole camp was in a celebratory mood. However, no food or water arrived for the prisoners.

'We are stuck,' said Tansy, talking softly to her friends whilst watching the two guard animals.

'As long as we are not on the menu,' moaned Ruffle.

'At least they seem to be ignoring us, for which I am glad,' Tansy added.

They said no more. The guard animals sat motionless, watching the friends and seeming ready to pounce. The friends had slept very little in their own camp and the night persisted. Despite their danger, tiredness overtook them and they fell to sleep. Other than a few guards, the Girngog had all found sleep much sooner.

Ceri woke several times and looked to check if the two animals remained on guard. They were there, as if they had not moved. Gradually, the rising sun roused all three friends. Though few Girngog were in sight, it was clear this was their base; they had no reason to be elsewhere. The tents and surrounding equipment bore the look of having been there for quite some time. It seemed likely that the fate of the three companions would be decided at this outpost.

When they awoke, the companions felt stiff and sore.

'I have bruises on top of bruises, I think,' said Ruffle.

'I need to stretch and find something to drink,' said Tansy. 'Can we try asking someone?'

'I think we should, but….' Ceri paused, looking ahead.

'Who is this?'

Walking toward them, carrying a water jug, was a man, a thin, scrawny twig of a man. He stopped in front of the tree where they were tied.

Ruffle stared at him and spoke.

'You're a Rall.'

'Indeed, I am. Spignib is my name. And I think you must be one too,' he smiled, which revealed a row of green teeth with two noticeable gaps.

'As for you ladies, I don't think you are Rall, but I'm not sure. But first things first, would you like a drink?'

All three captives nodded.

'I will undo your ropes, Dumik said it would be fine. If you run, his pets here will catch you and they have a nasty bite. Besides, there is nowhere to run to and they haven't been fed yet,' said Spignib, chuckling to himself as he untied their ropes.

'What are you doing here?' Ruffle asked, feeling confused and suspicious.

'I cook for them. There were three of us, all from Stonehelm; it was either cook or go down the mines. We chose to cook, but they sent us away from Stonehelm to this wilderness. The Girngog got bored and some ended up eating the other two Rall. They were bigger than me, you see, fatter if you like. I am skin and bones. The Girngog prefer something with more meat. But I am happy to see you. We have very little meat left. Plenty of spuds and carrots and onions and the like, but not a lot of meat. Not a lot to catch round here. So, I've been worrying that they might turn on me. But with you here, I can relax for a bit, I can spread you out for some while.'

'What do you mean by that?' asked Tansy.

'Well, Dumik, he's the boss, is posted here to guard the land north of Stonehelm, but there is nothing here, no threat to them. You probably noticed there are not a lot of farms. The ones that were here had sheep, mostly. But they have gone now, eaten. Though they did last a while. So, as the lads here missed a bit of meat, they turned on my helpers. After all, it's just meat,' said Spignib.

'That is a terrible thing to say,' objected Tansy.

'Sorry, dear, but that is how it is. But your being captured spying hereabouts has changed things. It's a good thing they caught your horses too, or it might have been your turn tonight,' said Spignib as he passed the water jug to Ruffle.

'We were not spying. Just travelling home,' said Ceri.

'Where might that be then?' queried Spignib.

Ceri realised that she did not wish to answer that question; she did not trust this bony man. She changed the subject.

'What do you mean, it might have been our turn tonight?'

'Well, they got two horses when they caught you. So, one will be feeding the camp tonight. Then tomorrow it might be the second horse or one of you lot. But as usual, they are arguing as to who they eat first. They like eating women; they find them more tender, and they need less cooking. But some want to keep you as their wives. Though the Girngog women don't like that idea, not a lot of them are here in camp. I reckon they will eat one of you and keep the other. Though I hope whoever they keep can't cook. You might do me out of a job!'

'I am not going to be the wife of any Girngog. They can cook me first,' spat out Tansy, clearly offended by the thought.

'Good. There's usually an argument about that, so it's good of you to volunteer. Would you prefer to be on the spit or in the pot? The lads don't mind either way. I hope you choose the spit, it's less cleaning up for me,' said Spignib. 'But I don't need to know just yet.'

'I wasn't volunteering,' Tansy snapped back.

'Well, we can get by on one horse tonight, maybe eat the Rall next night, then the other horse and then you. That way it's a little bit of variety for the lads. So, you can cheer up, you might have three days yet, so best I keep you fed until then, aye. I might see if I can stretch you lot out a bit longer. Nothing personal, mind, it just keeps me safe if I keep their bellies full,' said Spignib.

'You're a traitor,' said Ruffle, clearly annoyed with Spignib.

Spignib stood up straight and looked at Ruffle.

'Don't you go accusing me, I'm alive, ain't I? I seen others eaten and it's not a pretty sight. These Girngog don't care; they eat anything and anyone. My chances of surviving here are not good, but I will keep going as long as I can. You're already finished anyway. You should not have let 'em catch you. Tis your own fault.'

'They came from nowhere, we had no warning, we didn't get caught on purpose,' said Ruffle.

'Well, more fool you. They been watching you. They saw you were coming this way and they was happy when you went in the trees, making it easy for them. Clever in their own ways, some of them,' mused Spignib.

'Would you help us escape?' asked Ceri.

'Now, why would I do that? I just told you how glad I am that you are here. Besides, there is nowhere to escape to. Yasrall is now part of Gritol. You run away and these dog things here will find you and believe me, they are nasty; they will tear you to bits. Horrible sight. They sit there all quiet, but they want you to escape, so they can catch you; 'cause they don't get fed regular, keeps 'em hungry. If they catch you, then they get a good chew. So, young lady, that was a stupid question, sorry to say, but you got nowhere to go.'

Spignib continued.

'Anyways, I will get you some porridge. As for today, it's your horse on the menu, not you, so you can rest easy, enjoy yer day. I will leave the jug here and go get you breakfast.'

The spindly man walked away. The three watched him and pondered on what he had said.

'Extraordinary. I wonder how much he has had to endure,' said Ceri.

'Whatever he has endured, it has not been a wash. He stinks. No Rall should be helping the enemy. As a fellow Rall, he should be helping us,' said an angry Ruffle. 'He should be ashamed.'

'I think he has given up. He does not believe anyone can help. And clearly, he has no intention of helping us. But I do not intend to just wait here and be served up as a Girngog dinner. Whatever it takes, I am getting out of here or perish trying,' added Tansy.

'So, you would leave me to become a Girngog bride? Thank you,' said Ceri.

'I think you would make a lovely Girngog bride,' said a smiling Tansy.

'If there is no other choice, then I will take my chance at outrunning those nasty-looking beasts who never stop watching us,' added Ruffle, glaring back at the two guard animals.

A short while after, Spignib returned with a pot and some bowls. He sat with the three friends as they ate the weak, lumpy porridge.

'You might be thinking of running off, but I seen those animals run and they are fast. They make a mess of what they catch. In days gone by, the runners who survived their mauling had to be cooked the same day. To be honest, if there was a way to escape, I might have taken it myself before now, but there ain't.'

'For now, you'd best eat as much porridge as you can; likely they won't feed you again until nightfall. They won't share any of the horse with you. They don't even share any with me. But I can keep your water jug filled,' said Spignib.

'This porridge is just about acceptable, I was expecting something much worse,' said Ruffle, trying to befriend his fellow Rall. 'And having water would be appreciated. Tell me, do those animals ever get taken for a walk?'

'Sometimes, but usually they let them loose at night to go and hunt their own dinner. Mind, they won't do that until they return from their patrols. The first patrol today will head out of camp soon. Mostly they come back with nothing to report, so you see why they were so happy to find you lot.'

'How many Girngog are here?' asked Ceri.

'Oh, don't know really, maybe about fifty or a hundred, I'm not the best with numbers. Only half go out on patrol, so don't think you might be left alone. There is plenty remaining here and they will make any excuse to lop off your arm or hand. With so little happening here, you are their entertainment now. They're all talking about what the best seasoning is for cooking you. They won't even take my advice as a cook! Though it's me who gets the blame if they don't like it.'

'I have had enough talk about cooking,' said Tansy. 'What will you do when the Girngog are defeated? How will you explain helping them?'

'Don't you worry about me. For a start, the Girngog won't be defeated, there's too many of 'em, and I told you before, I have no choice but to help them if I am to stay alive.'

Spignib stood up and stretched his arms. Tansy thought he looked like a scarecrow.

'I better get back and sort things out for dinner tonight. You just sit here and relax, it's your horse that should be worried,' he grinned.

Collecting their empty bowls, he made his way back to the middle of the camp, quietly whistling.

Watching him go, Ruffle said, 'I don't think he and I would have been friends in Stonehelm even if the Girngog had never arrived.'

The companions sat by the tree all day. No longer tied up, they occasionally stood to stretch, but each movement was met with a menacing growl from the ferocious beasts set to guard them. In the morning, they watched one Girngog patrol leave and later return, followed by the departure of another. Spignib had been correct; the companions were not fed. They saw him with one of the horses, leading it to a tent from which pots and knives hung. They presumed it was the kitchen tent. The afternoon patrol returned and the noise levels increased with laughter and arguments spreading across the camp. Several times, Girngog walked over to look at the prisoners, pointing and obviously discussing their preferred fate for the captives.

'I am very glad that I do not speak the Girngog language,' said Ceri. 'I don't think I would wish to hear what they are saying.'

'I definitely agree with you,' Tansy nodded.

'We have been here all day and between us, we have not come up with a decent plan of escape. That is what concerns me more than anything. I know we won't be cooked tonight, but we must do something. We can't just sit here and await whatever they plan for us,' said a very frustrated Ruffle.

The sun was slowly sinking and the heat of the day was seeping away. The companions felt stuck. They discussed and agreed that there were too many Girngog to fight. If they ran, then the two beasts watching would give chase and the land offered few places to hide. They would inevitably be caught. They were feeling the situation was hopeless. Their conversation dried up.

The evening was drawing in. The two animals guarding them seemed to be increasingly restless, each standing up and looking about.

'Those things look on alert, or maybe they're hungry and need feeding!' suggested Tansy. 'Like us they have not been fed today.'

Ruffle lifted his head and looked at his friends.

'Listen. What was that?' he asked.

'I can't hear anything,' replied Tansy, puzzled by Ruffle.

'There, I felt it and I think I hear something.'

'What did you feel? What did you hear?' Tansy insisted.

'Hush, just listen.'

They sat still and listened, but other than the racket from the camp, none could make out any other sounds.

'Feel the land,' Ruffle said, as he put his ear to the ground. 'I am sure….'

Ceri did so.

'I can feel vibrations. What is it? An earthquake?'

Tansy lay flat and listened.

'I feel it too.'

'It's getting louder, like a rumbling thunder, but not from the sky,' observed Ruffle.

The two animals guarding the companions had apparently also heard something. They had both stood up and were looking out beyond the camp. Saliva dripped from their mouths, teeth bared, they were ready to fight.

Then, shattering the quiet of the early evening came a cacophony of horns, blowing loud and clear, accompanied by the sound of thunder. But it was not thunder, it was galloping horses. Out of the gloom burst an army of cavalry, wearing silver armour decorated with black dragons. Their lances and swords cut through the air as they charged.

Horses reigned up close to the companions, Soldiers brandishing swords, leapt down and surrounded the friends. Then one of the cavalrymen removed the face mask and spoke to the friends.

'Apologies that we are so late, but it seems we are at least in time. This is the Sudoorn.' It was Adella.

A group of Sudoorn had alighted and thrown a protective ring about the companions, the two beasts that had been guarding their prisoners growled, barked and ran at the companions. They did not get very far, dropping to the ground almost immediately, punctured by arrows from the soldiers and now lifeless.

Adella could see that the companions were in shock and immobilised by confusion as to what was happening, so she took charge.

'Stay here, nothing for you to do, the Sudoorn will take care of matters and we will stay with you.'

The companions watched, surprised and shocked, but more than anything else, impressed. The Sudoorn were clearly skilled and experienced warriors. The black dragon emblem of Tebira adorned their flags, armour, shields and horse colours. Upon seeing the

Sudoorn charge through the camp, most of the Girngog ran. In a short while they were dispatched, their camp overrun, trampled and demolished. The Girngog leader was slumped and pinned to a tree by a lance.

The horse that had been destined as the main course for the Girngog supper stood whinnying and untouched, still tied beside the tent. Later, the companions searched for Spignib and found him pinned to the ground by a Girngog spear. A fight had taken place among the Girngog before the arrival of the Sudoorn. It was judged that Spignib had been slain before the Teb descended. After the raid only two Girngog had survived. These were now being interrogated.

'How did you find us?' Tansy asked Adella.

'I had you followed. Whilst I understood your impatience to do something, I also surmised that it could be more dangerous than you anticipated. So, two of my people followed you at a distance and kept out of sight. When they saw that you had been captured, one sped back to us whilst the other continued on your trail. Fortunately, the Sudoorn had arrived at Xynnar sooner than expected. In fact, we here are merely a small group sent to rescue you. The bulk of the army is behind us, but will catch up very soon. I feared that if we delayed, we might find you on a campfire spit!'

'Well, I am so glad that you didn't delay. We were at a loss as to how we could escape. And I for one have had enough of being captured by Girngog,' said Ceri.

'Well, it is time that my soldiers fed, freshened up and rested, as we rode hard once we knew you had been taken prisoner. From now on, please temper your eagerness and remain with us, that way you might reach your home intact. Tomorrow, we all ride with the main Sudoorn force and make for Stonehelm. I am sure the Girngog will be there and ready to greet us. With what is remaining of the night, we will make a camp and take the time to rest,' Adella concluded and went off to organise matters.

'I think we should definitely do what Adella suggests. I for one will stay close to the Sudoorn,' said a relieved Ruffle.

'After tonight, you will get no disagreement from me,' said Ceri.

'I wonder what seasoning they had in mind for me?' smirked Tansy.

28

The Unexpected Arrival

At Castle Black, the siege towers of the Girngog were proving to be a partial success. Wheeled forward as close as the moat would allow, arrows could be fired from its small horizontal windows. Being so narrow they also afforded protection against incoming arrows. Once in position, platforms could be extended from the top of towers to the castle walls. It meant that the Girngog would be able to walk from tower to castle.

The weakness of this tactic was that those crossing on the platforms were easy targets for the castle bowmen. Many Girngog perished trying to reach the castle, but it seemed like an endless supply of the invaders were willing to try and cross. As one Girngog fell, another simply replaced him. The enemy just kept pouring out of the towers. Those who did manage to scurry across and reach the castle wall, found themselves outnumbered and got no further. The castle held fast, but the intensity of battle had increased.

However, it was not the loss of soldiers that persuaded the enemy to cease using this tactic, but burning arrows. Oil-soaked shafts had no impact on the towers, as it seemed they had been painted in something that prevented the wood from catching fire. But the platforms which extended from the towers on which the attackers would run across, had not been treated; as a result, they caught fire and the Girngog had to retreat. They then had no option but to hack away the burning platforms, which fell to the ground.

The success of this tactic deterred the use of 'walk – across' platforms for several days. Then they reappeared, and this time the platforms had been treated with the flame-resistant substance that had been used on the siege tower walls.

Whilst the castle defenders had to repel the Girngog attacking from the towers, simultaneously they also had to contend with bolts and boulders launched from machinery on the ground. Consequently, the castle ramparts were fully occupied, repelling the different forms of attack. The fighting was intense with little respite.

However, the one constant the Venterrans could rely upon was the castle. The structure of the castle was never truly threatened - the rocky missiles would simply bounce off the thick walls and fire could not take hold on the black stone. Nonetheless, the relentless assault would repeat day after day. As a result, the castle defenders spent much of their time either finding cover or engaging the enemy, sometimes face to face when any managed to cross the platforms.

Intensifying their assault, the Girngog adopted a further tactic. They brought small craft - carried upside down for protection from arrows - which were then launched into the moat. They acted like floating platforms, allowing their soldiers to reach the castle walls. From the bobbing boats, grappling hooks were launched onto the ramparts. Hauling themselves up from the floating platforms, the invaders tried to scale the smooth walls. Inevitably, the Venterrans flung the grappling hooks back down into the moat. Boiling oil and water were tipped onto those who persisted in trying to climb up. Very few Girngog made it as far as the top. For those that did, they were outnumbered by the defenders and quickly seen off.

This pattern of attack and defence repeated each day. The enemy made no progress in penetrating the huge fortress. But both sides suffered casualties. It was a stalemate just as many had expected it to be.

One thing that was noted within the castle, was that many of the Girngog did not return to their camp when the fighting stopped each day. It was realised that they were using the broken buildings of Duskhold as shelter. The King had noted this development and spoke to it when his war council met one morning.

'It seems that many of the Girngog now take cover within the ruins of Duskhold, much too close for comfort. In effect, they hide within our own town. Being so close means that we have much less warning each time they launch an assault. The first lesson that we learn from this, and it is one for the future, is that when we rebuild Duskhold, it will not be so near the castle.

Before anyone could respond, a knock on the door of the meeting room preceded the entry of a soldier.

'What is it?' asked the king.

'Your majesty, the Girngog have begun their attacks today.'

'Thank you. You may go,' replied the king.

Turning back to his officers, seated around a long rectangular table, he continued.

'Well, another day begins. Keep them at bay and do....'

He stopped as he heard a growing clamour and shouting from outside. Walking over to the window, he looked down upon the large courtyard below and saw everyone running for cover.

'What is going on?'

'Fibert, go and see what is causing that commotion,' he ordered.

Commander Fibert pushed his chair back, stood and walked out of the room. The king sat down again, hand stroking his bearded chin.

'We will resume when Fibert returns. I want him involved.'

The king drummed his fingers on his chair whilst the council members mumbled little conversations. Within a few short minutes, footsteps were heard and a breathless Commander Fibert stepped into the room, though still holding the door ajar.

'Sire, I think you had better see for yourself what transpires,' he suggested as he regained his breath.

'I hope this is not some foolish errand, Fibert,' uttered the king as he rose and followed his officer.

The other council members followed, curious as to what was happening. They made their way downstairs and into the courtyard. The king looked about, nonplussed as to what all the fuss was about, but noted that all in the courtyard were looking to the sky.

'There, sire,' said Fibert, pointing upwards.

Circling high above the castle flew a creature of myth. A creature that brought dread to most within the castle. One officer, with his hand shading his eyes from the glare of light as he looked up, said what many were thinking.

'What is it, a demon summoned by the Girngog! How do we fight that?'

'No, that is no demon, that is a dragon,' replied the king with a slow smile. 'If I am not mistaken, I think it might be a welcome surprise.'

The dragon circled, dropping lower and lower. Its emergence had quelled even the Girngog, who also gazed to the sky. It slid down from the clouds in decreasing circles and landed in a most gentle fashion in the middle of the castle grounds. It was enormous, its scales deep green in colour. Its body throbbed, mouth snorting, though not releasing fire, just a little smoke escaping from its nostrils. Once landed, its big eyes scanned the surroundings. It will have noticed, sheltering around the courtyard, ready to flee, stood hundreds of people gaping at a creature risen from tales of old, now come to life.

Many stared with mouths wide and others with swords drawn. But the smile on the face of the king reassured the onlookers. The words 'I never believed that dragons were real' were heard repeatedly amongst the throng. Unsurprisingly, the younger children were either frightened, thrilled, or a mixture of both. A few appeared eager to rush towards the monolithic creature, only to be restrained by wary mothers and fathers.

Perhaps just as big a surprise as the creature itself, was the sight of someone sitting astride a green basilisk. The dragon rider uttered something that no one there understood and the beast lowered itself, allowing the man to slip from its back down onto the ground. He was dressed in silver armour, patterned with images of a green dragon. He seemed to recognise the king and walked over to him and bowed.

'My name is Zetz, Your Majesty and I come on behalf of Tebira, your ally and good friend. We have learned of the Girngog aggression and I am here to discuss what assistance we might offer.'

On his travels in Tebira, the king had learned of the dragon riders, though he had never met one or seen a dragon. Zetz was one of a handful of Teb that the dragons allowed to ride them. He was also aware that the dragon riders were revered in Tebira. Delighted to see the dragon arrive the king wore a smile that never dimmed as Zetz introduced himself

'If we may, can we talk, Your Majesty?' requested Zetz.

'By all means. Your unexpected arrival is very welcome. Does your dragon require anything whilst we talk?' the king enquired.

'The dragon who has brought me here is Cherigg, the daughter of Vazzorg. She will be fine as she is, though I would caution your people not to touch her.'

The king instructed his soldiers to keep people from encroaching on the huge beast.

The dragon laid its head on the ground, closed its eyes and appeared to be sleeping. Those watching within the courtyard could feel heat emanating from its body and no one was inclined to approach the living furnace. The warm welcome the king had given Zetz had reassured most about the intention of this fiery legend resting among them. Fears had reduced whilst curiosity had increased. The awe and fascination had turned into a low murmur of chatter amongst the audience.

Outside the castle, even the Girngog had been affected by the arrival of Cherigg. Upon seeing the dragon land within the castle, they had ceased their assault. There was an expectation that they would hear screams and a clamour of panic as the dragon set about devouring the castle inhabitants. It never came.

They were unsure what this meant for them and a loud hubbub rather than the clang of weapons arose from within the enemy ranks. Had the Venterrans befriended the creature! If they continued to attack, would the dragon help the castle dwellers? These questions and more fed uncertainty and confusion amongst the Girngog. They hesitated, then halted their assault, waiting for instructions from their leaders.

Inside the castle, the king and Zetz talked for a good hour. They were then joined by the war council, who sat about, eager to learn how the Teb might help. The king explained to his War Council some of the news Zetz had brought.

'You will recall the two Chimbles, Ceri and Tansy, along with Ruffle the Rall. Well, the good news is that they are alive. Most of you know that they attempted to traverse the Ironspine in order to return home. They did not succeed, but with the help of some other friends, they were rescued and taken to Tebira. To keep this brief, they made Tebira aware of the Girngog aggression and asked for their help. We owe them a great deal and we must never forget that.'

'Happily, Queen Polleema and her ministers agreed to answer the plea. The Teb do not go to war easily, so it is a true sign of friendship that they have chosen to help us. I think most of you know that when I was away, I spent time in Tebira and one result of this was the signing of a treaty between Venterra and Tebira. In honouring that treaty, Tebira has sent its army, known as the Sudoorn, into Yasrall. Zetz has come here to inform us of this. The magnificent animal in our courtyard is Cherigg, one of the few remaining dragons from Dragon Mountain in Tebira.'

'So, does that mean Cherigg will fight with us?' asked Commander Valaya.

'No. The dragons in the family of Vazzorg have decided that they no longer choose to fight in the disputes of men or Girngog, or in fact any other races. Though I think Zetz may offer some indirect assistance as he and Cherigg depart from us,' answered the king.

'But I am confused majesty, how can the Teb reach Yasrall, they are separated by the Ironspine mountains?' questioned Commander Fibert, who knew the land better than most.

It was Zetz who replied.

'The Tebira War Council decided that, for the final time, they would open the old road which connects the two lands and was built by the mountain dwarves. This road runs through and under the mountains and has been closed since the dwarves went away. It lies empty, abandoned and sealed off. One day, the dwarves may return and reopen the road themselves, although most do not think that is likely. As yet, they have not done so and perhaps never will. So, a Teb with the knowledge to unlock the entrances has reopened the road. And as we speak, our western army, the Sudoorn, are entering Yasrall on that road.'

Soon after, the meeting drew to a close. All returned to the courtyard and found Cherigg seemingly asleep. Still brimming with curiosity, the inhabitants of the castle stood about watching the dragon and feeling the heat emanating from its long green body. Unnoticed at first, a child of no more than eight slipped past the guards and crept towards the beast. The king was about to call the child back, but Zetz stayed his arm as if to say there was no need. So, the child crept closer until she was within touching distance of the dragon's head. She reached out, touched the scaly head, turned and looked back at her audience. She grinned, then turned and touched the dragon again. Without the child noticing, the large eye of the dragon that she now stood directly underneath, had opened and seemed to be peering down at the intruder. Then there was a great rumbling which clearly came from within the dragon, the mouth opened slightly and the girl fled back to her mother as fast as she could. Zetz and the king, together with those watching, all laughed.

'Cherigg knows she is a creature of wonder for many and she would never hurt someone who is merely inquisitive, said Zetz.

They walked over to the dragon, the king gave a letter to Zetz and they exchanged farewells. Zetz climbed into his bespoke saddle, which he explained also gave him protection from the heat generated by the body of the huge mythological being.

'You would be better to stand back some way, Your Majesty, whilst Cherigg gains some height,' advised Zetz.

The whole courtyard and many more who had now appeared at the windows, watched as the dragon flapped its wings hard, took some steps and began to rise, climbing upward into the sky. The wind and the heat issuing from this take off, made the king appreciate Zetz advice.

'To the battlements, ' the King directed his war council. 'But Your Majesty…' started Fibert.

'You will see why, follow me, Fibert,' said the King before setting off up the stone steps to the castle wall.

Meanwhile, Cherigg had gained height and flew in circles high above. The Girngog remaining by their war machines were watching, as transfixed as those in the castle. To the surprise of everyone, the dragon stopped circling and began to fly down toward the Girngog. It swooped low with increasing speed and roared as it sped along the front of the castle, spewing fire at the siege towers and ballista. Even the repellent coating protecting the towers from the castle's arrows caught fire as the Girngog fled. The dragon then turned and repeated its sweep, intensifying the fire that was destroying the siege machinery. The red-hot tongue of flame burned all that it licked.

A great cheer sounded from within the castle, encouraged by the sight of the Girngog fleeing into the ruins of Duskhold. Yet the dragon was not finished. The green beast flew over the town dwellings closest to the castle, pouring a tsunami of flames that the crumbling buildings could not withstand. More Girngog, who had hidden within the broken-down town, joined those running away and back toward their camp.

After what seemed merely minutes, Duskhold was half-demolished and would no longer provide the invaders with the shelter they had enjoyed so close to the castle. The 'indirect assistance' proffered by Zetz had accomplished more in minutes than months of resistance could have done. Its work done, the dragon flew up, circling and circling until it appeared no larger than a big bird; and then it swept away toward the Ironspine mountains, seeming to fly in and out of the clouds.

Allowing a few minutes for the cheers on the battlements to subside and the excited chatter to calm, the king reconvened and addressed his War Council.

'The Teb have come to our aid and this changes things. We should consider what our strategy may be going forward and if maintaining the siege is our correct course of action. The Sudoorn are in Yasrall and from my knowledge, there are few that can match them. So, we should be optimistic that they will have an impact. Do the Girngog yet know of the Teb intervention? We do not know. We will have to observe them and see if there is any discernible response.'

'Is the Teb army coming to aid us here, your majesty?' asked Fibert.

'I believe that they are, but it is a long march, so we must be patient. For the time being, there is a great deal for us to consider. To begin with, I would welcome your ideas and considerations as to what we might do next. Then, how best might we prepare for the arrival of the Teb?'

29

The Sudoorn

The companions had been impressed by the rout of the Girngog during their rescue and that impression increased when they met up with the main contingent of the Sudoorn.

'Well, I'll blow out candles, this is mighty encouraging,' said Ruffle, staring at the ranks of Sudoorn. 'I have never seen such an army.'

Ceri and Tansy agreed with Ruffle. The Sudoorn had come in great numbers. There were cavalry and infantry, with wagons at the rear chocked with quivers of arrows, swords, spears, medical supplies and all kinds of provisions. This army was organised and equipped. The green dragon emblem was emblazoned everywhere on their silver armour, their saddles and their flags. The 'green dragon army' was the colloquial name by which they were known. Within a very short time, they had set up camp, were cooking and preparing for the next day.

Speaking with Adella, Ceri shared her amazement.

'I have not seen many armies, it's true, but certainly never one as magnificent or in such numbers as this. And they seem so well organised.'

'Thank you. We have not always maintained such a large army. However, a long time ago, we were in dispute with Skovelenbar, a vast land with a massive army. We were not ready to adequately defend ourselves in the beginning against the Skove and had no option but to increase our own forces to prevent being conquered.

Thus, three armies were created across Tebira and the Sudoorn was the largest. It grew in size and has remained large ever since, though thankfully not engaged in warfare very often,' said Adella.

'Have you fought the Girngog before?' queried Ceri.

'Historically, I have, but for the majority now serving in the Sudoorn, no. But our army is always meticulously prepared and will know what to expect from the Girngog. That said, I know from my own service in the Sudoorn that no matter how well prepared one is, it can never be a true substitute for the actual experience. War is brutal. Nonetheless, you should be confident, I would back the Sudoorn against any foe.'

The efficiency of the army was demonstrated the very next morning when breakfast had been consumed, tents packed away and the Sudoorn was ready to move, all before the morning was very old. The companions felt a ill at ease as they felt they were being treated like royalty. They given pride of place, riding at the front of the army alongside Adella and the commander of the Sudoorn, General Therkon. Scouts were dispatched ahead to discover what lay before them. The General explained that they were heading for Stonehelm and expecting to encounter Girngog along the way. Yet by midday, they had encountered no one.

Yet there was abundant evidence of the Girngog invasion. All the farms they saw were destroyed, buildings broken, crops ravished and the land burned. The only Rall they saw were long dead, now scavenged by the crows. There were no animals, although the area of Yasrall they were passing through was renowned for its sheep and cattle herds. Ruffle's heart was heavy upon seeing how devastated his homeland now was.

Despite the destruction wrought by the Girngog, after two days riding, they had seen none. On the third day, less than three leagues from Stonehelm, they met a small group of Girngog. But there was no parley; upon seeing the green dragon army, the Girngog did not seek to talk; they simply fled.

'Do you think that all the Girngog will run at the sight of this huge army?' Tansy asked Ruffle.

'I hope they do, but I fancy not. The best thing would be that they surrender or negotiate peace! I don't know if that's likely, though,' he replied.

It turned out that both thoughts were wrong. Whilst the Sudoorn continued to move forward without any obstruction, their progress eventually came to a sudden halt. Just a league or so from Stonehelm, the Girngog reappeared. This time, they were in far greater numbers and plainly ready for a fight; they were noisy, stomping both feet and weapons, all to a background of banging war drums. Their faces were painted and as intended, they were a fearsome sight.

General Therkon ordered the three companions to be escorted to the rear of the Sudoorn. They were told to stay amongst the wagons and the medical people, who were preparing to undertake their work with the inevitable wounded who would come their way.

'I should be fighting, it's my land they have invaded,' snorted Ruffle.

'You are not a soldier, Ruffle. Your heart is brave, but I fear this will be a fight that we can do little to help. The Sudoorn know what they are doing. Besides, we need you here,' said Ceri.

Whether she knew it or not, Ceri was right. A ferocious and bloody battle exploded before them. There seemed to be little evidence of any battle plan from the Girngog, who simply charged at the Teb army.

The Sudoorn were excellent soldiers and highly organised. They had anticipated this kind of clash and they were battle-ready. The Girngog were wild, like rabid animals who scented a kill. With msd grinning faces and screaming war cries, they presented a terrifying sight. Although the Sudoorn had superior numbers, not all of them could be brought into the battle at the same time. There was insufficient land space to make that advantage count.

Strangers to warfare, the three friends could not make out what was happening or who was winning.

'It is horrific, ' said Ceri, who sat astride a horse observing from afar. She was stunned by the sound and the sight of so many in close combat. 'How can anyone survive?'

Tansy and Ruffle were equally appalled. The screams of pain, shouts of aggression and the sight of everyone splattered in blood, caused the friends to turn away.

'I can't watch such slaughter. Perhaps we can find something helpful to do,' suggested Ceri, gesturing toward the wagons and turning her horse.

They decided to help out at the medical tents. Soldiers were being brought from the battlefield to those whose job it was to tend to their injuries. It was another sight none of the companions had ever witnessed. They were shocked at the wounds, blood and pain all around them. Whilst feeling sickened and numb, they immersed themselves in trying to help the wounded.

Ceri had been learning about medicine and healing in Chimbleton, but had little experience of traumatic wounds. Nonetheless, she administered what assistance she could to the stricken soldiers, including helping with some surgeries. Tansy and Ruffle were lifting and carrying soldiers groaning with pain, fetching bandages, ointments and offering their help however they could.

Eventually, a cheer went up as word spread that the Girngog were defeated. The battle had lasted less than three hours, but it felt much longer, observed Ceri. The Girngog who were still standing had run back toward Stonehelm. General Therkon decided at that point not to pursue them, wary of what traps he might find in the town, he opted to focus on his own wounded and their care.

Adella had distinguished herself on the battlefield, returning unhurt, smattered with blood and exhausted. She found the three friends in the hospital tents. They were busy with their nursing and did not notice her enter. They, too, were covered in blood, but not their own. She could see that it was not theirs, but she could tell from their demeanour that they were in shock and reeling from the barbarity of conflict.

'Come along, my friends, you have done what you can. Let us clean up, eat and then I have some questions for you,' said Adella as she gently ushered the companions away from the groans and tears within the makeshift medical tents.

It had been the first major battle the three companions had seen close up and each confessed that they hoped it would be their last. Now, they sat together in a tent, washed and fed.

'Talking about war and being involved in one are two very different things,' said Ceri. 'Any king or queen starting a war should have to be involved in the fighting, then they might think again as to whether it is a good thing to do.'

'You are right, Ceri; war is utter folly. But if one side takes up arms and is aggressive, then the other side either gives way or defends itself. I think you will find that most would choose to defend themselves or their land or whatever it is at stake,' Adella calmly replied.

'For my part, today has hardened my resolve to become better at yielding my sword. Hopefully I will never have to wield it in Chimbleton or in such a battle as we saw today,' added Tansy.

'What are you thinking, Ruffle?' asked Adella.

Ruffle had been unusually quiet and privately, Adella was worried for him and his reaction to what he had witnessed that day.

'I am not clear as yet as to what my thoughts are. I am horrified by battle, that is true. I have seen violence before, in particular from the Girngog occupying Yasrall. It revolted me then, but it was not like this. And whilst I wish that there would be no more fighting, I know such ideas are just wishful thinking. But I will take up arms if I must. I will defend my land and my home. I would not have travelled to see King Cadmus or be here today if I were not prepared to do what is needed. For certain, I am not inclined to become a warrior, but I will fight if it is necessary to defend what matters to me. Though I realise such violence will damage me inside. That is my answer to your question. It's as much as I can say, as my own thoughts are still disturbed. However, it is the best I have at this moment,' Ruffle concluded.

They talked a while longer and the companions gradually relaxed, enough for Ceri to enquire as to the next step for the Sudoorn.

'The General has decided that we will continue into Stonehelm in the morning. Our expectation is that progress will be slow, as the buildings there will provide hiding places for the enemy. He expects we will be preoccupied with a lot of street fighting, which will slow our progress. Once the town is clear of Girngog, we will continue onto Bridgemouth,' she explained.

'I hope nobody takes a detour toward Chimbleton,' said Ceri, not sounding very hopeful.

'Yes. And where are the Rall captured by the Girngog?' Tansy wondered aloud.

'Indeed, that is something that concerns me,' said Ruffle, 'where are my people? I am hoping that they are unharmed and in Stonehelm. Though I fear that many have paid a terrible toll in losing their homes and probably their lives.

'Yes, I am afraid there is likely to be an unwanted truth in your words. Despite that, we will need you to be strong tomorrow. Although the General will not allow you to be at the front of the push through the town. However, your knowledge of Stonehelm means that it will make sense if you are close by. I am thinking that it may also be necessary to call upon you to help reassure any Rall that we discover or rescue. Would that be an acceptable position for you, Ruffle?' asked Adella.

'Absolutely, it would. Thank you for the thought. I would welcome the opportunity to see my people as soon as I can,' responded Ruffle, clearly pleased to be asked. At the same time, he dreaded the despair he expected tomorrow would bring.

After the battle, the main activity amongst the Sudoorn was to prepare for the next day. They attended to the injured and made ready to transport those who could not fight back to Tebira. The companions spent an anxious evening as they speculated on what they might discover over the next few days. Consequently, sleep was hard to come by.

30

The King's Last Charge

In Castle Black, the King listened to the differing views of his War Council. The debate went back and forth. Some advocated caution, whilst others proposed risk. He had heard enough. He raised his arm to signal silence.

'I think enough has been said and I thank you all for your contributions. My conclusion is this. Providence has presented us with an opportunity. The dragon has destroyed the war machines of the enemy and they are in disarray. They have retreated to their camp. It is our turn to grasp the initiative. Whilst they remain a larger force than us, they are ill-disciplined and I would assume, currently demoralised. They need time to rebuild their war machines and will wonder if the dragon might reappear.'

'It is our moment to break the siege. I propose that we ride out in the morning and get among them in their own nest. We must rout them and set them running back to Gritol. The urgency is to act now before they reform and attack the castle again. So, what say you? Is there anything to dissuade us from this strategy? Please speak freely.'

There was silence for a few moments and then Commander Fibert spoke.

'Your majesty, it is the strategy I hoped for. The cavalry will be ready and keen to send the enemy back to the hills.'

Commander Valaya spoke.

'Majesty, despite their chaos, they still outnumber us by a big margin. Is it wise to launch an attack when they are gathered together?'

'Wise words, but we may not get a better opportunity to seize the initiative,' said Fibert.

The word 'agreed' was repeated around the table. It was clear that this was the favoured strategy. Valaya nodded. The consensus was clear, it was a move that could wrest control back for Venterra.

'It seems we have an agreement, so let us now attend to the details. Commander Valaya speaks wisely, we have to make this foray count,' added the King.

With the strategy settled, the King left his commanders to thrash out the details. The Venterrans had the element of surprise on their side, as the Girngog would not expect to be attacked. The plan was to devastate their camp, then pursue the enemy to Bridgemouth before driving them back to Gritol.

So, it was necessary to organise the support required to ensure the pursuit was not hampered by a lack of provisions. Many within the castle would find themselves busy throughout the night, readying the wagons with supplies. The commanders delegated responsibilities as news spread that tomorrow would bring forth a battle.

So it was, that early in the new morning, the king stood on the battlements with his oldest son, Lorin and his brother, Prince Hewl. They peered through the morning mist toward the Girngog camp. Lorin was nineteen years old and eager to play a part in the conflict. As his eldest child and heir to the throne, the king was reluctant to allow his son to fight, but he included him wherever he could. He wanted Lorin to understand why and how decisions were made. It transpired that Lorin was popular within the castle, not only for his merry manner, but also because he had shown himself to be a fair and sensible prince. And unbeknownst to his father, he was a very competent swordsman.

'The enemy shows no signs of movement, but we must assume that they are considering how they continue the siege. It is imperative that we do not afford them the time to regroup and certainly no time to rebuild their siege weapons,' said the King, standing on the ramparts and straining his eyes to observe any activity.

'I will be by your side, brother,' said Hewl. 'That shapeshifter has made a fool of me and I intend to make amends for that on the battlefield.'

'You have nothing to make amends for on that matter, Hewl. There are a few that could ever recognise that they are in the presence of a shapeshifter and those that can are usually wizards. Although the faerie possesses the uncanny sense to recognise when one is present.'

'I thank you for your kind words, brother, but it is like an embedded splinter under my skin that brings constant pain, so I welcome the opportunity to repay such trickery,' replied Hewl.

'Well, I have a particular role for you, Hewl. Once we are amongst the foe, I foresee a number fleeing to the Pancake Lands. I would like you to lead the troops on that flank and when they try to escape that way, prevent as many as you can. It may mean taking in a good number of prisoners, but I think that will be true for all of us once they are routed and running.'

'Father, what can I do? I am eager to play a part,' said Lorin.

'You will, my son. I want you to oversee the garrison within the castle. Of course, we cannot engage the whole army in battling the

Girngog or in ushering them back to Gritol. Some must remain here. The castle will be at its most vulnerable. The gates must be closed and the people kept safely within until we return. There are good officers and administrators who can continue to manage the activities within the castle, along with the guards. But they will need a leader and that shall be you. I trust you are ready for such a role!'

'Definitely father. I will be efficient and fair. I will make you proud,' said Lorin.

'I am sure you will. But now we must get ready, we open the gates in less than an hour,' said the king. The king strode ahead, whilst Hewl walked alongside his nephew.

Hewl whispered, 'You will do fine, Lorin.'

'Thank you, uncle,' whispered Lorin, smiling.

On the grassy knoll outside the castle, the siege weaponry smouldered, almost extinguished. A blackened and crumpled catapult sat blocking the main road leading from the castle, close to the moat. It was the work of the dragon. Very little of Duskhold was intact, its smoky ruins no longer offering effective shelter. But the road needed to be clear for the Venterran army. So, soldiers were already at work clearing debris from the main thoroughfare that ran through the demolished town.

Early in the morning, the castle gates quietly opened and the Venterran army filed out. There was no fanfare or cheering, just a steady procession with a serious intent. The time for trumpets and war cries would come once they were in position to attack. At the head rode the King with his commanders and the royal guard, followed by the cavalry. Behind them came the bowmen and infantry. A long column of sombre figures departed the castle, steadfast in their purpose and fully aware that not all would return.

The king cast an imposing figure on his jet-black horse. The crest of Castle Black adorned the shields that most carried, with flags and the pennon tied at the end of the lances. Lorin watched from the high inner battlements, proud of his father and wishing he were by his side. They marched ten abreast across the road until they were out of the charcoaled detritus that was once Duskhold. At that point, the army spread wide, readying for the charge into the enemy camp. The morning mist still lingered, affording them cover from prying Girngog eyes.

Nonetheless, the Venterrans were surprised at the lack of response from the Girngog camp. Commander Fibert summed up what many were thinking.

'Before we reached this point, I expected that they would come out to meet us; after all, they must have spies on lookout. Perhaps they think that the dragon is still with us!'

'Yes, this is rather unusual for them. Nonetheless, we will continue with our plan. Though I think we might expect something unexpected. Be ready,' uttered the king.

The line of cavalry walked their horses nearer and nearer toward the Girngog camp. The morning mist was clearing and the Girngog camp lay before them, quiet, as if asleep. Still, there was no response. Commander Fibert gave the signal. Trumpets blew, ripping through the silence, flags were hoisted and the cavalry prepared to charge. Lances were lowered and they were off. Gathering speed, they galloped toward the black tents. Thundering hooves and wild shouts contributed to a cacophony of sound surging through the air.

Finally, the Girngog responded. They had not been sleeping. Soldiers who had lain hidden in the long grass now jumped up, pulling ropes that lifted and revealed wooden spikes planted directly in front of the charging cavalry. The obvious intention was to injure the horses and break up the charge. At the same time, many of the black tents collapsed to the floor, revealing rows of archers who immediately loosed a storm of arrows toward the Venterran cavalry.

The wooden spikes set in the ground were spread so that a horse could not jump over without landing on more spikes. The leading riders had seen this and signalled to slow up the charge. This proved difficult and some went into the deadly obstacles, though most managed to stop just before. Inevitably, this created confusion with horses facing in different directions. The danger was further compounded by a torrent of arrows falling from the sky.

The king had been in the leading group but had pulled up in time. The Girngog were the other side of the spikes, jeering and screaming. They had appeared as if from nowhere and had plainly anticipated the Venterran strategy. They had set a trap and the king had fallen into it.

'Get some ropes on these contraptions and pull them away,' ordered the king. But there were no ropes to hand. The charge had been halted, with the cavalry at a standstill and vulnerable. Shields were raised to fend off the bombardment of arrows. Then it was the Girngog who pulled some of the mounted spikes away to clear a passage in which they pushed through, shouting their own war cries as they began to attack the horses.

Some of the cavalry were unseated, others dropped their lances and drew their swords. But the group around the king were not being assaulted by the enemy on foot. It soon became apparent why. The Girngog archers now concentrated their fire on the king.

'Fall back, we must fall back,' shouted Commander Fibert.

It was a desperate plea as the arrows rained down upon the Royal Guard. Fibert tried to lead the way back, but it was slow. The Guard had to shield from the arrows as best they could, but a number were hit. Then the king and his horse both fell. The horse had several arrows sticking out of its neck and body. The king had fallen as his horse had collapsed. Though he had also received two shafts, one in his thigh and another in his side.

'Majesty,' screamed Fibert.

Immediately, several of the Royal Guard dismounted and using their shields, formed a protective circle around the fallen king. Suddenly, the stream of arrows stopped, as if turned off like a water tap. The Girngog had flooded through their own defences and now turned their attention to the king's group. Many of the Venterran cavalry had ridden back to their own lines in order to regroup. The effect was to leave the king's guard separated and surrounded.

Commander Valaya had seen the disarray of the cavalry and now the Venterran archers were sending their own torrent of bolts down on the Girngog. Yet they dared not fire too near the King, for fear of striking their own. Prince Hewl, seeing what had transpired, rallied his infantry and led them streaming across the grass in a desperate bid to join the fray and reach his father. But they met with fierce resistance and struggled to make headway.

'I am alright, but my beautiful Bess, my beloved horse. I believe they made us a target,' said the king, stroking his deceased horse.

'Your Majesty, can you stand?' asked Commander Eleen, who was in command of the Royal Guard. 'We need to get you on a horse and away from here.'

At the same time, the commander realised that trying to ride through the Girngog would make the king an easy target. She did not persist with her suggestion.

'We are surrounded, but I see our infantry is trying to reach us. We have little choice but to stand our ground and pray our soldiers arrive in time,' suggested Commander Fibert to his counterpart, Eleen.

The king was trying to stand up.

'Break these damn arrows, but do not remove them,' he asked of Fibert, referring to the two protruding from his leg and side.

Fibert broke both arrows close to the skin where they stuck out of the king; he knew that extracting them completely would cause increased blood loss. This was all that could be done for now. Cadmus was helped to his feet, leaning on his sword. He was in a circle of about twenty guards who were holding off the raging and baying Girngog. There was a cry and a horseman trying to reach the king had fallen from his mount. Immediately, he was surrounded by infantry trying to protect him. The king had seen the incident and recognised the wounded horseman to be his brother. He did not realise it, but the prince had been speared in the stomach, whilst another deep cut seeped blood from a wound in his chest.

'Oh no,' whispered the king to himself. He knew that he could not reach his brother. The infantry was slowly fighting their way through to the king, but Hewl had ridden ahead and alone from the soldiers he commanded, impatient to reach his brother.

Looking about, Commander Valaya was doubtful that the cavalry or infantry would reach them in time to save the king. She realised that there were more of the enemy pouring out from their camp. It was clear that the Girngog had anticipated this response from the Venterrans.

'If this is to be where I perish, then I will not go easily,' said the king, struggling to stay standing. The wound in his side made it difficult.

'Fibert, grab me another sword to lean on and put my own sword in my hand,' he ordered.

'Majesty, you are wounded. I will defend you,' he said.

'Thank you, but if you are occupied, I still wish to defend myself,' retorted the king. 'Come, let us take some of these awful creatures with us.'

'Yes, Majesty,' Fibert replied as he handed the king another sword to lean on and placed his own sword in his hand.

'If this is to be my end, I will fall by the side of my king, and be proud to do so.'

With the help of Fibert, the king stood up, barely able to put any weight on the leg embedded with an arrow. Upon standing and looking out over the battle around them, both the king and Fibert saw an enormous Girngog scything his way through the bloody melee. He was coming from the black tents and heading their way. Bigger than the king and swinging his axe effortlessly was Trumvek. His voice could be heard even amongst the cries of war and the jarring of weapon striking weapon.

'I am coming for you, old man,' the voice of Trumvek boomed out, looking directly at the king and mercilessly slaying all before him.

'It is time for me to slay that ugly giant,' spat the king. Though Fibert was aware that the king could barely stand. Saying nothing, he instantly decided that he would be the one to confront the approaching monster, not the king.

As if to signal the drama unfolding, the bleakness of their plight, the sky darkened and a huge clap of thunder rolled across the land. The sun shone down in tunnels of light in between the clouds. Then a tumultuous sound rang out that stopped most on the battlefield where they stood. Many a heart stopped beating as it rang through the air.

It was the call of hundreds of horns singing together. Silver reflections of light came from the same direction. The Girngog had paused, even Trumvek. Drawing closer to the battle with every second, the ground reverberated from the pounding of hooves. The illusion that an army had ridden out of the heavens was crowned by the dazzling light bouncing off hundreds of raised swords. Gloriously leading on a white horse in white armour, the person leading held a gold sword aloft. The faerie had come to battle.

King Cadmus stood leaning on his sword and smiled.

'Fibert there rides the lady of legend, Queen Tixlodel. Once again, her timing is perfect. What a welcome sight, my friend.'

Renowned for their gentle nature, the forest faeries show a different face when threatened. They wore that face that day. Without hesitation, the faerie charged straight into the midst of the fighting. The faerie queen and her guard rode directly toward King Cadmus. Trumvek was close to the group defending the king and ready to smite those who stood in his way. He was eager to strike down Cadmus before he could be saved.

But he drew to a standstill as a large white horse pulled up in front of the king to block his progress. It was Queen Tixlodel. In one swift movement, she had slipped out of the saddle and stood facing the immense Girngog. He was twice the size of the faery queen.

'Go home whilst you can and take your minions with you,' the queen said firmly.

Looking down at the faery standing before him, the Girngog roared with laughter.

'Little pixie, run along, before I step on you.'

The king was watching and smiling. He turned to Fibert and said, 'That was a mistake.'

'So be it,' said Tixlodel in a quiet and serious voice.

Trumvek swung his axe above his head and charged the faerie queen. Tixlodel moved so quickly she made the Girngog look clumsy. She feinted and struck with her sword. The Girngog dropped to his knees, blood seeping from behind his right leg. He leant on his axe to haul himself up.

'I will roast you alive and eat every last bit of you,' he said in an angry tone and raising his axe.

'Enough, little man,' taunted Tixlodel.

She stepped in and quicker than the eye could follow, swung her gold sword. Again, Trumvek fell to his knees, both legs bleeding. Even on his knees, he was taller than the faerie queen. He lifted his axe again, but that was his final motion. The queen moved close and delivered a flurry of strokes with her gold sword. Trumvek stopped and fell forward, his head rolling away from his body.

The fall of Trumvek was dramatic and instantly fractured the confidence of the Girngog. Their willingness to fight evaporated and steadily they began withdrawing from the battlefield, running in all directions. The pressure on those around the king was gone. Several of the king's guard who had continued to fight, now collapsed through exhaustion and wounds. Almost instantly, scores of infantrymen arrived and surrounded the king in protection.

Queen Tixlodel walked over to the king, smiling.

'Cadmus, I told you some years ago, you are too old for this now.'

'I now believe it,' he laughed.

'Are you badly hurt? Do you need my healers?' said the queen with concern.

'I have two of their damn pins stuck in me, but I think my own doctors can fix me.'

'Well, if we are needed, do not hesitate to tell me. What is your name, young man?' asked the queen.

'I am Commander Fibert, your majesty.'

'I hold you responsible, Fibert, do not allow your king to worsen with his wounds. Do you understand me?' said the queen. 'Tell me immediately if your healers cannot help.'

'Yes, your majesty. We will take the greatest care, I promise,' replied Fibert.

'I will be fine, I must see Hewl; I saw him felled from his horse. Tixlodel, your kindness is appreciated,' said the king. 'It is so good to see you and your timing, as ever, could not have been better.'

'Well, I cannot stop to talk, for I do believe the Girngog are not yet defeated. I will talk with you later, but for now, I must ensure this victory is complete. Straight away, Fibert, get your king back to the castle,' Tixlodel ordered as she mounted her horse.

Her own personal guard was mounted and ready, waiting for her. She sped off to join the faerie army, who were routing the Girngog.

31

Surrender

In Yasrall, the Sudoorn were marching on Stonehelm. Outriders expected to find Girngog entrenched and ready to fight. Instead, they reported that the town was deserted.

'This may be some kind of trickery, I find it hard to believe the enemy would simply retreat,' General Therkon said to Adella.

'It is most odd, General. Do you think that we should wait until the outriders have scouted the whole town?' queried Adella.

'No, we should proceed. But I confess I am suspicious; we must be watchful.'

More outriders returned and each confirmed the initial reports. The Girngog had vacated Stonehelm. Upon seeing the Teb army enter the town, its remaining residents began to emerge and many confirmed the enemy had fled. It seemed that most had run toward Gritol, whilst some had gone in the direction of Bridgemouth. Upon learning this, General Therkon made the decision to leave half of his force in Stonehelm, whilst the other half pursued the Girngog, fleeing to the port.

The town was broken and dilapidated. Why, wondered Ruffle! It seemed unnecessary, given that no battle had occurred there. He concluded it was an act of wanton vandalism, intended to demean and dispirit the Rall. Yet worse revelations awaited. They soon discovered that most of the captured townsfolk and farmers had been forced into the mines dug around Stonehelm. Resolute, Ruffle chose to accompany the Sudoorn in the liberation of the Rall still held in captivity.

The network of mines was more extensive than anyone expected. Large areas had been decimated to create the holes in the ground. And there they found many Rall imprisoned. It seemed the bulk of the population was kept there, including children. All were hungry, dirty and exhausted. The Girngog guarding them had fled without explanation. The mines had been created to extract precious metals and ore. However, it was evident that the Girngog were not natural miners. Tunnels and shafts had been built haphazardly. A good number had caved in whilst being created and many Rall had perished.

Freeing the imprisoned Rall was both joyous and sad, with so many gone. Families were reunited wherever possible, but the painful count of those missing began. The people of Stonehelm were in shock, their homes and lands deeply damaged. Much work would be required to overcome, restore and rehabilitate Yasrall. Most of Stonehelm would need to be rebuilt. Ruffle was profoundly affected and made the decision to stay in Stonehelm to help, rather than continue with the Sudoorn making for Bridgemouth.

Ceri and Tansy were dismayed to see such violence and destruction. They understood Ruffle choosing to remain with his people; but for them the journey was not yet over. They elected to travel with the Sudoorn to Bridgemouth and would make their own way to Chimbleton at some point along the way. Their concern for Chimbleton had increased. They worried, had the same fate befallen the valley?

It was an emotional farewell between the companions; no time for reminiscing. They were surrounded by distress and their own journey now felt secondary to helping the people of Stonehelm. The three friends parted, agreeing to meet in Clinglewood Forest and catch up with Jevell at some point in the future.

Unsure whether to go straight to Chimbleton or accompany the Sudoorn to Bridgemouth, the two Chimbles chose the latter. When the Sudoorn rode out of Stonehelm in solemn silence, the Chimbles rode with the leading group. It was a procession of virtual silence amongst the Teb. It seemed everyone had been deeply affected by the destruction of the land and treatment of the Rall.

As the Sudoorn wended its way to Bridgemouth, Adella noticed Ceri and Tansy quietly conferring. The road was passing close to a forest of large trees on the left. To the right were slowly ascending hills. Adella was curious.

'Is this place familiar to you?'

'Yes, we know this area,' answered Ceri.

'Do you think we are in danger of ambush? That the Girngog might be hiding amongst those trees?' queried Adella, looking at the large forest.

'Not if they know what is good for them,' replied Tansy, chuckling.

'Forgive her giggles, for that is part of Clinglewood Forest and is protected by a great wizard whose favourite friend is a giant dog. The Girngog would be fools to even try to enter those woods,' explained Ceri.

'I take it that you are not teasing me? What would be the name of this great wizard?' asked an intrigued Adella.

'It is Master Jevell, have you heard of him?' said Ceri.

'Jevell. The Jevell?' Incredible. Everyone knows of Jevell; he is a legend in Tebira. And you say he lives there,' said Adella, clearly impressed.

'Yes, we know him,' beamed Tansy. 'A jolly nice wizard he is, makes lovely tea.'

Adella's eyes widened, 'then it is no wonder that you are confident that no Girngog will be within those trees. I am surprised he did not come to the aid of Yasrall.'

'He is sworn to protect Clinglewood Forest. He has cast spells to facilitate this, but he must also remain there to ensure that they work effectively. The forest itself is full of life. Shadow is the name of the giant black dog that helped us; then there is Worro, a massive bear, but we have yet to meet him. Then there is the Professor and…' said Tansy, who was clearly taken with the inhabitants of the forest.

'Well, it seems Jevell has his hands full,' interrupted Adella. 'I would hope that one day I have the pleasure of meeting him.'

Adella now looked upon the forest with different eyes. But silence resumed as they marched. It was plain which way they had to go as there was only one road. Shortly after passing Clinglewood, they came upon a crossroads, where a narrow road led off to the town of Midmoor. Outriders brought news that the Girngog were no longer there. Sadly, the enemy had wreaked similar destruction upon the small town just as they had done at Stonehelm. The General sent some soldiers to Midmoor to assess and report back later in more detail, whilst he continued to lead the bulk of his force onto Bridgemouth.

The port and the bridge were both within sight when they halted. The General spoke with Adella, but not close enough for the Chimbles to hear the conversation. However, she turned about to inform them what was happening.

'It seems the Girngog have barricaded the bridge and that many more are congregating in the town on both sides of the water. Large numbers have arrived through the Ghost Mountains and from Springhaven, apparently escaping from Venterra.'

'Tell me, Adella, if they are leaving Venterra, do you think that means they are in retreat and failed in their siege of Castle Black?' wondered Ceri.

'A good question, Ceri, but one for which I have no answer. I think it may be something the General wishes to understand before taking further action. But it would explain why they are gathering here.'

'Oh, I do hope that they are retreating, for surely that must mean things have gone well in Venterra,' said Tansy, clenching her hands together.

'I think the General is of a mind to make camp here and assess the situation. In fact, as you can see, some of our tents are already being erected. I think we should take the opportunity to rest the horses and eat something. We have soldiers watching for any developments within Bridgemouth,' said Adella.

It was not long before the Sudoorn had assembled a very large tent which was to be used as a dining hall. An hour later, Ceri and Tansy were inside eating bread and soup when Adella joined them. She sat down smiling.

'You were right, the Girngog are in retreat from Venterra. They are scuttling away from Venterran soldiers and if I am not mistaken, the Faerie. I have never met a faery, but I think I spotted some on the other side of the lake,' explained Adella.

Tansy and Ceri hugged one another in delight.

'That is such good news to know that the Faerie have come to battle. We met quite a few, you know. Though I never thought that they would become involved in our battle,' said Ceri.

'I wonder if King Cadmus is with them?' pondered Tansy.

'From what we can see across the lake, I do not think so. But as we speak, a boat has been commandeered and some Venterrans and Faerie are to come across to speak with us,' said Adella. 'And what is impressive for me is the bridge. I can see why they call it The Necklace; it looks wonderful all lit up. Despite being full of Girngog.'

'We learned that the bridge spans the narrowest part of the lake, for if one travels north, the water grows wider and wider,' said Tansy.

'I am glad to have seen the bridge for myself. Few Teb have done so. The 'necklace' as you call it, is by far the longest bridge I have ever seen,' said Adella.

The next day was a flurry of activity and the Chimbles saw little of Adella until mid-afternoon. They had found a small hillock where they could sit and watch what was happening at the bridge and in the port. The town was chock-full with Girngog, but to their surprise, no fighting appeared to be taking place. Adella spied the Chimbles and joined them, sitting on the grass.

'Sorry not to have kept you up to date, but events have been moving quickly. You will be pleased to learn that there will be no more fighting. The Girngog have sued for peace, which has been accepted. As we speak, they are surrendering their arms. There will be a formal peace parley tomorrow. A gentleman by the name of Beklok is arriving from Gritol to act on behalf of the Girngog.'

'Goodness me, I did not expect this,' exclaimed a surprised Tansy. 'I thought the Girngog were renowned for fighting to the end. But it seems that is an exaggerated myth.'

'You are not the only one puzzled by this turn of events. Many of us are suspicious of what is really transpiring here,' agreed Adella.

'Even I. unused to war, am surprised by this surrender. I was told that the Girngog have a reputation for fighting to the end. But now, after marauding through the Kingdom, they seem to have suddenly decided that they are done fighting. Very odd,' added Ceri.

'Yes, it's almost as if they wanted to surrender as soon as they could,' mused Adella.

'But the good news must be that the fighting is over, no more loss of life,' said Tansy.

'Yes, you're right, Tansy, it has all been more horrific than I expected and thankfully shorter than I thought it would be,' agreed Ceri.

The next day, Beklok arrived, escorted by Teb soldiers who had ensured that he simply travelled from Gritol to Bridgemouth. A treaty of surrender was drawn up. Present at the meeting were Queen Tixlodel; Commander Fibert, accompanied by Prince Lorin; General Therkon and Adella; Beklok of the Girngog; the old mayor of Stonehelm, Pilbuft; and to the surprise and delight of the two Chimbles, was Ruffle Cragstone representing Yasrall.

In truth, there was little to be negotiated. Essentially, the Girngog had no option but to accept the terms imposed upon them. There was much discussion as to why the Girngog initiated an invasion in the first place, but little meaningful explanation was forthcoming from Beklok. Finally, the terms were agreed upon and included the following:

All captured Girngog were to be disarmed.

Further aggression by the Girngog would result in all other parties moving to occupy Gritol.

Gritol would have to make good the damage done to Yasrall and in particular, its rebuilding.

The old fort that sat partway between Stonehelm and Gritol, would be restored and rebuilt. It would be an outpost where Venterra could oversee adherence to the treaty.

Gritol would be left to resolve its own internal differences.

It was also insisted that Merektar attend the surrender meeting

In the discussions, it was never said, but neither the Teb nor the Venterrans dispelled the impression held by the Girngog that a dragon could again be pitted against them in an instance of more aggression. They felt it was useful for the Girngog to assume the Teb had a dragon ready to fight; albeit the Teb knew the dragons would not involve themselves in any further conflict between the races.

The Girngog also insisted that Merektar was gone and so could not attend the negotiations.

Many more minor issues were discussed, but they were matters that concerned Venterra. The Faerie and the Teb withdrew from the talks, each party eager to return home.

Surprisingly, Ceri and Tansy did not know that Ruffle would be involved in the thick of the peace discussions. He had arrived with Pilbuft early in the morning for the parley. They saw him very briefly. They spoke just enough to reiterate their agreement to meet up in Clinglewood in a week's time. So, once they learned of the conditions of the surrender, the Chimbles decided that it was their turn to go home.

'We can't put it off any longer, we have to face whatever awaits us in Chimbleton,' said Ceri.

'Yes, I know,' agreed Tansy.

The road between Bridgemouth and Stonehelm was unusually busy, mostly with soldiers going back and forth. The Girngog had been disarmed and escorted back to Gritol by Teb and Venterran soldiers. When escorting the defeated Girngog back to Gritol, one significant development was discovered. Something that the Girngog had quietly accomplished that surprised all.

The land between Stonehelm and Gritol was flat and barren, commonly known as the Grim. It was regarded as part of Yasrall, although only a handful of Rall had ever settled in that area. The Ironspine mountains ran along the northern and western side of Yasrall and were, in effect, the boundary that separated them from Gritol. The mountains were steep and difficult; nobody attempted to climb what was effectively a high natural border wall. There was just one way through the mountains into Gritol. It was a V-shaped valley through which ran the only road. It was the only way to access Gritol from the Old Kingdom.

The development that surprised everyone was not the road, but that a great gate had been built across its entrance. This huge gate could be closed to prevent any access to Gritol. It now sat wide open to receive the defeated Girngog returning home.

Adella later acknowledged that none of the allies knew of this gate when they were discussing the terms of surrender. Beklok had said nothing of it and it no doubt influenced his attitude in negotiations. For Adella, this contributed to her own suspicions. She realised if it was closed, there would be no way to reach the Girngog.

The Chimbles joined the exodus heading to Yasrall. They walked, mingling with the throng, not wishing anyone to notice their leaving. In all the meetings and greetings at Bridgemouth, no one had mentioned Chimbleton, which pleased them. They preferred to interpret it as a sign that nothing dramatic had occurred in their homeland.

With no fuss and no fanfare, they simply strode away from Bridgemouth. They walked most of the morning before they stopped and lay on the ground to rest. They moved away from the road into the long grass, enjoying the heat from the sun and the quietness, though still in sight of the road.

'I really do enjoy being away from the noise of so many people,' said Ceri as she chewed a long piece of straw. 'It is tiring being around so many all the time.'

'I agree, it is soothing to have just the birds to listen to,' agreed Tansy, eyes closed and drifting into a hazy sleep.

Shortly after, Ceri suggested that they should get going again. Looking around, there was no one close on the road, so they seized the chance to veer off onto the hillside. It would have been very hard for anyone to have followed them, so adept were they at disappearing within their own lands. As they climbed the gentle slopes, they became nervous and cautious.

'What if the Girngog had attacked and plundered the valley?' said Tansy aloud. 'Would anyone realise it?'

Ceri looked at her friend, but said nothing. She was filled with dread and lost for words.

After a long day walking, they eventually emerged along the same path they had taken with Ruffle. Big Sprout was there, same as always. Tense and watchful, they walked back toward their homes. To their relief, Chimble Thistle looked just the same, as if they had never been away.

Leaning on her gate, Mrs. Duckle looked at the two companions walking by.

'Now, where you girls been? What you been up to, eh? I hope you been behaving 'selves!'

'Just been for a walk, Mrs. Duckle,' replied Ceri.

'A walk! Fiddlesticks. You been up to somethin', me thinks. You been gone somewhere's and took your time.'

Turning to Ceri and grinning, Tansy whispered as they walked past Mrs. Duckle.

'I am so happy to be home.'

'We definitely don't need any warring here, Mrs. Duckle is enough to keep us occupied and long may things stay this way.' replied Ceri.

They found their homes thick with dust and their gardens overgrown, yet otherwise just as they had been left. Ceri threw open her windows and set about searching for a duster. Tansy had come with her, not yet ready to begin the task of restoring her own dwelling.

'I must get some fresh herbs and have a clear out,' muttered Ceri to herself as she began cleaning her kitchen.

'You need to prioritise Ceri. Firstly, I think you should put the kettle on, find some biscuits and sit down. It's always the best place to start,' smiled Tansy.

32

Agreed Suspicions

Before leaving Bridgemouth, Queen Tixlodel had sent word to King Cadmus that she would return to meet with him. There was a lodge, large and sumptuous, that the king would occasionally visit, where he could spend time with just his family. It was away from the hustle and bustle of his court. It was within the woods on the eastern most side of Venterra. Hidden within the trees, few knew of it. That is where the king would sometimes meet with Queen Tixlodel. But not this time. The king was wounded and confined to his bed, so Tixlodel would make a discreet entry into Castle Black.

Once again, the gates of the castle were open. The people of Duskhold had ventured back to their charred and broken homes to salvage what they could. There was little remaining and the worry of Girngog returning meant that the majority preferred to continue sleeping within the safety of the castle walls. It was already proclaimed that the ruins of Duskhold would be fully knocked down. A new Duskhold would be built and it would be positioned further away from the castle.

Blanketed by darkness, a hooded Queen Tixlodel, accompanied by two of her royal guards, met with Commander Valaya and made a quiet entrance into the castle. The faery queen found King Cadmus propped up in bed. The arrows had been removed and he was bandaged. He had lost much blood. He was gaunt and clearly tired. His physicians worried that he would not rest properly. Nonetheless, he was happy to meet and talk with the Faerie queen.

'Those physicians' fuss about me, but I will live. I feel my age; that much is true, but at least those darts were not poisonous. So, do tell me what has transpired.'

Queen Tixlodel explained how matters had unfolded after the rout of the Girngog in Venterra. He was intrigued to learn that the Teb had used the old road running beneath the Ironspine to cross into Yasrall. He was further delighted to learn that the three companions had survived and proud to know that his son, Lorin, had attended the surrender of the enemy.

Tixlodel explained that it had not been her intention to be involved in peace talks, but as Cadmus was not present, she felt obliged to do so as the most senior, experienced and ranked person.

'Cadmus, I wish to share a thought with you. Something that troubles me. Namely, I think we have been led by the tail. I believe that there is more to this campaign by the Girngog than it would seem. They are renowned for their sheer aggression and fighting to the finish, but in this conflict, that was much less evident. Some things were just not typical of the Girngog. It could be that it is now a long time since the end of the Dragon Wars and they may have changed. But I strongly doubt it. We had all assumed that, having been vanquished, they would return to fighting amongst themselves, as their tribes have traditionally done. However, it seems we were wrong. The tribesmen fought alongside one another in this short campaign. They seem united once again.'

'You know Tixlodel, I think the reason we get along so well is that we think alike,' laughed the king, though it caused him some discomfort to do so. 'I confess I am of the same mind. I have had time to think, being confined to this bed and I also do not believe that the Girngog brought all that they could muster to this war. I wondered why not and I fear that they have a deeper purpose yet to be revealed. This Girngog campaign was strategic in intent and we remain ignorant of its purpose.'

Tixlodel was nodding her head in agreement as she replied.

'The rumours say that there is a mage manipulating the Girngog and we know all too well who that could be. Merektar was never found after Olbus and the wizards defeated the Girngog in the last war. Here again, my instincts tell me that there is a deeper and darker mind scheming this latest invasion. To what end I know not, but that is my suspicion, voiced only to you. Most worryingly, I suspect it is the work of Merektar.'

'Yes, it would answer the suspicions that I have, if it were so. Yet, I remain puzzled. Why would the Girngog start a war that they were not fully committed to? What devious plan might Merektar have conjured? What is he seeking?' pondered the king.

The queen leant back in her chair and brought her hands together.

'Well, let us consider where we are. I spoke with Adella and she informs me that whilst the Teb were willing to help in this conflict, they are reluctant to leave the old mountain road open for any length of time. The Tebiran Council consider it makes them vulnerable. It is their wish to close it for good. They hesitate as they are unsure if the Girngog aggression has run its course.'

'She is very sure that we will no longer receive any assistance from the dragons. They have suffered so much in the wars of men, Vazzorg has affirmed that they have no intention of becoming involved in any future conflicts.

'On the more positive side, Castle Black remains intact and your future king is developing good experience. I know you must be proud of him, though it is a mixed time with Hewl now gone.'

The king slowly nodded his head, but said nothing. Tixlodel continued.

'It is my thought that for the time being, we need to listen and watch. My people are very reluctant to become embroiled in another war. There is a growing consideration in Earthroot that we should move out of the west side of the great forest and confine ourselves to the eastern side. I doubt this would happen, as it would leave the west side of Earthroot vulnerable. It is more that my people are weary of war. We Faerie live long lives and there has been too much spilling of blood in our lifetime. Yet, I am doubtful that the Girngog efforts to annex Venterra are done.'

'It was also noticed by many that the wizards did not involve themselves. Some say it was because it was a relatively short war, others suggest that they are too old or even dead. Others suggest that the time of the wizards has gone, they now belong to history.'

The king spoke, at the same time fidgeting to find a less painful position in his bed.

'Unfortunately, there is little that I can add to the speculation. I know Jevell lives in Clinglewood and I believe he would have made his presence known if the forest had been threatened. But I have no idea where Arc or Ralissa now live, or what occupies them. Though I suspect none are dead. Wizards live an awfully long time, you know. I also thought Olbus lived in Earthroot, but you would know that if it were so,' said the king.

'Yes, you're right, he does reside in Earthroot. In truth, I am the only one who knows where he is. He lives deep within the trees and keeps to himself. I have seen him on a few occasions and he always asserts that he will not be in Earthroot forever. He insists that he will never be involved in warfare again and he deeply regrets making the Instruments of Light and Power. My impression is that Master Olbus will be leaving Earthroot before very long. Though I don't know where he will go,' admitted Tixlodel.

'Will he disappear just like the Wizard Library? His wisdom and counsel is missed. Many believe him dead. I know our soldiers were disappointed not to see the Instruments wielded again in this campaign,' observed the king.

'Yes, I have heard that said, but as none of the wizards appeared, it was no surprise that nothing was seen of the Instruments. As far as I know, they are still in the possession of Olbus and the Master Wizards. I can also testify that Olbus is far from dead,' replied the queen.

'You are likely aware that a duplicate of the Crown of Connection has been held here in Castle Black. It had no powers, of course. And, as Olbus had predicted, it was stolen. When I was away in Tebira, a shapeshifter duped Hewl and made off with it,' explained the king as he winced with the pain from his wounds.

'A shapeshifter and a half-hearted war, it increases my suspicions, Cadmus. Something may be coming and it reeks of Merektar. But we have yet to grasp what is afoot. I am of a mind to suggest that we keep in closer contact. It seems that we are as one in expecting that there is more to befall us. Unlike many of my kind, I believe Earthroot cannot close its eyes to the world away from the trees. It is not done with us yet,' said Tixlodel.

'I agree. Some precautions must be taken. Reopening the old fort in Yasrall will help to monitor Gritol a little, but we need ears in places where tongues are loose. The more knowledge we can gain, the better we can prepare. And I do believe we will have to prepare. Though for what we prepare, I do not know. Like you, I also think this is not finished,' added the king.

'Do you know what Merektar ultimately seeks?'

'No, I am afraid I don't. The only thing I feel sure in stating is, that the warring is not concluded, the Girngog will return.'

'Will the wizards help us?' posed the queen.

'Honestly, I don't know. I find it hard to imagine that they won't. At least we can hope they do,' concluded the king.

The two rulers talked further of more mundane matters. Then, despite the late hour, the queen and her guards set off back to Earthroot. The king lay in his bed, thinking and cursing his wounds, which made it difficult to sleep. His thoughts went round and round as he pondered what was happening. He could not find a satisfactory explanation and he was a long way from basking in the joy of a victory. His overwhelming sense was that he was sitting on a volcano, one that he knew would erupt, but he knew not when or where.

33

Sorcerer

Sitting alone in the Blue Tower, legs outstretched, he smiled to himself. As always, he was dressed in black, and being alone, he was warming his bare feet by the fire in his room. Bright jewellery and rings holding precious stones complemented his dark appearance, as did his eyes, which were almost black. He cut a figure of someone made from the fabric of midnight. Amongst the Girngog, he was known as the 'eyeless one' - though it was never said in his presence. This was Merektar and the Girngog were in thrall to him.

He sipped wine, feeling content and satisfied. Unlike some of the tribal leaders, he regarded the recent Girngog campaign as a success. His main objective in waging this latest incursion had been to gather information that he felt vital to his truer, more ambitious intentions. He had achieved this.

Foremost in his plans, he wished to gauge if the Grandmaster Wizard, Olbus, and his three Master Wizards were active. None had appeared during the invasion. What could he deduce from that? Had they left the old kingdom? Were they still alive?

He was quite sure Jevell lived in Clinglewood Forest, but maybe he had become reclusive, confining himself to the woods and solitude? According to his spies, he had not been seen outside Clinglewood in a long time. He had not intervened as Yasrall was put to the sword. He wondered, had the wizard lost his powers?

Another question that intrigued him - what was he to make of the fact that nobody had wielded any of the Instruments of Light? Where were those tools of power? Had they been destroyed?

Perhaps they were hidden? Could Olbus have taken them away? His own shapeshifter, Opik, had seized a replica crown, but what significance did that hold? There had been no discernible reaction to the theft of the false crown.

It was said that only a wizard, at the level of a Master, would be able to control the power that each Instrument contained. But he was encouraged that no wizards of such calibre had been seen for years. So much so, that Arc and Ralissa had almost become mythical, for they too were absent from the Old Kingdom.

The strongest rumour that he thought credible, was that Olbus had taken the Instruments to the Wizard Library. But then, where was the library? It had disappeared from the edge of the Pancake Lands and nothing was now known of its whereabouts. His spies could find no information that it still existed. Perhaps the domain of the wizards was crumbling and with it the Wizard Library, may be gone forever!

The biggest surprise of the short Girngog campaign had been the appearance of the Teb. Their arrival had been significant. With the mountain dwarves long vanished, he had not expected any interference from the north of Yasrall, where the land was scarcely populated. The Ironspine formed a natural boundary between Yasrall and Tebira. The doors to the old dwarf road that ran through the mountains were closed. He did not know where to find them as, ordinarily, they were invisible, hidden within the rock. Merektar had assumed that the passage was sealed for good, that is, until the Teb opened the doors once again.

The surprise arrival of the Teb represented a weakness in his scheming, as they were the greatest threat to his ambitions. However, he was comforted when he learned from his cohorts that they intended to close the mountain road again and this time permanently. The Teb had been the ones who repelled the Skove invasion during the Dragon Wars. They possessed the largest well-trained army in the Old Kingdom. He wondered if his own Girngog forces were now a match for the Teb, but decided that his plans would be stronger if he waited for the road to be closed again. And once the Teb had no easy access to Yasrall, there was less likelihood that any dragons would reappear. He knew what a big difference a dragon could make to a campaign. The appearance of Cherigg at Castle Black had demonstrated that.

He had mistakenly discounted interference from the dragons living in Tebira, as he knew that they had forsaken intervening in the conflicts of humankind. Thus, he had been surprised to learn that a dragon had helped break the siege of Castle Black. But he gauged that the arrival of Cherigg was an isolated occurrence. He deduced that once the road to Tebira was closed, the dragons would remain at Dragon Mountain. Then, when the time was right, he could deploy his own surprise.

He was in no rush to complete his preparations, having spent considerable time plotting and planning. He was prepared to bide his time until all was in place and he knew that the time was close. Meanwhile, his spies would be deployed far and wide, collecting information about the Instruments of Power and his treasured tome – the Book of Shades. For this, it was important for him to know the whereabouts of the Wizards and their Library.

His particular labour of love was the Book of Shades, which he had personally embellished from stolen spells and potions held at the Wizards' Library. As an apprentice wizard, he had betrayed the trust placed in him. He had copied and stolen material intended to remain at the library. He was a natural sorcerer and his intention was to become the most powerful wizard. However, before he had finished secretly adding to the Book of Shades, he had been discovered.

Consequently, before he could complete his malevolent work, he had had to flee. Annoyed with himself at being found out, he took the book he cherished with him. Pursued by the library guards and wizards, and despite being cornered and confronted on numerous occasions, he had defeated and overcome all those pursuing him. All that is except for one. Now titled Grandmaster, it was Olbus who had caught up with him and recaptured the book. Though Merektar had given up the book to create a diversion by which he could escape. The loss of the book burned deep within him. He would never forgive Olbus. His thirst for revenge and to regain the book became an obsession. But where was Olbus or the book, he no longer knew.

In all his scheming, his most acute curiosity centred around the Wizards' Library. It was where mages progressed in becoming wizards. It held a vast accumulation of knowledge, including all things magical. He felt that it was the most likely place that the Book of Shades would be held. It would be the logical thing to return it to the library. He calculated that it was also the most likely place where he could find Grandmaster Olbus.

Merektar had apprenticed at the old Wizard Library in the Pancake Lands. But that was already turning to dust, having been abandoned. The mystery for Merektar was, did a Wizard Library still exist somewhere? He believed it did, but exactly where, nobody seemed to know. There was nothing to help him, no news, no whispers, no clues. Just rumours. However, he doubted the grandmaster would allow all the knowledge and artefacts within the library to disappear or be demolished. No, he could not accept that. All his instincts told him that the Wizards Library still existed and it would be where he would find the Book of Shades and the Instruments of Light. He was determined and prepared to do whatever he must to find it.

Once he had regained the book and the Instruments his ambitions extended this. His scheming was on course. He had designed the recent Girngog invasion as a means to help gather crucial information. For Merektar, the invasion was a 'false campaign' for he never expected a permanent victory. He had convinced his own mages and the tribal leaders of the Girngog that a limited campaign was necessary to gauge the strength of the enemy. He needed to assess the response he might expect once his true campaign launched. For, unknown to all outside of Gritol, he had been organising and building the Girngog forces for a long time.

The Girngog were truly under his spell. They relished his false interpretation of history. He had persuaded them that Gritol had been wronged, that it had once been an empire reaching far beyond the Old Kingdom. He had the Girngog believe that defeat in the Dragon Wars had resulted in their lands being stolen and their tribes being confined to Gritol as punishment. It was all fabrication.

He spun this myth as he needed the Girngog motivated in order to fulfil his own plans. Within himself, he had tasted defeat and denial. He now wanted revenge and a permanent victory. Conquering and ruling the Old Kingdom was his first objective, but his lust for power extended far beyond the old boundaries; he planned to destroy the Wizard Library, to become the greatest sorcerer and create an empire.

34

Jack

As arranged, the three companions met in Clinglewood Forest a week after the surrender discussions. They spent a joyful few days with Jevell and brought him up to date with all that they had seen and experienced. More light-heartedly, Ruffle was especially impressed with a pie that the wizard made on their second day. Yet, despite his general good humour, the Rall owned up to an underlying sense of gloom. This was derived from the scope of damage that the Girngog had inflicted upon Yasrall. There would be no quick and easy fix.

It was a subject that Jevell spoke about as he led his guests on a stroll through Clinglewood.

'Sadly, the cost of warring conflicts lingers long after the spilling of blood. And it would seem that Yasrall has suffered the highest cost. But let me say, I am proud of you all. You set out facing unknown dangers on behalf of others; and many things have been achieved due to your bravery and persistence.'

'Thank you, but I did not prevent what has happened in my lands. I was too late. Now I am not sure how much can be healed, both within my people and our homes. So many of our dwellings are destroyed,' commented Ruffle.

'Time and serendipity can help,' began Jevell.

'And you cannot blame yourself for any of that. One could say that it was because of you that Yasrall was liberated,' said Tansy, interrupting.

'I don't know if we should rebuild or find an alternative solution to the destruction,' wondered Ruffle.

That was part of a conversation that had occurred some three years past. Ruffle had then returned to Yasrall, determined to lead the rebuilding of his land. Ceri and Tansy had resumed their lives in Chimble Thistle. They were all preoccupied with day-to-day life and had not met with Jevell since.

Having travelled well beyond their valley for the first time, it was comforting for the Chimbles to be back home. But their adventures had ignited something within Tansy. She was not aware of it at first, not least because she was preoccupied with restoring the condition of her house. She had returned to find the garden overgrown, the house covered in dust, and many little repair jobs that she had previously put off, still waiting for her.

Then there were her neighbours, endlessly curious as to where she had been. Equally as interested to know more was Chayde, whose wish to begin courting Tansy had not waned. It was not long before Tansy felt that she was once again immersed in the cut and thrust of daily life in Chimbleton.

Imagining the response that they might expect upon their return, Ceri and Tansy had agreed that they would share limited details regarding their experiences. They doubted many would believe the more fantastic episodes of their adventure. And they did not want their fellow Chimbles worrying about conflicts in the Old Kingdom. However, the more inquisitive Chimbles were not sated by the explanations they received. So, over time, the accepted tale became one that had them staying with friends in Yasrall, more like a holiday. This was more comfortable for Chimbles to hear. It was uncommon for Chimbles to leave the valley and it was a long time before the truth was learned in Chimbleton.

Generally, Tansy did not talk about where their adventure had taken them, other than to Ceri. But she found that she thought about such things often. Slowly, she realised that she had the urge to travel again. It was quite unlike a Chimble to have such a wish, for above all else, they treasured their peaceful valley and the contentment it brought. Few thought that going travelling was an attractive idea. So, unsure what to do with such thoughts, she decided she would not talk about it. Opting to keep such ideas to herself.

Being more pernickety than Tansy about her surroundings, Ceri had returned aghast at the state of her home. Things needed repair and cleaning, so like a whirlwind, she swept through the house mending and tidying. She held the simple view that a tidy house made for a tidy mind. She also felt she needed to have a 'spick and span' house in order to continue her study of herbs and healing. She knew she could think more clearly when her surroundings were orderly.

However, once word spread that she had returned, a steady stream of children began arriving at her door. Ceri had been the most popular teacher within the valley and many children wanted to recommence their learning with her. Just as many, of course, longed to hear about her time away. To the children, the notion of anyone leaving Chimbleton was extraordinary, an adventure in itself and they were keen to know what she had encountered beyond the valley.

Inevitably, her neighbours chatted and gossiped, eager to bring her up to date with what had happened of late in Chimble Thistle. They also reminded her, through compliments, how they missed the wonderful cakes she would create. So, Ceri found herself busy and quite quickly integral to the daily 'to and fro' of her village. Yet despite being swiftly re-immersed into the Chimble way of life, she found that her thoughts often harked back to the uncertainties of her travels. Gradually, it dawned upon her that she, too, had the urge to travel once again.

However, discussion about any further travelling rarely emerged between the two companions. Both adventurers fitted neatly back into Chimble life, like pieces that had been missing from a patchwork quilt. So, more than three years had slid by and they had not met with Ruffle or seen Jevell in all that time. Though three years is not long in the life of a Chimble.

The little house that Ceri called home had a wooden porch at the front. It spread across the width of the dwelling. It was decorated with lanterns and wind chimes, with two rocking chairs looking out on the world. Sitting at the front of her home, the chairs looked right down the valley, which, as Chimble Thistle was set slightly higher than most of Chimbleton, afforded wonderful sunset views.

It was a regular thing to find the two friends sitting on the porch, gently rocking on the chairs and reflecting on life. The sun would slip from the sky and it would be the turn of the stars to shine. The two friends would talk for hours, whilst watching the transition from day to night. On one warm summer evening, just before sunset, the two friends sat sipping summer wine.

'I have been thinking, it's been too long since we heard from Ruffle. Shouldn't we contact him, or maybe go visit him?' wondered Ceri.

'My dear Ceri, have you been reading my mind? I have been thinking the same thing of late. I wonder how he is and how well Yasrall has recovered? And yes, I confess I would welcome the chance to go and visit him. As content as I am being home, I confess to having itchy feet. A little travel would be very acceptable.'

'Indeed. Have you been reading my mind, for such thoughts have occupied me of late. But do you have the time, now that you are courting Chayde?' chuckled Ceri.

'I am not courting Chayde. It is true that he has asked me to step out with him, but I am undecided. Besides, the opportunity to travel once again would be more my priority than courting at this moment. If you were not so embroiled in your herbs and teaching, then you would be courting, too. I happen to know that there are plenty of potential suitors for you, Ceri, though I also know that you frighten others with your independence.'

They both laughed.

'Hello, what's this? Tansy muttered quietly.

Ceri looked in the direction that Tansy was staring. Something was moving swiftly across the ground, though it was difficult in the failing light to ascertain exactly what it was. Speeding down the road and heading in their direction, it stopped immediately in front of where they sat. With its arms on the ground, its eyes looking all about, and panting to catch its breath, stood a large hare.

There was silence as they looked at the hare, who happened to be wearing a black bowler hat. When it seemed that the hare had caught its breath, it spoke and the friends jumped in surprise.

'This must be the place, they look likely, perhaps they're asleep,' said the hare, apparently speaking to itself.

'Hello, can we help you?' Ceri asked in an attempt to be friendly. Both friends had stopped rocking and sat still, watching this unusual visitor.

'Of course not, I should be asking the questions,' the hare replied rather haughtily.

A hare is usually bigger than a rabbit, usually, and this was a large hare. Unusual in size, this hare also stood out for other reasons, namely, that hares do not typically wear black bowler hats or talk.

'I am trying to find a 'Tazi' and 'Kiree' who live somewhere hereabout,' he said.

'There is no one I know of with those names,' replied Tansy, who immediately suspected the hare had the names confused. 'Unless you might mean Tansy and Ceri.'

'Indeed, that's what I said, of course,' replied the hare, standing on its hind legs and adjusting its hat with its front paws.

'Well, you are in luck, it just so happens that we are Ceri and Tansy.'

'Excellent. How clever of me. Right, I need to be off very soon. It's that time of year and I do this as a favour; it's not my business, mind you. Now that we are done, it has been very nice to meet you.' And with that, the hare turned as if he meant to go.

'Was there something you needed to tell us or ask of us?' queried Ceri, who was trying hard not to giggle at the fidgety messenger.

'Of course, why would I be here otherwise?' The hare replied, sounding a little offended. He turned to face the Chimbles. He moved closer and bent his head forward, 'Take my hat, please and look inside.'

Ceri took the hat from the hare, having first to lift it high over its ears as they protruded through holes in the inner brim. Looking inside the hat, she saw a piece of paper tucked into the inner band. She carefully slipped it out, noting it was addressed to her and Tansy. Before she could even begin to read what it said, the hare bent his head forward and spoke.

'Would you kindly replace my hat? I can feel the draft already. Then please read the note.'

Tansy took the hat and settled it back onto the hare's head, carefully sliding its long ears through the holes cut into the brim. The hare then sat looking at the two friends, tapping its right foot, as though expectant, clearly waiting for something.

Ceri unfolded the paper and read the contents before passing it to Tansy.

Dear Ceri and Tansy, if you are reading this, then it means Jack has found you. Jack is a friend and possibly the quickest hare in Yasrall. He carries this message as a favour to me.

It has been too long since we last sat together and much has happened. I write to suggest that we should meet up and catch up. I will be in Clinglewood Forest at the house of Jevell in three days. May I be so bold as to suggest that you join me there in three days?

Why so suddenly, you may wonder, well I am leaving Yasrall and thereafter it will be more difficult to meet up, as I will be going a long way away. So, I thought I would take the opportunity to meet with my dear friends before I go. It has been too long since we were together.

Just tell Jack yes or no; he would not remember much more than that.

I hope to see you there; I have missed your company.
Signed, Ruffle

The friends took a few seconds to absorb the message. Tansy gave a quick humph as she said, 'Typical of Ruffle to ask something of us and give us so little time to respond.'

'Well, it may not be an adventure, but I would like to see both Ruffle and Jevell again; it has been much too long. I think I can say immediately that I would dearly like to go, how about you?' Ceri asked Tansy.

'Definitely, it's a lovely idea,' Tansy replied with a big smile and a little surprise that Ceri had responded so positively so quickly.

The big hare was sitting there, front paws now folded, clearly ready and waiting, its right foot still tapping the floor silently,

'Your name is Jack?' said Ceri.

'Who else would I be? I certainly would not be Jill, she is waiting for me and I am late as it is,' came the reply, in which the hare made no effort to hide his impatience.

'Well, Jack, please tell Ruffle that our reply is yes,' said Ceri, 'do you want me to write that on this note?'

'Of course not, and thank you,' he responded. 'You did say yes, am I correct?'

Ceri nodded. 'Yes.'

The hare nodded too, turned and then sped off at a terrific pace, which left the Chimbles open-mouthed as he bounded over the ground, barely touching it.

'Crumpets, I have never seen anything move so fast,' said Tansy. 'No wonder he has his ears tucked into his hat; at that speed, he would lose it otherwise. Do you think he will remember the answer we gave him?'

'Surely he will, I mean it's not a lot to recall, is it?' replied Ceri, though her voice betrayed her uncertainty.

Disappearing into the dimming dusk light, the hare was gone and silence cloaked the two friends. They both sat staring into the fading light and marvelled at this friend of Ruffle. Then Ceri lit a lantern and several candles.

'Now I did not expect that, I think a pot of tea might be in order,' she said, gazing into the descending gloom in the direction the hare had gone.

'Indeed,' replied Tansy, 'and perhaps the occasion calls for a biscuit too.'

'What occasion would that be?' queried Ceri.

'Why the occasion of deciding that we are going on a journey, albeit it is not an adventure, we are nevertheless venturing out of Chimble Thistle once again,' said Tansy, smiling. 'And I am quite tickled at the prospect.'

'Yes, Tansy, you are correct. I had not really thought about it, but even travelling just to Clinglewood is rather appealing. Seeing Ruffle and Jevell will be wonderful. So, my dear friend, I think a biscuit and even a slice of hazelnut cake might be exactly what is needed', laughed Ceri as she made her way to the kitchen and the kettle.

Tansy sat for a few moments more, then followed her indoors. She sat at the kitchen table, watching Ceri as she took the biscuit box from the pantry.

Ceri ran her eyes along the shelves filled with large boxes until she found the one she was after, 'There you are,' she uttered to herself as she lifted a box down and set it upon the table. The label on its top read 'Hazelnut'. The boxes on the shelves all contained cakes, a variety to suit any palate – strawberry, carrot, blueberry and so much more. In truth, Ceri gave away more cake than she ate. Her neighbours often contrived excuses to drop by, secretly hoping for a slice of one of her scrumptious cakes. Ceri was well aware of this, yet took no offence; she delighted in sharing her delicious creations for others to enjoy.

'How long do you think it will take us to travel to Clinglewood Forest?' asked Tansy.

'I think a little bit more than half a day, but there is no hurry. So, leaving the day after tomorrow after breakfast will be fine' suggested Ceri as she sliced the hazelnut cake.

'Which means that we can prepare tomorrow and leave the next day!' said Tansy. 'That should be enough time for me to sort a few things out before we leave.'

Ceri stopped, looked up and was clearly thinking.

'If we take today as day one, tomorrow as day two, then the day after is the third day. So yes, let us go with that. We can leave mid-morning, which should afford us plenty of time to reach the forest in daylight. Just in time to rendezvous with Ruffle,' she said, thinking out loud and before continuing to cut a cake.

'I wonder how changed they are? And where is Ruffle going to?' pondered Tansy.

Ceri laughed, 'no doubt he is off on another adventure and we will accompany him!'

'I doubt it, but it will be lovely to see him again,' Tansy decided.

35

Together Again

So, it was the day after, when the two friends set off for Clinglewood Forest. They walked to the Wishing Well near Big Sprout and took the same path that they had once taken with Ruffle. This time, there was no sense of urgency. The two Chimbles were excited; the invitation had arrived at a good time. It chimed with their growing urge to travel once again. They passed lots of budding blackberries, but it was too early in the season to pick them. They reached the foot of the hill and stopped to look about, a habit they had developed when fleeing from the Girngog. This time, there was no one in sight.

They went at a leisurely pace, crossing the fields and arriving early afternoon at the outskirts of Clinglewood Forest. The cottage of Jevell lay deep within the trees and there was no path to follow. Their simple plan was to start walking into the forest as far as they could and hope that Shadow would find them. That was how they had found Jevell the first time and they hoped to repeat it.

Off they went, stepping over fallen branches, getting very warm and swiping away the many buzzing insects. After a couple of hours, Tansy felt hot and bothered and stopped. There was no sign of Shadow.

'I am not sure this plan is going to work!' she said.

It was a warm sunny day, though the canopy of trees created a rather gloomy light.

The ground was hard and they consistently crunched dry twigs underfoot. It seemed very little rain had penetrated the high cover for some time. There was no wind to bring any coolness and Ceri felt just as frustrated as Tansy.

'Unfortunately, I think you may be right. We've been walking and walking and getting nowhere.'

'Let's just rest a while,' suggested Tansy.

So, they sat on a large fallen tree. They each dug out a flask from their knapsacks and took a long swig of cool water. They were hot and lost. They had known that they would get lost, but as they expected to be found by Shadow, they had not been overly concerned.

'Do you think we might have to spend the night amongst the trees?' said Tansy.

'It's a good while yet before the sun goes down, I think we should keep walking and hope we hit upon a path,' replied Ceri.

'I don't think there are any paths in Clinglewood. Maybe we should have sent a message to Jevell," suggested Tansy as she wiped her brow with a yellow handkerchief.

'How could we do that? I don't know how to do that' replied Ceri. She took another drink. 'Although the forest probably tells Jevell once anyone enters.'

'I think that is something that you should remedy for the future,' said a deep, warm voice coming from the darkness between the densely packed trees.

The two Chimbles started in fright, momentarily unsure whose voice they had heard. Then out of the darkness between the trees stepped a huge black dog, as large as a horse, like something you could imagine in a nightmare, except this was Shadow, Jevell's dog.

The two Chimbles sprang up and ran over to hug him. As delighted as they were by his appearance, his vigorously wagging tail made it plain that the feeling was mutual.

'Oh, Shadow, we are so pleased to see you; we hoped you might find us,' said Ceri, clinging to his large right leg,

'Have you grown bigger?' asked Tansy, clinging to his left leg and looking up at his face.

Shadow laughed a deep, throaty laugh that they had never heard before.

'Well, my friends, I don't think so. But perhaps you both have' the dog said. 'Still, I would suggest that you climb on my back and we make haste to join Ruffle and the Master.'

'Is Ruffle already here?' asked Tansy

'Yes, like you, he was wandering in the woods this morning. The red squirrels alerted us and it was a surprise, because Jevell was not expecting him' replied Shadow.

'So Jevell knows we are arriving?' asked Ceri.

'He does now. He is very happy to have you visit him again and he sent me out to find you, realising you would never find his cottage otherwise,' said Shadow.

'Wonderful', exclaimed Ceri, rubbing her hands together in anticipation.

Shadow sat down on all four legs to allow the Chimbles to climb on his back. As he stood up, the friends gripped the fur of the dog. Shadow walked a little and then gathered speed. Despite knowing what to expect, the passengers sat with mouths agape as the graceful dog ran and the branches moved aside. It was as if the woods saw him coming and made way. Before very long, they had arrived at the clearing, which looked like a large overgrown garden.

And there, sitting in the middle of the clearing, was the cottage of Jevell. From the outside, it looked rather small, constructed of wood and stone with a dark green door on which sat a bright red knocker in the shape of an apple – both Chimbles felt it was all rather welcoming.

The two friends threaded their way through the flowers onto the small path that led to the cottage door. Despite the warmth of the afternoon, smoke billowed from the chimney. They knew from previous visits that the world inside the cottage was a little different from that outside. They were in an enchanted place. The obvious example being the small square cottage, which was a completely different size inside, where large rooms and corridors could be found. Long ago, they had decided it was some form of wizardry and accepted it.

Standing by the door, the two Chimbles looked at one another, both smiling, both happy to be visiting Jevell again. Tansy reached out for the apple knocker and before she could touch it, the door opened. Standing in front of them was a grinning, bearded Ruffle.

What followed were countless hugs and repeated cries of 'so good to see you'. Then the large figure of Jevell appeared, joining in the joyful greetings. They moved into the cottage and sat down in the seats spread about the fireplace, all still beaming at the pleasure of being in one another's company.

'Have you been here long?' asked Tansy of Ruffle.

'Not really, I arrived late morning, thanks to Shadow.'

'We also owe thanks to Shadow, I doubt we would ever find the cottage without his help,' laughed Tansy.

'Well, the good thing is that you are all here safe and sound,' said Jevell, 'but first things first, let me make some tea and find some things to nibble, then we can sit outside and enjoy the remainder of the afternoon whilst we catch up.'

'Sounds like a good plan to me,' agreed Ceri.

They congregated in the garden around an old oblong pine table, comfortable wooden chairs and a surplus of soft cushions. The wizard served strawberry tea, along with a bowl of red grapes, a loaf of bread and scones, all complemented by several jars of various jams. A dish in the form of an open flower held some shining white cream. Pride of place and sat in the centre of the table, was another dish shaped like a miniature replica of the small cottage, which, when its roof was lifted, revealed a deep yellow hunk of butter. On a plate patterned with flowers sat the scones. Tumbled into a little woven basket, brought out from a cake tin and not an oven, they were inexplicably deliciously warm. More wizardry thought Ceri.

'Tuck in,' encouraged Jevell, which they did, needing no second invitation.

'So, tell me, did anything in particular prompt you to visit with me at this time?' he asked.

The three guests each had a mouthful of scone, jam and cream, making it difficult to speak. So for a few seconds there was no reply. It was Tansy whose mouth emptied first and she broke the silence.

'Well, I think we were overdue to visit with you, and it is lovely to be together again. But credit must go to Ruffle, as he sent the note suggesting we all meet here. And he did so via a very unusual postman.'

'Yes, he sent our invitation carried by the quickest hare I have ever seen and one that could talk,' explained Ceri.

'Oh, well done, Ruffle,' laughed Jevell.

'The hare was called Jack. And do tell us, Ruffle, how do you know him?' asked Tansy.

Originally, he recognised me from when I got lost in the rabbit holes, whilst escaping the Girngog; although he never spoke to me then. In fact, I didn't realise that he had seen me as I never saw him. Then long after the war had ended, I came across him out in the fields and he took me by surprise. When he saw me in the field he simply walked up and started talking. I confess it was the last thing I expected to happen. It was quite a shock.'

'In particular, he asked me how I had gotten out of the rabbit tunnels. So, I explained what had happened but made sure he understood that it was due to good luck, as I could never find my way back through the tunnels. I wanted him to know that I would never be venturing in the there again. Since then, I have met him on several occasions and I noticed how swift he was. When the idea of meeting up came to me, I thought he would be able to deliver my message more quickly than any other options I had. Happily, he agreed to carry my message to Chimble Thistle. I also thought you would enjoy meeting a talking hare!'

'Did you give him the hat?' asked Ceri.

'Yes, truthfully, I doubted he would remember a spoken message. So, I offered him the hat, which he liked. Then I attached the note inside and he agreed to be my postman as his way of showing appreciation for the hat.'

'Well, he certainly gave us the impression that he liked his hat when we met him,' said Tansy.

'And Ruffle, was there anything that sparked you to choose this particular time to get together?' asked Jevell.

There was no immediate reply as Ruffle had just bitten into another scone and his mouth was full. He wiped the cream deposited on his beard, and chewed as quickly as he could. He finished his munching, took a drink of tea and apologised, 'Sorry about that, it's all so delicious'. Everyone chuckled as the happiness of meeting up again still infused their mood. Ruffle continued.

'I think if you will bear with me, I ought to give some background to explain why I suggested we meet now.'

The others nodded as they happily took their turn to devour scones while waiting to hear what he had to say.

'Well, following the war and the return of the defeated Girngog to Gritol, there was much to repair in Yasrall. Things were broken, destroyed and depleted. Our land was in pain and still is. If I had not seen it myself, then I would have found it difficult to believe that so much destruction could be inflicted. Most of the buildings were beyond repair. It became clear that we needed to give nature time to heal and at the same time rebuild Stonehelm. We could not farm or grow things as before; it was as if the Girngog had poisoned the land. It would take time, a long time. And many Rall were fearful that the Girngog would reappear.

During the telling of the story, Ruffle could not disguise the anguish it caused him; it was evident in his face and through his voice.

'This presented us with a problem. As Rall, the sense of who we are comes from the harmonious relationship we enjoy with the land. Although our ancestry stems from the dwarves who live within the mountains, we are different. Our affinity is with the land in the outer world. We have always worked alongside nature and now the best thing we could do was to leave the land to heal in its own time.'

'To add to this, the fort established near Gritol to watch over the Girngog, gradually became unused. In the first year after their surrender, the Girngog were employed to make good the damage they had inflicted upon our towns. For a while, the old fort became useful once again. However, a point was reached where the Girngog labour was no longer wanted or helpful. So, as required by the peace treaty, they kept within Gritol and stayed away from Yasrall.'

'The arrangement at the fort involved changing the guard every four months, after all, the Grim is a thankless place to be posted. There is little there to occupy the soldiers. To begin with, everything went as planned. But, before very long, the number of soldiers posted to the fort reduced. The Girngog stayed within Gritol which meant that there was so little to do. It was an unpopular posting for the soldiers and eventually deemed unnecessary. So, now it sits empty.'

'It was true that for some time, we had seen very little of the Girngog; they kept behind the great wall that forms the border to their land. However, within months of the soldiers finally abandoning the fort, the Girngog reappeared in Yasrall. Nothing significant in terms of numbers, but then some began staying at the abandoned fort. Something very few Rall noticed or cared about.'

'Meanwhile, after more than two years, it was realised that the land would still need much longer to repair itself. We had done what we could to facilitate the healing, but more than anything, it simply needed to be left alone. This was a dilemma for all Rall. How could we make a living? How could we survive when we could not farm? These were questions that challenged us. Plus, the reconstruction of buildings was far from complete.'

'Fortunately, since the war, contact had been maintained with Tebira. The old road through the mountains had not yet been closed.

The Teb have been invaluable in our recovery. In fact, they came to understand, perhaps even before we did, that we would have to make some radical decisions. Too much was irreparable.'

'It was then that the generous and noble spirit of Tebira shone at its brightest. They offered us land, plenty of land, for all Rall to go and settle in Tebira. There was no fee involved, no price to pay; it was sheer generosity. Since then, I have learned much more about Tebira, not least being that it occupies a huge mass of land. Most of it enjoys a climate where food can be grown naturally, even in its winter months, which are mild. They are also people who possess many skills and create beautiful things. Whilst we too are skilled craftsmen, the opportunity to learn from one another is very appealing.'

The friends could see his mood lighten as he described the invitation from Tebira; the future for Rall appeared brighter as his story unfolded. Ruffle went on.

'Their offer was so magnanimous that it could not be refused. So, after some discussion, it was decided to accept this wonderful opportunity and almost all Rall have agreed to move to live in Tebira.

'It is a wonderful opportunity and is also a safer choice for Yasrall. Tebira has excellent soldiers and being bordered by mountains, it is unlikely their land would ever face a threat from the west, even from Girngog. Yasrall would become its own community within Tebira, which is so large as to barely notice our settlement. Of course, moving away from the shadow of the Girngog was an appealing element of this offer, and Tebira has decreed that it will close the old dwarf road through the mountain, once we have moved. They intend that it never be opened again. For me personally, there is just one drawback, it will mean that I would move much further away from you all and it will make visiting one another much more difficult.'

Nothing was said, the Chimbles knew this to be true and seemed to be reflecting on his words.

'Even as I sit here, some Rall have already begun moving to Tebira. It will be the turn of my family soon, so I decided that before I make the move, it would be a good time to meet up. That is why I suggested it now. Perhaps it is a little selfish of me, but for a long while I have wanted to enjoy your company again. We have had too little contact these last few years. So, there it is, that is what prompted me to contact you' concluded Ruffle.

There was silence; all were wrapped in their own thoughts. Jevell rocked slowly on his chair, appreciating that it was not the time for him to speak. He knew Ruffle wanted to hear from his friends first and foremost.

'Well, your story fills me with a mixture of feelings,' said Ceri, 'I feel sad about Yasrall, the destruction and damage it has endured, but joy that Tebira have come to your aid'.

'Me too,' said Tansy. 'I think Tebira is a wonderful place and I believe you could be happy living there.'

'I agree, it will be a long journey for us to visit you in Tebira compared to Yasrall, although it is a place I do wish to return to,' added Ceri, managing a smile. 'However, I understand why you thought it a good idea to meet up and I wholeheartedly agree. I am very glad you suggested it.'

'What worries me in your tale is the Girngog. I did not expect them to venture beyond their borders for many years yet' observed Tansy. 'Do you know any more about them and what is happening?'

Before Ruffle could reply, Jevell spoke.

'I have much to say on the matter of the Girngog. There are things I believe it is time you learned, my friends. There is a larger picture that you should know of. But let Ruffle conclude his story and then I also have a tale to tell you.'

'I have nothing more to add,' said Ruffle. 'It is my intention that after leaving here I will re-join my fellows and make my way to Tebira'.

In the telling of the tale, his face had betrayed a range of feelings, sadness, joy and hope, but by its conclusion, he looked crestfallen.

'I did not realise how much destruction the Girngog had inflicted on Yasrall,' said Tansy. 'It seems the wounds of war do not end when the war stops.'

'Very true, my young friend, very true,' agreed Jevell.

Responding to what Tansy had asked, Ruffle spoke again.

'Something else I would tell you. One of my cousins ventured out to the abandoned fort and being a nosy Rall, he rode further on, nearer to Gritol. He said he got close to the wall that seals Gritol into the valley and, surprisingly, saw no guards or activity. He turned back for home and had not gone far when the gates within the wall opened. He saw a big group of Girngog march out and so he galloped away, hoping he would not be seen.'

'That night, he stopped at the fort, intending to continue on to Stonehelm the next day. But he was awoken by the sound of chanting, which turned out to be Girngog. He realised they were making for the fort. So, he quickly stole into the night and watched as they took over the empty building. He did not attempt to sleep any more, but under the cover of darkness, he began the rest of his journey home. He asked me if I knew what they were there for? I confessed I was surprised and could offer him no answer.'

'It is no surprise to me and I am sure that your cousin speaks the truth,' said Jevell. 'I think it will make more sense to you once my tale is told, but firstly, let us have a break and something to chew.'

The three companions were intrigued, happy to enjoy the hospitality of the wizard and very eager to learn what Jevell had to say. Meanwhile, the Chimbles engaged Ruffle in chat, hoping to alleviate the sadness that had enveloped him.

36

How History Matters

The scones had long since disappeared and the tea had grown cold. So, they removed the plates and cutlery, as Jevell went to the kitchen to boil another kettle of water and prepare some food. Conversation switched to happier things, as they stretched their legs strolling among the kaleidoscope of colour displayed by the flowers spread across the garden. It was still warm though evening drew closer. They returned to their seats as Jevell set down a fresh pot of tea, a plate of blueberry and oat biscuits, and a large jug of juice. To Ceri, it felt almost like a picnic, though the subjects they discussed today were far more serious and troubling than their usual picnic chatter. Normally, this was the point at which she would drift into a nap for an hour or so, but not today. They had just regrouped around the table when Jevell began his tale.

'In order for you to fully understand what is happening today, we must delve into history. I wonder if you have ever heard of the Wizards Library?'

The three attentive listeners nodded.

'Yes, though I think we know next to nothing about it,' said Ceri, qualifying their nods.

'Well, it is the place where magic is written down and histories are recorded. It is also a place of training for wizards, where they can learn their craft and acquire a mentor. The library is protected by sentinels, many of whom are wizards in training. Of all the endless books and papers stored in the enormous library, there were two large books more valuable than the rest. Pride of place is The

Book of Wisdom, a tome that records every spell ever devised. It is an amazing treasure. In fact, many say it is alive, for it grows and changes as you read it. Any new spells created anywhere will automatically appear in the book, be they good or evil. It was and still is the depository of all magic. Also, as you turn the pages, the book itself never grows larger, even as new spells are added; it is as if the pages that one read then became thinner once turned. Yet if you checked back at the pages that you had previously read, they will be the same size and thickness as they had been before. This very special book is the favourite reference for all wizards, old or new. I believe there is only one of its kind.'

'But there is another book that few know had been created. This book is titled the Book of Shades. It is a beautifully illustrated volume that contains the spells a wizard might use in acquiring such things as power or money and so forth. Or in creating creatures crafted from one's nightmares. It is regarded as a corruption of wizard magic, almost evil in purpose. It is considered dangerous and kept under lock and key in a part of the library accessed only by wizards who have reached the level of Master. Thus, most students do not know of its existence. No one knows whom the original author was or why it was created. Fundamentally, it is unlike the Book of Wisdom, as new spells or charms do not automatically appear on its pages. In this dark book, someone would need to scribe any new additions. However, unbeknownst to the librarians, dark spells from the Book of Wisdom had been copied and added to its contents. Unsurprisingly, it was rarely looked at or checked. So, for a long time, nobody noticed it had grown and thickened.'

'In the past, efforts had been made to burn it, or tear it up, or find some way to destroy it, but it had proven resistant to everything. It could not be destroyed, which is why it was locked away.'

'It may have been complacency, but it was considered that the library was virtually impregnable with so many wizards in residence and thus the Book of Shades got little attention or particular protection. Nonetheless, it was the job of sentinels to protect the library; the sentinels were mages who sought to progress to the level of wizard.'

'Within the library, there were locked rooms and both of these large tomes were held there. It was only Master Wizards who could enter, although as part of their training, advanced mages were allowed to use the Book of Wisdom for reference and research.'

'Then one day it was found that both books were missing. It soon became clear that they had been stolen. This had been thought impossible. But it transpired that it was one of their own who was the thief. The Guardians of the Library had never expected this. The thief was identified as Nevan, an unusually strong mage, with the innate skills of a sorcerer. He seemed very likely to develop into a Master Wizard. Which is why part of his training afforded him access to the room where the books were kept. But he clearly had other ideas. In fact, unbeknownst to all others, he had been copying spells from the Book of Wisdom into the Book of Shades.'

'Nobody knew how long he had been adding to the dark tome or plotting to steal the books. His demeanour had always been appropriate and he was liked by many. However, he had been careful not to share his intentions with any confidant. Acting alone, when he fled from the library with both books, no one knew where he had gone.'

'Alarmed, there was deep questioning amongst the Guardians of the Library as to how he had accomplished the theft. Was there a misjudgment in allowing him access to the books and why had no one detected the motivations he clearly possessed? The community of wizards were upset with themselves for not noticing what Nevan had been doing.'

'The reputation of the Sentinels had been sullied. The system of allowing wizards in training to be sentinels was questioned. Aside from learning magic, the sentinels were trained in combat skills. So, they were the ones charged with going out into the world and recovering the books.'

'The majority saw this as an opportunity to restore their good name. Twenty-nine sentinels went out into the world. Their search was long and wide as Nevan disguised his whereabouts very cleverly. It took time to find him. How and where they did so, is a tale in itself. What befell those brave sentinels, as twenty-eight tragically perished in the quest will be told one day. Ultimately, just one person outwitted and outfought Nevan. He succeeded in recovering both books. But Nevan was not captured or slain. He escaped. He crafted a dilemma which meant either he was captured and the books lost, or the books regained but Nevan escaped. The brave and wise wizard who entrapped him chose to save the books. Thus, Nevan got away, diminished but alive.'

'The wizard who succeeded where so many failed had been the mentor of Nevan and he blamed himself for failing to spot the corruption in the thief. It was someone you now know, Grandmaster Olbus. However, it had taken him a long while to accomplish the recovery and during that time, the Wizards' Library had vanished. Previously, it could be found on the edge of the Pancake Lands, close to Venterra. But by the time the books were recovered, it was gone. All that remained was an empty building, windswept and dusty with sand. Had its contents been destroyed or had it moved elsewhere, quite simply, no one knew. Few knew that it was not the only or the original site of the Wizard Library.'

'In a similar vein, Grandmaster Olbus and the two precious books disappeared. Where he was and what happened to the books, was unknown to most. So, for a long time, there was little wizardry in the world, or so it seemed. The pervading impression was, that the Old Kingdom was at peace. Though this was not a view held by the Master Wizards. Then the First Girngog War began and all changed.'

'Now there are some things you should appreciate about the Girngog. The land that we know of as Gritol is a vast area of land, with high mountains, many rivers and large flat plains. It has a long coastline on its western side that few have ever visited. For a long, long time, it was inhabited by tribes with their own territories who were frequently in conflict with one another. But they did not seek conflict with the world outside Gritol. In fact, it was wild and big enough for a few people from other lands to settle there and make a life. The tribes of Gritol did not war with the new settlers. Indeed, there were dwarves and men living in Gritol alongside one another. It was like an unmanaged frontier, with no common rules or shared beliefs. It was rather chaotic, yet by and large, it seemed to work well, even without being governed. At least that was the impression outsiders held.'

'Then one day a leader emerged amongst the Girngog, regarded as the father of the Gritol that we know of today. He went by the name of Bereldun, a fierce warrior who led one of the largest tribes. He had a different approach. He did not set out to conquer all the other tribes. In fact, over time, he persuaded the leaders from the different tribes that their best interests lay in working together. It took time, but he is credited with uniting the Girngog and forming them into one entity. He introduced the name Gritol, which we use today. He led the Girngog to declare that men and dwarves were no longer welcome to settle in Gritol. In a relatively brief time, new settlers either left or were driven out, or worse.'

'For many years, Bereldun ruled and Gritol became a land increasingly unknown and inaccessible to outsiders. The Girngog tribes were united under his leadership and internal conflict diminished. After he died, many others tried to assume his throne, but all struggled to bring cohesion amongst the tribes. Gritol slid once again into a mix of warring tribes. Fortunately, just with one another. Then a new leader arose and things changed again. This leader was a powerful sorcerer known as Merektar, affiliated to no particular tribe. His strategy was to direct the tribal bickering outwards – as Bereldun had done - by creating the fallacy that Gritol had once ruled the lands that we now refer to as the 'Old Kingdom.' His strategy was not only to keep Gritol pure but to regain what had been lost. The approach was effective and the tribes united again.'

'To facilitate his plans, he established the Night Wheel, a group of mages whom he trained and led. He taught them wizardry in his style. Whilst this group gained a fearsome reputation within Gritol, the true power lay with Merektar. He held sway and the Girngog adored him. It was a long time before anybody realised that Merektar was none other than Nevan, the same mage who had stolen the books from the Wizard Library.'

'Unbeknownst to anyone outside Gritol, in a few short years, he assembled a huge army. Meanwhile, the Girngog traded with the mountain dwarves and eventually with Yasrall. At that time, Yasrall was quite a different place, busy, prosperous and growing. The prosperity stemmed from trade with Venterra. This occurred overland and through Bridgemouth, as boats regularly crossed the Great Lake and wagons traversed the Necklace. Yasrall also enjoyed the rewards of its own thriving farms.'

'Nobody paid much attention at first as the Girngog mingled into the world around Yasrall. At that point, they were few in number. There were many traders from different lands visiting Yasrall, so the increasing number of Girngog were barely noticed. Then one day, without warning, a great horde marched out of Gritol and overran Yasrall. It took them all by surprise. It was the first step that sparked the Girngog War.'

'Of course, Yasrall resisted and there were bloody skirmishes across the land, but it seemed that the Girngog were endless in number. Yasrall had never sought conflict and had no army as such. The pockets of resistance defending against the Girngog proved futile, but did provide time for the rest of the Kingdom to become aware of what was happening. They were awful times and the Girngog were merciless in their invasion, wreaking havoc and destruction. It was this carnage that has deterred many from ever returning to Yasrall in any meaningful numbers. It signalled a decline which has seen Yasrall towns reduced to villages and its large houses emptied. In fact, Stonehelm is the only large town remaining. Even Midmoor is now reduced to the size of a small town.'

Jevell paused, looked skyward and the companions did not interrupt. They each suspected he was remembering the past events he was now describing. Then, after a few moments, he resumed the story.

'For a while, the Girngog seemed invincible. They spread across Yasrall, marched over the Necklace, took Bridgemouth and swarmed along each route over and through the Ghost Mountains. At the same time, knowing no people lived in Clinglewood Forest, they began to cut down trees and hunt its animals. They advanced up to Springhaven, close to the Pancake Lands, where a fierce battle took place. The town was surrounded by Girngog, but the Venterrans drove back each assault; however, the assaults never relented. Eventually, there came a point when those remaining in Springhaven knew all was lost. Many escaped across the Pancake Lands. They were pursued, of course and the story goes that only a handful of people made it across that hot deathbed of land to reach Duskhold.'

'Each assault by the Girngog had been coordinated by wizards from Merektar's Night Wheel and included a range of vicious creatures. Surprisingly, giants were used. It was unusual, for giants are singular beings, rarely gathering in numbers, let alone fighting alongside one another. More peculiarly, the giants had never previously involved themselves in the wars of others.'

'In addition, the evil minions of Merektar had created many beasts of destruction. Especially dangerous were the Pelicrons, large slobbering doglike creatures, with long teeth and bloodthirsty appetites, held to spearhead many attacks.'

'In what seemed a short time, the Girngog reached Castle Black and positioned an army on the edges of Earthroot. They seemed unstoppable. Entrenched outside the castle, it was then that Merektar showed himself. He joined his main force camped south of Duskhold. It was clear that he believed he could breach the castle, though no other before him had ever done so. It was their declared intention to capture Castle Black, overthrow King Cadmus and destroy Earthroot. The ambition and bloodlust of Merektar knew no bounds. The speed of the invasion and the sheer numbers of Girngog had favoured his plans. Plans that had plainly been in the making for some years. However, this arrogant and evil sorcerer had not calculated on something which, at that point, he knew nothing of.'

'Was it Chimble Thistle, were Chimbles a secret weapon?' asked Tansy, leaning forward in her chair in anticipation.

'Don't be silly, Tansy,' said Ceri. 'But this tale is very similar in part to what happened when we were involved.'

'Well, as for Chimbles, I am sorry, Tansy, Chimble Thistle was too small and out of the way for the Girngog to bother with. Which was probably a very good thing,' replied Jevell.

Tansy sat back, not really surprised at the answer. Jevell continued.

'The next part of this tale is different, Ceri, as you will understand. Deep in Earthroot, where Tixlodel is queen of the Faerie, lived someone that Merektar must regard as his nemesis. You know him as Grandmaster Olbus. He taught me wizardry. He is my tutor and mentor. A wise and compassionate man, as well as the same wizard who had caught and defeated Nevan. Few knew that he lived in Earthroot; he enjoyed the anonymity and peace of living deep within the forest. He personally protected the two precious books retrieved from Nevan. Whilst living in Earthroot, his own studies deepened and his abilities flourished; he felt it vital that he pass on his knowledge and so he took in three wizards whom he felt could become Masters. His judgment and choices were sound, thus in time they fulfilled their promise, becoming distinguished and accomplished Master Wizards in their own right, but always students of the Grandmaster Wizard. Those fortunate wizards were Arc, Ralissa and myself.'

'Over time, the Grandmaster had become less and less inclined to get involved in the affairs of humankind, so his excursions outside of Earthroot were rare. But when he learned that it was Merektar and his so-called Night Wheel wizards who had masterminded the Girngog invasion, he was angry and his attitude changed. He blamed himself when he learned that their leader, Merektar, was none other than Nevan, the thief and student whom he had taught.'

'He always believed that wizardry should only be yielded for good purposes. In recovering the two tomes of magic from Nevan, they had fought and Olbus wounded his foe and thought that he had perished from his injuries. He hadn't. Olbus was angry with himself for not ensuring it was so. The price of that oversight had now manifested in a bloody war in which, like a phoenix, Nevan had returned. He had assumed the guise of Merektar, but he was also more powerful than he had been when previously vanquished.'

'Immediately after learning the news of the invasion, Olbus disappeared into his study. Sparks and bangs, bright lights, shouting, smoke, little explosions, hammering, and more, all came from within, but he allowed no one to enter; and then, after several weeks, he emerged from his isolation with what came to be known as the Wizards Trinity, or more commonly the Instruments of Power and Light. Three instruments each delivering different kinds of power.'

'He had toiled to create these Instruments specifically to defeat Merektar and his followers. They consisted of a sword, a crown and a wand.'

'The sword is now known as the Sword of Light and was forged from an unbreakable metal, the like of which had never been seen before or since. It glowed with a silver light and sliced effortlessly through anything it smote. Other swords would be broken by its touch.'

'The second instrument was the Crown of Connection. It was a band of gold studded with three stones of different colours, some say are rubies and diamonds, but I do not know. More amazingly, it had the quality of slowing time. Whoever wore it would experience that everything roundabout slowed. Any blow or arrow coming toward the crown wearer could be seen long before it struck. Whilst the world moved slowly for the wearer, for everyone else, it was as if crown bearer moved too quickly to lay a blow on her. A wizard wearing the crown and wielding the sword was invincible.'

'The third instrument was the Red Wand. In some ways, it was similar in powers to the wands that many wizards use, but this was much more powerful. Whoever held the wand had instant access to any spell that was needed from the Book of Wisdom. The wearer simply had to think of what she required and the spell was immediately on her lips. Thinking of the intention was enough without needing to recall the words of a specific spell. A very powerful tool. What is more, when used it rendered all other magic ineffective. So evil magic conjured by the sorcerers of the Night Wheel would be useless against the holder of the Red Wand.'

'Each of these Instruments could be used singly and of itself be a powerful force, but all three used together would make the bearer unstoppable.'

'The creation of the Instruments was timely because by that point victory for the Girngog seemed imminent, even though their advance had slowed and Merektar was frustrated at how long it was taking to tear down the walls of Castle Black. Hundreds and hundreds of Girngog lost in futile attacks were of no matter to him; he had thousands more he could bring forth.'

'The giants and war machines he employed inflicted grievous damage to the walls of the castle, but they held. Although it held at a price, as bricks broke and crumbled, the great gate was splintered in several places, and the continuous onslaught from the Girngog catapults and arrows was incessant. Ropes were continuously thrown, some managing to hook onto the battlements and the enemy climbed, only to be pushed off down to the ground. This assault occurred before the moat around the castle had been built.'

'The soldiers on the ramparts could see that the Girngog were busy constructing more wooden belfries with which to scale the walls. The earlier ones had not been high enough. They were being rebuilt and adapted to overcome such obstacles.'

'In wave after wave of attacks, the defenders of Castle Black had leased torrents of arrows on the Girngog - their wounded and dead lay all about, including giants and pelicron, who were not impervious to showers of arrows and spears, albeit it took many to cause any damage. At night, under the cover of darkness, the fallen Girngog and their creatures were removed from the field. And every night the drums of the Girngog would beat incessantly, keeping many in the castle from sleeping.'

'King Cadmus had kept spirits high inside the castle, but privately, he expected that Merektar had more plans to breach the walls. Holding his thoughts to himself, he was unsure how much longer the castle would survive. Weapons and provisions were being reduced. It had been the longest siege any had experienced and it was taking a toll on morale.'

'After much discussion, the Faerie had begun their fight at the edges of Earthroot. Whilst the Faerie may be the most skillful of fighters, they too were facing a quantity of foes larger than any they had ever encountered before. Like an army of red ants, the Girngog were relentless; they kept coming and coming.'

'Fighting alongside the Girngog, the giants swung axes and smashed trees with their heavy clubs. The splintering of the revered woodland was loud and frequent. At the same time, the Girngog launched countless arrows, many alight, requiring the Faerie to constantly douse flames before they could spread. Burning the ancient forest was a tactic the Girngog knew would most anger the Faerie. In the thick of the battle, Queen Tixlodel led by example, swinging her sword and smiting any enemy close to her.'

The audience of three plus a giant dog, Shadow, had listened without uttering a peep. Hanging onto to every word Jevell spoke, they were brought back to the here and now when the wizard said - 'Time to breathe. Let us have a break, I will continue soon.'

37

The Instruments of Olbus

The companions sat spellbound and silent. It was a history of which they had known little. They did not want the wizard to pause in his telling; they were itching to know more and what happened next. But the break was timely. Tansy needed the toilet and Ruffle had pins and needles in his left leg; he needed to move about.

Jevell rose and made his way to the kitchen. Soon the kettle was boiling, fresh tea was brewed, fruit was squeezed for juice, and warm bread was placed on the table. Jevell confessed with pride that bread was his weakness—he loved both making it and sharing it. He spoke of the many kinds he could bake, though the loaf before them was a dark brown with a hint of oat. A plate of white cheese was set out, and the wizard added a slice to the bread, topping it with small onions he had scooped from a glass jar.

'This is one of my favourite indulgences,' he smiled. 'Help yourselves.'

His three guests needed no further encouragement and copied their host.

'I would like the recipe for this bread, if I may,' said Ceri.

'Of course, of course,' replied Jevell, 'it is rather delicious, don't you think. It is….'

He was interrupted by Ruffle, who nearly choked, as he had too much in his mouth to be doing anything other than chew. Having partaken of the bread, cheese, an onion and strawberry tea all at once. Once the Rall was recovered, Jevell seemed ready to continue his tale.

'So, let me continue with my story, which nears its end.'

'Jevell, much of what you say is familiar to us. Our experience of the more recent Girngog invasion seems almost a repeat of what you describe. I am puzzled by this repetition,' said Ceri.

'They say history often repeats itself and I can see why it would seem so here. The thread that links these wars is the instigator, Merektar. But allow me to finish my story, as there is more that you should know.'

Ceri leant back in her chair, eager to learn what happened next in Jevell's recounting of the Girngog wars.

'As I recall, we rode through Earthroot, the Master and we, his three pupils. It took us some time to reach the edge of the great forest of Earthroot. It is so vast that the Faerie refer to it as the Infinite Wood. We each had our own swords and wands; we were strong wizards in our own right, whilst the Master carried the three Instruments.'

'We arrived at the edge of the wood to find the faerie in the midst of battle. It was chaotic and raw, as fighting typically is. Trees were damaged, some burned and many broken branches lay scattered across the ground. Shouts of pain, the screeching sound of metal upon metal, roars of aggression, slain Girngog, wounded faeries, the smell of charred trees, it was mayhem. There are many shortcomings amongst humankind, but war is perhaps the worst of gifts to have been brought into this world. It had been the sheer number of Girngog that had kept the faerie from advancing out of the forest.'

'The Master was greeted by Queen Tixlodel. After a quick conversation, he told us to remain where we were; instructing us to assess for ourselves when we should follow his lead. Immediately, he donned the crown, held the sword in one hand and put the red wand in a pouch on his belt. Instantly, we felt the air change, an incredible energy pulsed all around Master Olbus. Sitting upon his horse, he slowly strove forward, the sword shining brightly, heading straight into the thick of the fighting.'

'He took out the wand and spoke, but not so loud that we could hear his words. For a few seconds, there was no discernible difference, and then it felt as if a weight had been lifted from the world. The dark, foreboding mood induced by the battle was lifted. A wave of optimism washed through us and the faerie.'

'Then we witnessed a display of swordplay and combat that I would not have believed had I not been there. The Master Wizard moved amongst the enemy so quickly that I could not be sure where he was. The Girngog fell like skittles, the trolls and ogres roared in pain. Both Girngog and creatures began to flee. In little more than an hour, the Girngog attack was halted. The Master smote them down at will, which encouraged the faerie. Confronted by the sight of the white-bearded wizard felling Girngog as though mere scarecrows, panic swept through the invaders. The superior skills of the faerie finally told in their favour. Swords and knives clattered to the ground as the invaders fled.'

'At the back of this fleeing horde stood two black robed figures incanting spells, trying in vain to get the retreating army to turn and fight. The Master made his way toward them. They saw him approaching and together turned their attention on him, pointing their wands and mouthing their fury. Quickly they realised that their efforts were futile and their magic useless. In disbelief they charged Olbus, who with the Red Wand in hand struck them down.'

'That signalled the end of all attempts by the Girngog to assail Earthroot; they had failed and scampered away as fast as they could. There was relief and sadness amongst the faerie, but crucially, they had defeated the barbarous aggressor. The Master returned to the trees to a hero's welcome. Arc, Ralissa and I had gotten involved and fought alongside the faerie; but it was Master Olbus who had turned the battle and led the rout of the enemy.'

'He was never one to bask in victory but took to the Queen's tent to rest. We went with him and saw that he was truly exhausted. Clearly, his amazing efforts in the battle had taken a toll. Privately he spoke with us and I recall his words.'

"Wielding the three Instruments together is more difficult than I anticipated, but I must do it again tomorrow. We must relieve the siege at Castle Black before it is too late. After that, I will ask each of you to wield an Instrument and take to the battle. You must help end this war as swiftly as possible. For the moment, I need rest so that I have the strength to do what must be done tomorrow".

'That was our first insight into the enormous effort it took, even for the most powerful wizard, to use the three Instruments which, thereafter, were referred to as the Instruments of Power.'

'The next day, we rode from Earthroot toward Duskhold and Castle Black. This time, there were just the four of us. The faerie remained to tend to their wounded and the damaged forest. For many leagues, the road was empty, until we spied the camp of the Girngog hordes. Their camp was vast, stretched all around the castle and occupying the town. They were ositioned beyond the range of the castle bowmen. Duskhold was then a smaller town and the Girngog had inflicted much wanton damage. They had used the clay and bricks of the buildings to throw at the castle walls.'

At the point that we arrived, it was near the middle of the day and the fighting had not begun. The Master told us to ride alongside him and stay close. He took out the Instruments, put on the crown and waving the wand, uttered a spell. Nothing seemed to happen, but he assured us that the Girngog or their mages could not harm us. We then rode straight into the Girngog camp. To begin with, there was quiet, as they appeared shocked that we should do such a brazen thing. 'There's only four, chop 'em down' was heard from many, but nobody attempted to stop us. They crowded around us, growling, grumbling and shouting abuse, but did not attempt to prevent us riding through the camp up to the gate of Castle Black.'

'We saw the black robed wizards of Merektar emerge from elaboratively adorned tents and I think the sorcerer was among them. They pointed wands and seemed to be uttering incantations, but too far away for us to hear. However, nothing happened; their words were lost in the wind.'

'When we reached the gate of the castle, we turned about in order to face the Girngog and their leaders. By then, King Cadmus and the soldiers lining the battlements were watching, many calling out warnings to help us. But most were no doubt wondering how we could ride right through the enemy untouched.'

'Then the Master called out in a booming voice that no ear could hide from. I recall his words -

'*Merektar, you have caused enough pain and destruction, take your army and go home. I have returned to smite you once again if you proceed. I offer you this one chance, let there be no more bloodshed. Girngog, you may save your lives if you leave now. Go back to your families whilst you can.*'

'Merektar laughed, and then seeing his response, others began to laugh until most of the Girngog joined in, creating a loud mocking chorus. Merektar then raised his arm and the laughter ceased.

'*You are a fool wizard, age has addled your mind, I will take my revenge and strike you down and all those who stand behind you. This is my time, this is my dominion, so run now and I will let you shrink away. Though not before you return what you stole from me. Tell those in the castle to surrender and I will let them live. This is the final chance I offer you.*'

'The Master replied, '*You have made your choice, Merektar, I do what I must now, but I do it without relish.*'

'He took out his sword, which shone brightly, and with the red wand in the other hand, he turned to us and said, '*This is not why I took you on as my students, but the world needs us to act. For today, use your skills as warriors.*'

'Merektar was shouting at his minions of the Night Wheel, who in turn were yelling at the Girngog commanders. Some Girngog ran forward as if to attack us and the Master swept his sword toward them and they tumbled to the ground and lay still. The energy and power we had experienced yesterday were back as the Master strode forward on his white horse. He waved his sword in one direction and then another, without needing to touch the enemy and they fell down. Everything they tried to throw at him could not reach him; it was as if he was protected by an invisible wall. Many arrows, spears, and swords dropped to the ground, as the brilliance of Olbus advanced.'

'He looked so large on his horse, shining like a bright star and moving inexorably toward Merektar. Cheers were ringing from the castle walls and we three students of the Master followed behind, dispatching those who had escaped the swathe of his sword and were trying to attack us from the side. Uncertainty and fear were palpable, it could be tasted. No one had ever witnessed such a display of power. Many were running away.'

'Their flight was turning to panic, as they pushed one another and any objects away from their escape path. Their vicious animals ran yelping, though some attempted to attack the master and were slain. It was chaotic. There were some Girngog who attempted to war with the Master but were soon dispatched and that included wizards from the Night Wheel.'

'Nobody noticed but Merektar disappeared. It must have been his worst nightmare. The one who had defeated him previously had returned and beaten him again.'

'It was a long way back to Gritol and many of the enemy who were spread across Venterra had not witnessed the power displayed by Master Olbus at Castle Black. In fact, large numbers of Girngog still stationed throughout the land continued to occupy areas of the Kingdom, unaware of the retreat of their leader. So, although the invasion was effectively over, many invaders did not know it. It was still necessary to confront and rid the land of the remaining Girngog.'

'It took some time, but they were pursued and vanquished by a combination of soldiers from Venterra and Earthroot. Battles and skirmishes were fought at Springhaven, in Yasrall and on the Ghost Mountain roads. Good soldiers were lost, but the war had been won. Though it took time to finish it completely.'

'The Girngog spirit had been quelled, their armies in disarray and their only desire was to return to Gritol and refuge. Several wizards from the Night Wheel had fallen. Merektar had been exposed as vulnerable. He was not the all-powerful sorcerer he had boasted of being. In the panic of retreat, he had vanished. We wondered if he had gone for good or perhaps even perished, but at that point, nobody knew.

'Summoning the power to wield the Instruments had exhausted the Grandmaster. Once the Girngog had begun to flee the battlefield in Venterra, he took us aside. He gave us each one instrument to use and he retired from the fighting. To Ralissa, he gave the sword, to Arc the wand and to me the crown. We each used the Instruments in pursuit of the remaining Girngog to extinguish the embers of the invasion.'

'The Master returned to live in Earthroot, where we later joined him. Wielding the three Instruments together had taken a great toll on him and he needed time to recover. His experience had taught him that very few possessed the strength to be able to use the Instruments together. The realisation came to him that if there was anyone who could use all three, then they would be unstoppable. This possibility frightened him. He did not want the Instruments to fall into the wrong hands. It was not long after that he confessed regret that he had ever made them.'

'We could all understand this. Taking our own turns to use just one of the Instruments, we had found them powerful, but very exhausting. In our different ways, the sheer power of each had made us unbeatable. The Master then tried to destroy each and found that he could not. No fire, force or spell could inflict even a scratch upon the Wizards' Trinity. Master Olbus feared that he had unintentionally created Instruments of doom. He was in despair at what he had done.'

'So, taking his three faithful students into his confidence, he devised a plan. I will tell you something of this plan now and in so doing, I take you into my confidence because something tells me that it may come to pass that you have a part to play. If I confide in you, then you must be sworn to secrecy; it is vital that no word of this plan should ever be shared with anyone. Can you agree to this?'

The three companions looked at one another, still absorbing what Jevell had told them. What did it mean? It was Ceri who first gathered herself together.

'I thank you for considering that you can bring us into your confidence, Master Jevell. For my part, I will have no difficulty keeping whatever secret you wish to share with us. But are we the right people to be sharing in this secret?' she asked.

'This secret is both an honour and a burden. There are but a few I would entrust with it. Yet I have no doubt that each of you can be relied upon to keep this information safe,' said Jevell, a faint smile touching his lips.

'Well, I know that I am excellent at keeping a secret. There are things that I have not even told Ceri and she is my closest friend,' enthused Tansy.

'Like what?' asked an open-mouthed Ceri, staring at Tansy, who simply raised her eyebrows and smiled.

'And I am not known to be someone who gossips, or shares loose words even with the birds, so be assured, master Jevell, any secrets are safe with me,' said Ruffle.

'Good, I expected as much from each of you,' responded Jevell, sitting upright and now with a serious demeanour, he continued.

'Master Olbus was determined that he must safeguard the world from what he had created, so he decided that he would devote his life to finding a way to destroy these Instruments or at least place them somewhere so they could never be found or used again. His regret for having made them at all ran deep.'

'His first thought was that they should be kept separately, to reduce the possibility that they could be used together. Thus, he gave his three pupils one Instrument each to keep safe and away from the others. As each Instrument was powerful in its own right, he made it a condition that none of us would ever make use of them. He warned that using any of them would alert the world to their existence and whereabouts. He also had in his possession the Book of Wisdom and the Book of Shades, though few knew this. Of course, we all agreed to play our part. So, now I share with you the secret knowledge that I have sworn that you keep solely to yourselves.'

The three companions waited with bated breath.

'The safekeeping of the Instruments meant that the sword was given to Ralissa, the wand to Arc and I was given the crown. Master Olbus also entrusted me with the tome, the Book of Shades. He kept the Book of Wisdom. And besides ourselves, there were only two other people who knew of this arrangement – King Cadmus and Queen Tixlodel.'

'When the Master had appeared and led the victory over the Girngog, most did not know who he was. The mystery surrounding him was deepened when he vanished. Some said he had gone in a puff of smoke, whilst others believed that he had been killed in battle. Likewise, few appreciated that he had wielded Instruments never seen before. Most regarded them as magical devices, as might be conjured up by wizards just like that! A notion that was reinforced somewhat when Arc, Ralissa and I deployed them in the pursuit of the Girngog.'

'It was other mages who understood that the Instruments constituted new tools of magic never seen before. Master Olbus believed that once others appreciated that the Instruments actually existed, then some would seek them out to copy or steal.'

So, a plan was hatched. A replica of the Crown of Connection would be made, possessing no power whatsoever. It would be kept at Castle Black and guarded as if it were the real thing. The intention was to deceive and focus the attention of anyone who might be curious and tempted to steal the Wizards' Trinity. If any tried, then they would reveal their identity in the process.'

'Meanwhile, Master Olbus would continue living in Earthroot and persist in trying to find a way that the Instruments might be destroyed.'

'Unrelated to that plan, Arc, Ralissa and I have all gone our own ways. So much so, that I confess it is too long since I have met with my dear friends. I often dwell on the thought that we spend too long apart. I doubt it is a wise choice. However, I have the pleasure of your company and you do have an uncanny habit of appearing at significant occasions. This serendipitous quality you bring coincides with the visit of another guest who is due here today. He has a significant part to play in this unfolding tale. He undertakes a very special quest and I believe carries some momentous news. I look forward to introducing him to you later,' concluded Jevell.

'But, Jevell, I have some questions that…' uttered Tansy.

'I appreciate that Tansy, yet there is more to tell which may satisfy your questions. Meanwhile, I ask you to have some patience. When our guest arrives, it will all become clearer when I explain what he is here to do. Now, more tea anyone?' said the wizard.

38

The Quest Passed On

And with that, Jevell rose, stretched his arms and strode into the cottage. The three friends continued sitting in the garden, enjoying the warmth of the setting sun. Quietly, they watched as bees still flitted amongst the flowers, and drank in in the subtle scents all around. The day was shrinking, the light fading. They had learned a great deal in the last few hours, much more than they could have imagined or expected.

'I feel honoured that Jevell entrusted us with that information and I have no concern about taking that oath to keep it secret. It feels important. I can imagine that much of what he told us would be pure treasure for an enemy,' remarked Ceri.

'The hairs on my arm tell me that there might be more to this. As Jevell stated, I wonder if we have a part to play. I am not saying that Jevell has anything planned for us, for he cannot have known that we intended to visit with him this day. But is it a coincidence that, at the same time that we arrive, he is also expecting a visitor with momentous news?' queried Ruffle, now sitting back in his chair, legs stretched out and puffing away on his thin pipe.

'For my part, I think it is a coincidence, yet I respect that the hairs on your arm may be accurate,' smiled Ceri.

'I am not sure about the hairs on your arm, but something I am puzzled about, is that when the Instruments were used to defeat the Girngog, why didn't they push on into Gritol? It may have prevented the subsequent war that we later experienced. In fact, I think I shall ask Jevell to explain that decision,' queried Tansy.

'Yes, and you could ask the same question again after the conflict in which we were involved. The Girngog were allowed to go home without effective oversight of their subsequent activities!' added Ruffle.

'Well, perhaps it was felt to be merciful? They may have been thinking that signing a treaty of surrender and helping repair Yasrall was sufficient retribution? Or maybe Venterra did not wish to oversee the whole of Gritol, what with the practical challenges that that would bring. Then again, the Girngog may have seemed so defeated that the idea that they would ever start another war appeared highly unlikely. Although, admittedly the Girngog may have then interpreted it as a sign of weakness! Oh, I don't know. I think you are right; we will have to ask Jevell,' said Ceri.

'We must also remember that after the first war, their leadership was routed with the Night Wheel shattered and Merektar vanished; indeed, many suggested he had perished. So, the likelihood of another war must have seemed implausible at that time,' said Ruffle.

'Yes, and it was many years after that War before the Girngog ventured out of Gritol again. The memory of the Master Wizard and the power he wielded would surely have deterred them from considering another attack. But why did they start the first war? What were they trying to achieve? Were they simply under the control of Merektar, or are they naturally war mongers?' asked Ceri.

'Well, they say Merektar disappeared after the first war and yet the Girngog did attempt another invasion, the one that we experienced ourselves. And many think it is again the hand of Merektar behind it all. So, I reckon that everything points to the Girngog as natural war mongers,' decided Tansy.

'You may be right,' Ruffle muttered quietly. Smoke rose from his long pipe; his hands were clasped and resting on his belly, and he seemed deep within his thoughts.

'They may well be war hungry, or being controlled by Merektar, assuming he did not perish. It could be that his scheming instigated the war that we were caught up in. Though to my knowledge there was no sighting of him. I am of the view that no one really knows, people just speculate, just as we are doing,' said Ceri.

The conversation dried up. Each of the friends was absorbed in their own thoughts and Tansy got up and wandered about the garden. The tea, bread and cheese had been consumed several hours earlier and so by the time Jevell called out that dinner was ready, they all agreed that it was welcome.

Ruffle stood, stretched his arms wide, ready to greet the food.

'We seem to do nothing but eat and talk, what a splendid way to spend the day.'

Everyone ushered themselves inside and gathered around the table. Jevell appeared to be his usual calm self and the conversation during dinner touched on many topics, including questioning Ruffle as to when he had taken to smoking a pipe.

During the laughing and the teasing, they managed to consume a large vegetable pie, a colourful variety of fruit, two big bottles of wine and the freshest water they had ever tasted to wash it all down. Each guest sat back, sated and content. Ruffle even picked up and played a mandolin that sat in a corner of the room. Ceri and Tansy were impressed, as was Shadow, who pricked up his ears and stared at Ruffle.

'First, he smokes a pipe and now he serenades us with music, is there no end to the talents of this man?' joked Tansy.

It was mid-evening when the meal was finished and Ceri asked Jevell when the other guest would be arriving.

'I thought he might have been here by now,' said Jevell.

No sooner had Jevell spoken when there was a scratching on the door; he opened it to reveal a red fox standing there. Jevell knelt down close to its face and after an exchange of noises with the fox that no one else could understand, he stood and beckoned Shadow, whispered something to him and then both dog and fox sped into the night.

'Is all well?' queried Ceri.

'Essentially yes, but it seems my visitor is delayed. Shadow has gone to help him find his way here' replied Jevell.

Now visibly in a more serious mood, Jevell busied himself collecting small bottles and balms, before arranging them by a cot positioned at the far side of the room. The three friends recognised the concern in the mood of the wizard and decided it was best to refrain from asking more questions of him at this point. However, it was not very long before their silent curiosity was answered and noises could be heard outside.

'Shadow must have found our guest; his name is Zellfon and he hails from Earthroot,' the wizard proffered as explanation for the noise outside.

Almost instantly, the door opened and in limped one of the Faerie, supported by Shadow. The reason for his limp was immediately obvious; he had three arrows protruding from his right thigh and one from his shoulder.'

'My apologies, Master Jevell. I would have arrived earlier, but I was delayed by an attack on my good self from what seemed to be a gang of Girngog. Though some will not be pursuing anyone any longer, they did manage to leave their mark upon me,' said Zellfon, wincing with pain.

'Never mind that, we can discuss Girngog later, let me tend to your wounds first,' said Jevell as he led Zellfon to the cot on the far side of the room.

As he lay on the bed, Jevell pulled a curtain across and the friends could not see what was happening but they could hear the discomfort the faery was in.

'Can we help?' asked Tansy to nobody in particular, but looking at Shadow.

'No, the master will be fine, I think staying out of his way would be the best course of action,' said the big dog.

At that, they all sat down in the armchairs positioned about the fireplace and Shadow slumped in his favourite spot in front of the fire.

'He mentioned Girngog,' said Ruffle, 'I wonder where he met them, surely not in Clinglewood! We didn't see any.'

'I didn't think the Girngog were anywhere near Clinglewood,' pondered Ceri, arms folded and wearing a thoughtful expression. 'I wonder what is happening!'

'It all smells a bit odd to me and not a smell I like,' said Tansy.

There were a couple of occasions when they heard a painful call from Zellfon, but mostly they could hear the comforting words of Jevell, although not what he was actually saying. Then, after an hour or more, the wizard emerged, went to the kitchen, and returned to join the companions sitting about the fire. He stretched out his long legs, lit a pipe and stared at the dancing orange flames. The wizard had said nothing and Tansy was about to enquire about the faery, when he spoke.

'Hopefully, Zellfon should recover, though he will need much rest. I believe that I have managed to remove much of the poison that tipped those arrows. They were Girngog arrows and likely from a hunting party. He carries several items of important news, which I told him could wait until tomorrow, but he wishes to share them with you all straight away. He remains in pain, but he wishes to speak tonight. It is information that was meant for my ears alone, but I have decided that you all should hear what he has to convey, so we will join him in a short while.'

Ten minutes later, they had arranged themselves around the bed where the faery lay. He was conscious but plainly weakened by his plight. Jevell slipped an extra pillow beneath his head so that he might see them all. It was plain that the faery was fighting to stay awake.

'My apologies, friends, I did not expect to arrive in this manner,' said Zellfon.

'No need for apologies, it is a pleasure to meet you, though perhaps not in this manner, with you wounded and all,' said Tansy.

'Yes, indeed,' replied Zellfon, as he shuffled his body weight to find some comfort. 'It was not my intention to catch any of those cursed Girngog arrows.'

'Are you sure they were Girngog?' asked Ruffle.

'Let us save our questions for later, Ruffle. I only want Zellfon to impart his news and I should be able to answer any questions later. I want this fellow to find sleep as soon as he can,' said Jevell.

'I will come to the purpose of my visit shortly, but I think it better if I tell you of other matters that seemed to have occurred before the need for my visit here,' started Zellfon. 'I realise you are a Rall, Mister Ruffle, so you may know this already. Over the last few years, many Rall have moved to live in Tebira. They are being generously welcomed and the land they have been allotted is near Dragon Mountain, a very large mountain so named because that is where the dragons of Tebira live.'

'Unfortunately, in the early days of this relocation, there was an attempt to steal a dragon egg. In the commotion of the move, many Rall visited Dragon Mountain and it was first thought a Rall had taken the egg.'

'By all that is sacred, I never thought one of my own would be so nasty,' roared Ruffle, 'I will find the thief myself and teach him a lesson. What terrible news you bring me.'

'Slow down, all was not how it seemed. In trying to discover what happened, wizards in Tebira investigated and uncovered something quite surprising' replied Zellfon. 'It took a little while, some unusual spells and the help of some smell hounds, but it was discovered that this was no Rall but the work of shapeshifters.'

'Shapeshifters!' exclaimed Ruffle.

Zellfon went on, 'Yes, unfortunately, when tracking these shapeshifters, it was realised that they had escaped back into Yasrall and the scent was lost. As the Rall have no shapeshifters, the current and worrying thinking is that he came from Gritol.'

The three companions were shocked, not only because of the Girngog involvement, but each had thought shapeshifters were merely the stuff of stories, not actually living amongst them.

'How can you recognise a shapeshifter?' asked Tansy.

'That's just it, you can't,' said Jevell. 'They can walk among you and nobody would know. Some wizards can sense when a shapeshifter is near, but not always. However, smell hounds can sense their presence and they react, which is why they were used.

Although their scent is disguised to humankind, the hounds can follow their trail very effectively.'

Zellfon continued.

'It is because shapeshifters can take on the form of whoever they wish that they were able to fool the guards. In fact, they probably assumed the guise of a Teb rather than a Rall in order to get close enough, as I believe visitors are not permitted to be near the dragons.'

'Why would they want a dragon's egg?' asked Ceri.

'Well, one was stolen some years ago and never recovered. When an egg hatches, whoever first cares for the young hatchling will become a parent or the master of that dragon, which would enable them to control it. And that seems most likely the reason behind the theft,' suggested Jevell.

'But for what ends?' persisted Ceri.

'If it was stolen by the Girngog, then surely that would mean they would bring a dragon to war?' surmised Tansy.

There was fidgeting amongst the listeners as the potential ramifications of Tansy's words were absorbed.

'The dragons have long ceased engaging in the wars of people, but a dragon raised in Gritol is not likely to learn that. It could, in effect, become a rogue dragon to be used in conflicts. But that assumes that there is anyone native to Gritol who could control a dragon and I am doubtful any Girngog could do so,' added Jevell. 'But, before I say more, please continue, Zellfon, we can discuss our speculations later.'

'Happily, the theft was foiled. We were told that, by coincidence, smell hounds were accompanying the Rall group and alerted their handlers to the presence of a shapeshifter. Although he was not captured, no egg was stolen. Some are saying that shapeshifters are members of the Night Wheel that emerged in Gritol under the control of Merektar. Whereas others do not believe this, as they say the Girngog War destroyed Merektar and his circle of wizards. Whatever the truth, there is evil afoot.'

'Which brings me to the true purpose of my visit here. Jevell tells me that you already know something of this matter. It concerns the Instruments of Power.'

'You are correct, Zellfon. As my friends now know, the three Instruments of Power were divided amongst the Master Wizards serving the Grandmaster Wizard,' added Jevell.

'As I have learned, the Grandmaster Wizard who lives in Earthroot has finally created something to do with these Instruments, something that he has strived to create over many years,' said Zellfon.

'Allow me,' said Jevell, as he took the small bag Zellfon had carried and pulled out an ordinary-looking brown belt. It was a plain leather belt with a dull metal buckle. The companions expected that he was now about to bring out some shiny magical implement, but there was nothing else. Meanwhile, Zellfon was struggling to stay awake.

Jevell held the belt in two hands.

'I am told that its purpose will only reveal itself when the true name of the Grandmaster Wizard is spoken. However, I am aware that few know his given name. I believe it is only Master Wizards who do so and that is one reason why Zellfon is here visiting me, so I can voice his full name.'

The companions were somewhat bemused and puzzled at this point. It appeared that the work of many years had culminated in a leather belt! It was a well-made belt, no doubt, but Ruffle was sure he could make a finer one himself! No one was sure what to say. Ruffle thought he best say nothing; he might sound rude. Then Jevell stood up, saying, 'Excuse me for a few moments', and strode off, taking the belt into another room.

'I suspect he does not wish any of us to know the name of the Grandmaster, which is probably sensible,' suggested Ceri.

'Yes, I agree,' said Zellfon, barely conscious and struggling to speak. 'The fewer people that know his name, the less chance this belt, or whatever it is, can be used for evil purposes. None of us could reveal the name to the enemy if we didn't know it. I certainly don't know it.'

'It can't just be a belt. Anyone could make a belt. It may have a message hidden on it or maybe it turns into a snake, a friendly snake, I hope,' said Tansy.

'Or it could just be to keep your breeches up!' added Ruffle with a chuckle.

Despite Ruffle's attempt to create a more light-hearted mood, silence descended until just the crackling of wood on the fire could be heard. The large figure of Shadow dozed in front of the fire, seemingly oblivious to what was being said, though Ceri doubted he was truly asleep. In an attempt to keep Zellfon awake to speak with Jevell, Ruffle asked him a question.

'So Zellfon, did you expect to meet any Girngog?'

'Well...' but before Zellfon could reply, he was interrupted by Jevell returning.

'So, my friends, the Grandmaster Wizard has done well and I will share what I can soon, but here let us take some refreshment,' said Jevell, setting down a flask of wine, some water and a pot of tea. 'Zellfon, here drink this,' he said as he lifted the head of the faery and gave him a separate drink from the wine. 'It will help you heal.'

'Thank you, but now I must continue my story as I can feel sleep calling on me. And I will sleep more soundly knowing that I have passed on my message,' said the faery.'

'Well, please continue,' said the wizard.

'Queen Tixlodel took me aside and explained what I have told you so far. She confided that Grandmaster Olbus wished to destroy the Instruments and he had found a way. She said I could play a part, starting with the delivery of that belt to Master Jevell. She thought that if I travelled alone, I would be much less conspicuous. I concurred and set out just five days ago. In that time, I have barely seen anyone. I kept to the trees and avoided villages wherever I could. The only occasion that I was visible to others was when I crossed the Necklace. And I now suspect that I was followed from that point.'

'However, I must have been about half a league from Clinglewood before I first noticed that I was being followed. I lay low, hoping that whoever it was would pass by. We faerie are especially adept at not being seen. But my pursuers had spread out to search as they proceeded, anticipating my ploy. There were about ten of them and despite their attempts at disguise, I noted at least two were Girngog. Unusually for Girngog, they were adept at hiding and I lost track of where they all were. I saw no other choice but to make haste into the forest.'

'So, as quietly as I could, I took flight. However, that placed me more in the open. I knew they could not catch me in a race and I suspect that they realised the same. Hoping I had not been seen, I started to run. Almost immediately I was having to dodge arrows. I halted briefly and returned fire with my bow. Several of them fell. But I was still outnumbered and so I set off running again. I was actually quite close to the trees of Clinglewood when I was hit by an arrow. I stopped and was about to pull it out when I received a double thud and I fell down in pain. I had arrows in my leg and in my shoulder. I lay there for a while gathering what strength I could muster before scrambling the remaining distance into the trees. I saw several of them running toward me before I found cover. As I had hoped, they ceased to chase me once I was amongst the trees. They were wary of the forest and perhaps aware of its enchanted history.'

'I tried to walk, but I sensed that I had not only been wounded, but poisoned too. I was too weak to move far. I sat back against a tree and suddenly became aware that a red fox was standing in front of me and staring, as if he were asking me what I was doing there! Though neither of us uttered a sound. It then ran off. I fell in and out of consciousness until the next thing I saw was a huge black dog. It stood looking down at me. I thought I was about to be eaten. Or was I dreaming? Then, it spoke, suggesting that I scramble onto its back. I had heard of a huge dog that could talk and lived in Clinglewood from my queen and so I hoped it was he. I was reassured when he said he would bring me to Jevell, so with some difficulty I climbed onto his lowered back and in what seemed next to no time, he delivered me here.'

Zellfon lay back with eyes closed, clearly exhausted after recounting his tale. Jevell rose and went to the kitchen, returning with a bowl of broth. Though weary and in some discomfort, the faery managed to eat with the wizard's help.

'Let Zellfon conclude his tale and then he can rest and we can talk,' said Jevell.

But Zellfon already had his eyes closed, so Jevell continued the tale for him.

'The plan had been that Zellfon would come here and I was to show him what the purpose of the belt is. Then he would undertake the task of finding Ralissa and Arc. It is clear he cannot do that now. He needs my help if he is to live. Alas, it will take time for the poison to leave his body and for his body to repair.'

'I am sorry,' uttered Zellfon, opening his eyes, but Jevell touched him on the shoulder to reassure him.

'Nothing to apologise for, we must deal with events as we find them,' Jevell said. 'And one thing we do know from recent events is that something is afoot. Was it you, as a faery, or was it something else your pursuers sought? We do not know. Yet we would be fools to imagine that the attempted theft of a dragon egg and the presence of Girngog near Clinglewood are not telling us something. I fear events are moving quickly, although we do not know for what purpose. However, this knowledge suggests that the task bestowed on Zellfon would seem more pressing now. So, it's something I have decided to explain to you.

'I would appreciate that, as I am a little confused as to what is afoot. I don't understand why Zellfon was coming here or what his purpose was!' said Ceri.

'I will explain matters, but let us leave Zellfon to sleep; we can move to sit about the fire,' said Jevell.

They did as the wizard suggested and congregated around the fire.

'You will recall I told you earlier that the Wizards Trinity, the Instruments, were shared amongst the three wizards serving Master Olbus,' said Jevell.

'Having created such powerful Instruments, Master Olbus discovered that he could not destroy them, and feared that their power could be used for the wrong purpose. He decided that he wanted them kept apart. This was to lessen the possibility that if one were stolen, the other two could not be used in conjunction with it. So, he separated them and entrusted the responsibility to his three most able wizards. This plan was to be a temporary arrangement, until he could discover a way to either rid the world of them or ensure they could never be used together again. This is what I told you earlier, do you follow me?'

'Yes, I think so,' said Ceri.

Tansy nodded.

Ruffle muttered, 'Yes.'

'Well, it is now time to remind you of the oath of secrecy you took. What I now tell you is part of that oath. The Master Wizard has finally found a way to bring the Instruments together and destroy them. This ordinary-looking brown leather belt is the key. When the right words are spoken, the belt transforms into something else. It becomes a vessel intended to hold the three Instruments. In this form, it is disguised as a belt. Only those who are privy to its secret function would know its true purpose. For everyone else, this is just a belt.'

'The objective is to gather the Instruments together and have them placed inside the vessel. Once they are all collected, then they have to be taken to a place that Grandmaster Olbus has chosen. In his mind, it is imperative that no wizard, sorcerer or warlock should ever be able to use these conduits of power again. Once at this chosen place, they will either be destroyed or made unobtainable.'

'This was the task that Zellfon was chosen to fulfil, to gather the Instruments and transport them to their final destination. A most dangerous mission for anyone, but now we must consider what the alternatives are, for Zellfon is clearly no longer able to complete the mission.'

With that, Jevell brought the conversation to a halt. Zellfon had long fallen asleep. The wizard gently covered him with more blankets and indicated that they should leave him to sleep.

'Now I need a few minutes to think and I will make some light refreshment whilst I do so,' said the wizard as he took himself into the kitchen and started to prepare supper.

The three friends sat facing the fire in the hearth. They talked quietly so as not to wake the injured faery.

'And I thought we were simply meeting to share some good food and catch up with one another, how wrong was I?' said Ruffle, gently moving in a rocking chair.

Ceri leant back on a padded armchair, looking up at the ceiling, hands behind her head. Tansy sat on a stool, legs extended and crossed.

'Well, we are catching up with one another. Though, as always seems to be the case whenever we are with Jevell, we learn a lot more than we expected,' chimed Ceri. 'I feel quite honoured that he has told us so much, he has trusted us.'

Tansy stood, walked over to the chopped logs by the hearth, then added another to the well-established fire. Ruffle had taken out his pipe and was trying to light it, but was having a struggle to do so.

'You know, there is a bigger question that we must ask ourselves?' Tansy suggested.

'Yes, indeed there is,' replied Ruffle, still fighting with his pipe and giving off a grumpy attitude.

'But I am not sure Jevell wants us to ask that question, assuming we are all thinking the same thing. After all, Zellfon was picked to complete his task and I imagine for several good reasons. Not least for his battle skills,' said Ceri. 'I may be presuming too much, given that we do not possess the skills I imagine Zellfon has, but I would prefer our considerations to be more plainly spoken.'

'Before I get confused, I take it you are referring to the matter as to whether we should offer to replace Zellfon and undertake his mission!' stated Tansy. 'Is that what we are all thinking?'

'Yes, unless there is someone else Jevell has in mind who is better suited to take over from Zellfon? If he has, then we can step back from dwelling on that question. But I think the quest needs completing as soon as practicable, and clearly the faery will not be well enough to resume his task for some while,' said Ceri.

'To put it bluntly, are you inferring that we are not equipped to undertake such a mission?' asked Ruffle.

'Well, yes. Or no. I am not saying we should decline to help, but perhaps Jevell has someone else in mind. If we were to volunteer to take the place of Zellfon, Jevell might be uncomfortable turning our offer down.'

'I think you are making a mountain out of this molehill. Jevell would say no, thank you, if he needed to. He is not someone who hesitates to do the right thing. But maybe we should offer our services anyway, he is likely to say no thanks,' said Tansy.

'Consider, it would involve going to places we have never been. I imagine it would be more complicated than our last adventure. And are we really capable of taking care of that vessel? It may all be beyond our capabilities,' suggested Ceri.

'In which case, I have no doubt Jevell would tell us so,' added Ruffle. Having finally produced smoke from his pipe.

'For my part, I would look at the matter differently. Uncertainty is unavoidable in life. We succeeded once before when getting our message to King Cadmus, when we had no idea what to expect. So, why couldn't we undertake another quest? I do concede that there may be things Jevell is yet to tell us that could rule us out, but as yet we don't know,' said Tansy. 'I am also ready for another adventure,' she grinned.

'Well, before we go offering our adventure skills, why don't we listen to some more of what Jevell has to say?' said the Rall. 'Then we can find out if he has someone else in mind or not.'

'It makes sense, Ruffle. At home, we do not take many risks; it's not the Chimble way. But I have good memories of our working together. It seems to me that when we work together, we can get things accomplished!' add Tansy.

'You are an inspiration, my dear Tansy. I am abashed by my attitude and you have woken me up. We learned before that the world is larger than Chimbleton and for a while, we took our place in the wider world. But like a hedgehog, I had slipped back into hibernation. I think it is time for me to awaken. In fact, if you are both willing, I would go so far as to suggest that we at least offer our services to Jevell. Of course, he may not need our help, but it seems the thing to do!' said Ceri.

'I think you know my answer. I am more than ready for another adventure. So, if Jevell will accept us, then let it begin,' asserted Tansy.

'Well, I have much to attend to at home, but if you think I would allow you two to go off without me, then you underestimate me, my friends. Besides, you would get lost wandering the world if I weren't there. Count me in,' said Ruffle.

The three laughed, stood up and exchanged hugs.

'Well, I think we must offer our services to Jevell as soon as we can. Although, be prepared, he may not want our offer, so we should not be offended,' cautioned Ceri.

With that, their conversation fell away, and they sat in pensive silence, each lost in their own thoughts, watching the dancing orange shadows cast by the fire decorating the cottage walls.

Jevell returned with a tray of biscuits and a fresh pot of tea. The friends were impatient to put their offer of help to the wizard, and it was Tansy who spoke even before the tea was poured.

'Jevell, we have been talking and there is something we wish to say to you,' she said.

The wizard kept pouring the tea.

'What might that be, Tansy?'

'We have discussed the matter and we all agree that we would like, if you would like it, of course, that as Zellfon is no longer able to fulfil his task, and given that there is some urgency, to offer our services in helping to fulfil his mission.'

'Yes, we all agree,' concurred Ruffle. 'I could not have put it better,' he said, suppressing a giggle at Tansy's expense.

'You offer this without truly understanding what is involved and how it is fraught with risk?' asked the wizard.

'Yes, we wish to help,' said Ceri. 'Of course, we may not be suitable and that is fine, if that is what you think. But perhaps you might tell us a little more of what is required before a final decision is made.'

The smile on the face of the wizard was kind.

'Allow me to be clear on this. You are offering to take the place of Zellfon in order to fulfil the task that he was set. You do this knowing little of what is involved. And from what was said earlier, you do at least appreciate how important the task is?'

'I think we do, but we also realise that there is more to know,' said Ceri.

'When you talked of the Wizards Trinity that impressed upon me how much is at stake,' added Tansy.

'Quite bluntly, there is a great deal of risk involved in securing the Instruments and delivering them to Master Olbus. At this very moment, others are likely plotting as to how they might find and gain these Instruments. For anyone, this is a quest beset with danger. Plus, there is little I can do to assist you; truthfully, I have no idea where such a venture will lead or what obstacles you might face,' explained Jevell.

'Maybe we should withdraw our offer!' said Ruffle.

Tansy glared at him.

'I am joking, it's dangerous and full of unknowns, just what we excel at!' smiled the Rall.

'Seriously, we do have some appreciation that it is a dangerous quest, but we are agreed that we want to help,' said Ceri.

Ruffle and Tansy nodded their heads to show agreement. The three friends turned to Jevell, awaiting his reply.

Jevell remained silent, his hand stroking his chin in a familiar pose of thought.

'Is the room getting warmer or is it me?' whispered Ruffle.

None of the friends felt it was appropriate to speak. They knew that it was Jevell who must respond and so they waited, feeling increasingly uncomfortable amid the silence.

Finally, Jevell spoke.

'Firstly, I am grateful for your offer; you are brave souls. You do this knowing the mission will be filled with jeopardy, likely much more than we can presently anticipate. You also know that Zellfon was selected because of his abilities as a warrior. Though even warriors can be struck down by the shaft of an arrow. Secondly, you come here as guests, looking to enjoy one another's company and wholly unprepared for any quest. It is impolite of me to put you in a position of potentially great danger.'

'Having said all that, it is no longer a surprise to me that you respond so swiftly to what you find. You have had so little time to consider matters, but knowing you as I do, I do not say this lightly. I know of no more valiant souls so fitted to fulfil such a mission. My pause in replying to your generosity was my reluctance to ask you to step forth into such a hazardous situation. It may not always be straightforward, but you do have a way of getting things done. So, despite my misgivings about placing you in danger, I will gladly accept your offer. Thank you. It is a joy for me knowing that you are within this world.'

'Splendid,' uttered Ruffle.

'Adventure, meet your friends,' said Tansy.

The tension amongst the companions was released and they all shook hands and swapped hugs.

'Thank you,' said Ceri.

'It is I who must say thank you. But more pressing is that we must lay the table and eat a little supper. Then, my friends, although the night is upon us, we should discuss matters. There are things I need to show you, things I must speak of and finally we have to plan,' concluded the Master Wizard.

'Here we go again, though it seems to me a lot more is at risk,' said Tansy.

'Maybe this time you will get to fight a dragon!' grinned Ruffle.

457

Thank you for travelling this far. When you're ready, the sequel awaits, and it holds the answers you've been searching for.